-------------------------------------------

# Ashes and
# Awakenings
## by Kathryn Kramer

-------------------------------------------

Harlin,
I wrote this after the
death of Elijah. We
need more love in this
county and not hate!
Here's hoping the future
is one of truth and
hope
Kathy

ASHES AND AWAKENINGS

**Historical Romance**

Copyright 2020 by Kathy Lynn Kramer

To Bob Eccel a treasured friend who has been so supportive of my efforts to write this book and who has listened patiently to my story ideas and plot twists and turns.

And to Elijah McClain whose life was brutally taken away on the streets of Aurora, Colorado.  How I hope you are now playing violin for the angels and that at last you will receive justice...........

"We know through painful experience that freedom is never voluntarily given by the oppressor it must be demanded by the oppressed."

Dr. Martin Luther King

"For the human soul is virtually indestructible, and its ability to rise from the ashes remains as long as the body draws breath."

Alice Miller

"Sometimes, the most profound of awakenings come wrapped in the quietest of moments."

Stephen Crane

# KATHRÝN KRAMER

## Author's Note

The Civil War was a devastating tragedy. Approximately 620,000 lives were lost in combat, by accident, from starvation or from disease. Families were torn apart. Lives changed forever. At the war's end there was a monumental amount of destruction left as the "Old South" died and the Reconstruction began. The Reconstruction Acts of 1867 and 1868 placed the majority of Confederate states under military rule, requiring Union Army governors to approve candidates for election as well as appointed officials.

Warfare had left desolation – railroad tracks and bridges had been torn up, houses and barns burned or looted making it necessary to do a great deal of rebuilding. Confederate currency and war bonds were worthless, and property once valued at billions of dollars, the slaves, no longer counted as property at all. Slavery had been abolished, but tragically now many blacks found themselves homeless and hungry when they had been promised a great deal. The dream of "forty acres and a mule" never was fulfilled as promised. Black codes were put in place to control the behavior of former slaves. These codes required blacks to sign yearly labor contracts which limited economic options and reestablished plantation discipline.

The cohabitation or intermarriage between racial groups was regulated by state law and was known as *anti-miscegenation laws*. The idea of a black man marrying a white woman frightened many southerners

5

so that it was magnified into "a great threat to society." It was further stated that as a result of freeing blacks, white women might be raped, defiled and sullied by these savage "jungle" animals.

There were even terms to designate degrees of "blackness." A person of mixed race who was half white and half black was called a mulatto. A black person with a white parent and one mulatto parent was a quadroon. A person with one white parent and one quadroon parent was an octoroon. The "one drop rule" designated that any person with even one ancestor of black ancestry (one drop of black blood) was to be considered "colored" or black.

Although attempts were made to redress the inequities of slavery and the social, political, and economic legacy, it was a task that was complicated by bitterness and anger. The problems arising from the readmission of the eleven states that had seceded from the Union was responsible for the far-reaching changes in America's political life as new laws and constitutional amendments permanently altered the federal system and the definition of American citizenship. All persons born in the United States were now defined as national citizens who were to enjoy equality before the law. In an effort to discourage any rebellious individuals, citizens were required to recite an oath of allegiance to the Constitution in order to vote.

The quest for learning prompted former slaves to seek education, which they saw as an important step towards achieving independence, equality, and prosperity. They were dedicated to learning despite their poverty, the anger this caused, and the obstacles white people put in their paths. Learning to read became a symbol of their freedom because as slaves they were more often than not denied access to any kind of education in an effort to justify and maintain the institution of slavery. Unfortunately, there was a shortage of teachers and buildings that could be appropriated as schools, so churches were often commandeered.

Southern landowners struggled to keep their land, fighting against carpetbaggers and "scalawags." The political revolution of Reconstruction sparked organizations, such as the Ku Klux Klan (from the Greek word "kyklos, meaning circle and the English word clan) that committed terrorist acts in a violent backlash to restore white supremacy. The South was in turmoil. Then yet another hardship occurred. A banking firm collapsed and caused the Panic of 1873 and a period of a depression. Thousands of business failures and unemployment affected people both North and South. Many fortunes were lost, and a few gained during this period and the move "westward" which had already begun, attracted more people as a last resort to keep body and soul alive.

**Note:** The White League, White Line, and Red Shirts unfortunately were real and did exist during the Reconstruction era. They described themselves as defenders of "hereditary civilization and Christianity and stated their purpose as the "extermination of the carpetbag element and restoration of white supremacy. They targeted local officeholders who supported the northern attempts at reconstruction for assassination and terrorized black people to keep them from voting, organizing politically or getting an education. Unfortunately, 123 years later our nation is still grappling with white supremacist organizations and racism still exists in many areas of the country.

# KATHRYN KRAMER

## PROLOGUE May, 1859

The river was turbulent, rocking the small boat to and fro. Fighting against the waves, the frail, worried man worked frantically with the oars as the water pounded viciously against the stern. He had to outdistance his pursuers. He must!

The wind whipped at his face, chilling him to the bone as he pulled and pushed at the oars with all the strength he could procure. Hastily looking over his shoulder to discover his whereabouts, he heard a whimpering noise and looked down at the child wrapped in his jacket.

"Be quiet, little one. Everything will be all right."

The eyes that looked up at him were huge, her expression trusting.

"I must do everything I can to protect you, for there is no telling what they might do to you if they catch up with us now."

Nervously he looked over his shoulder for any sign of the men who were following them, and thought he saw the faint outline of their boat in pursuit. He sighed with relief as he thought how easy it had been in all the confusion to slip over the side of the larger boat with the child in his arms. The had a head start.

"Murderous bastards!" Oh, yes. They had noticed the missing dinghy and were following their prey. Squinting his eyes, the man sighed as he searched for any sign of land, of safety. Alas, because of the fog all he saw was an endless span of water.

"Mama!" The little girl whimpered as she clutched her doll in fright. Slowly she crawled closer to the man, wanting to be comforted, but he gently pushed her back with the tip of the oar.

"No, no, little one," he said. "Stay back. We must not take a chance of your falling out of the boat. I will take care of you later."

The large hazel eyes of the child mirrored her trust as she obeyed, then widened to reflect her renewed fright as the wind gusted, tossing the drifting boat back and forth even more violently. Suddenly the boat capsized, and the child found herself engulfed in icy blackness.

"Jemma!" In blind panic the man searched their watery prison for her but to no avail. "No!" Praying beneath his breath he dove again and again, trying to catch even a glimpse of her.

As if his prayers were answered, he saw her small body being swept under by the river a few yards away.

"Jemma!" With surprisingly strong strokes he approached her sinking form. Grabbing her arm, pulling her to him, he fastened her arms around him. "Hang on to me, child, and don't let go no matter what happens," he ordered between gasps. The river appeared to be almost endless as he put one arm before the other, stroking the waves, fighting against their watery prison.

"Joseph...." The little girl hugged the man tightly, shutting her eyes against the sting of the cold water.

Though he wanted to whisper words of comfort to the child, he could not take time. Instead, he fought the strength of the current, struggling desperately for survival.

"I'm cold.....!"

This time he did answer. "Hang on to me tightly. It's only a little further. You must somehow find the strength."

The little girl choked as she swallowed some of the dirty frigid water, but she obeyed him and grasped him even more tightly around the neck.

"Please God! Help us. The child is so young. Her life is still ahead of her. Please!"

As if in answer to his prayers, the flow of water rose to aid in his combat with the elements. They were drifting with the strong current. Squinting against the sting of water he could see land! Just a little further. They just might make it after all.

A rock struck his foot as the man at last stumbled upon the shore. Gently he set Jemma down, watching as she scrambled out of the wet jacket and flung it upon the wet ground.

Digging her toes in the wet sand, Jemma exhilarated in the feel of the dirt beneath her tiny feet. It felt so good to be on land again! She wanted to laugh; to cry but the sound that escaped her lips was a blend of both emotions.

Turning to her rescuer she smiled at him, but instead of returning her smile, he looked at her with a strange expression. His eyes rolled back in his head as he frowned. It was a look of sheer horror as his mouth opened wide, as if in an endless scream. Somehow, he managed one word.

"Run!"

Confused, Jemma watched as he slumped forward, a knife protruding from between his shoulder blades. Someone in the clump of trees nearby had thrown with deadly aim.

"Joseph!" She wanted to help him. He was hurt. The red that oozed from his back reminded her of the time she had fallen and scraped her knee. It had hurt so....

"Run!" The command was a choked gurgle.

Jemma saw a man step out from the trees. She stared. Never would she forget his face. His mouth was crooked, his nose as large as a bird's beak, his eyes small and angry. Instinct told her to run, that this man would harm her, just as he had harmed Joseph.

Run. Run! Run!

He was coming towards her, his arms outstretched as if he already held her in his grasp. All the while, he screamed at her over and over again, saying words her mother would have gasped at. Swear words. Hurtful words.

Angrily he took a swipe at her, but Jemma nimbly escaped his grasping hands. She sprinted down the sand as fast as her legs would carry her.

Jemma could hear the man's breathing as he closed the distance between them. She felt him pull at her hair and she screamed as she tugged free of his grasp. If only she could make it to the clump of trees, perhaps she could hide. Hide! She remembered how she liked to play hide and seek and how no one could ever find her. Her life depended on that game now.

Looking behind her, she expected to see her

12

pursuer hovering close but saw instead his sprawled form upon the sand. He had stumbled and fallen over a rock in his path. He quickly rose to his feet again, however, to renew the pursuit. Screaming and shaking his fist at her, he was indeed a frightening sight.

Jemma was far ahead of the man now. Slipping easily between the branches of the trees, she weaved this way and that, and then climbed to the top of the largest tree. Stealthily she hid in the foliage. The bird nosed man would never find her now.

Resting her head against the tree trunk, she at last gave vent to tears. What would happen to her now? Where was her mother?

"Mama!"

She remembered visions that were frightening. Two men had grabbed her mother just as Joseph had picked Jemma up in his arms. Tears stung her eyes as she thought of how they had pushed her mother down roughly to the deck of the big boat, her mother screaming all the while. They had hurt her, she knew it.

Softly she started to sob. Her eyes fluttered shut. She reached for her doll. "Emma..." Her pretty little doll was gone too, and she remembered that it had fallen into the water. Joseph had not been able to save Emma. Emma had drowned. "Poor baby....."

A rustling sound alerted her that her danger was not over. In anxiety she peered through the leaves of the tree hoping to catch a glimpse of the bird-nosed man. She felt a sense of immense relief that he had seemingly disappeared.

A hand slipped over her mouth.

13

Jemma tried to scream, but the hand was clasped to her lips too tightly. Terror pricked her heart as she struggled and kicked furiously. It was to no avail. She was a prisoner.

*"Please don't hurt me,"* she thought as she looked into her captor's eyes.

It was not her enemy who held her, however, but another man. A man with skin the color of her own. But his eyes were blue. Piercing eyes. Eyes that gazed at her, yet strangely held a look of kindness. Even so, she struggled to escape from his grasp. His hand was shutting off her air. She couldn't breathe!

*"Mama....."*

Holding her tightly against him the man slid down the tree trunk. Furtively he dodged in and out of the trees. Where was he taking her? She could not wonder for long. In fear and exhaustion, she tumbled into unconsciousness.

KATHRYN KRAMER

# PART ONE:  The Mystifying Women

## Richmond, Virginia, and Surrounding Area

## Spring 1873

"A man gives many question marks, however, a woman is a whole mystery."

Diana Sturm

# ASHES AND AWAKENINGS

## Chapter One

The streets of Richmond were oddly deceptive and showed few signs that just eight years ago there had been a war. The air buzzed with noise—voices of women strolling along the sidewalks, modeling their finery, laughter of children at play, the rattle of wheels on the road. Taking off his large-brimmed hat, Derek Cameron paused as he walked along the street and ran his hand through his shock of blonde hair, breathing in the smells of the city as he did so. He loved this city, the old stone house on East Main Street that had been George Washington's headquarters, Capitol Square with the statue of Washington on horseback, the spire of Saint Paul's Church, the view of Manchester across the James River, the bridges and islands, the Richmond theatre. He loved all these places. Coming to the city was exciting, a sharp contrast to the rural areas.

Located at the falls of the James River, Richmond was a blend of magnolias and mills, a provincial town, and yet at the same time an industrial city. Iron and tobacco were significant industries. One could see the smoke from the Tredegar Iron Works from miles away, could smell the aroma of tobacco. Always the air smelled of it. It was Richmond's lifeblood. It even colored the pavement and bricks with its brown stain. One seemed to see and smell tobacco at every turn. Tobacco. Brown gold. It was here in Richmond that Cameron tobacco was processed and sold. And it was here that carpetbaggers, the drudge of the South, were as thick

16

as thieves. Carpetbaggers and scalawags.

"Damned Yankees! Damned opportunists!" he said beneath his breath. The unscrupulous robbers had come to the South with just one purpose. To profit from the misery the war had brought to those they termed "the losers." If the reconstruction was bitter medicine for the southerners, it was a tasty elixir for the vultures that had come from the north.

For just a moment it was as if the days of the turbulent past were unfolding right before his eyes. Was it only twelve years ago that the war had started? Derek shook his head. Hard to believe that he had just been a boy with minimal understanding of what the war would mean to his family. He had never realized then that warfare would take the life of his brother Bevin or that his family would nearly lose everything they had worked so hard to attain. Nor would he have every dreamed that even before he had reached manhood, he himself would have stubbornly run off to fight for the South. Such a foolishly brave venture.

Looking up he saw his boyhood friend, Moses, coming towards him and he waved. Once Moses had been a slave in the Cameron household. But to Derek he had been a friend, a companion, a confident, and someone to whom he had shared all his secrets. He had grown up with his friend, thus it had been heartbreaking when he had learned that his father planned to sell Moses as punishment because a houseguest had told a bald-faced lie. Derek's father had refused to take the word of a slave. But Derek's sister, Allegra had saved the day when she had concocted a plot to make use of the Underground Railroad to spirit Moses and his family away to seek safety in the north. Derek had thought never to see him again but during the last days of the war when he was in grave danger of being captured by the Union army, Moses, now a Yankee soldier, had returned the favor and saved Derek from being taken prisoner. Together they had come back to Winding Oaks, the Cameron plantation.

"Were you able to get the loan?" Derek asked, feeling a sudden surge of desperation. Someone was trying to steal Winding Oaks out from under their noses. Someone with friends in high places. But the Camerons were fighters.

"Can a crow fly?" Moses grinned from ear to ear as he reached in his satchel and brought forth the papers. "Thank goodness for the Freedman's Bank." The Freedman's Savings and Trust Company had been created to assist newly freed slaves and Negro soldiers at the end of the Civil War.

"Thank goodness for *you!*"

Proudly Moses held out the documents. "There is my signature. Moses Abraham Douglass!" Since slaves usually didn't have last names Moses had given himself one. Douglass. After Frederick Douglass, abolitionist and statesman, the most respected Negro north or south.

"And you are sure you really want to give me *your* loan?"

"As sure as I am that we will always be friends." Moses gave him a playful pat on the shoulder.

Derek felt guilty taking money meant for Moses, but his friend had insisted. It would be a way to pay off the debts the Camerons had incurred and play the scalawag, who wanted the plantation, at his own game. In return, Derek had insisted on giving Moses a large tract of land on the Cameron Plantation. If his father Charles was upset by the transaction, well so be it.

"Then we will shake hands on it!" Suddenly Derek felt relief sweep over him as they grasped hands. He felt in the mood to tease. "Did y'all get dressed up to impress the men at the bank or is there a lady who has caught your eye?"

From the top of his dark-haired head to the toes of his black shining shoes Moses was every inch the gentleman. He looked as if he'd walked straight out of the pages of a catalogue. It wasn't just his clothes. He wore the dark blue suit, vest, and tie as if he'd been made for them. The severe cut of the coat showed off the width of his shoulders, the slimness of his waist and hips. Moses was tall and it appeared that were he to harness his strength, he might be a fearsome man to reckon with.

"None of the women has caught my eye just yet, but I'm looking." Moses winked.

"That makes two of us," Derek admitted. They had both been so busy trying to keep body and soul together that neither had been anywhere near a female, with the exception of Derek's mother, Honora, that is.

Looking down at his own clothes Derek laughed as he thought how his work clothes – the tobacco-leaf stained blue shirt, tan overalls, and boots was a contrast to Moses' fine garments. They were in fact a study in contrasts. Moses had skin the color of chocolate while Derek had light skin that had been tanned by the sun. Moses had dark brown curly hair, Derek's hair was long, blonde, and straight. Derek had blue eyes and Moses had eyes that were a light brown. Each was handsome in his own way although neither one was overly proud of their manly good looks.

Plopping his hat back on his head, Derek pointed in the direction of his wagon. "Although I'd like nothin' better than to go celebrate, I think we had best get back home." His grin was lop-sided. "Though it seems that dressed as y'all are a fine carriage would be more to your likin'."

Taking off his coat, loosening his tie, Moses shook his head. "Carriages are for carpetbaggers, politicians, scalawags and the ladies."

Derek laughed. "Livin' up north has made you talk like a carpetbagger."

"And by staying down here you have kept that southern drawl that would drive the ladies crazy up north. They would be on you like bees to honey," Moses countered.

Derek dusted off his trousers and exaggerated his accent for fun. "Do *y'all* think so?"

Moses elbowed him in the ribs. "I know so."

Derek could see that Moses looked tired. "Are you certain you want to go back in my wagon?"

Moses laughed. "Even if you slung me over one of your horses' backs it would be just fine. All I want right now it to get out of these clothes and put on something that doesn't have such a stiff collar."

The two men headed off in the direction of the wagon but a throng of people, who were crowded around the street vendors, blocked their way. The vendors were calling out to passersby, hawking their wares.

"Fish. Caught fresh today. Fish."

20

"Ripe melons! Juicy and fine. Ripe melons. Buy mine."

"Red rose tomatoes. Green peas. Sugar peas!"

Each vendor chanted a melodious singsong in an attempt to sell his wares. It seemed that on the streets of Richmond all the vendors were musical, singing out over the sounds and noises of the street. There were even quacks, who called themselves doctors, selling the latest tonics which were guaranteed to cure any ailment.

"Some things never change," Derek observed, doing his best to push through the crowd. "Still like it was when we were boys."

"Blackberries, fresh from de vine. Blackberries. Don't you want mine."

Giving in to the temptation, Moses bought a small basket of blackberries from a young woman and shared the fruit with Derek as they walked along the way. In rapt conversation they talked about the "good ole days" when life was so much less complicated.

"When we get everything under control at Winding Oaks I'd like to go fishing again," Moses was saying. "I remember....."

Suddenly from out of nowhere a buggy careened right towards Moses, spattering dirt from the road on his coat. It would have grazed him had Derek not reacted quickly, shoving his friend out of the path of the buggy's wheels.

"Ape! Dressed in yer monkey suit," shouted out a gray-haired man in a mocking tone.

"That's what happens when you let them Nigrahs off of their chains," his younger companion cajoled.

Infuriated by the insult, Derek started to run after

21

the buggy with the intent of forcibly teaching the men some manners, but Moses held him back. "No harm done. Sticks and stones may break my bones but words from the likes of them will never harm me."

"Damn carpetbaggers from the looks of them," Derek grumbled, raising his fist in the air in a gesture of defiance. "Hell, they can be an annoyin' and insultin' lot."

Brushing off his coat, Moses shrugged. "And dangerous....."

Derek's voice was infused with anger. "Only if we let them be." Whispering several swear words under his breath, Derek headed for the wagon, Moses following only a few steps behind. For the moment, the unpleasant incident was forgotten.

*       *       *       *

The small wooden schoolhouse was situated outside of Richmond, at the bottom of a hill. The building was rustic, hardly more than a cabin made of rough lumber and whitewashed well-chinked logs, yet it held a certain attraction for Amelia Seton. It was her dominion, the one place where the brutality in the world could not intrude. The large bell at the top of an old dead tree was used to call the children to classes and to announce the day's end.

Inside the schoolhouse wooden tables and benches in neat little rows filled the room. At those benches sat the offspring of the sharecroppers who worked on nearby plantations. After the war and the freeing of slaves there were many farmers who had become trapped in the new system of economic

22

exploitation known as sharecropping. Lacking money and land of their own they had been forced to work for large landowners. The tragic thing was that even though they worked their fingers to the bone, although they struggled, they always seemed to be poor. The sad thing was that instead of blaming the greedy landowners they resented the Negroes who were often competition for their jobs.

Standing at the front of the room Amelia studied her students just as intently as they were raptly staring at her. Reaching up she brushed at a stray lock of her thick reddish gold hair to put it back into the tight bun atop her head. Although the strawberry blond color was not to her liking, others had complimented her on the rarity of the color.

"I think we have had enough of numbers for the day. Let's do a bit of history." Amelia offered her students a smile. She could smile prettily when she chose, and her straight white teeth were one of her best features. Unfortunately, she did not smile very often. Perhaps because she had always thought that her mouth was much too wide for her face, a criticism that had been espoused by her Aunt Lucinda for as long as she could remember.

Amelia's aunt had in fact prattled on for so many years about her niece's lack of beauty that Amelia believed her, though in truth she was far from being plain. Had she but known, all of the older boys in the classroom had a crush on her—and half of the younger ones as well.

"Sam, who is the president of our country?" Before her words were completed, a pigtailed little girl in the front row held up her hand. "You seem to know the answer, Suzy."

Before Suzy could answer, Beauregard Johnson in the back row piped up. "Jefferson Davis."

"No." Susie was indignant. "Grant!" she countered. "Ulysses S. Grant...."

"Grant is a damn yankee......" Beauregard spit out the words as he sneered.

Amelia shook her head, wondering if the children saw her as a "damned yankee" also. The anger that was still held against the northerners was understandable. So many men had been killed or maimed. Amelia's own father and brother had been killed in the war fighting for the Union and her mother had been so devastated that she had taken her own life. That was why Amelia had been forced to live with her father's sister.

"Be that as it may, young man, we have to be realistic. Suzy is correct. It has been a long time since Jefferson Davis held that office. Grant is our president now."

"Ha, at least Grant is better than that pig, Johnson was," another boy shouted out.

"Not much better," Beauregard insisted. "Besides, if not for him, Robert E. Lee would have won the war and then we'd be up north stealin' land from *them*."

Amelia put her hand to her temple. She was starting to feel a headache coming on. It was stuffy in the room and there was only one window. That window, however, could not be opened for fresh air. Perhaps that is why her answer to Beauregard was curt. "Well we didn't win the war and that is *that* young man."

"Hell, we ought to start another war." Tommy

Winslow, always defiant, stood up. "Hell, from what I've seen of 'em they are all a bunch of sissies with their silly top hats and fancy clothes. We could lick 'em this time. We could." It was obvious the boy was mimicking words he'd heard at home. At her stern look he changed the word to 'heck.' "Ain't no better men than my uncle and my pa."

Amelia quickly moved on to other matters, outlining the history of the United States. It was only fitting that the children learn at least a few facts about the early days of the country. History was a subject that had always fascinated her.

"George Washington was from Virginia," she said, writing his name up on the small chalkboard. "And Thomas Jefferson....."

"My daddy says the landowners who founded this country all had slaves. Is that true?" Beauregard had a smug expression. That he was up to no good Amelia sensed right away.

"Yes, because once many here in the South had slaves but that was several years ago, and no one has slaves now. Which is a good thing." Hurriedly erasing the chalk board, she pointed to a large pull-down map. "Now.....who can point out Maryland for me?"

The morning passed by quickly despite the fact that Amelia devoted much of it to her least favorite subject—geography. She was determined that the children learn all the names and locations of the states. Although she had been in such a hurry this morning that she had neglected to bring any food with her, an abundance of apples on the top of her desk assured her that she would not go hungry.

Early in the afternoon it was time for the boys to

go back to their work, so she called it a day. Walking back to her Aunt's house nearby she let her eyes roam over this land she loved so well. Her brother Andrew had died at Antietam and her father had died fighting the Second Battle of Petersburg. So long ago. So tragic. Her father had held such hopes and dreams, but it was for others to carry on those dreams now.

*Oh, Papa*, she thought, *if only you had not been killed*. But he had, and there was no use torturing herself with that fact. Still, she could not forget his handsome face, his chestnut hair and laughing green eyes, eyes so like her own. He had been her sun and moon, showering her with affection. Then suddenly he had been taken from her when she was still too young to fully understand such things. But she had her memories. As to her mother, Amelia wondered if she would ever be able to forgive her for just giving up and leaving Amelia all alone to fend for herself.

The rattle of wagon wheels interrupted her musing and Amelia looked up, surprised to see it rumbling down the road at a time when most men and women were working. Shading her eyes with her hand she could see two riders, one with blonde hair dressed like a sharecropper and the other a well-dressed Negro sitting on the seat beside him. Strange. She had never seen either man before and she stiffened as she wondered if they were northerners.

As the wagon caught up with her, Amelia felt uneasy. There were numerous stories about carpetbaggers ill-treating women. Despite the fact that both men waved in a friendly manner, Amelia picked up her skirts and ran as quickly as she could to a grove of trees where a wagon couldn't go. She did not hear the two men's comments.

26

"She was pretty as a picture. Wonder who she is?" Derek craned his neck to catch a glimpse of the woman as she headed off into the trees. "If she hadn't run off like that, we could have offered her a ride to wherever she was goin'."

"Whoever she is she took one look at you and skedaddled." Moses laughed. "Maybe you need to brush up on your manners."

"Me?" Derek elbowed Moses in the ribs. "I think she was runnin' from you. Seeing you in that suit she probably mistook you for a real scalawag!" He turned his head to see if he could still see the young woman. "Guess it doesn't matter. We most likely will never see her again."

"Too bad. I was looking forward to playing cupid." Moses pretended to shoot an arrow into the air.

"For me or for yourself?" Derek asked with a laugh.

A scowl distorted Moses' face. "Not for me. Do you think I want to be hung from a tree with a noose around my neck?" For just a moment a shiver passed through him as he thought of what had happened to other black men in the area who had trifled with white women. Times were dangerous and tensions were high.

An awkward silence followed as they continued on their way home. Derek regretted the walls that sometimes separated the two of them because of the difference in their skin color. Because he was not prejudice, he often forgot the hatred that seethed all around them. But it was real, and he knew the two of them needed to be cautious lest they, too, became victims.

# ASHES AND AWAKENINGS

*     *     *     *

The vivid blue sky shimmered with rays of golden light. The bright sun cast a shining halo on the earth below as woodland creatures scampered about, finding breakfast for their families. Pausing for just a moment a brown squirrel stared in fascination at the young woman lying upon her back looking up at the sky. Sensing that this human posed no threat, the rodent chattered away in conversation, then returned to its task of food gathering.

Breathing in the fresh clean smell of the earth, mingled with the perfume of wildflowers that grew in abundance in the woods, Forest Faulkner smiled as she watched the animals scamper around. It was peaceful here in the woods, away from the noise, commotion and staring eyes of the townspeople.

"If you ask me, the upstanding citizens of Richmond could learn a few lessons in manners from all of you......" she whispered, addressing the feathered and furry creatures who shared her afternoon.

Indeed, Forest's opinion of the people who sometimes crowded curiously around her foster father's wagon for a look at the seldom smiling, opinionated man and his "daughter" whenever they had to go into town, was scathing. They could be rude and unkind, particularly the so-called ladies. They made no secret of the fact that they were shocked at her manner of dress - men's breeches, cotton shirt, and boots. They stared and twittered behind their hands and fans, curious about her attire. Forest had heard their whispers and wonderings about who and what she was.

"Nobody knows who she really is.... She lives in that cottage in the woods with that...that strange man."

"I heard that they were living up north during the war and then just suddenly appeared here last year."

"As if out of nowhere, just like the rest of those *northerners*."

"Her skin is a bit dark and I don't think it's from the sun."

"I think they both might have been escaped slaves......"

"Slaves! How utterly shocking......" she had heard them whisper.

"Well, now, don't be telling any tales. No one really knows for sure..... They both *could* be white."

The way they talked made the truth about her situation hurtful. Although she had been just a child when Quentin, her foster father, had rescued her, she remembered enough to know that her name wasn't really Forest. Once upon a time she had been Jemma. And once, so long ago, she had had a mother and father who had loved her. Parents who had risked their very lives to be free so that she, too, could live without the bonds of slavery.

Although she had tried so hard to remember all that had happened that day so long ago, the images in her mind were hazy. What she did remember, however, always made her feel downhearted. She wasn't really certain what had happened to her mother and father. Had they been punished? Killed? Returned to their owners? Whatever had happened they had been separated from her, a sacrifice they had

29

made to see that she at least would find freedom by traveling on the Underground Railroad.

Forest remembered the turbulent river, remembered running—fleeing from that frightening man who was following her. A slave patroller no doubt. A real breathing living Simon Legree. She might have suffered a horrible fate if not for Quentin and his timely rescue of her. Like a giant angel he had swooped down as if from nowhere and had taken her to safety where her pursuers could not find her.

Even though she was just a child Forest had known that she had Negro blood, though how much surged through her veins she did not know. Nor did it really matter because even one drop meant that she was considered a Negro, at least in the South. Quentin had told her that he suspected that she was a *mulatto*. That was why Quentin had changed her name once they had reached the safety of Pennsylvania lest they be captured and returned to one of the slave states.

"All because of a hateful law," she whispered, remembering when Quentin had told her about the danger they were in and that she must never tell the truth about her heritage. The Fugitive Slave Act, it had been called and it required that slaves be returned to their owners even if they were now living in a free state. The act had even made the federal government responsible for finding, returning, and trying any escaped slaves they might find. Although Quentin had not been a slave "Jemma" had been and so her fate had been hanging in the balance.

They had been relatively happy in those days and even during the war. Because both she and Quentin had light skin, they had been able to pass for white.

30

That he was a man of knowledge who was sought after for his advice on important matters enabled them to continue in the charade. Forest had even had a few friends in Philadelphia, but that was then, and this moment was now.

Quentin had always said that money was the root of unhappiness and greed and Forest had found out just how true that was when financial uncertainty had swept over the country at the beginning of the year. Business failures, unemployment, and tightening credit heightened class and racial tensions. Suddenly those who had depended on Quentin's expertise no longer had need of him. On a sinking, economic ship it was every man for himself. Bundling up all their possessions, taking all his money out of the bank, Quentin had made the decision to go back to live on the land he had owned as a free man near Richmond.

One of the things Forest had always admired about her foster father was his determination and the fact that he knew his own mind. He was secure in himself whereas there were times when Forest felt insecure. "I want to know about my parents. Myself. Who am I?" All she knew was that once her name had been Jemma and that she had been loved. Though she had asked Quentin so many questions he couldn't answer her because he didn't know. He said he had not even a clue whatsoever about her past or true identity. Though she tried to tell herself that it just didn't matter, it did.

With a sigh she rose to her feet, making her way to the edge of a pool nearby and curiously peered at the reflection of an olive-skinned girl with dark curly hair, and hazel eyes, a young woman who loved the outdoors. A streak of dirt was visible on her nose

31

and she hastily wiped it off with her hand.

"Who am I......?"

When she was much younger, she had fantasized that she was really a princess in disguise, but now that she had grown up, she had to admit the truth. She might never remember anything about her past or her parentage, except in her dreams. Something would always be missing in her life, a sense of real belonging and love. Sometimes she felt such loneliness, such longing.....

Not that Quentin hadn't been good to her. He had. He had raised her, fed her, clothed her, and taught her all about nature and life. The simple pleasures. He was her friend and her mentor, a philosopher of sorts. To him learning was nearly as important as breathing. It was what separated a man from the animals he had said. A lack of education was what had kept the slaves in bondage, he had told her. Under his tutelage she had learned to read, write, and do her sums and much, much more.

Quentin had a way of thinking about the world, the universe, and society that was different than how other people thought. He asked questions about the nature of people's thoughts, the nature of the universe, and the connections between them. He had told her how much he admired a man who lived long ago. A man named Socrates. He had told her that because of his studying that philosopher he had learned to do critical thinking. Quentin was sure that he knew the meaning of life and it was his desire to one day teach that meaning to others.

"But what if other people don't want to learn?" she had asked Quentin. "People can be so cruel and so stupid....."

Gazing into the water Forest remembered an incident that had happened the last time she and Quentin had gone into town. She had been humiliated by two bullies who had thought her to be a boy, dressed as she was with her hair tucked under an old hat, her face smudged with dirt from the road.

One of the boys gave her a punch on the shoulder, sending pain up and down her arm. Even so, she had put up her fists. They had snickered at her and pushed her to the ground. Eying her up and down one boy had callously called her an uppity mulatto.

*Mulatto*. Just a word and yet the way they said it, as if it were the worst insult in the world, had made her feel frightened and ashamed. It reminded her that she didn't really belong in the world of the Negroes or in the world of the whites. Not here. Not now. Perhaps she never would belong.

Fighting against her tears Forest had not realized that a rescuer had appeared, until she heard a voice say, "here, you two, leave the boy alone." The man had a low, very masculine voice, mistaking Forest for a boy because of her clothing.

Reacting to his intrusion, the two boys had run away, like the cowards that they were. "Are you alright?"

Forest had felt the firm pressure of the man's large hand as he touched her arm. Looking up, her eyes were met with an intent blue gaze.

"I'm.....I'm fine...." she had answered. "Thank you."

"Are you sure?" He had looked hard at her, as if seeking to see her face through the dirt and smudges wrought by the scuffle.

Suddenly tongue tied she had nodded in answer.

"Good. I'd be ever angrier if you were hurt." He shook his head. "I hate bullies, don't you?"

Again, she had nodded. There were so many things she had wanted to say but the sight of a middle-aged women coming his way caused her to remain silent. She looked towards the woman with the wariness of a wounded doe.

"Derek!" The woman had come forward, waving her hand as she called out. It was then that Forest had taken to her heels, running from the certain disdain she knew would follow. Better to keep to herself. She didn't need anyone. Not now. Not ever.

Swirling her hand in the pool's waters she sought to chase the insecurities from her mind. Life was peaceful at Quentin's cottage in the woods. There was no one to laugh at her, taunt her or pick a fight. She and Quentin would be just fine. She would take care of him and he of her and life would be grand! Rising from the grassy bank she walked to where her horse grazed. Patting his head, she climbed upon his back and headed back to the cottage.

## Chapter Two

A warm, soft breeze swirled down upon Winding Oaks, cooling the air, and rustling the leaves of the tall oak trees the plantation had been named for so long ago. Amidst these glorious giants stood the Cameron home, a huge two-stored white manor with six columns soaring into the air. There were several rooms in each wing of the house—four wings in all-- the east, west, north, and south wing. Two floors, the bedrooms being on the second floor along with the nursery. On the ground floor were the servant's quarters, dressing and bath rooms, dining room, kitchen and drawing room. The wine cellar and storage rooms were down below the kitchen and it was there that the family had hidden from hostile Union soldiers at the end of the war.

Once it had been one of the finest homes in the county filled with family and slaves, every inch the symbol of the South. But during the past nine years since the end of the war its beauty had diminished much like a woman losing the blush of her youth. The broad porch, once decorated with potted plants and carved wooden benches was sadly in need of paint, the window shutters of forest green were broken and threadbare. But it was home and despite all the hardship of the past few years it still belonged to the Camerons. And now, thanks to the money Moses had been able to get from the bank, it would be in the family's hands for at least another year, or until they could think of a plan.

Derek pulled the reins on the wagon's horses and

pulled to a stop. "Do you want to come in, Moses? I'm sure Father will be grateful for your help."

The expression on Moses' face said more than words could ever say. "Hell no. I'd just as soon face the devil himself." Moses could never forget that it was Charles Cameron who had sold him to another plantation owner. If not for Derek's sister, Allegra, Harriet Tubman, and the underground railroad he would have faced a dubious fate. For just a moment Moses' memories were rekindled. Closing his eyes, he could almost see the events of that fateful night as clearly as when it had all happened.

It had been a very dark night. Running in and out of the shadows, he and his mother, Sarah, and father, Jacob had headed for the carriage house.

"You'll be safe in here," Allegra had promised, holding open the lid of the chest so that he could crawl inside. "There are holes cut in the sides to let air in. But you must keep quiet. Don't make a sound."

Sarah was dressed in Honora Cameron's clothing while Jacob donned the butler's garments.

With skin a light shade of tan and her hair a light shade of brown, it was hoped that Sarah would have no trouble passing herself off as a lady. Jacob was to pretend to be her slave. They were to travel to Richmond by carriage then seek passage on a train.

"Just be careful," Allegra answered, her expression reveling her emotions. "Now listen carefully to what I tell you. There can be no mistakes."

Moses had listened intently as the detailed plan had been revealed. Sarah was to pretend to be Amanda Cameron, Jacob who had dark skin was to take on the persona of her butler. But with horror

36

Moses had realized that he would be inside the trunk for the entire journey lest he be discovered.

"These papers give proof to your identity and also prove that Jacob is your slave. Above all, Moses must stay hidden." As Allegra caught him peeking from beneath the lid of the chest, she repeated the words. "Stay hidden." Moses remembered how he had wanted to tell them he couldn't do such a thing. He had wanted to just run away and hide, but he had no alternative but to do what they insisted.

It had been no easy task to arrange for the necessary papers to send Jacob and Sarah and their child through Virginia to Washington, D.C. There had been so little time for the forger to do a careful job. If anyone took a careful look it was feared they might detect an error, but it was too late to think about that now.

What had followed was the worst moments of Moses' life. Darkness. Hardly any air. The insecurity. The fear. Was it any wonder that he now was claustrophobic?

"I can't say that I blame you. Father can be as grumpy as an old bear. But I promise you he has mellowed." Derek's expression was pleading. "After all, he has to be grateful to you for helpin' to keep a roof over his head."

Moses said just one word emphatically. "No!"

"Fine friend you are. Leavin' me to face him all alone." Derek pretended to be peeved though he understood his friend's reluctance to go inside. Moses helped Derek unhitch the wagon, then taking their leave of each other, promising to meet up the next morning, they went their separate ways.

Derek walked towards the house with a bearing

straight and proud, belying his nervousness. He had always been more than a little bit intimidated by his father but that was no surprise. Charles Cameron was stubborn, stingy, critical, demanding, cranky and he refused to admit when he had been wrong.

Reaching for the big brass knob on the front door Derek thought back to the time when the door would have been opened by a tall, gray-haired Negro dressed in a blue swallow-tailed coat with large brass buttons that glittered in the sunlight. But there weren't any butlers now, or anyone else to open the door. The Camerons were on their own. One by one when the money had run out the house servants had left the household. Unlike the slaves they had not been obliged to remain.

Walking through the entryway Derek had a strange foreboding feeling. A feeling that intensified as he made his way to the drawing room and saw his mother hovering over the figure slumped in the over-stuffed chair. It was obvious that the man had passed out. "Mother, what's wrong?"

"It's your father. He fell into the well." Although she tried valiantly to hide her anxiety it flickered in her eyes.

"What?" It was the last thing Derek could ever have imagined.

"He wanted to fetch a bucketful of water but leaned too far over the edge and tumbled right in. If not for one of the sharecroppers, he might have drowned."

Honora Cameron, unlike the mansion, had weathered quite well. At fifty-four she was still a lovely woman. Her dark honey blonde hair was streaked with gray, worn back in a chignon that emphasized the delicate planes of her face. Her lovely blue eyes had just a few lines at the corners. Her lips, usually smiling, were tightly clamped together, and frowning now. Wearing a full-skirted dress of indigo blue that had been mended several times, she was still the very picture of good breeding and femininity.

"Is he...is he, all right?"

"Yes. Though he has a bit of a lump on his head."

A blending of concern and annoyance were obvious in Derek's voice as he asked, "had he been drinkin'?" It seemed Charles Cameron just couldn't stay away from his brandy and bourbon of late.

Honora stared to tell a lie, then thought better of it. "Yes. He was drunk as a skunk. I had to undress him and put him in dry clothes"

"Damn!" Narrowly Derek held on to his temper for his mother's benefit. "His timin' couldn't be worse. I can't run this place all on my own. I need his help."

Once Charles had been strong, stubborn, and determined to make Winding Oaks profitable, but the war, the death of his favorite son, Bevin at the age of twenty-four in the war, then the hardships and pressures of the reconstruction had taken their toll. He just couldn't seem to cope as Honora and Derek had. Feeling like a failure he had sought the bottle to get him through the day.

"You just have to be patient...."

"Patient!" Patience was something that was in short supply in the southern part of the country.

The period of restoration was supposed to be a time of healing of wounds. The state of Virginia had begun its slow climb to recovery. The slave system had produced unhealthy economic conditions – false standards and gross inequalities-- but the war had brought poverty to everyone and because of this progress had been slow.

"Your father has been tryin' to accomplish an impossible task, tryin' to bring this plantation back to its former glory." Honora closed her eyes, fighting back tears.

"And I have been right here doin' everything I can to help him. But I am only one man. I'm not a miracle worker." Derek sat down on a chair across from where his mother was. The past few years had been like a nightmare, for the war had not determined what the future relations of the southern states to the Federal Government would be. Nor had there been answers as to what the future relations of the Negroes would be to the whites. The questions which preoccupied many minds had been on what conditions should the former Confederacy states be readmitted to the Union and what position former slaves would have in Southern life.

"I know you are not, Derek. No one expects you to do anything else but just what you have been doin'. But I want you to understand how difficult this has been for your father. He has been up against new neighbors, northerners, who still think the South should be punished for its actions in the past."

"We *have* been punished." Plantations, including Winding Oaks, had been reduced in size and land redistributed which doubled the number of farms. Former poor whites and small farmers had benefited the most by this redistribution. Sharecropping and tenant farming had appeared, and Negroes had been allotted small shares of land. Because of Derek, Moses had been allotted acres that had once been part of Winding Oaks. Charles Cameron had been furious, but his anger had done him no good. In the new government's eyes, he wasn't any more important than any of the others.

"We haven't had it quite as bad as some." The war had left desolation. Railroad tracks and bridges had been torn up, houses and barns burned or looted. Fields left to grow up in weeds. Livestock had been senselessly slaughtered. Forests denuded. There had been a great deal of rebuilding necessary. "And your father certainly didn't help matters...." Honora chastised.

Derek knew what she meant. Angry by the turn of events, Charles Cameron had made things difficult for his new neighbors, especially those that were dark of skin. Hoping to make amends Honora had done all she could to make up for her husband's spitefulness. She had shown kindness to the sharecropper's families and had even helped renovate an old cabin at the far end of the plantation so that it could be used as a school for the children.

Derek couldn't seem to keep from pacing up and down in the room. He had been so hopeful when Moses was able to procure the money but now he couldn't help but feel uneasy. He couldn't work a plantation, or farm as it was now called, with hardly any workers. So far, he had pinched pennies, worked as many hours in the day as he could manage, had hired a few field hands but it all came back to the matter of finances.

"Money, money, money. It all boils down to that," he said under his breath. Was there ever

41

enough of it? He remembered how the bottom of the world had seemed to drop out beneath the family when confederate currency became worthless and war bonds which many southerners, including his father had deemed so valuable, were suddenly not worth the paper they were printed on. The South was basically an economic wasteland, completely at the mercy of northern financiers for economic survival.

"I wish I had more jewelry to sell, but I'm afraid what's left is imitation and…"

"You've done more than anyone could expect, Mother." Honora was a shining light in a world gone dark. Hurrying over to her he took her hand. "I will find a way to manage. I have to find a way. And Moses will help me. Despite how Father treated him he has always been my loyal friend."

"Damned that ungrateful Nigrah!" Awakening from his deep sleep, Charles Cameron sat up with a start, his gaze riveted on Derek. "Did you help them escape? Was it you who betrayed me?"

Honora grabbed Charles by the sleeve and pulled him back down. "Hush, Charles, you must have been dreamin'."

"I was going to sell that boy to ole Jensen. I looked like a fool when he just up and disappeared." Turning his head, he seemed to be looking for someone in the household. "Where's Hannah?"

As Honora's gaze met Derek's it was obvious, they thought the same thing. "Hannah has been gone for almost ten years, Charles."

"Gone?" He shook his head as if to clear his thoughts. "What about Ole Thomas?"

Now Derek knew he had reason to be worried.

"Thomas died over ten years ago, Father." Despite his previous anger his voice softened. "Don't you remember we lost all the slaves after the war was ended."

"All of them?" As if sensing that his comments had caused alarm, Charles nodded. "Ah, yes. I remember now. Gone and it's a damned shame. Those Nigrahs were valuable. Even Ole Thomas."

"We have to pay men to work for us now. I have pinched every penny until the coins shrieked, but the rates from those northern bankers is so outrageous we don't have much hope of payin' it back. Or at least we didn't until Moses got a loan. He's keepin' some but he has let me borrow a large sum."

Charles bolted to his feet again. "You borrowed from that Nigrah? Give the money back. I just won't have it."

Derek felt as if he were going to explode with anger. 'You won't have? You *won't* have? You ungrateful *bastard*!"

"Derek!" Fearing a severe confrontation, Honora stepped in between the two men. "Apologize to your father."

The sound of the Grandfather clock ticking off the time was all that could be heard in the room. Tick, tock, tick, tock. At last Derek was able to calm his ire. "I will apologize because of you, Mother. That's the only reason." The words seemed to stick in his throat and when they did come out his mouth tasted like bile. "I am sorry for calling you a bastard. I have no intent on insulting my grandmother."

Sensing that was as good an apology as Derek was going to give, Honora nodded. "That will do for the time bein', but I don't ever want the two of you to raise your voices in this household again."

"Yes, Mother." Derek looked down at the piece of paper in his hand but instead of saying more, he tucked it inside the waistband of his pants, then with a mumbled oath headed for the stairs. He would deal with it tomorrow.

\*     \*     \*     \*

Winding Oaks Plantation had been Moses' home until he had been forced to escape on the Underground Railroad. Several miles to the northeast of Richmond, it once had been a prepossessing, widespread area of gently rolling countryside that contained over one thousand acres of land. Upon that land stood not one house but two, the original house, referred to as the Avery Mansion, and the present Cameron mansion, which dominated the scene. Twenty-four rooms in all, it stood in the center of the plantation grounds and looked with its pillars like a Greek temple. When Moses was just a boy he had dreamed of living inside that house or a house just like it someday.

Along with the two houses stood barns, curing sheds, smokehouses, a carriage house, stable, and the twenty wooden cabins that had once housed the Cameron slaves who had worked the plantation. Moses remembered that at one time the Camerons had owned over seventy-five slaves. Now there were only a few whites who worked the land and just two Negroes who lived with their families in houses no better than shacks upon the premises.

Several roads ran past the plantation grounds, through the woods of pine, cypress, and oak, past the

44

fields of tobacco and on up to the orchards and planting fields, where the assorted fruits and vegetables that sustained those who lived in the wooden cabins nested. There were chicken yards, water wells, and fenced-in stalls that housed the small amount of livestock the Camerons had been able to afford.

"Poor Derek. He has his work cut out for him." he whispered now, looking out over the area from atop a hill in the middle of the acreage, as if strategically placed by human hands. "I don't envy him now." Although he had once wished that by magic he could trade places with him. What would it be like to be white if only for a day, he had thought then.

Moses guided his horse back towards the stables, dismounted the animal, and set out on foot towards the fields as he had done routinely the past few days. He liked to walk. As long as a man had use of his legs he could face any disaster, he reasoned, heading for his own acreage and the small stone house he had built with his own two hands from the rocks and stones he had found in the fields. Derek and some of the sharecroppers had helped him and if it wasn't a mansion, well at least it was "home."

The sun beat down upon his bare head as he stood in the fields watching two field hands cutting and pulling at the thick weeds that threatened the tobacco plants. He had learned much more about the growing of tobacco since he had returned than he ever could have imagined. Enough to know that many a fortune had been made from the leaves of these plants, plants that needed rich black soil, plenty of water, and careful tending.

45

# ASHES AND AWAKENINGS

Feeling lost among the six-foot plants and exhausted by the heat of the day Moses reached down, picked up a straw hat that was lying there on the ground, and put it on his head. How he pitied those poor slaves who had had to work all day in this heat in days gone by. There had been no respite from the toil unless they were ill. Nor had they been allowed to stop work on Sundays. They had been forced to go to their church in the evening after their work was done. Sadly, there were so many Southerners who didn't own slaves but were still just as insensitive. Cruel. Uncaring. As if the slaves had been little better than the horses.

He thought about Charles Cameron and how he had once thought of him as a father figure. He had once wanted to be just like him. "Like him? Ha! A man who went about buying and selling human beings? But he had to let bygones be bygones. Derek was his friend, and he was determined to help him rejuvenate the premises. Besides, he had always loved Honora Cameron, with her kind heart, gentle ways, and friendly smile.

Turning around, shielding his eyes against the sun, he saw several horsemen riding through the fields. Dodging in and out among the giant plants, plants with oval-shaped leaves, they seemed to be in a hurry, but he didn't think much about it.

'Tobacco. Brown gold, he whispered. Remembering Derek saying "guess we should thank ole Christopher Columbus. If he hadn't found the Indians smokin' tobacco through hollow tubes and taken some of it back to Europe with him, we'd all most likely be workin' in some factory."

How ironic that the word "factory" had come up

46

when they were just boys playing around. Little did Moses know then that was exactly how he would spend his time up north where industry was king. Moses had had to compete with the immigrants flooding in who had provided cheap labor. Men, women, and children had worked in dimly lit, dangerous, and filthy "sweatshops" as they were called. Like the others, Moses had worked long hours for low pay. In some respects, his life was worse than it had been on the plantation.

Looking out over the acreage he was thankful to have what he had now. In the city housing conditions had been poor – crowded and filthy. Crime and disease spread rapidly, and fire had been a constant threat. What had surprised Moses the most, however, was that just like in the South the Northerners were hateful towards Negroes. They said they were not in favor of slavery, yet they didn't like those with dark skin moving to their towns and cities, taking away their jobs. Over and over again Moses had been told that his natural inferiority to white men would keep him from attaining any kind of success. If not for his mother, Sarah, God bless her he might have even believed it.

"Your skin is just an outer wrapper, Moses, and inside you have a good heart, a kind soul and a quick mind. If you work hard and believe in yourself no matter what others may say, you can do great things. A mother knows."

Passing by a peach tree, Moses picked the ripest and ate it as he walked towards his house. As he went along, he tried to remember the names of a few of the Negroes he had briefly met in town who might be persuaded to come work for the Camerons even though Charles Cameron had a terrible reputation. It was said that he was cheap where the white workers were concerned and condescending where the Negroes were the ones in his employ. But somehow, someway, Moses had to put together a working crew.

Passing by the small lake where he and Derek had fished when they were small, he smiled. Once things were going smoothly, he would challenge his friend to a fishing contest. When they were boys Derek had been frustrated because Moses had always seemed to catch the largest fish until he had told Derek his secret. Crickets. The fish preferred the insects over worms.

Seeing his stone house up ahead, Moses was anxious to get inside where it was shady. He would get water from the well behind, strip down and pour it over his head. A shivery shower of sorts that he had learned from Derek. The promise of the cool water caused him to quicken his steps until at last as he was coming up the walkway. Suddenly he paused in disbelief. No. It couldn't be. But it was. There in red paint, the letters marring the white paint of his house were the words every black man abhorred. "Go back to Africa, nigger." Nigger. Such a disgusting hateful slur that was meant to do just what it did—cause fear and anxiety. Looking around Moses was unnerved. Who had done this hateful thing? He was at a loss to come up with even one name.

"Go back to Africa......" The words were hurtful as well as stupid. Most of the freed slaves had been born in America and had never even been to that dark continent of their ancestors. And yet he had heard that Abraham Lincoln had toyed with the idea of doing just that with the freed slaves.

Determined not to let the incident get under his skin, Moses went to the barn, thankful that it looked like he had enough white paint to cover the hateful words. Hurrying into the house to change into his working pants, he set about restoring the house. For the moment, all thoughts about finding laborers was gone as he moved the paintbrush up and down, determined that in the coming days he would be careful, cautious and watch his back. Somewhere out there he had an enemy or two, perhaps the horsemen he had seen riding through the fields. Best to be on alert and keep his rifle handy.

# ASHES AND AWAKENINGS

## Chapter Three

Streaks of coral and red appeared upon the horizon, glowing with the light of the dawn. Tiny specks of sunbeams hung suspended and golden, as if bouncing across the bed to greet Amelia Seton as she opened her eyes.

"Morning already!" she groaned softly, passing her hand before her face. She was so tired, yet it was her own fault. She had done it again, stayed up late to finish reading a book. Now she would have to pay for her folly by suffering weariness throughout this long day. Yet she knew it was worth it. Nathaniel Hawthorne's *The Scarlet Letter* was an enthralling story about imperfect people, sin, and guilt. Though she did not know why, Amelia felt a kindred spirit with Hester Prynne, the heroine of the story. Perhaps because Hester had to deal with being criticized, yet through her dignity and strength survived. Amelia knew that she, too, was a survivor. Someday she would prove her worth to her Aunt Lucinda.

"Amelia, are you up!" Aunt Lucinda's shrill voice startled Amelia. Pushing aside the bedcovers, Amelia hurried to get out of bed. She didn't want another quarrel with her aunt about her lack of discipline.

"Yes, I'm up!" she lied. "Thank you." Well, it wasn't really a lie because she was up now. Hastily she went about her toilette, pouring water in the small china basin then washing her face and brushing her teeth.

50

Amelia was grateful that her aunt had taken her in after she had lost her entire family. Although her mother had received a meagre pension for her husband's part in fighting the war, the money had quickly run out. Facing poverty and loneliness had been too much for her mother, Jenny. She had procured belladonna from an unscrupulous doctor and set about to poison herself.

With a shudder she remembered that she had merely thought her mother had a fever until the hallucinations had made it evident that something was seriously wrong. Though she had run all the way to the doctor's house, by the time she was able to get help for her mother it was too late. Penniless, Amelia had been terrified that she would be put in an orphanage until good fortune shone down upon her and her father's sister, a woman she had never met before, agreed to take her in.

Reaching for a brush to put some order to her thick hair, she thought again how much she owed her aunt, who was a widow herself. Having scandalized her family by running off with a southerner, Lucinda had done quite well for herself as a seamstress. Amelia hoped that the few dollars she made teaching school helped the household finances at least a bit.

Amelia stared into the mirror at her reflection as she arranged her hair, parting it in the middle and forming it into a tight bun at the back. Waist-length with a hint of curl and thick as a horse's tail, it was difficult to manage, requiring a dozen or more hairpins, yet somehow, she tamed its unruly locks. Slipping on her chemise, under-gown and drawers, Amelia couldn't help but wonder why nature had been so unkind as to give her breasts which were so difficult to hide. Aunt Lucinda decried her niece's figure as a disgrace, making several tight bodices to flatten such shameful curves. The tightness of the bodice made Amelia extremely uncomfortable.

Choosing a bright blue dress and comfortable leather shoes, Amelia finished dressing and hurried down for breakfast. She could smell the freshly baked blueberry muffins and bacon which emphasized how hungry she was.

"Good morning, Auntie. Her aunt looked very pretty today with her dark blonde hair pulled atop her head. Hadn't Lucinda often told her that she had been the belle of Richmond in her day. Taking a seat opposite her aunt at the table, she didn't talk much as she ate. But that didn't keep her aunt from indulging in a one-sided conversation.

"I don't know why you don't get a teaching job in Richmond. You do have your faults but being stupid isn't one of them. You could be teaching at a fine school instead of bothering with those sharecroppers' ragamuffins. Lordy, lordy, you might even meet an eligible man. You aren't getting any younger, Amelia."

"I'm not husband hunting, Auntie." Taking another muffin, she stuffed it in her mouth packing both her cheeks like a squirrel. It was a small gesture of defiance, knowing how much Lucinda hated bad manners.

"Well, you should be." Her expression was disapproving. "If anything happened to me you would be right back where you started when your mother died. And this time there wouldn't be anyone to take you in."

"I like teaching children who really need me,"

Amelia answered with her mouth full. "I hope to make a difference in their lives so that they can better themselves." She washed the muffin down with a gulp of tea.

"Better themselves. Ha! No doubt they will be stuck doing exactly what their poor fathers are doing whether or not you teach them how to add and subtract." Wiping her mouth with a napkin, Lucinda left the table to wash the dishes, waving Amelia away when she started to help. "No, you go on. You will be standing on your feet all day. Best get on your way"

Finishing her tea, Amelia picked up her schoolbooks and put them on the seat beside her, then stepped up into the buggy. Today she was too late to walk all the way to school.

The buggy ride was a pleasant one, through winding streets, past flower gardens which bloomed with bright reds and pinks, near the creek bed, its sand and rocks begging for rain. It was perhaps the highlight of Amelia's day, a time when she could enjoy the world around her and think her own thoughts. A time away from Aunt Lucinda.

Amelia's life, if not exciting, was a well-established routine. Monday through Friday, from eight o'clock until four, she taught her charges reading, writing, and arithmetic. Saturday morning was spent cleaning the small house she shared with her aunt, the afternoon was a time for tea with the ladies of her aunt's age and views, Sunday she sat in the tall steepled wooden church and listened to the Reverend Mr. Apple's sermon and tried not to yawn. But the nights belonged to Amelia, her companions the characters she met in her books—knights in shining armor, aristocratic Englishmen, or men of daring deeds. If she was not living a life of excitement herself, she lived one vicariously. She was content.

Arriving at the schoolhouse, Amelia was glad that she had arrived before the children so that they didn't have to wait outside until she arrived to unlock the door. Untying the horse and securing the buggy, she was stunned to find the lock broken and the door ajar. She would have to see about getting the lock fixed as soon as possible. Opening the door, she was surprised to see a young Negro boy sitting on the floor gazing at one of the schoolbooks in such rapt attention that he didn't hear her come in.

"Hello." Her voice startled him, and he dropped the book. Since she was between the boy and the door he was trapped.

"I ain't doin' nothin' wrong," he rasped, his eyes darting towards the door and back again.

Her voice was gentle. "Of course, you're not. Reading is a very, very good thing to do." Moving to where he was seated, she picked up the book. "You can have this book if you would like. Then you can read it at your leisure."

He looked sad. "Oh, I can't read, Missy. I just saw the door was open and…and I like to look at the pictures of the animals and such." The books were elaborately illustrated in black and white.

She was going to ask him if he had broken the lock but that was a ridiculous question. It would have taken a lot of brute strength to pull it apart.

He looked sheepish for a moment. "I have come by here before and seen the others and I wanted to come in, but I was afraid".

"Afraid." Amelia knew that before the war slaves were forbidden to learn to read by their masters. And now there was still a hostility towards Negroes going to school. A wave of sympathy swept over her. Reading was such a joy to her that she just couldn't imagine not being able to enjoy the written words. "Would you like to learn to read?"

"Learn to read?" His smile said more than any words ever could. "I would give my eyeteeth to know what the words said."

On impulse Amelia said, "then stay for the lessons. I can teach you. It will unlock a whole world of wonder." She had felt an immediate bond with the boy. She wanted so to do something to brighten his life.

Frantically he shook his head. Fear was reflected in his eyes. "Oh no. I couldn't. The others are all white of skin. Besides, I have my chores to get to."

Amelia was determined. "Well, what if I come to school early and give you lessons before the others arrive. Reading is easy. It won't take you long to get the hang of it." When he didn't answer she said, "an hour in the morning. Each morning."

A grin was her answer. "Sure, sure, I can do that, Missy."

Holding out her hand she sealed the agreement with a handshake. "It's almost time for the others to come. How about starting tomorrow."

His smile seemed to brighten the drab room. "Tomorrow. I'll be here." Standing up he moved towards the door, then turned back. "Thank you. Maybe there is a way I can return the favor some day."

"We'll see." She smiled. "Tomorrow." It was just a small act of kindness. Amelia liked to think that it was fate that she came across the boy when she did. She supposed that her offer to help him would affect both of their lives.

\*     \*     \*     \*

It looked to be a pleasant day. Forest had gotten up early so as to finish all her chores so now she was rewarded by the leisure of spending a few moments enjoying the view of the rolling hills and trees outside the kitchen window. The cottage was isolated. Quiet. The same kind of "cottage in the woods" that were always written into fairy tales. But here there were no wicked witches, nasty stepsisters, ogres, or giants. No magic. Just all the wonders that nature could provide.

A large wood-burning cookstove stood in the center of the room, used for heat as well as cooking and now Forest hurried to light it, striking a match on the sole of her shoe. She fed the fire with wood from the pile just outside the front door then stood watching the intricate mica window in the stove door until she could see the flickering flames dancing about behind it.

Boiling water, she poured it over grounds in the upper part of the coffee pot so that it would slowly drip through a cloth filter into the lower chamber, then stepped back to enjoy the aroma. It amused her that although she didn't like the taste of coffee and rarely drank it, she loved the smell, even when the grounds were not fresh. Making a note on the kitchen chalkboard that more coffee was needed, she ran her fingers through her curly hair, letting the tresses fall to her shoulders.

She didn't hear Quentin come up behind her until he said, "seeing you with your hair out from under that hat I am reminded of what is said about a woman's shining glory.'

Quentin Faulkner was a large, powerfully built man whose physique belied his emphasis on matters of the mind and not on his prowess. Though his shoulder length hair and beard had once been dark they were now almost all gray.

"Do you really think I have nice hair, Quentin?" She smiled as she toyed with a strand absentmindedly.

"Definitely. It is a different shade of dark brown. Like burnt umber." As usual he had a newspaper placed under his arm, his link to the outside world. If it was more than a week old, he didn't seem to care. News was news as he always said. "It is unfortunate that you keep it tucked under your *chapeau*. But in these times, you are safer maintaining a sense of anonymity. Perhaps one day when the world has regained its' senses you will be able to feel free to expand your horizons."

Forest sighed. "With so many strangers among us and all the turmoil, I'm afraid I will be a little old lady before everything gets back to normal." *If it ever did.*

A frown wrinkled his brow as he poured himself a cup of the just-brewed coffee. She couldn't understand how he could drink it black, without cream or sugar. "Do you miss our old home up north?"

Feeling her chest tighten, she tried to put old memories out of her mind. "Sometimes. But I realize we had no other choice. A person cannot exist without money. Particularly in the city. But here we can be self-sufficient." As if to emphasize her words she reached in a basket to take out several freshly laid eggs from their five chickens and put them in a bowl. "Will scrambled eggs suffice?"

"Mmmm, yes. I think perhaps that is my favorite way of eating them." He grinned and she could feel a lesson coming on. "You know people in this great country are like scrambled eggs." He pointed to the eggs in the bowl. Some of them were brown, some white, one was tan and there was even a blue one. "Different colors on the outside but all are eggs just the same. And when you put them all together and mix them up, they come together to make a tasty meal. If only human beings realized that just like the eggs, we are all the same." He touched his chest where his heart was. "Inside here…"

"There are some who just don't see it that way. They like to keep their eggs separate." Breaking six of the eggs into a smaller bowl she added chopped mushrooms and wild onions and whipped them together with just a dash of cheese and cream. "I wonder when people started eating eggs." Using just a bit of lard in the frying pan, she poured the mixture in the pan to cook, carefully tending the eggs with a spatula.

As always Quentin knew the answer. "Eggs have been eaten since the early days in China and Rome and perhaps even before." He laughed, a deep throaty sound. "That's because unlike other food the eggs couldn't fight back."

Forest politely laughed at his joke as she scooped the eggs out of the pan and onto two plates. She also put wild raspberries and blueberries on the dish, a pleasant surprise she found growing behind the cottage. Sitting down at the table across from him, she quickly said grace then started to eat.

"What would you think about me writing a book. I think we have a fine story to tell. About our journey on the underground railroad and the importance of freedom?"

Forest wasn't surprised by his question. It was something she had heard him mention before. "I think it is a fine idea. More people need to know about Harriet. She must have saved at least a hundred souls. I don't know what would have happened if she hadn't helped us."

As they ate, they engaged in a discussion about the hardships they had experienced and the people they had met on the journey to freedom. For just a moment in time they had all been merged together on their trek. It had been like a gigantic family.

"I wonder what happened to the old man and woman who were going to join their son in Maryland. Or the young mother who had just given birth but braved the journey with her child anyway." Memories of the journey were as vivid in her mind as if it had happened yesterday.

"Or the girl who was running because she had been caught reading and was going to be sold as punishment." Quentin grimaced as he remembered.

"I remember the mulatto who was traveling with her supposed butler. I felt so sorry for their son, forced to hide inside that trunk the whole distance. I would have been so afraid"

Reaching out, Quentin affectionately patted her hand. "As I recall you were very kind to him and brought him your portion of sweetmeats. And I remember the times you secretly read to him while I stood as a lookout, just so he wouldn't be alone. Kindness never goes amiss."

"I like to think that his family arrived in Maryland safely." She didn't even want to contemplate the fates of those few who got caught. Hurriedly she set about cleaning up the dishes and tidying the small kitchen, then went to the cellar to check on their supplies. There was only half a bag of the one-pound sack of flour, three potatoes, a small sack of carrots, a few turnips, and a sweet potato.

Quentin poured another cupful. "How's the supply of coffee?"

"About enough for another day or two," she called out.

Quentin Faulkner savored his coffee. He said it was the only thing that would keep him awake when he was intent on finishing a book late at night. He'd invested in his own coffee grinder, a smaller version of the one he had seen at a hotel in Richmond. It had a wheel that needed cranking to crush the coffee beans. The grinder was his pride and joy.

"We will need to go into town. While we're there I want to stop by the library and pick up another book or two."

"Or three or four," she teased.

He stood up, towering over her as he did so. "A person can never have too many books. So much to learn. If I had another lifetime, I couldn't even begin to read them all."

She didn't want to spoil his reverie, so Forest kept her feelings to herself, but she dreaded the idea of going to town. There was, however, no other way to get the needed supplies. Besides, Quentin was always the happiest when he had discovered new manuscripts. Tucking her hair under her hat and brushing herself off, Forest followed Quentin out the door.

*    *    *    *

Moses ached in every muscle. There had been trees to cut down and stumps to be removed. Tough roots which were impossible to burn had to be pulled or dug out. It was arduous work, but he was determined to make something of the land he had been given. An additional problem was that the tobacco crops originally planted nearby depleted soil nutrients, although not as much as cotton crops did. He would have to be critical about what he replanted.

"Perhaps I should try to grow peanuts." The crop would take about 120 days to mature and could easily withstand the fall frosts. All he would need was fresh, raw peanuts in their shell and loose dirt. As for planting, as a child he had helped plant tobacco plants and had also helped Derek since his return.

All the while Moses was working, he tried hard not to think about the incident at his house. Never-the-less it was obvious that it had not been any accident. The words hadn't appeared out of thin air or been written by a ghost. Leaning on the axe, he paused for a minute to breathe in the fresh air and nearly became intoxicated on the invigorating scent of pine oak, white pine, crapemyrtle, and beech mingled

61

with the mustiness of the earth and the fragrance of wild flowers.

He treasured the land. It was beautiful. Made a person see things in a whole new light. Living close to nature made a person appreciate the simple things, most of all freedom. Closing his eyes, he remembered the days when his people had been held in bondage. But no more. Never again.

Inspired, he started to work again. What he had done was just the beginning. There was still plowing to be done, peanuts and other seeds to be sown, a chicken coop to be built, fences constructed, firewood stacked. And on top of that he wanted to honor his promise to help Derek whenever help was needed. Which reminded him of the fact that he needed some help. He couldn't do this all by himself. It was a grudging admission.

The day was especially sunny, or so it seemed to Moses as he put down the axe and stacked the cordwood. Even without his shirt on he was hot. He felt exhausted beyond belief, and thirsty. Very, very thirsty. Picking up a bucket, he went in search of water, finding the perfect place in an area where several large rocks purified a small stream. Filling the bucket to the brim and drinking his fill, he quickly retraced his steps.

He started back to work after the pause but as he looked up, he saw a buggy or a wagon coming down the seldom used pathway, stirring up quite a lot of dust. Whoever it was they were riding at a life-threatening pace. Remembering the incident with his house, he was on alert scolding himself for not bringing his rifle. He smiled in relief as he saw that it was Derek.

Pulling at the reins to bring the wagon to a stop little more than a foot away from Moses, Derek said cheerily, "I brought you some freshly baked bread, a dish of just-churned butter, a jar of cherry preserves, a small ham and a few other things Mother decided you would need."

"Honora is always so thoughtful." Moses appreciated the mothering.

Jumping down from the wagon and handing Moses a huge basket he asked, "so, how is this farm of yours comin'?"

"See for yourself." With unsuppressed exuberance, Moses made a sweeping gesture and let Derek assess what had been done. Taking the basket from Derek, he set it on a large wood stump then flicked his fingers through his thick dark hair, brushing it free of the wood dust his chopping had created. He thought about telling Derek what had happened at his house but thought better of it. Derek had enough on his mind.

"I'm going into town to try and find some workers. Thought you might want to come with me. We can make use of a man or two and share their time between your place and the plantation." Despite the new designation as a farm, Derek always thought of Winding Oaks as a plantation.

Moses eyed the food. "Only if we can eat first. Your mother's cherry preserves, and bread are calling to me." Picking up the food and getting into the wagon, Moses hitched a ride back to his house. Inside it was obviously a man's domain because there was just the bare minimum of furniture—a threadbare sofa, a lone wooden chair in the living room, a wooden bed made out of logs with a yellow blanket and a pillow atop the mattress. It was the kitchen, however, that was starkly bare. There was a stove, a sink with a water pump, a cupboard that was mostly bare, a table and two chairs.

"I think you need a wife," Derek mumbled, looking around at the plates that needed washing and the floor that hadn't been swept in at least a week.

"And I think you need to mind your own business," Moses retorted, cutting the bread, and buttering a piece for himself and one for Derek. "I was a slave once I don't need to find another master." An unpleasant memory of being told to call his friend "master Derek" when they turned nine, flashed through his mind and he frowned. "What about you? Isn't it time you sired a child to continue the mighty *Cameron* line?"

Remembering the argument, he had with his father, Derek grimaced. "I have my hands full with my father." Taking his portion of bread, Derek spread it with the preserves but declined to join Moses in partaking of any ham. He didn't have as much of an appetite as he usually did.

They ate quickly and silently, each thinking his own thoughts, then washing their hands and putting the left-over food in an underground cupboard, hopped into the wagon. The ride into Richmond was pleasant—the road a wilderness broken by occasional farms and clearings. It was a good time to enjoy the beauty of the countryside, but Moses and Derek were troubled with too many thoughts to enjoy the view. At last they came to Main Street and were just going to turn onto Fourth when Moses spotted a living ghost from the past.

"Wait. Slow down."

Derek looked in the direction of Moses's gaze to see a tall, bearded man with gray hair and his young companion. "It's a small world. I remember that lad too. Saved him from a lickin'"

For just a moment Moses felt as if he couldn't breathe. He wasn't mistaken, it was them. "That's not a boy." His breath came out in a loud sigh. "Although it's been thirteen years or so I would remember them both anywhere. He's *her* father." He leaned forward for a closer look and was satisfied that his eyes were *not* deceiving him. "We traveled the Underground Railroad together. I could never forget."

It was a memory they both wanted to forget. "That was so long ago......." Derek took a closer look. "But why were they.....?"

"Moses knew what Derek was thinking. "They both are light skinned so they were never in any real danger of being retaken. Not like I was. If anyone had found me hiding out in that chest....." A vortex of unpleasant memories whirled in his mind, tampered by the one good memory.

"I'm sorry you had to go through that." It was a tragedy that had also devastated Derek, to lose his friend because of a lie. "Everyone believed you were telling the truth except my father. He wanted to make an example of you."

Moses was staring too intently at the two as they loaded up their wagon with supplies and a stack of books. He wasn't paying attention to what Derek was saying. "I was locked in that trunk in the back of the train. I was frightened out of my wits. Alone. Neither my mother nor father dared to come anywhere near me for fear of me being discovered in that old chest, fearful of anyone guessing what

65

deception we were all involved in. I was spooked by every sound. Sure that we were all going to be caught. I couldn't help myself. I started sobbing."

"God save a goose!" The expression had been a favorite one in their youth. "You could have been discovered."

'I was. By the prettiest young girl I have ever seen." He smiled as he remembered. "Though we were both little more than children I think I fell a little bit in love with her." A flood of emotion swept over Moses as he remembered. "She came to visit me and let me out of that trunk. She brought me food that I suspect was her portion." His emotions welled up in his throat and he choked out the rest of the story. "She gave me something to look forward to. She read me stories. We talked about so many things. I was sorry when we reached our destination and had to say goodbye."

Looking behind him Derek realized that they were blocking several wagons in the roadway behind them. He started to guide the wagon towards the man and girl, but Moses grabbed the reins. "What are you doing? You need to reacquaint yourself with her. Otherwise you may never have another chance."

"No." More than anything Moses wanted to see the girl named Jemma again but unlike Derek he knew she was as unattainable as reaching for the moon. The Negro community had a social differentiation among themselves as strict as between those of the whites. A class structure that was developing even more acutely after the war. The whites distinguished between "bad Negroes," "good Negroes" and "uppity Negroes" but among themselves the lighter Negroes had the upper hand.

They were the ones who were the political leaders, teachers, and businesspeople. They had an advantage because the white people didn't abhor them as much as they did those with darker skin.

"What's gotten into you?" Derek tried to recapture the reins, but Moses held on too tightly and only handed them back to Derek once they were further down the road. "You are a fool. You've missed your chance."

Moses shook his head sadly. "I never *had* a chance. Besides, I think she and her father passed." When Derek looked at him questioningly, he said, "passed for white. And mostly likely they are doing so now. Knowing me could complicate her life."

Quickly losing patience Derek insisted, "I think you are wrong. I think we should go back." If anyone knew how stubborn Moses could be it was Derek. At last he gave in. "All right then."

Turning his head for one last look, Moses felt a sense of great loss. But what was the point of going after a dream that would melt away with the dawn. He had made his choice and no matter how this moment in time might haunt him it was a choice he would have to live with.

## Chapter Four

The early morning air smelled of flowers, fresh grass, and the river as Amelia hurried up the pathway to the school. Just as she had promised, she had come to the school very early for several days now, so that she could teach her favorite pupil. The young Negro boy's name was Jedidiah, the youngest child of freed slaves. He had a thirst for knowledge that seemed unquenchable and she never ceased to be amazed how quickly he had learned how to read. At least twice as quickly as the other students.

Before the reconstruction, while slavery still existed, it had been illegal to educate slaves and Amelia thought how fortunate it was that Jedidiah was now free to learn. He was a child strong in body and mind and she had a feeling he could brave the obstacles the whites would put in his path. She was determined to at least help him attain the tools that would aid him on his educational journey.

Amelia had asked one of the children's father, a sharecropper, to fix the lock and get her an extra key for Jedidiah so she wasn't surprised that the boy was there before she arrived every single morning. Today was no exception. Opening the door, she found him sitting at one of the desks immersed in a book, his lips moving as he read the words. He stumbled over a few of them but sounded them out just as she had taught him to do.

"O come and see J..Jane feed her p..pet lamb."

"Bravo, Jedidiah. Bravo." Taking off her bonnet and hanging it on a small hat rack by the door she urged him to continue.

"It has fine soft wool as…."

He was having difficulty, so she said the word. "White. White as snow."

He scowled. "But wool and w..white aren't spelled the same. Why do they sound alike?"

*Out of the mouths of babes she thought.* "I have often struggled with such things myself, Jedidiah. Unfortunately, you will find many times when words don't sound like they should. Just do the best that you can."

He continued, doing quite well for just learning. Her praise was well earned. A little while later he looked up from the book. "I don't think I have ever seen a lamb. But I've seen horses, cows, and pigs."

"That's because sheep aren't as prevalent here in Virginia as they are other places." She remembered sitting with her mother as they looked out the window at the falling snow. They had shared the woolen shawl her mother had just finished knitting to guard against the chilly air. "Where it is cold the people rely on wool sheared from lambs to make sweaters and cloth."

He was intrigued. "I'd like to touch a lamb some day. I'll bet it's soft, Missy."

"Very." She remembered seeing sheep up close at the fair. "And the wool is spun into cloth."

He was intrigued. "Like they do with cotton?"

She didn't really know the process used. "I would suppose."

# ASHES AND AWAKENINGS

Amelia had brought her father's pocket watch to mark off the time, knowing how important it was to end Jedidiah's lessons before the other children arrived. There were still many whites who were determined not to help the Negroes get an education and she didn't want to take the chance of Jedidiah's feelings being hurt. Some of the children, like Beauregard, had viperish tongues. Still as the two of them read together and she witnessed the joy on the boy's face when he learned to read new words, she found herself mesmerized by his intelligence and delighted with giving him the gift of knowledge.

"Hmmm. Quarter to eight. We'll have to wait until tomorrow to do more reading." When she saw the dejected look on his face she amended, "but you can take the book on farm animals with you if you would like."

"Can I. Can I really?"

His delight was shared with her. "See if you can figure out some of the words on your own and I'll test you tomorrow." She watched as he gathered his meagre belongings and happily ran out the door and down the pathway.

"And that is why I became a teacher...." She said to herself as she watched him disappear through the trees. Then it was time for the school day to begin. Amelia took a role call as each child sat at their assigned desk. It was the fashion of the day that girls were separated from the boys, but Amelia thought it best to sit the children all together, alternating boy, girl, boy, girl. It kept the girls from gossiping and the boys from playing pranks on each other.

"Good morning, class." Amelia forced a smile.

It looked to be a tedious day. Beauregard had

already reached across the aisle and punched Robert in the arm, then pretended that he wasn't the one who had done the deed. Although she had often made him wear a dunce cap and sit facing the corner, it hadn't done a thing to curb his mischievous behavior.

"We'll read today from the National Reader."

"Miss Seton, look what I found." Suzy Thompson's high voice interrupted the lesson. "It's a dollar bill." Holding the money up for all to see she giggled in glee.

Amelia gave a sigh of exasperation but walked over to take a look at the girl's discovery. "It's a Confederate dollar bill. I fear they aren't worth even a penny now."

"Whose picture is that?" Beauregard was interested in anything Confederate.

"Clement C. Clay." She could see Beauregard's disappointment that it wasn't Jefferson Davis. "Where did you find it, Suzy?"

"In this book as a bookmark." She held up a book about Cinderella.

The schoolroom dissolved into chaos as the other students reached out to try and get possession of the bill. Pounding her podium with a ruler Amelia at last had the students quieted. Hoping to keep them occupied she set aside reading and told them to take up their slates to practice handwriting.

As usual it was hot and stuffy in the room. Amelia tried to loosen the high collar on her pale-yellow dress and had to unbutton the top two buttons. She watched the bent heads of the children as they toiled over their slates. Willy always grumbled that he was going to be a farmer and didn't need to know how to write. Timothy had such a scrawled hand that she wondered if he would ever learn to write at all. Mary's writing was so tiny that Amelia could barely read it. Belinda had the clearest writing of all.

History, arithmetic, writing, and back to reading and yet the day seemed to drag on. Amelia strained her ears to listen as each child took his turn to recite. Since each child varied in skill, she gave each a different book to read from. Jimmy stumbled even over simple nursery rhymes and she couldn't help but feel sorry for the lad. His father was from a family descended from the elite who had come to Richmond during the turn of the century. Too much was expected of the boy, and she knew he could never fulfill his family's ambitions now that their lives were in limbo.

Last to recite was Mary, who read from *Alice in Wonderland.* As a teacher Amelia tried her best to be impartial with the children, yet something about Jedidiah tugged at her heart. She was so deeply sorry that she couldn't bring him into the classroom and take the time to teach him all the things she knew would delight him. She thought to herself that she didn't think she would ever understand why people judged human beings by the color of their skin. What a strange world it would have been if animals did the same and a white rabbit thought itself superior to a brown, black or gray one.

Amelia put her thoughts quickly out of her head, reaching for her watch to look at the time. She treasured the watch more than any other of her possessions. "Classes are through for the day, children. You may go home. Jimmy, would you like to ring the bell?" Eager to be outdoors, Jimmy raced to the bell and loudly rang out the end of another day.

Placing her father's watch on the desk, Amelia straightened up the tables and benches and wiped the slates clean, mindful of the promise to her aunt that she would not be late. She was surprised to see Beauregard still inside the room when she looked up. She started to move past him, but he blocked her way.

"I saw you very, very early this morning," he said, his mouth set in a smug grin.

"Saw me. And why not. My coming to school is not a big surprise." She stiffened, wondering just what he meant.

"My pa would be upset ifen I told him what you were up to." Like the bully he could often be, he took a step towards her.

"And just what is that?" Somehow, she knew in her heart just what he was going to say but she hoped that she was wrong and that he was merely teasing.

He pointed a finger at her. His attitude oozed belligerence "I saw you sittin' beside that nigger boy, teaching him to rea...."

On hindsight Amelia would realize that she had done the wrong thing, but on impulse she clenched the ruler she held in her hand and swatted him on the finger wagging right before her nose. Just a tap in warning. "I don't ever want to hear you use that word again. Do you hear me? It's vile."

His voice was taunting. "Why? That's what he is?" He started to say the word again but seeing the angry look on her face he backed down. "My pa says they have no business tryin' to read and write. He says you might as well teach a donkey."

"It's none of your father's business," she shot

73

back, trying to keep her temper in check. Beauregard's father didn't have a thing to say about what she did or didn't do.

He shrugged. "Maybe not. I was just lettin' you know that I know your secret now. If  y'all are smart you'll trade me an "A" for keepin' my mouth shut."

She tried to tell herself to remember that despite his size, he was still a boy. But a voice whispered in her ear that he was a bratty little weasel.  A treacherous mini version of his father. "You are a little young for blackmail," Amelia said dryly. She wanted to say more but now that he had warned her, he turned and walked through the door.

Amelia just stood watching him retreat and was surprised to find that she was trembling all over. The confrontation had shaken her to the core, and she felt a mixture of outrage and alarm.  She was afraid, not for herself, but for Jedidiah. She would have to be cautious in the future and not take anything for granted.

*       *       *       *

Derek didn't know things could go so quickly from bad to worse, but they had!  If it wasn't bad enough that his father had continued his bouts of drunkenness, Charles had insisted on working in the tobacco fields, to show the new laborers how it was done. Disregarding that he was now in his older years, he had pushed himself to the point of exhaustion and had suffered what the doctor had said was a bout of apoplexy.

Derek had found him doubled up on the ground

near the tobacco fields, his hands covering his face. Although his drinking often caused slurred speech, difficulty keeping his balance and mental confusion this had been different. In an instant Derek had known that something was very wrong with his father. Never before had his father shown fear but as he had battled the assault to his body, Charles Cameron had actually cried.

Derek remembered his father reaching out, trying to communicate that he couldn't see out of one eye, couldn't coordinate his arms or legs and that he had a blistering headache. Although Charles Cameron's newly acquired girth made him a large bundle to manage, somehow Derek had been able to lift him up on the back of his horse and ride back to the house. Leaving him in the capable hands of Honora, Derek had ridden into town at breakneck speed to fetch the doctor. The week-long vigil that had followed had been unsettling, emotional, and tragic. To see anyone fight for their life was like a journey into your own soul.

Coming in from the fields Derek knew he needed to clean up before he looked in on his father so he paused at the well to fill a bucket, then washed the dirt and grime off his hands, face, and arms as best he could, allowing the sun to dry him off. His emotions were in a turmoil. On one hand he was relieved now that he and Moses were sharing the work of six additional field hands; on the other he was still concerned about finances. Ever since Grant's second inauguration earlier in the year the nation seemed poised on a downward spiral even worse than after the war. At the back of his mind was the fear that he wouldn't be able to stretch the money to make the tobacco fields profitable again and therefore he would be unable to pay Moses back for the loan he had so generously granted him.

"You are borrowing trouble," he whispered to himself, quoting a saying his mother always used when he was morose. Tobacco was as popular as bread. If he could produce a crop there would be a market for it.

Plastering on a smile for his mother's benefit, Derek opened the front door, surprised to find her still engaged in conversation with Doctor Adams. "How is Father?"

As always Honora came right to the point without sugar-coating her words. "I fear your father is more seriously ill than was first suspected."

Guilt flashed over Derek as he remembered the argument he had had with his father concerning the loan from Moses. He should have just ignored his father's tirade and not called him an ungrateful bastard. Two words he wished he could take back.

"He has pneumonia," Dr. Adams said matter-of-factly.

"Pneumonia." In addition to his apoplexy. It was a two-edged sword. Pneumonia was a leading cause of death.

"We'll have to do everything we can to remove the excess fluid from his lungs. And of course, we will use leeches. Bloodletting is a valuable aid."

Bloodletting. Derek grimaced at the very thought of having those disgusting leeches attached to any part of *him*. He pitied his poor father.

"I've been giving him warm tea with fresh ginger and it seems to reduce his pain and his coughin'." Honora drew a deep breath. It was

76

obvious that she was exhausted. She was pale and her eyes had dark circles.

Derek's attention now centered on his mother. "You can't take care of Father all on your own. You need help. Let me contact Allegra. She can take the earliest train…."

"No." Honora could be just as stubborn as Derek. "Your sister and Reeve have enough to worry about with his new job as a lawyer and their four children."

Though he seemed to give in to her refusal for help, Derek had other ideas up his sleeve. He had heard about one of the wives of the sharecroppers being a healer. Perhaps he could find out who she was and enlist her aid.

*　　*　　*　　*

It was a quiet night except for the chirping of field crickets and the occasional hooting of an owl. Watching as several fireflies lit the darkness with their pulsating flashes of light, Forest wondered what cruel twist of fate had been responsible for Quentin crossing paths with a man from the past. The man was a northerner who they had crossed paths with the morning they had ridden into Richmond for supplies. He had come upon them while they were loading up the wagon. He was a man Quentin had once advised on political matters in Philadelphia. The man had been exuberant to run into her foster father and had somehow convinced Quentin to get involved in politics.

Though at first Quentin had reneged on the idea,

# ASHES AND AWAKENINGS

Matthew Stewart had talked and talked until he had convinced him. The South needed honest men like Quentin, he had insisted. Together they could help form a coalition during these turbulent times. A party to break the power of wealth and established privilege among the planter elite; a correct political party could give all men, no matter what the color of their skin, a chance to better their lives by getting an education. To open up the scholastic door, Stewart had said, they needed funding and that meant "one of theirs" being elected.

Matthew Stewart knew Quentin's soft spot for book learning and teaching others and so he had renewed her foster father's interest in political matters. He had reminded him that the Fifteenth Amendment to the United States Constitution had been adopted three years ago giving the right to vote to male citizens without that right being abridged or denied on account of race, color, or previous condition of servitude. He had told Quentin that it was his duty to do everything in his power to change Virginia for the betterment of all.

Although she couldn't say why, Forest just didn't trust Matthew Stewart. Not that he had done anything obviously wrong. No. It was just an inner voice, an instinct that told her traveling down this new path would not do her and Quentin any good in the long run. People could be petty, ambitious, selfish, and cruel and she feared that although he was a brilliant man in so many ways, Quentin was naïve when it came to reading other people's ulterior motives. She, on the other hand, had witnessed first-hand how ruthless politicians could be. She felt in her heart that Quentin would be hurled into the lion's den.

78

# KATHRYN KRAMER

She remembered hearing the ladies in Philadelphia talk about their husbands. She recalled how they had talked about tumultuous meetings in smoke filled rooms, about heated arguments, money being tossed around as if it was confetti, about secret deals, grudges against those who didn't play the game, vendettas, and payoffs by those pleased that they could buy themselves a senator or congressman. Politics was dirty business. She had heard that bandied about all the time in Philadelphia. Wives always knew their husband's secrets but didn't always know when to keep it to themselves.

"This is the calm before the storm," she whispered, her voice being carried off by the light summer breeze. "Everything is safe and peaceful away from people like Matthew Stewart." But once they were thrown into the whirlwind nothing would be the same. They would have to play their game of pretend again and somehow lose who they really were. Once Forest had thought that they were happy in Philadelphia but the seclusion of the cottage in the woods had helped her think more clearly. In Philadelphia she had been playacting, trying to be like the others even though deep inside she knew that she was nothing at all like them. But what was the use of re-living the past? One thing she had learned from Quentin was to never look back but try and look forward to a better future. Could she do that now?

Wrapping her arms around her body she thought about Quentin and all he had done for her. She fully suspected that his decision to jump into the fracas was for *her*. He was trying to secure the future so that she wouldn't have to live far away, isolated from civilization like he had done for so many years. You are young, not an old goat like me, he had said. You

79

need to be around people of your own age.

"But I'm happy here," she sighed, then felt a twinge of guilt as she suspected that she was being selfish. In their exile-like existence they had been secluded and sequestered without a care about the outside world. They hadn't had to answer to anyone else or give in to other people's whims. Now Forest feared the intrusion that would follow. The secrets that might be revealed. What if there were those who wanted to learn more about Quentin and the young girl thought of as his daughter. Forest knew from those days in Philadelphia that there would be political organizers, newspaper editors, and hangers-on who would be intruding into their privacy and into their lives.

Reaching up she combed her fingers through her hair uneasy as she realized that eventually she would have to stop masquerading as a boy. Their uncomplicated life was going to become complicated. Once again, she would have to wear skirts and petticoats and watch her manners so as not to create a scandal. And once again she would hope that there wouldn't be any suspicions as to her real identity. Most important of all she feared what would happen if anyone found out that once upon a time she had been a slave.

## Chapter Five

It was a cool and crisp morning, much chillier than usual and though Amelia wore an aqua-blue linen dress, she felt the need to pull her shawl about her shoulders to ward off the cold air. Strolling along the pathway to the school she looked frantically for Jedidiah but didn't see him. The fear that somehow something had gone wrong assailed her. Dear God, what if Beauregard had made good on his threat to cause trouble. What if Jedidiah had been bullied or threatened. What if he was afraid to come to the school?

A sound behind her startled her for just a minute but turning around she saw Jedidiah's smiling face and she felt relief sweep over her. "Oh, Jeb, I was afraid you weren't coming this morning."

"Not come to school?" He shook his head. "The only way I'd not be here, Missy, is if I were dead."

The very idea shook her to the core. "Don't even talk about death, Jedidiah. You are just a boy. Wait until you are an old man."

Jedidiah laughed. "Heck, by the time I am gray in the whiskers I'll know so much the devil will be jealous." He had both hands behind his back but as he spoke, he held out his left hand. "You are such a fine teacher, Missy. I was late this morning because I was finishing this."

The item that he held out to her was a wooden carving of an angel with wings, a halo, and a book. Amelia was amazed at the workmanship and talent the carver had to make such a beautiful object. Looking closer she was almost brought to tears as she noted the angel was wearing her hair in a bun and had a face that looked amazingly like Amelia.

"You carved this?"

He flashed her a toothy grin. "Yes, Missy, I did. I learned to do that from my father."

'It's beautiful, Jedidiah. I had no idea you had such a talent." She carefully took it from his outstretched hand, running her fingers lovingly over this new treasure. "I'll keep it with me at all times for good luck and to remind me of a young man of immeasurable skills and a very loving heart."

Together they walked into the classroom, sitting side by side as Jedediah read out loud. This morning they read from *At the Back of the North Wind*, a fantasy centered on a boy named Diamond and his adventures with the North Wind. In the book the boy traveled with the mysterious *Lady North Wind*.

"I have been asked to...to t...t...tell you about the back of the North W..W..Wind," he read, "an old Greek writer m..m..mentions a people who lived there....."

The book told the story of a young boy named Diamond who made happiness everywhere he went. One night, as he was trying to sleep, Diamond plugged up a hole in his loft bedroom wall to stop the wind from blowing in. He soon found out, however, that the plug was stopping the North Wind from seeing through her window. Diamond befriended her, and North Wind let him fly with her, taking him on several adventures.

As he read, Amelia was caught up in the spell of the adventure, almost as if she and Jedidiah were traveling with Diamond. Suddenly she was brought back to the present. Looking at the watch she realized that the other children would be arriving at any moment.

"That's all for today, Jed. We'll start where we left off tomorrow."

Wishing they had more time, she watched Jedidiah hurry down the pathway. Turning around she had the unnerving feeling that she was being watched. Had she seen a shadow behind that tree? Yes, she was certain that she had.

"Jenny? Billy? Johnny?" She laughed at her fears. It was no doubt one of the children--who else could it be? No one but her students ever came this far.

"Beauregard?" How like him to spy on her again. "Show yourself, whoever you are."

The bushes rustled, the branches of the tree crackling as a tall man obeyed Amelia's request. He was dressed in tan trousers, which hugged his muscular legs like a second skin, a white cotton shirt with the sleeves rolled high above the elbows, and knee-high brown leather boots. A sharecropper she supposed by the way he was dressed. That he was also very handsome, she would have had to be blind not to notice. Brushing a hand through his wind-ruffled blond hair, his blue eyes appraising her, he just stood looking at her with a bewildered look on his face.

"Well I'll be damned. If you are indeed the school marm, y'all aren't like any of the ones who schooled *me*."

She was taken aback. "I beg your pardon." Self-consciously Amelia put one hand up to the neck of her light blue cotton dress while the other brushed stray tendrils of hair out of her face.

Fearing he had been much too bold; Derek took a step backwards. "I didn't mean any offense. It's just that I was assuming you would be much older and not so pretty."

The compliment caused her to blush, and she found herself unable to think of what to say. For a long, drawn out moment they just stood staring at each other. At last Amelia asked, "can I help you with something?" She immediately thought he must be the father of one of her students. Suzy perhaps? The blonde hair was similar. She looked behind him to see who he was with then realized he was all alone.

Derek came right to the point. "My father suffered apoplexy and now he has pneumonia. He needs constant care and a miracle." He shook his head. "My mother is a sweet, stubborn soul who won't admit that she needs help caring for him."

"I'm so sorry." Now that she looked at him more closely, she could see the concern in his eyes. "How can I be of help?" She folded her arms across her chest. "I'm afraid I don't know anything at all about nursing."

Seeing that she had misunderstood him Derek hurried to clarify just what he was looking for. "I've heard that one of the sharecroppers has a wife who is a healer. I was hopin' you could help me find her so as to enlist her aid in helpin' my father."

"A healer." Amelia thought for a moment. Even though she didn't know him she felt an obligation to help him. "I think I've heard Jimmy O'Leary talk about the potions and remedies his mother has made. I can ask him today as soon as school is under way."

Relief swept over Derek. Finding a woman who might be able to help his father had been easier than he had hoped. "If y'all could do that I would be immensely grateful." He wanted to say more but was annoyed to find himself tongue tied. "Be sure and let it be known that I can pay the woman for her services." He didn't want her to think he was a pauper even though he knew he must look like one dressed as he was.

"I...I will." The children were starting to crowd through the school door and Amelia was regretful that she couldn't stay and talk with the blonde man longer. "How can you be contacted?"

Derek wondered where his manners had gone. "I'm sorry not to have introduced myself. "I'm Derek. Derek Cameron."

"Cameron." Anyone in the area who wasn't a carpetbagger knew the name. For generations, the Camerons had been wealthy and had owned one of the finest plantations near Richmond. Many of the sharecroppers whose children she taught in school were employed by Charles Cameron or were sharecroppers on his land.

"And you are..?"

Amelia tried hard to focus but somehow she was mesmerized by his good looks. "My name is Amelia. Amelia Seton." Oh, if only she had known they would cross paths today she would have worn one of her best dresses, not the faded cotton.

"A northerner by your accent." He smiled, amused how those from up north always said the southerners had accents when clearly it was just the opposite.

"Originally, yes." Looking towards the door, she

could see that some of the boys were squabbling. Regretfully she realized she had to go inside to restore discipline. "Once I find out who you are looking for shall I have her contact you at your…your house?"

"Well yes, that would be perfect." He really regretted that their time together was coming to an abrupt end. He wanted to learn more about her. It was clearly time to leave, however. One glance at the boys sticking their tongues out and making faces told him that. "Thank you so very, very much."

"You are very welcome." Picking up her skirts to avoid tripping, she started walking up the pathway to the doorway. Turning around, she saw that he was watching her intently. For just a moment her aunt's criticism came to mind and she hoped he didn't find her too unattractive.

"Thanks again," he called out, flashing her his winning grin.

Amelia started to answer but to her horror she tripped and only by the grace of God somehow managed not to fall. Regaining her balance, she stiffened her shoulders, held up her head and walked through the door of the schoolhouse without another backward glance.

*     *     *     *

It had been a long time since Forest had seen Quentin all dressed up. Determined to look his best for a meeting with Matthew Stewart and some of his political friends, he was wearing a dark brown three-piece suit along with a tan and green striped vest, white shirt, and a top hat. His waistcoat was short in front and extended to the knees in back as was the fashion when the garments had been tailored for him in Philadelphia a few years ago.

"Do I look presentable?" He was nervously preening in the mirror, an action she had never seen him do before. He was the least vain person she had ever met. "With all your good cooking I have put on a few pounds but thank the good Lord I still fit into these clothes, though I fear the pants are a bit snug."

"You'll have to be very careful not to split them if you bend over," she teased, then complimented him. "You look very distinguished. Like a mighty well-dressed giant." He had even trimmed his beard and had Forest trim his hair.

Forest was waiting for Quentin to chastise her for still wearing men's pants and a long-sleeved shirt, but so far he had not said a word. Perhaps because he sensed that she was not quite ready for a metamorphosis. During the time they had been together, he had learned to sense her emotions.

Turning away from his reflection he asked, "are you coming with me?"

She wanted to, very much. "Isn't it forbidden for females to even step inside that stuffy room?"

"You will have to be extremely careful. If some of those old boys get wind that there is a woman in the hall, they might have apoplexy." Nodding his head, he signaled for Forest to adjust his tie.

As she untied then re-tied his cravat, she hurried to assure him. "I'll be as quiet as a tiny mouse. I'll shrink back into the shadows. No one will even notice me."

He laughed his deep, booming guffaw. "Even

87

dressed as you are you are noticeable. Why the other day in Richmond two men in a wagon drove by our vehicle and they were staring a hole right through you. I don't think your boy's garments fooled them for a second."

For just a moment she was concerned but she laughed it off. "Perhaps I should glue on a mustache."

Quentin laughed again. "Oh, my Lord no. Just swagger in and act as if you belong there."

"I should. I think it is foolish that men don't allow females at their meeting places." Grabbing her hat from the rack, she put it on her head, hiding her pinned up hair. "And I'm not alone in what I believe. All the women in Philadelphia felt much the same."

Taking her gently by the shoulders, Quentin turned her to face him. "I think the same thing, but you must be patient. We of Negro blood have had to wait a long time for even a smidgen of a chance for equality. I feel in my heart that one of these days women will get the rights that they deserve. It has to be."

His words lightened her mood. "I hope that day is soon." Together they left the cottage and stepped up into a small buggy Quentin had bought from a neighbor. It would be useful in the coming days, he had insisted. Traveling in the wagon was demeaning at a time when he wanted to garner respect.

"Let me take the reins," Forest requested. "I might as well start acting as your manservant.

He laughed. "The prettiest manservant in all of Virginia. I'll be the talk of the City." Although it was said in jest, Quentin didn't know how right he was or how much their lives were going to change.

KATHRYN KRAMER

## Chapter Six

Amelia had told herself a hundred times that she wasn't interested in Derek Cameron. Even so, she had taken the trouble to find out about his marital status from Rebecca James when she had discussed with the older woman the need for someone skilled with herbs and potions at the Cameron house.

"Derek Cameron?" Her mother's friend Rebecca had a knowing look on her face. "Why he is free, Amelia dear. As free as a bird. Why do you ask?"

Amelia had blushed. "No reason. I just wondered if there would be any Cameron children coming to the school any time soon."

That he was eligible opened her up to daydreams of a courtship and the hope that she would see him again. He was such a fine-looking man. But there was something else as well. His concern for his mother showed he had a kind heart and to Amelia that was the most important thing. That kindness had shown brightly in his blue eyes. Eyes that had seared her soul.

"I do declare, Amelia, if you don't stop peeling that same carrot you will have it whittled down to the size of a hair." There was more than just a hint of annoyance in her aunt's reproach.

"What?" Amelia flushed as she looked down at the unfortunate vegetable. "Oh!"

"Something's on your mind." Lucinda paused. "You're not yourself this evening. What in heavens name are you thinking about?" Her eyes were searching, as if she could read Amelia's mind.

"It's...it's nothing!" Amelia picked up another carrot. She wanted to tell her aunt about her meeting with Derek Cameron, needed her advice, but knowing that Lucinda could be condescending she held her tongue.

"Nothing?" The graying eyebrows shot up in disbelief.

Amelia was quick to respond. "I was just worrying about one of the students, that's all. He is so disruptive in class that I have had to discipline him several times this week." Thinking about Beauregard she almost nicked her thumb.

"Hmm. A naughty student is taking up your time. How foolish." Lucinda picked up a long wooden spoon, stirring the bubbling iron pot of stew. "Well, if you would listen to me you would set your cap for a wealthy husband and then you wouldn't have to bother with someone else's little monster. You would have brats of your own."

Amelia immediately went on defense. "I've told you time and time again that I don't want to trap any man. As a matter of fact, I don't want a man at all."

Putting an onion down on the chopping block, Lucinda gave vent to her peevishness, slicing it into several tiny pieces. "Not now perhaps, but you will one day. And then it might be too late. You're not a pretty woman, Amelia. Time is running out. That's why I took the liberty of asking Edward Cutler to dinner."

"No!" Amelia definitely was not in the mood.

Lucinda's face flushed. "I'm a hopeless matchmaker."

"And you're wasting your time." Putting the knife and peeled carrot down, Amelia wiped her hands on her apron.

"Your objection has come too late." Lucinda wiped her face with the bottom corner of her apron. "He will be here any time now and I expect you to entertain him while I put the finishing touches on this stew." With a snort she went back to her cooking, stirring the pot so vigorously that Amelia feared she would break the spoon.

"Entertain him. We have nothing in common. Besides, I don't like bankers. They are too…."

Lucinda was nodding her head towards the doorway where the red-headed Edward Cutler was standing. Since no one had answered his knock he had apparently let himself in, a bold move that to Amelia was annoying.

"Shush. He's here. Now go!"

Reaching up, Amelia took a stack of plates from the kitchen, carefully balancing them as she walked. "I'll be polite but please get rid of him by seven. I need to get to sleep early tonight." Her eyes moved to Edward. He was a pleasant enough looking fellow of average height and build, well dressed in a suit, but something about him left her cold. A man of all smiles, he tried to instigate a conversation.

"Your aunt tells me you are a *teacher*." His tone of voice was condescending.

"Yes, I teach several of the sharecroppers' children. Reading, writing and arithmetic. Geography. History."

He brushed at his lapel as if it was dirty. "It must be unnerving trying to teach a rag tag group of children. I commend you."

Amelia stiffened. 'There is nothing to commend. I enjoy helping young people expand their knowledge." Putting the plates down on the table, she looked up into his beady brown eyes, thinking to herself that those eyes looked almost feral.

"Good. Good. Nice to know." He reached up and adjusted his red tie. "I'm from the north, just like you and your aunt. That is, I'm from there originally. Now I consider myself a son of the South."

She thought to herself "carpetbagger" but didn't say it. "How long have you lived in Richmond? I assume that is where you reside."

He thought a moment. "Seven years. I came right after the war ended sensing there would be *opportunities* for an enterprising man." He nudged her in the ribs and winked. "As it is things have worked out even better than I could have ever hoped."

Amelia chided herself for thinking unkind thoughts about him just because he handled money. "How fine for you. I'm sure there are many businesses and families that depend on you for financial help."

He looked down at his feet. "Well, I don't know that I am of help to them. My main job is calling in bad debt, especially loans. That's how the bank makes most of its money."

"I see." It was just as she had first thought. He was a vulture, just like so many of the others. The South was wounded, and his kind always seemed to smell the blood.

93

# ASHES AND AWAKENINGS

Taking a seat at the table, Amelia had to work very hard to be amiable as he took a seat beside her. It was going to be a long and tedious evening. Even though her aunt's cooking was at its best, she didn't seem to enjoy the meal. Putting the spoon up to her mouth again and again, she hardly even tasted what she ate. There were so many of the sharecroppers who had dreams of owning their own land and it was men like Edward Cutler who shattered their dreams. All the while padding their own pockets.

If Amelia was put off by their dinner guest, however, her aunt was obviously impressed. It was Lucinda that did most of the talking at the dinner table, telling Edward all about her niece and how accomplished she was. Compliments she never gave to her niece. Amelia thought sarcastically that her aunt might as well have wrapped her in paper and put a bow on her forehead. It was obvious that she was offering Amelia up as a marriage prospect for the eligible banker.

At last the meal was ended and Amelia's aunt insisted she would clean up the kitchen so that "the two young people" could be alone. As Amelia moved towards the settee, so did Edward, taking a seat beside her. Somehow it seemed another lifetime ago that she had left the schoolhouse. Edward's soliloquy caused the time to move like a turtle trying to cross the railroad tracks. Abysmally slow.

Reaching in his pocket, Edward pulled forth a wrinkled-up piece of paper which upon closer inspection proved to be a map. He traced a line on the map with his finger. This is the property I have my heart set upon."

Amelia moved closer, trying to see. Female intuition told her this wasn't just chit chat. "What do you mean?"

Flicking at the map with his finger, Edward's voice lowered to a whisper, as if he were revealing some deep dark secret. Perhaps he was. "Right here sits what used to be one of the richest plantations in this area. But they have fallen on hard times. Too much debt. Too many loans. A drunken owner....."

"You want to purchase it?" If he was trying to impress her his babbling had the opposite effect. Talking about taking advantage of another's hardship was disgusting.

"Purchase it?" He laughed. "I won't have to. All I have to do is play the waiting game."

Amelia was used to looking at maps. At school she had used them many times to help with her geography classes. Squinting she examined the map, taking note of an "x" representing the schoolhouse. She noted that it was at the end of the property in question. That meant that the banker had his eye on the very land she crossed every day on her way to school.

Edward Cutler traced the penciled line that represented the boundaries of the property he coveted. "There are only two mansions to speak of, the Avery Mansion," he pointed to its location. "And the main plantation house." He moved his finger to where he thought it would be. "I plan to build a third that will be even grander than either one."

She wanted to tell him then and there what she thought of him but instead said, "you are talking about the Cameron Plantation." She wanted to make sure she was right in her calculations.

95

He moved closer to her like a predator stalking his prey. "The Cameron farm as it is called now." He lowered his voice to a seductive tone. "If a pretty woman like you played your cards right you might be living there like a queen."

"And you would be the *king*," Her loathing for him knew no bounds.

"I would be." As he reached out to touch her, she stood up, just managing to elude his grasp.

"I would think you are more like the joker," she exclaimed, throwing back her shoulders so that she stood tall and strong. "And a fool if you really think you can wrest that land away from its rightful owners." Derek Cameron's image flashed before her eyes. Though she had just met him she didn't want him to lose what he was working so hard to maintain. Unlike Edward Cutler she had heard that Derek was a fair man, a good man. No one she had talked with had a bad word to say. And his mother, Honora, was said to be a saint.

"A fool?" Edward Cutler looked as if he were choking. "See here…."

"I don't want to *see* anything more," she said gesturing towards the front door. "We are through here, Sir." Ignoring her aunt's flustered questions, she ushered the banker out and closed the door behind him. She was determined to pay a visit to Derek Cameron as soon as she could. Someone had to warn him.

\*     \*     \*     \*

The air was thick with the mingled smells of

peppermint, eucalyptus, onions, and garlic, as well as other strange odors. As he stood at the door watching as Mrs. O'Leary patiently tended his father, Derek's eyes watered from the aromas in the room as well as his emotions. He smiled through the tears as he thought about the schoolteacher he had met and how she had kept her promise to find someone who could help his mother take care of his father.

"Leeches be damned!" It was an opinion that was shared with Catriona O'Leary who had been so bold as to shoo the physician attending Charles out of the room.

Derek couldn't help but chuckle as he recalled the scene. Doctor Adams had just delivered Charles Cameron's prognosis, telling Honora that Charles was very weak and most likely would not last the week. Giving him a dose of laudanum to eliminate the cough, he had declared that the rest was up to God.

"I'll return tomorrow morning to see how he is doing," he had said. The doctor had not been prepared for the likes of Catriona, however. Picking up a broom from its resting place in the corner, she had wielded it like the fiercest weapon.

"No. Don't be coming' back here with your failed and outdated treatments, bringing that sad face and dire predictions. You are pawning your duties to the poor Lord above who is overburdened already. We have no need of you." That said, she had pushed him out the door with the bristles of the sweeper.

Honora Cameron had been much too astonished to speak. She had kept silent as Catriona O'Leary had taken her place next to Charles' side and then taken his hand. Her voice was low and comforting as she uttered words of promise. She had told Charles

Cameron that he was going to recover because he was much too stubborn to give in.

Derek might not have fully believed her then, but he did now. Beyond a miracle his father's ashen face had taken on a bit of his former color and the ragged breathing and hacking coughs had subsided.

"You are a miracle worker, Catriona. He's showing signs of life for the first time thanks to you."

Reaching up to brush her bright red hair from her eyes she shook her head. "I don't work miracles; I just use what God has provided. Peppermint, eucalyptus, and fenugreek tea. Helps ease the pain and inflammation and helps the cough a bit." She turned to Honora. "When he gets back some of his strength, I'll have him gargle with warm saltwater. I would suppose you have some in the kitchen."

"We are well stocked. Both Derek and Charles, I fear, won't eat anything that isn't covered in salt and pepper. Even grits." Reaching out Honora touched Catriona's arm in a gesture of gratitude. "Thank you from the bottom of my heart. I know that words are not enough but somehow we will find a way to reward you."

Derek could have sworn that the woman blushed, but it was difficult to say with her ruddy complexion. "You are the ones who should reap a reward for fixing up that schoolhouse and teaching my Jimmy."

"We just provided a meeting place. It's the teacher--Amelia who has set a good example." Her face came to his mind and he thought about picking some flowers from the garden at the back of the house and taking them to her. He couldn't deny that he wanted to see her again.

Immersed in his own thoughts he didn't hear

98

Catriona's instructions to his mother until she said, "soaking the body in lukewarm water may help cool your husband down if his fever returns and starts to heat up his body."

Deciding that his father was being well cared for, Derek turned and left the room. There was so much work to do that he couldn't let any more time escape. Today he had to repair some damaged storage sheds, use a divining rod to find a place for a new well, and cut down a few dead trees. He would have to think about Amelia Seton some other time.

Hastening outside Derek hurried to the toolshed to get a hammer and nails then headed to the storage sheds. He was relieved to find that the wood had not been warped or damaged to the point where new wood was needed, thus it was relatively easy to pound the nails back in to keep the slats in place. Pausing, he looked in the direction of the fields thankful that he wasn't toiling with his field hands, at least today.

*Tobacco*, he thought scornfully. Hell, he didn't even smoke, but the leaves of that damnable plant ruled his life. First there was the planting with tiny seeds that needed temperatures of at least seventy-five to eighty degrees before they were put in the ground. Then the plants had to be tended to as carefully as a woman tended her babe. The plants were vulnerable to climate variations, diseases, and parasites. Then there was the harvesting when the tobacco was ripe. It was a leaf by leaf process, starting from the foot and picking up two or three leaves every two to three days, choosing each by the right ripeness. When that was done the leaves were hung in curing barns and allowed to dry for a month or two if needed. Drudgery pure and simple. And now the responsibility of keeping the "farm" running profitably was all on his shoulders.

For the life of him he didn't know why he hadn't just turned around and walked away when his father had insisted on keeping the plantation running. Farming was just not in his blood, or his heart, or on his mind. And yet out of a sense of family duty he had remained at Winding Oaks and convinced Moses to stay there too.

*So, I condemned us both to stay in the South when there were plenty of opportunities elsewhere,* he thought sourly as he wielded the hammer. Now he was wearing ragged clothes instead of wearing a fine suit and partnering at the law firm with his brother-in-law, Reeve.

Thinking about clothes caused Derek to realize it was hot and getting much hotter. Stripping to the waist he finished the task at hand then exchanged the hammer for an axe. Shirtless in the blazing afternoon sun, straining his muscles and getting blisters on his hands he turned his attention to cutting down the remainder of dead trees.

Even without his shirt on he was hot and soon grew exhausted beyond belief, and thirsty. Very, very thirsty. Picking up a bucket, he was going to go in search of water but had the strange sense that someone was staring at him. Turning around he was astounded to see Amelia Seton standing there like an alluring vision out of a dream.

Amelia couldn't help but stare. Although she hadn't seen a man half undressed before she knew he was as fine a specimen of manhood as existed. Well-muscled without even one inch of fat, his skin tan from the sun, his waist trim. Hurriedly she forced her eyes to look at his face feeling flustered to be caught staring.

Derek reached up to brush his sweat-damped hair out of his eyes, then smiled. "To what do I owe this pleasant surprise?" He made no move to put his shirt back on.

To her mortification her voice came out in a squeak. "I....I was just...just going home from teaching the children. I was at the school and....." She pointed towards where her horse and buggy were sheltered behind an oak tree.

"You came to see how my father was doing," he answered for her.

"Yes. Yes, I wanted to see if Catriona had been able to...to heal him." Her throat was parched, and she thought surely that was why she was having such trouble getting her words out.

Derek nodded returning her stare with one of his own. "His color has changed from ashen to normal and his breathing was not as raspy this morning. I owe you a heartfelt thank you." Watching as she licked her lips, he thought what a pretty mouth she had with full lips that looked very kissable. "Are you thirsty?"

"I'm parched," she answered.

Remembering his manners, he asked, "would you like to go inside? Mother could make you a cup of tea or pour you a glass of cider."

Noticing the bucket and guessing his intentions she told him not to go to any trouble. "Water would be just fine. As a matter of fact, a cool sip of spring water would taste like heaven's nectar." Realizing she

101

had sounded overly dramatic she laughed softly. "Thank you."

Derek went in search of water, finding the perfect place in an area where several large rocks purified the stream. Filling the bucket to the brim, he quickly retraced his steps, but before drinking he reminded himself to act like a gentleman. He offered the first dipper to Amelia.

"For you, sweet lady." As he held it out to her their hands touched and their eyes met for just a moment. But it was long enough for Derek to come to a conclusion. Amelia Seton fascinated him. The attraction he felt when he was around her was undeniably potent.

"Thank you, Derek." Taking the dipper, Amelia stepped back, startled by the strange shiver that rippled through her. A strange sense of excitement that had set her heart pounding. A giddy feeling. She had certainly not felt this way towards Edward Cutler.

Derek's intention to bring her flowers came back to his thoughts. "Wait here," he said, taking her arm and leading her to a shady spot beneath a tree. He gestured for her to sit on the tree stump that was the only reminder of the tree he had just felled.

Hurrying to the garden at the side of the house, he hastily picked a bouquet of bluebells mixed with a few strands of lavender and Blue Moon Wisteria. Returning to her side he handed the flowers to her. "I had intended to take more time in arrangin' flowers for you but perhaps this selection will suffice until I can offer you a more formal bouquet."

She was flattered by his thoughtfulness. "My favorite flowers. I love blue and the smell of Lavender has always given me a sense of calmness."

She was entranced by Derek Cameron's presence. But where did things go from here? Amelia was not the kind of woman to be overly forward.

Derek thought as he stood there just looking into Amelia's eyes that Moses would tease him unbearably because of his feelings. Feelings that he thought must be written upon his face. If only he had the time to pursue a relationship with this pretty young woman! Alas, that was a luxury that was not for him, at least not now.

Remembering why she had come in the first place Amelia cleared her throat. There....there was a banker at my aunt's house the other day. I thought you should know that he...he had a map of Winding Oaks and has his eye on getting his hands on it."

Her reminder of how precarious the ownership was of the plantation and how dire it would be if they could not pay back the loan sobered his lightheartedness. "Yes, I know."

His voice was so gruff that she took a step back. "I thought you should know."

Derek tried to force a smile. "And I appreciate that you thought to tell me." His pride goaded him to act as if nothing was wrong. "The situation has been handled. No banker will dare set foot on Cameron land, I assure you."

She sighed, relieved that he was not in any danger from a man like Cutler. "I'm glad."

There was an awkward silence between them. There was just too much work to be done and little time to do it in. Derek couldn't allow himself to be entranced by a pretty face. He was trapped by his promises, his responsibilities, and his determination to pay Moses back for every cent he had loaned to him.

103

And so, for the moment he didn't try to further any kind of relationship. With a sense of loss, he watched as she got into her buggy, picked up the reins and was gone with only a sad wave and a sigh.

## Chapter Seven

Politics was a disgusting business that seemed to bring out the very worst in men, Forest thought as she huddled in the back of the large meeting room. Pulling down her hat she tried to make herself as invisible as possible, the only salvation being the fact that the men sitting around, puffing their cigars and spouting their opinions were more interested in themselves than in any unimportant young *boy*.

Although Quentin had wanted Forest to dress like a young woman again, Forest had been adamant about keeping to her masquerade as a young male. The moment she revealed the truth about her masquerade she knew instinctively that she would have been banned from the "gentleman's" club and made to wait for Quentin outside.

"Women shouldn't worry their pretty heads about men's doings," she had heard several of the men say. They acted as if females had straw stuffed in their heads where brains were supposed to be and could only think of what to cook for dinner or what hat to wear to their afternoon teas. It was infuriating.

Politics had never been anything of interest before but the more she listened the more intrigued Forest became. From the speeches and discussions, she had already learned about the rival political coalitions that were gaining steam in the South. The most distressing were the "Redeemers" who Quentin told her were the Southern wing of the "Bourbon

Democrats". It was a conservative and pro-business faction that sought to regain their political power and enforce white supremacy. They wanted to oust the so-called Radical Republicans who were a coalition of freedmen, carpetbaggers, and *scalawags* led by former planters and businessmen. The Redeemers often disrupted meetings and political gatherings and worse yet sometimes used violence and threats of violence to get their way.

She had never seen Quentin so enthused about politics, but he was immersed in the new party being formed by Matthew Stewart. They wanted to help blacks and poor whites actually be able to vote without being intimidated, wanted to increase funding for schools and other public facilities, wanted to improve the railroads that had been rebuilt after the war but only constructed shoddily. They wanted to make certain that promises made right after the war was over would be kept, such as re-distributing property so that everyone had a chance. Quentin had told her that so far, few Negroes had gotten their forty acres and a mule.

Forest had learned from Quentin that Matthew Stewart, like them, had Negro blood as well as Indian heritage. While in Philadelphia he had been passing for white just as they had been. Now he wanted all people to be able to marry the person they loved no matter their blood. It was as Quentin had said, a noble goal.

The chair she was sitting in was getting more uncomfortable the longer Forest sat listening to the conversations flowing back and forth. Leaning back, she closed her eyes and tried to pretend that she was sitting outside the cottage this warm afternoon but

106

there were too many distractions to relax. Oh, how she missed the life she and Quentin used to have before he had decided to give aid to the politicians.

"You. Boy!" Although the words were spoken in a loud voice, Forest didn't really hear at first. She was immersed in her own thoughts. "Boy!"

Uncomfortable at having been noticed, Forest tried to shrink back into the shadows again but realizing that it wouldn't do her any good she stood up. "Yes, Sir."

He motioned for her to come closer. When she did, he handed her a folded and sealed piece of paper. "I want you to take this to the bank down the street and see to it that Andrew Wyatt receives it."

Looking down at her feet to avoid direct eye-contact and thereby possible detection, she reached out and took it from his hand. "Mr. Wyatt. Yes, Sir."

"He has the kind of face that no one ever forgets." Turning his back, he put the matter out of his mind as he returned to his jabbering.

Pushing through the doors of the meeting room and hurrying down the stone steps, Forest put her hand up to her eyes to adjust to the bright sunlight. The familiar sound of the venders tempted her to buy something to eat but she ignored their voices. That is until she was face to face with a vendor who sold her favorite treat. Hushpuppies. Fumbling in her pocket she found the correct coinage and exchanged the money for the deep-fried cornmeal dumplings. Munching on them as she walked along the street, she looked for the bank building.

"Merchants National Bank of Richmond." Brushing the crumbs off of her face she went inside.

# ASHES AND AWAKENINGS

It wasn't that she hadn't been inside a bank before but that had been when she was with Quentin. She felt conspicuous and out of place. All of the men inside were wearing suits and ties, a stark contrast to her garments. Standing in line she was impatient as she waited her turn to talk with the teller. When at last her turn came, she blurted out her determination to see Andrew Wyatt.

"Just what do you want with him?" He eyed her up and down, determining that she didn't look at all important.

"I have a message for him that is to be delivered to his hands only."

After a bit of hemming and hawing the teller disappeared. Through the open door of the office behind the counter, Forest heard him telling a man that there was a messenger out front. Tapping her foot in impatience she was getting more annoyed by the minute. At last she heard a voice.

"You have something for me?"

Looking up, holding out the folded and sealed piece of paper she nearly choked as she saw Andrew Wyatt's face. Mother of God it couldn't be. Her eyes were playing tricks on her.

"Well. Give it to me."

In panic she realized that she was clutching the paper like a lifeline. Hurriedly she let go, blinking her eyes, fully expecting to see a different visage. But no. Like a face from the past, the image that had haunted her nightmares for so long was right before her.

Never would she forget that face. His mouth was crooked, his nose as large as a bird's beak, his eyes small and angry. If the hair and mustache were

108

no longer dark but now touched with gray it didn't matter. That face was embedded in her brain. Forest remembered this man as the one who had chased after her that fateful day.

*     *     *     *

Shuffling as he walked, Moses felt like a man who had suddenly turned ninety and realized how hard he had pushed himself today. And yesterday. And the day before. But he was damned if he would stop now. With an oath, he picked up an axe in one hand and a shovel in the other. He had something to prove--to Charles Cameron, to Derek, and to himself.

Pushing open the barn door, he walked outside and stood for a long moment viewing the pink-and-purple horizon. Strange how many times he had looked upon a sunset lately. He had also viewed quite a few sunrises. They had lost their magic and were sadly becoming commonplace. Working from sunrise to sunset and sometimes beyond was normal for him now. In just a few years his life had changed significantly. He owned land. And on that land was a house. A barn. A well. And soon there would be a peanut crop. Peanuts that would need to be harvested.

It had been an arduous task planting the peanuts in the soil two inches deep, eight inches apart, bending over and staying in that position until you were certain you wouldn't be able to straighten up. But at last it was done and he could hardly wait to see the green leaves at last peek through the ground.

Breathing in the smell of the earth in the air, Moses felt as if he were embarking on a whole new life, as if the old Moses was gone and a new one had taken his place. He hadn't felt this optimistic since he had at last been freed from that old trunk and felt the joy of no longer being a slave.

Putting his hand up to shield his eyes from the setting sun, he looked out upon the land and groaned. Trees, as far as the eye could see. It would be an endless job to clear them. But if he followed through on the work there would be a profit from the lumber. Extra money to pay off the loan.

Walking across the area he had cleared just the day before, Moses put down his shovel, flipped the axe so that the smooth, curved handle slipped through his hand, and began to work. Disturbing the silence with the thump of his axe, he started to chop a tree but paused in mid-swing as he saw Derek riding up on his horse.

"How is it goin'?"

Moses' scowl seemed to say, not very well.

"Mother would say to us both that we have bitten off more than we can chew," Derek called out as he dismounted his horse and tied it to a nearby tree.

"And your mother would tell us both that we can be very stubborn. But it's gotta be done." Moses set aside his axe, relieved to have some respite from his toil. Seeing that Derek held a large sack in his hand he hurried towards him. "Don't tell me. A surprise from Honora."

"She made us a pound cake. Says she got the recipe from *Godey's Lady's Book*, though I don't know how she manages to work such wonders on that old kitchen stove with no...uh.... help...." He held up a whiskey bottle. "And she filled one of my father's discarded bottles with cider. She kept it cool in the springhouse."

110

Moses looked up to the sky as if looking towards heaven. "She's an angel. God, how I love her. She's always been so good to me. Like a second mother." Honora Cameron had even taught Moses how to talk like a gentleman upon his return from the war. It had been of immense help to him in business dealings with the bank.

It was difficult to find a comfortable place to sit so they had to make do by sitting on an old log. Derek poured the cider into two tin cups, then broke off a portion of the pound cake for each of them to share.

"How is your work going?" Moses asked, talking with a mouthful of the cake.

After taking several gulps of cider, Derek gave a fairly detailed account of his day—repairing the tool shed, cutting down several trees, and his good luck in finding the perfect spot for the new well that was so necessary. Breaking off pieces of cake with his fingers he remained silent as he ate, but once he had finished, he told Moses about the visit Amelia Seton had paid to Winding Oaks.

"She probably thinks I'm a total fool. I couldn't find much to say to her except to thank her for contactin' the woman who is helpin' my father." He looked down at his hands, brushing them together to get rid of the crumbs. "And I picked some flowers for her."

Moses choked on his cider. "You did what? You?"

"It wasn't anythin' fancy. Just some flowers from the garden." For a moment he looked away, remembering her face. "She is very, very pretty."

111

"The young woman we offered a ride in the wagon?" As Derek nodded Moses asked. "I would hope that you asked her if you can call on her in the near future."

Derek shook his head. "I don't have time to court any ladies. But I sure as hell wish that I did." He was preoccupied for a moment as he remembered how their eyes had met and caressed.

"If it were me, I would make time. You can't just work yourself to death." Finishing his cup of cider, he poured another drink. "She'll think you just weren't interested and go off with someone else. At least give her an explanation and ask her to be patient."

Although Derek knew that his friend was giving him good advice, he wasn't in the mood to give Moses credit. "You are a fine one to talk when you wouldn't even stop to say hello to the young women we saw with her father. You said she showed you kindness on your trek up north, but you acted like a crazy man, drivin' right past them."

Moses stiffened; his mouth set in a grim line. Then he said, "that's different."

"How so?" Derek was puzzled. Moses wasn't a shrinking violet. He wasn't afraid of much.

"You know. I told you. She and her father are *passing*. If I were to intrude into her life now it could have dire consequences for her. She is as out of reach as a star." He shook his head. "You are white. You just don't understand."

Derek couldn't argue. He had tried to empathize, but he had never had to *walk in Moses' shoes*, as his mother had once explained. "I'm so sorry, Mo. Like everythin' else down here it just

112

doesn't seem fair." Putting the bottle and cups back in the sack, Derek stood up. "I do believe, however, that you should give the young woman the chance to make up her own mind about your chances with her. You never know. Sometimes love can be colorblind."

Moses bolted to his feet angered by the situation. "Not down here its not! So, it is what it is. I don't want to hear another word about it." Picking up the axe he said curtly. "I have to get back to work and I know you have to do the same."

There was tension in the air, but Derek knew that Moses would soon get over his annoyance. Their friendship had weathered so many storms. Even being on different sides in the war hadn't ruined the bond they had always had.

"I do." He got back on his horse. "But if you need my help you know where to find me."

Moses nodded with his head. It wasn't just the young woman that had riled him it was the incidence with the painted words on his house in red. He should have told Derek. Why hadn't he done so. "I do and I will." He started to call out to Derek, then thought better of it. It was just one incident. It was better to just put it out of his thoughts. Or was it?

## Chapter Eight

Amelia awakened to the sweet fragrance of flowers. Sitting up in bed, she let her eyes scan the room, remembering how she had so carefully put the flowers in a glass vase the moment she had arrived back home. Such a precious gift. And a thoughtful gesture. How could she help but smile?

*Derek Cameron,* she thought, whispering his name over and over again. Pulling the covers up to her chin, she sought the haven of her pillows and thought about every detail of yesterday's brief encounter. His face hovered in her mind's eye. The way his hair brushed his forehead, the shape of his nose, the width of his shoulders, the way he walked and talked, all haunted her. And his mouth--full and artfully chiseled, possessing a sensuous curve when he smiled. Touching her lips, she wondered what his kiss would feel like and that sent a warm glow flickering through her body. Dreaming about what could be she slipped off to sleep hugging the pillow as if it were him.

Amelia awakened to a cheerful blending of early morning bird songs, a chirping that was accompanied by the sound of her aunt clinking cooking utensils as she prepared breakfast in the kitchen. Suddenly she realized how late it was. She had overslept. Grasping her father's watch from its resting place on the night stand she was horrified to see that it was already way over the time that she should have been sitting atop her buggy heading towards the school. Poor Jedidiah

114

would be waiting. Tugging at her coverlet, she rose from the bed and hurried to get dressed.

There was no time to be fussy, so she went about her morning toilette. Brushing her hair and fashioning it into a thick braid, she pinned it atop her head. Looking in her small closet she reached in and made the commitment to wear the first outfit that touched her hand. It was a green print calico dress with white lace at the throat and a matching green calico jacket. Informing her aunt that there was no time for breakfast, she put several biscuits in the pocket of her dress, took a gulp of tea then hurried to her buggy.

If horses could fly Amelia would have sent the horses soaring. As it was, she managed to urge them into such a frantic pace that when she hit a bump or two or three, she was almost sent hurling out of the buggy and over the horses' heads.

"Hold on Jedidiah, I'm coming." She thought to herself that she would make him laugh to think that she, who insisted on discipline, was late for their early morning ritual. A meeting that she looked forward to even more than he.

Jedidiah had come so far so quickly. He had a remarkable memory and learned everything she taught him in record time. She was certain that he had a very bright future, a future that she hoped would include either teaching or perhaps even politics. She could just imagine him standing behind a podium giving speeches that would long be remembered. There was just something about him, a certain spark, that made it impossible to ignore him. As the buggy rumbled along, she ticked off a list of books in her head that she would give him.

Amelia was so immersed in her musing and

guiding the buggy that she didn't smell it at first, but as she came closer to the school it assaulted her nostrils. Smoke! The odor was unmistakable. "A fire!" Squinting her eyes, she sought to see the source, thinking it to be among the fields. She knew that sometimes farmers burnt their fields to remove plants that were unwelcome but already growing. It was to help the plants that were about to come up.

"No. The trees perhaps." Sometimes a tree would be struck by lightning and a fire would ensue but there had been no storms of late.

Suddenly she saw what was on fire and her blood chilled in her veins. *Not the school. Please. Not the school!*

Voices. None that she had ever heard before. Hostile. Shouting. There was a crackling sound. A flash of sparks. Someone had set it on fire. She saw two riders through the haze, heading off in the opposite direction from her.

"Jedidiah!" He couldn't be inside the school. No. Surely, he had smelled the smoke and run outside where it was safe. Praying like she had never prayed before, she hoped that God was protecting the child.

Flames leaped in all directions, licking hungrily at the dry hay and straw scattered on the ground all around the school. It seemed that this had been a well-organized plan, a vendetta. But towards who? Her? That could be the only possible answer. But why?

Amelia watched, transfixed in horror as the fire spread rapidly moving to the walls of the school, devouring everything in its path. Like someone possessed she jumped out of the buggy before it had come to a complete stop and stumbling ran towards

116

the door without a thought about the consequences. She had to make certain Jedidiah was not inside. If he was his fate would be too horrifying.

"Jedidiah! Jedidiah!" Her voice was screaming his name.

Flames licked at the wooden outer walls and door of the schoolhouse threatening to engulf it in the carnage. With a strangled cry she moved in that direction, disregarding the danger. The fire would ravage the entire structure in no time. She had to make certain the child was not inside.

"Jedidiah!" She yelled his name over and over. "If you are inside break the window." A crash of glass answered her shout telling her that the worst of her fears was true. Jedidiah *was* inside the schoolhouse. She had to move now, and quickly, or he might be harmed.

Derek had also smelled the smoke and seen the flames as he was riding his horse towards the small building. He had thought about what Moses had said to him about Amelia and had ridden to the schoolhouse with the intent of furthering their relationship. Now to his horror he saw her running towards the burning schoolhouse.

"No. Amelia!" To his alarm Derek knew what she planned. "You'll be killed."

She didn't look back at him but called out. "Jedidiah is inside. Oh, my God. I have to go after him." Tearing off her skirt she used the cloth to brush at the fire as if she could put it out. Kicking at the door she tried to get it open, coughing and choking on the smoke that filled her lungs with a murderous fog.

It would only be a few minutes before the flames destroyed the entire building. Derek knew he had to

117

ASHES AND AWAKENINGS

save both Amelia and the boy before they both were
entrapped, and all was lost. He had to get Amelia
away before she was trapped, then he planned to push
his way in to get the boy.

Flames rose upward, threatening to demolish
everything in their way. Even the roof was on fire.
Timbers were crashing down as flames ate away at
the foundation. They had to get the child out before
the roof collapsed. "Amelia! You must get away from
there or there will be two of you to save. I'll get
Jedidiah!"

She faltered for just a moment, then realizing the
hopelessness of the situation and putting her trust in
Derek, she did as he said and fought the flames as she
retreated. And all the while the flames from the
burning school danced higher and brighter.

The smell of smoke permeated the air, burning
his eyes and obscuring his vision as Derek ignored the
danger and slammed his body against the door again
and again. At last it flew open and he moved toward
the small bundle near the broken window. He closed
his eyes for just a moment. When he opened them, he
gasped as he bent down and picked up the child in his
arms. Lifting him up he dropped him as gently as he
could through the broken window, only narrowly
escaping the sharp shards of the glass. Then diving
headfirst, he threw himself out the window, wincing
as he felt the glass graze his skin.

Struggling to his feet, Derek picked up Jedidiah,
rolling him over and over on the ground to put out the
flames on his clothes. Then he carried the boy to the
front of the building to make certain Amelia was safe.
To his horror he saw that she wasn't. Wisps of flame
had caught hold of her petticoats, but she didn't seem

118

to know it.

With a shout he gently put the child on the ground then lunged forward. Reaching up, he caught Amelia in his arms and falling to the ground rolled over and over until the fire was out. Without any sign of her own distress, however, Amelia pushed away from his embrace and ran towards Jedidiah. Frantically she tired to get him to open his eyes, but the boy was as still as a statue.

"Jedidiah! Jedidiah!" She pushed against his chest, willing him to breath. When he didn't, she put her ear to his chest. "I don't hear a heartbeat."

Gently Derek pushed her aside. "I was in the Confederate army. I watched doctors do this to bring back the dead." Bending his head down Derek fused his mouth to the boy's and breathed for him. Stubbornly he kept repeating the procedure, thinking to himself – *live. Live!* At last he turned to Amelia. "Breathing all that smoke suffocated him, at least that is what I believe. Despite the fire he doesn't have any serious burns that should have caused his death."

"Death!" The word had such finality about it that she gasped. "No. He can't be dead. It can't be possible." They had to make him breathe, had to get his heart to start beating again. Grabbing Jedidiah's shoulders, she moved the front part of his body up and down as if in rhythm to a heartbeat. All the while she was willing him to breathe. To live.

"Amelia." Derek's heart broke for her and for the boy. Whoever did this was a murderer.

Brushing at the tears running down her checks, she let go of the boy's frail body and reached out to brush at his hair in a loving gesture. She tried hard not to dissolve into total hysteria but only barely managed

119

to control her ravaged emotions. Meanwhile dark gray smoke swirled in the air like an ominous thundercloud as the flames burned themselves out.

"You risked your life for him." Her courage impressed him. He didn't think many women would have tried to go into a burning building.

"It's all my fault," she sobbed. "I was late this morning. If only I had gotten here on time this wouldn't have happened. I would have been here to protect him."

Derek wanted to wrap his arms around her to comfort her but realized it was an awkward situation. Instead he went over to the smoldering ruins and dug through the burned wood with a large stick he found nearby. What he found answered his suspicions. An iron bar lay on the ground near where the door would have been. It had locked the door from the outside, a deadly ruse.

"No, I think you probably would have been trapped inside along with him and you both might have died."

"I should have realized Beauregard would spread his malice. I should have known......"

Derek shook his head. "That someone could do this..this....." He gestured towards the ruins. "You never could have suspected such a thing. It's against all that is human."

"But I should....."

He walked over to her and put his finger on her lips. "You have no blame in this great evil. You were helping the boy."

"But...." She dissolved in a cascade of tears.

Taking her in his arms, he cradled her close

120

against him, surprised by how very quickly she had become precious to him. Thick smoke billowed through the air stealing their breaths away.

Amelia leaned her head against his chest and tried hard to stop crying. Her breath escaped in a long, shuddering sigh. Turning his head, he nuzzled her hair.

They stood there together in a self-imposed limbo. Then Derek's sense of responsibility took over. "I'll take his body to the family. You have been through so much already that I don't want...."

Amelia wiped at her tears with her sleeve. "No, he was my student. I will go with you. I want to tell them how very smart he was. If only....." Her hand touched his, squeezing it tightly. "Come....."

Derek gently picked up Jedidiah's body and put it in the back of the buggy, covering it with a blanket he found on the seat. He tied his horse to the back of the buggy, then took a seat beside her for the short ride to the house where Derek believed that Jedidiah and his family lived. They rode together in poignant silence, each immersed in their own thoughts. A tragedy such as the one that had happened gave a whole new perspective to the importance of life and the sadness of that time when it was ended. That Jedidiah was just a child made his death all the more heartbreaking.

\*     \*     \*     \*

Several dirt roads ran past the plantation grounds, through the woods of pine, cypress, and oak, past the fields of tobacco and on up to the orchards and planting fields, where the assorted fruits and vegetables that sustained all the people, white and black, who lived upon the plantation grew. There were chicken yards, water wells, and fenced-in stalls that housed the livestock. It was a longer journey than Derek had calculated but at last they came to a small house made out of logs.

Derek was correct in where Jedidiah lived. His father and mother were both sharecroppers on the Jensen plantation that bordered the Cameron land. Like Winding Oaks, the Magnolia Hill Plantation had fallen into disrepair, some of the land sold off to pay delinquent debts. Unlike on the Cameron land, however, the sharecroppers were not treated as well and it appeared lived in squalor. Derek had heard "through the grapevine" that many of the sharecroppers here had once been slaves on this very plantation. He wondered if they had signed a binding contract with the owner that kept them in servitude nearly as cruel as slavery.

Finding a shady place under a Weeping Willow, Derek alighted from the buggy, secured the horses then helped Amelia step down. In spite of the sad circumstances he couldn't help but notice the feelings she inspired just by the touch of her hand.

"I wish I would wake up and find that this has all been a nightmare," she whispered. Straightening her shoulders, she prepared herself for what was to come as a petite Negro woman walked towards her.

"Can I help you?" the woman asked.

Taking a deep breath, Amelia took the woman's hands and squeezed them very gently. "There's been an....an accident," she said softly. "At the schoolhouse."

"An accident." The woman looked behind Amelia, searching for Jedidiah. "Where's Jedidiah. Where is my son?"

Derek took a step forward. "There was a fire. Jedidiah was inside."

"My baby!" Jedidiah's mother started to panic. Pushing away from Amelia she gasped, "please don't tell me he was harmed." She looked critically at Amelia, only then noticing that she was in her petticoats. Dusty. Dirty. Grimy with ashes from the fire. "No!"

"We did everything possible to save him but….." Derek somehow couldn't seem to find the right words.

"But…..!" The word hung in the air like a shroud.

In morbid syncopation all eyes turned to the back of the buggy, at the bundle covered in a faded blanket.

"Dear merciful God. No! No! Nooooooooo…….." With a heartbreaking wail Jedidiah's mother ran towards the wagon. Lifting the corner and seeing Jedidiah's face she recoiled as if she had been burned herself. Collapsing on the ground she hugged her knees, rocking back and forth as she keened.

Amelia knelt down beside her. "Your son was the brightest light, the best student, a joy to teach……"

Looking up, Jedidiah's mother rasped, "I wanted him to learn. I wanted him to be able to do the things I never could. That's why I encouraged him in spite of everything to learn to read and write. It was forbidden when I was a girl. But now….."

She might have said more but the intrusion of a tall, broad-shouldered black man with no discernable hair silenced them all. "What's going on, Delilah? Why are these white folks here?"

"It's our little Jeb. Oh, Ben, the schoolhouse burnt down, and he was inside. He's dead." Deliah stood up and threw herself into her husband's arms. For a long, long while they stood molded together, silently mourning.

At last Ben disentangled himself and glared at Amelia and Derek as if they had purposefully done the deed. "I knew keeping company with white folks was a mistake. I should have forbidden Jed to go to that...that school. But he wanted to go so badly. And now he has paid the price just as all of us have during these many years."

Amelia spoke up. "He was so smart. He learned so quickly. I am so, so sorry."

The dark eyes staring back at her were filled with anger. "A lot of good his learnin' did him. He's dead! And that's that. No amount of words can bring him back." When Derek started to speak, he put up his hand as if to physically stop him. Then he walked slowly to the wagon to retrieve his son's small body, uncovering him from the blanket and holding his lifeless body in his arms. "This is a private time for mourning," he grumbled. "Please leave and give us our solitude." That said he nodded to Delilah and the sad family retreated to the privacy of their log house.

Derek gently took Amelia by the arm and led her back to the carriage. "You will need to get back so that you can take care of the other children," he said gently.

"The children!" It was as if for a moment she

had forgotten the others existed. "Oh, what am I going to do. I have no place to conduct my lessons. I don't...."

"Yes, you do." The answer had come to him in a flash. "There is a house--the Avery House." That the house was filled with tragic memories he failed to reveal. "It is unoccupied at the moment. You can teach the children there." It seemed the least he could do for her.

"Thank you!" His kind offer touched her heart and although it was just an offer of friendship, somehow Amelia had the feeling that it could blossom into much more.

## Chapter Nine

*Andrew Wyatt.* He haunted Forest's dreams at night and dominated her thoughts in the daytime. His name, his face, his voice, and the chilling memory of that fateful day when she had nearly been captured had suddenly become very vivid in her life. It was as if she were reliving that moment over and over again. And yet she had not said a word to Quentin about having seen him and she didn't know why. Fear that Quentin might confront Andrew Wyatt in his quest to protect her? Perhaps.

Going about her daily tasks she tried very hard not to let Quentin guess that anything was wrong either by her expression, her words, or by moping about. He had enough on his mind trying to keep the new political party together. From the times she had been with him at the meetings and the bits of information she was able to pry from him when she was not by his side, she had learned that there was a great deal of rivalry going on among the politicians. They were in a grim competition with each other for control. Each one of them wanted to be the leader. They wanted power as much as they wanted air to breathe, Quentin had said. But just what was Andrew Wyatt's role in the politics of the day?

Remembering that Andrew Wyatt had been chasing after her on that day so long ago she suspected that once he had been a *slave catcher,* or a member of the paddy rollers, as she had heard the slaves on the Underground Railroad call them.

126

Whatever he was called, she thought he must surely have been in an organized group of armed white men who monitored and enforced discipline upon slaves and who dogged the tracks of escaped slaves to bring them back to their owners—dead or alive.

Picking up a wet dish rag, she wiped it back and forth across the kitchen table, her thoughts all jumbled in her brain. If only she could remember more details of her childhood perhaps she would know where her parents had come from and where they might have been returned to right before the war. Were they still alive? Had they stayed in Virginia or gone elsewhere, perhaps to start a new life. Not knowing the answers plagued her, tormented her.

What a strange quandary she found herself in. On one hand she was fearful of Andrew Wyatt recognizing her but on the other she wondered if he could be the key to finding her parents. Did she want to stay out of his reach or did she want to confront him with the truth and hope to find out her parents' fate.

"Forest, my dear, you are going to wear a hole in that poor table."

Looking up she saw Quentin standing in the doorway to the kitchen. "There is a stubborn spot, but I think I rubbed it out," she replied casting the dish rag aside.

"A stubborn spot?" He laughed and in that moment she knew that he had read her emotions as easily as the books he studied so intently.

"All right." She shrugged. "I have been thinking about my parents a lot lately. Wondering if they are still alive and if so where they might have gone after the war was over."

The corners of his mouth went quickly from a smile to a frown. "How I wish I could help you but alas, all I know is that your name was Jemma and that you were being chased by enemies. And that you were the prettiest little thing I had ever seen." Coming over to where she stood, he put his hands on her shoulders. "I know I can't take the place of your parents, Forest, but I want you to know that you have brought me more happiness than I ever knew existed."

What more could she wish for than to have this man as her father? For the moment all her fears were cast aside and she concentrated on tidying up the cottage. She couldn't change the past, but she could look forward to a bright future with Quentin as her guide.

*I won't think about Andrew Wyatt again*, she told herself. It was safer that way. Feeling lighter of heart, she finished her work, including mending one of Quentin's shirts, and sat with him after dinner as he read her his speech for the next evening's political meeting.

*I don't believe in Santa Claus, or the Easter bunny, the tooth fairy, or a pot of gold at the end of the rainbow. And I don't believe in the fairy tale that our founding fathers who were wealthy white men and slave owners believed all men are created equal. Nor do I believe that our country has a spotless history. The United States of America has a brutal history of genocide, slavery, indentured servitude, land-grabbing, broken treaties, warfare, and brutality. But it also has a history of brave pioneers, dedicated soldiers, industrious workers, hard-working farmers, and creative thinkers. History tells the stories of all*

# KATHRYN KRAMER

*types of people—bad and good-- who came together to form this country.*

*Now is the time. The time for the truth. A time to put aside prejudice and self-seeking and come together as a nation. A time to not only look back into the past but reach out towards a better future for all. A time to tear down walls and blockades that separate us. A time to abandon statues that are tributes to wrongful men and wrongful deeds. A time to instead venerate the true heroes of our society. A time to realize, that in God's eyes, we are all created equal. Life is precious. Black or white or of mixed color our lives matter. Because we are all members of the family of man.*

He looked up from the piece of paper he was reading from and waited for her response.

"I love it! The words ring so true. We *are* all members of the family of man. If only others could see that." Taking him by the hand she pulled him up from the sofa and together they went on their evening walk around the lake. For the time being Forest thought that the past was locked away and wouldn't come back to haunt her. She didn't realize how quickly that hope would blow away like the nightly breeze.

Later that night Forest readied herself for bed— brushing her hair a hundred strokes, brushing her teeth with baking powder and fresh spearmint from the garden. Putting on her nightshirt she slipped into bed and closed her eyes to sleep.

Forest willed herself to dream sweet dreams of butterflies, flowers, and candy, but her dream transitioned into a vision of cloudy skies, a misty fog, and a boat in the middle of a vast river. Faces sped by

129

her. She glimpsed her mother and father, but though she tried to touch them they eluded her, fading away in a cloud of light. Colors blended into each other until the features on the faces were indistinguishable from one another.

"No. Come back........"

Suddenly she was on land, darting from shadow to shadow. She had to hide. Her enemy was after her. Grabbing her doll, Emma, she moved towards the trees. She had to save Emma. But it was as if she were walking in one place, never going forward. Waving her arms frantically, trying to keep her balance, she turned just as the ground dropped out from under her feet. She was falling downward into a great gaping hole.

"No....!"

Hands reached out to grasp her. "Jemma......" A voice whispering her name.

"Mama?"

"There she is! Catch her!" Out of the fog several men appeared, pointing their fingers, leading a group of scowling men towards her. She had to find a place to hide.

"Quentin!" He was up ahead of her beckoning her to come to him.

"Help me!"

"She's a slave!" A chorus of voices gave warning. "Catch her!"

"Please. I'm not......! I'm not......" Oh, but she was!

Bright daylight played across her face, teasing her eyelids awake. Rubbing her sleep-filled eyes, Forest propped herself shakily up on one elbow and looked around her. *Dear God! A dream. Just a silly dream after all. And yet.........*

She remembered bits and pieces of the dream and shivered. How easily she had put her parents out of her mind all these years. Never in her wildest dreams had she ever thought there was a chance to find them. But there was no excuse now.

Forest knew what she had to do. She had to confront Andrew Wyatt and find out about her past. There could be no future for her if she didn't know about her past and what had happened to her family.

She sat up so quickly it made her head spin. Today she would go into Richmond and confront Andrew Wyatt. He had no power over her now. Slavery had been abolished by law. The chains that had bound her to an owner had been severed. There could be no retaliation. Not now. Not ever.

*I have to know the truth*, she thought. Maybe Andrew Wyatt would have information to help her find her mother and father. Maybe he would not. So much time had passed but that didn't matter. She had to try and find them or spend eternity wondering.

*      *      *      *

It was a dark and cloudy day and as Amelia looked out the window of the house she shared with her aunt, she thought how the day matched her mood. At least, however, her tears had stopped, if only for the moment. But they welled up in her eyes again when she looked at the small table by the bed and saw the wooden carving of the angel that Jedidiah had made for her. It brought back the memory of how tragically he had died.

*No, not died*, she thought. He had been murdered. The fire at the school hadn't been an accident. It had been carried out by hateful brutes, vicious monsters intent on causing fear, sorrow and pain. And they had succeeded in their detestable quest.

Amelia had spent the last few days in a haze of grief, with no awareness of time or of those about her, remembering Jedidiah's small body lying so still on the ground. Over and over again she remembered that moment when she had realized that he was dead, his promise of a future taken from him because of prejudice and hatred. That there would not be retribution for the act sickened her. Although she suspected that Beauregard's father had a hand in the matter, she had no proof. Worst of all was that what had happened was not a unique occurrence. Jedidiah's death would be just one of many. The area was filled with haters.

Cloistering herself away, Amelia had fought hard not to let her anger devour her. Hatred was evil and poisoned all those who fed on it. And yet when she looked at the carving and remembered a little boy so intent on learning to read, a rage welled up inside her and she had to take several deep breaths to regain her poise. Now, however, Amelia realized that she could not hide away any longer. There were other children to think about and so much to do so that school could begin again.

*I will need to find books*, she thought, wondering where on earth she was going to find some suitable for her students. She would need a chalkboard and

132

chalk. And desks, or at least chairs where her students could sit while they listened to the lessons.

She thought about Derek Cameron and how kind he had been. He had offered the use of the Avery Mansion on Cameron property and had promised to make it suitable for her needs. His offer of friendship was the only light in the darkness of the past few days.

"Amelia, you're staring a hole through that window!" Amelia heard her aunt's voice and closed the curtains. "There, that's better. I'm tired of your moping."

If Amelia had thought that her aunt would be sympathetic about what happened she soon found out that she was wrong. She had received only harsh words and a disapproving scowl. Her aunt's first words to her had been, "Amelia Jane Seton, you look frightful! Your clothes, your face, your hair! You must have been crazy to try to go into a burning building. What on earth was wrong with your wits?"

With her nagging and her scolding, Aunt Lucinda had tried to manipulate Amelia just as she had done before, but Amelia wouldn't and couldn't abandon the other children no matter what her aunt said. She didn't want to find a teaching job in Richmond and that was that. Her aunt was strong-willed, but she could be too. Perhaps, then, it wasn't any wonder that she and her aunt were hardly speaking to each other. When they passed on the stairs, Aunt Lucinda would sweep aside her skirts, muttering under her breath, "I've tried, God knows how I've tried. But you must want to end up an old maid."

Her aunt's unkind words seemed to act like an elixir. It was time that she visited Derek Cameron to offer her assistance in tidying up the building that was to be the new school. With the thought of visiting the handsome Cameron heir, Amelia decided to wear a dress of light coral muslin with a high lace collar. As to her hair, she decided not to wear it in the usual way but to just let it hang freely about her shoulders. Just because she was a school marm didn't mean she had to look like one. Without casting her aunt even a backward glance, Amelia left the house, hitching up the horses to the buggy. Then she was on her way, hoping she could remember the way to the Avery Mansion.

She found out that she didn't have to worry. The grand house in early Victorian style with its white pillars and ornate shutters was visible from at least a mile away. Amelia remembered hearing about the Antebellum South when she had lived up north and she had seen many mansions in the area, including the Cameron Mansion, but this one was special. It was vine covered with trees growing all around it. It reminded Amelia of the kind of house that existed in many of the stories she had read.

Securing the horses and buggy, she opened the door and went inside. The interior of the Avery Mansion smelled musty and was covered in dust and cobwebs, but as Amelia opened the door she saw Derek busy at work with a broom. He greeted her with a smile and gestured for her to follow him.

"Mother found some books that belonged to Bevin, Allegra, and I when we were children. It will be a start until we can procure more books."

As she followed Derek Cameron around the house Amelia could see the possibilities that existed to transform several of the rooms into a schoolhouse. It would take imagination and determination, but she felt in her heart that it would work.

"I know you have work to do on your plantation," she said at last. "So, my appreciation is tenfold. I will never be able to find the words to express just how grateful I am for your kindness."

She knew she must have been imagining it, but she could have sworn she saw him blush. "It is the least I could do after all that happened," he exclaimed, forcing a smile. At the back of his mind was a list of all that he needed to get done to keep the plantation working smoothly. There were just not enough hours in the day.

Picking up a discarded broom she joined in, sweeping aside cobwebs and spiderwebs. As they worked side by side, Amelia's heart started pounding so loudly she was certain he could hear. The feelings he stirred in her were as potent as those of any of the heroines she had read about in her books. Perhaps more so.

"You are working much too hard, Amelia. Are you tired?" he asked at last.

"Not at all." It was a lie and she knew it. She had never been so exhausted. The mansion was huge and was suffering from years and years of neglect. It was going to take almost a miracle to restore it.

Loosening the collar of his shirt with a tug he asked, "are you hot?" Oh, how he wanted to just take off his shirt and be done with it, but he didn't give in to that desire because of her presence.

Amelia shook her head, regretting that she had worn a dress with such a high collar, but her modesty prevented her from making any adjustments to her garments. She would just have to suffer. Oh, but how she wanted to slip at least one of her many full petticoats off and discard them.

"But I *am* thirsty. Are you?" When he nodded, Amelia moved towards a bucket before he had the chance. "I'll bring you water this time," she said, heading for the spring. Returning, she held the dipper out to him, letting him drink first.

"Delicious!" Derek took time to compliment her on her hair. "I like it unencumbered. Your hair is an unusual shade." He wondered if it was as soft as it looked.

Something in his voice touched every nerve in her body, made her feel dizzy. She thought, how quickly time went by when you were with someone whose company you enjoyed.

Derek put her feelings into words. "I like being with you, Amelia." He wished he could think of something to say to her that was more impressive but something about her made him feel as if his brain had turned to mush.

'I like being with you too," she answered softly.

They looked steadily at each other for a long, long time. His eyes caressed her, embraced her as firmly as if he touched her with his hands. He imagined what it would be like to slowly slip the dress from her body, to bring her down to lay beside him and to.......

Hastily Derek looked away. He didn't like where his thoughts were going. Amelia Seton was a lady through and through. She had been through hell

experiencing the death of her student. She didn't
need some love-struck fool making an ass of himself.

"I think that is enough work for today," he said
bluntly, then amended his statement by inviting
Amelia to take a tour of the mansion. "This was quite
splendid in its day, almost as interesting as the people
in my family who once lived here."

Leading Amelia towards the hallway where a
gallery of paintings covered the wall, he pointed them
out to her. "The Cameron family. These paintings
used to live in the Cameron Mansion, but father had
them brought here and hidden right after the war.
Mother had them put back up again in this building."

If he had wanted her to be impressed he had
succeeded. All that Amelia had of her relatives were
a few tintypes. She paused in front of the first
painting of a dark-haired man with laughing eyes,
lace fronted shirt, and three-cornered hat atop his
head.

"This is Avery, who started it all. My
grandmother tells me that he settled in Virginia and
married a girl he literally bought, an indentured
servant." He pointed to the picture beside him of a
woman with flaming red hair, an upturned nose, and
provocative pout, a lady dressed in emerald green
holding a fan. "They had two sons, Simon and Owen.
Owen murdered his own brother just like Cain, for the
property and the treasure. It's a long story."

"Treasure?"

"Blackbeard's treasure. It has never been found.
I don't suppose it really exists. Although I wish that it
did." He pointed to the next two paintings. "That is
Victoria Cameron, my grandmother, and her husband,
Stephen. He was nearly fifty when the painting was

done, but still handsome I think."

Derek took pride in his ancestors, telling Amelia the story of each one—Merlin Cameron, Megan Cameron, Stephen Cameron, Elizabeth Cameron, and lastly Charles Cameron. It was a family tradition, it seemed, to have a portrait of each master of Winding Oaks and his wife. Charles was sandwiched between two lovely women, Honora and Bevin's mother, another lovely blonde."

"And each one has a story to tell," she whispered, wishing that somehow she could find out more about them.

"What would you say if I told you that the founding father of the Cameron family had been a pirate, that Jared Cameron had sailed with Blackbeard himself?"

"Blackbeard?" She had read about the infamous pirate.

"And what if I told you that Jared Cameron had taken Blackbeard's daughter as his wife?"

"Then you are....."

"Related to a notorious pirate." Derek laughed, enjoying himself for the first time in weeks.

Amelia's eyes took in the spacious foyer. All of the rooms were generously proportioned with high ceilings that helped keep the house cool during the long hot summers. A wide, magnificently built stairway rose from the center of the foyer. It was carpeted in faded red with a carved wooden railing. In each of the downstairs rooms hung large chandeliers that sparkled with a rainbow of color when they were lighted. She would have to make certain that none of the children disturbed them.

138

"Grandfather Stephen brought these chandeliers from France," Derek said, noticing the direction of her gaze. "He was always said to have an eye for beauty." His eyes swept over her and he thought to himself that his grandfather would have appreciated the soft kind of beauty that Amelia possessed.

Gently taking her by the hand he led her up the stairs. Turning to the room on the right he opened the door. Following him inside, she followed the direction of his finger as he pointed to a large chalk board hanging on the wall.

"Oh, my goodness!" It was perfect. Even larger than the chalk board she had used at the schoolhouse. "Where on earth did you get it?"

My father has a friend at Richmond College. They were renovating the school. I traded the board for some fine ole Cameron tobacco and the deal was made. It even came with a goodly supply of white chalk."

"Oh, Derek....." He was pleasantly surprised when she slipped her arms around his neck. Then her arms tightened. "Thank you, for your generosity and kindness."

Before he had time to think, he had gathered her into his arms, his mouth only inches from her own. Her heart hammered in her breast, beating in rhythm with his. She was giddily conscious of the warmth emanating from his body, aware of a bewildering intense tingle in the pit of her stomach.

Derek closed his eyes tightly and clenched his fists, taking a deep breath as he fought for control. He started to pull away, but she held on to him. He touched her then, moving his hand slowly up her arm from elbow to shoulder as he explored, caressed.

Then it was Amelia who initiated a kiss, as she slowly raised her chin.

Derek groaned, closing his arms about her as he pulled her into the curve of his hard body. Her hands reached out to touch him, and the feel of those hands was his undoing. They swept all reason and caution from his mind. Derek captured her shoulders and bent his face to meet hers.

The tip of his tongue stroked her lips as deftly as his hands caressed her body. She moaned, turning her head so that his mouth slanted over hers and his tongue sought to part her lips. She mimicked the movement of his mouth, reveling in the sensations that flooded through her. That kiss made her feel as if the entire world shuddered and shook.

Derek's desire was not any less fierce than hers. He had known desire before, but never like this. His reaction to Amelia's nearness, to the soft mouth opening to him, trembling beneath the heated encroachment of his lips, was explosive. He shook, giving in to a shiver that was nearly as violent as Amelia's had been. For one moment he nearly lost his head completely. His hands pushed her back slightly as his fingers fumbled at her bodice, searching for her soft flesh. Then just as suddenly he stopped. Pulling away from her he held her at arm's length.

"Go home, Amelia." His tone of voice was stern.

"Derek....." She was trembling. Never in all her wildest dreams had she realized how primitive and powerful desire could be. Nor how fiercely and how quickly her emotions could get out of control.

He looked down at her for a long, aching moment, thinking how sweet and untouched she appeared. "I apologize for what just happened."

"Apologize?" She didn't want him to. "Why should you when it was really I who kissed *you*."

Taking a deep breath, he calmed his rapid heartbeat. "Because I'm the one who knows only too well where a kiss can lead."

"Oh....!" She blushed, knowing full well what he meant.

"You don't know how it is with a man. And today isn't the day for you to learn." Taking her by the arm, he gently led her down the stairs and to the front door of the mansion. "We have both worked very hard today."

She couldn't hide her disappointment. "Yes, we have."

He could tell from her expression that she was frustrated by his curt dismissal. Gently taking her chin in his hand he raised her face towards his and looked into her eyes. "Together I think we can make this work. Just be patient."

"I'm afraid patience is not one of my virtues," she answered, then smiled. "But I'll try." She liked the word "together" because it told her that there would be other days like this. "I'll be here again tomorrow," she whispered, hoping that he would be there too.

## Chapter Ten

It seemed to Forest that anger and hatred were contagious; spreading throughout the South like a disease, dashing the hopes and dreams of so many people that it was tragic. On the ride into Richmond for Quentin's meeting with his political committee, it was impossible not to almost feel unease in the very air. Downcast looks and frowns seemed to be everywhere. There were still many southerners who mourned their old way of life and whose memories of "finer" days still lingered in their minds. Even those who had never lived in a mansion or had slaves seemed to mourn the past and the ostentatious way of life in days gone by. Quentin said that they wanted a scapegoat for their current state of unhappiness and so many blamed those with dark skin.

"I have told Matthew Stewart that we need to move slowly as to the changes we propose to make to the laws, but he insists on being bold. I fear that could be dangerous," Quentin stated as they pulled up in front of the Capitol building. "If we are not careful our hopes and plans could collapse as drastically as the gallery and floor in this building did and then where will we be?"

Forest knew what he was talking about. She remembered hearing that three years ago the gallery and floor of Virginia's state courtroom had collapsed killing at least sixty men. It was called the Capitol Disaster, an act of God it was said, and yet there were those who viewed the disaster as a reflection of the Reconstruction politics. That it had happened right after Virginia had just been re-admitted to the Union was said to be no accident.

"And what did Matthew say?"

Quentin swore beneath his breath. "He reminded me that numerous educated Negroes and free people of color moved to the South to work for Reconstruction and that I was not the only one."

"Ah, but you are the smartest one," she answered with a wink and a grin.

"We will soon see about that. Indeed, we shall soon see." Clutching his notes, grabbing the handle of his leather satchel, Quentin secured the horses and buggy and started walking towards the entrance to the Capitol building. He paused when he realized that Forest was not following.

Forest never lied to Quentin, but she did so now. "I have an errand to run, at the market. I'll join you when I am finished." She waited until she saw him walk through the front door then she headed in the opposite direction.

Hurrying down the hill, Forest was nervous about confronting the ominous man from the past. For just a moment she almost turned back but taking a deep breath she realized that if she didn't seek the answers now she might never know the truth. Pulling her hat down to make certain it wouldn't blow off in the breeze from the James River, she broke into a run. She had to hurry so that she could get back in time to hear Quentin's speech.

Forest was so engrossed in finding her way to the bank and thinking about what she should say to Andrew Wyatt that she was barely aware of her surroundings. Only when a brisk, strong breeze ripped the hat from her head was she brought back to reality.

"Oh, no," she murmured, watching as the hat flew away like a scrap of paper in the breeze. Self-consciously she reached up, trying to keep her hair from tumbling down. She had to get her hat. Without it she wouldn't be allowed in the room to listen to Quentin. Worse yet she would be revealed as a woman the moment she set foot in the chamber and the men caught sight of her hair.

In a strange twist of fate, Moses was also walking down that same street. He had volunteered to help Derek turn the Avery Mansion into a school and was headed to the lumberyard to purchase wood for desks. He was about to cross the street when he saw that a carriage was careening down the road, heading for a young woman dashing across the street. Uttering a curse, he hurried to intercept the carriage.

Catching up with the young woman, Moses reached out and gripped her by the waist. Forest felt herself being lifted off the ground as she was carried a short distance to safety. Like a bundle of straw, she was deposited upon the ground.

"What do you think you are doing!" she said in annoyance, showering scorn upon her attacker. Her hair tickled her face and she had to brush it out of her eyes as she looked at the culprit. She tried to maintain her poise despite her awkward position upon the ground but could not refrain from looking up.

A very handsome black man was staring down at her with a grim expression on his face, his square jaw set sternly. His brown eyes stared at her intently, his black hair blowing in the same wind that had stripped Forest of her hat. Even in her anger, Forest had to admit that he was one of the most attractive men she had seen in quite a while. Dressed in tight work pants

144

which clung to his muscular thighs and a white shirt that clearly defined his wide shoulders, he was very masculine.

Moses looked at the young woman and recognized her immediately. Her name came out in a hoarse whisper. "Jemma!" Nervously he looked for a way to escape her scrutiny. Would she recognize him now that they had both grown up? He doubted it. The only reason he had recognized her the other day was because she was with her father. There were so many things he wanted to say but all he could think of was how pretty she was.

Forest realized that he was staring at her and she brushed the hair from her eyes and brushed at her skirt. There was something familiar about this man although she couldn't remember having seen him in any of the meetings Quentin had attended.

"You should be more careful..." he was saying, pointing to where the carriage was lumbering down the street.

"I...I...didn't see it," she stammered, understanding that this man had saved her. Struggling to her feet, she was aided by the strong hands of the stranger, hands that were firm yet gentle.

"Are you all right?"

She was mesmerized by the man's face, fascinated by the shape of his nose, his mouth, and the way he tilted his head in such a proud manner. He was a bit arrogant but fascinating. Once again she thought to herself that there was something familiar about him. After a period of silence she blurted out, "do I know you?" The way he was looking at her made her tremble and set her blood pounding in her veins.

145

The bold brown eyes traveled over her slender figure and he smiled, revealing his white, even teeth. The effect of those eyes was mesmerizing. When he didn't answer she took a step closer. She recalled that he had called her Jemma yet she thought surely that it was just her imagination.

At last he said, "it is not important."

Oh, but it was. The longer they stood there looking at each other the more the familiarity tugged at her brain. Suddenly a name flashed through her head. So many years had passed and they had both changed yet she seemed to remember. "Moses."

His very expression responded to that name. It *was* him. So many memories came flooding back. She threw herself into his arms, hugging him tightly as she had when they were children traveling on that train.

"Oh, Jemma. Jemma." She smelled so wonderful, like summer flowers.

She looked up at him. "I'm not Jemma any longer. My name is Forest now." Realizing they were creating a scene because of the difference in their skin color, she took him by the hand. "Come with me. We have so much to talk about, so many years to catch up on."

"I will but first I need to capture your hat." Which was no easy task. The wind taunted Moses, floating the hat up in the air until it was wrapped around a small tree and he could grasp it. "Here." He plopped it on her head for her.

"Father will be so glad to see you. We often wondered how you had gotten along." She took his hand.

146

He didn't have the willpower to say no. Feeling light of heart he followed her up the street not really caring where they were going. For the moment it was as if the years had been wiped away and they were just two frightened children not knowing what fate had in store for them.

\*       \*       \*       \*

The large, carpeted room with chandeliers hanging from the ceiling and statues and marble busts of men Moses didn't know, was intimidating. Sitting besides Forest at the back of the room, he tried to get comfortable in the hard wooden-backed chair as they listened to long-winded discourses given by unsmiling men. Moses knew he should be listening to their words yet how could he when he was sitting beside a lovely young woman who, even dressed like a boy, was the embodiment of every man's dream.

"That's Matthew Stewart," Forest informed him as she bent forward in her chair as if to be able to hear every word. Except for the mumblings of the man it was so quiet Moses could hear his heart beat.

Trying his best to concentrate on what the Stewart man was saying, Moses was distracted none-the-less as he looked around the room at those assembled. With the exception of their fancy suits the men were not anything alike. Moses was surprised to see men of all colors present, from the darkest Negroes to men with pale skin and graying dark or blonde hair.

The man named Matthew spoke of the inequity of representative government, the need for improvements in education and other public services for Negroes and his plan on how to raise the money needed to pay back all the debt Virginians owned. The word "taxes" was bandied about receiving frown after frown from those assembled in the room. He also spoke of the need to have more Negroes in office.

All the while he was sitting there Moses kept thinking of all that he had to do before he drove his wagon back home. He still had to get the wood for the desks as well as complete several of his own purchases. He thought to himself that he should explain to Jemma and take his leave of her, but each time he looked her way he didn't have the heart to disturb the new camaraderie between them.

"Quentin advised Matthew on financial and other matters when we were in Philadelphia," she explained as Matthew stepped down from the small, carpeted stage where the podium was located. She would have said more if it had not been Quentin's turn to voice his opinion. Moses felt her gently grasp his hand and could tell she was caught up in the moment.

Moses was impressed by how skilled Quentin was at holding an audience in the palm of his hand. Instead of starting to speak immediately, he stood perfectly still for a long, drawn out moment, just scanning his listeners, turning his head just ever so slightly. Then he began to speak in a low, booming voice.

"Long ago a man much wiser than me said the following, and I quote. He who knows not, and knows not that he knows not, is a fool; shun him. He who knows not, and knows that he knows not, is a student; teach him. He who knows and knows not that he knows is asleep; wake him." He raised his index

148

finger and moved it as if touching each and every one. "Ah, but he who knows and knows that he knows, is wise; follow him."

Quentin stepped down from the platform so that he was on the same level as his audience. Putting his hands behind his back he walked back and forth as he spoke. "The problem with politics is that we follow the fool, a man who knows not and is ignorant and prejudiced. Following that kind of man is what brought the South into the divisive war for which Richmond, Virginia....all of the South has suffered a great deal because we were the losers. Everyone hates a loser including the loser himself. But if we begin to follow the wise man who knows, strives to learn more, and has an open heart and open mind, then we will turn defeat into victory."

He spoke about reaching out to everyone, including the poor whites who had been hurt by slavery just as much as the slaves themselves because they had been forced to compete for work on farms and plantations. He insisted that sharecroppers also had the vote and could be wooed and welcomed into the new party.

Looking over at Forest, he was surprised to see a frown on her face. Turning to him she said, "that is not the speech that we had prepared." As she saw the look of rapt admiration on Moses' face she said, "but it does seem that this off the cuff speech is working well for him."

Looking at Jemma, now called Forest, Moses could see the little girl in the woman as he thought about his journey on the Underground Railroad. He wondered if she was still as kind and caring as she had been as a child. He hoped so. Certainly, she had

149

blossomed into a beauty.

"It frustrates me how southerners so frequently respond to any criticism by playing the fear and the blame game in a time we the people should come together and not show hostility to others with different opinions. I am tired of this frenzy of anger, hatred, and division.....of putting people in boxes and vilifying those who don't think like you. In these times we need to let love rule and put hatred out of our hearts. And that, gentleman, will be the key to winning not only the upcoming election but all those that will follow."

After Quentin's speech there was a flurry of accolades and back-pounding. When at last the men had dispersed, Forest took Moses by the hand and led him to where Quentin was standing. "Look who I literally ran into today," she breathed.

Moses stood for a long moment, unsure of what he should do or say next. Always having prided himself on his appearance, he loathed being caught looking like a poor field hand or sharecropper. Nevertheless, he forced a grin, bowing slightly as he said, "It's a pleasure to meet up with you again, Sir."

Quentin's blue eyes shown with an undisguised happiness. "And to see *you*, Moses." He smiled. "How are you?"

In agitation Moses ran his fingers through his hair, then brushed at the dirt on his pants. "Better than I look."

Forest looked him up and down again from head to toe, wondering what Quentin would think of him. Even disheveled, he was a handsome man. She had not realized just how pleasing to the eye he would be one day. "You look fine."

150

So many questions ran through her head. What was he doing here in Richmond? How long had he been in the South? Where had he been the past several years? In all that time had he ever let his thoughts wander and think of her? As if reading her mind Quentin asked those questions for her.

Moses told them about working twelve hours a day in a factory up north in order to help his mother and father survive. He told them about joining the Union army, about the hardships, the fear, the survival skills he had learned. Then he smiled as he spoke of confronting a Confederate soldier facing the threat of being taken prisoner and suddenly realizing it was his friend. He told of how they had both deserted their armies and run off.

"Derek and I were fortunate because the war was over the very next week. Together we made the long trek back to Richmond and I have been here since then." He looked at Forest, then at Quentin. "What about you?"

Without thinking he reached out and squeezed her hand. His touch caused a strange quiver to dance up and down her spine. In sudden embarrassment Forest pulled away. She'd thought about him often, wanted to see him again one day. Now that he was here, however, she felt uncomfortable, ill at ease. Something had changed between them. Her feelings toward him were different. She was all too aware of the fact that they had both grown up.

Noticing the looks that passed between the two, Quentin held up his hand. "It's getting late and I am afraid our story is much too long." To Forest's surprise he invited Moses to visit them at the cottage the very next evening. To Moses' surprise, he accepted.

## Chapter Eleven

A pretty woman can soon turn a man's brain to mush. That is what both Moses and Derek decided as they each had to work extra hard to catch up with the hours they had lost spending time with the ladies.

After Moses had parted with Forest and her father, he had just barely arrived at the lumber yard in time to purchase wood before they closed for the night. Loading it in the wagon he had hurried back to Winding Oaks where he and Derek had worked late into the night constructing small benches and tables that were child-size. Perfect for Amelia's needs, Derek decided. Then it was up early the next morning to work non-stop.

"As Preacher Michaels says, there is no rest for the wicked," Moses taunted.

"Speak for yourself. I haven't been wicked yet," Derek declared, looking over at Moses with a grin on his face. "But I am beginning to worry that she may soon have me wrapped around her little finger sooner than I would like."

Moses' wiped the sweat from his brow with his hand. "I think Jemma had me wrapped around her finger the moment I set eyes on her all those years ago. I only hope that I am not making a big mistake by furthering our friendship."

As if in slow motion, Derek paused using his hammer while it was in mid-air. "Are you losing your mind. It can't be a mistake to spend time with someone you have feelings for."

They weren't able to talk more about it because several of the field hands had arrived to help them raise a flue-curing barn to hang the tobacco leaves in so that they would dry later on in the season.

The sound of pounding soon disturbed the quiet of the morning. Moses and Derek had cut all the wood the day before, taking great care that all the pieces would fit. Now the men were putting the pieces together. Their tools were few--a square, a compass, a straight edge, hammers--but their logic was abundant.

Long before the axe fell, a barn builder had to plot out the routes of sunshine and wind, the slopes of drainage, and determine how the seasons might affect the barn site. Living so close to nature made people 'weather wise.' Derek remembered his father talking to him about a barn being placed "well into the weather."

First, they set the foundation timbers in place with a heavy hammer called a commander. Then they assembled the pieces out on the ground. Because it rained frequently in the area, they used wooden nails knowing that metal nails would rust. Wood against wood also made a strong structure. Using ropes and pulleys, Moses and the men hoisted the barn walls and hammered them into place. Large wooden shingles completed the sides.

The roof likewise was assembled on the ground. The front and back rafter sections looked like a large triangle with a kingpost up the middle. It, too, was lifted up by way of ropes and pulleys until it rested atop the walls. The result was simple beauty without embellishment. After chiseling the date into a section, the barn was erected, and a branch was put atop the new barn to bring good luck.

"Thanks to all of you," he said to the men. As a reward he went into the mansion and brought forth several bottles of cider that Honora had made. If he had spiked them with some of his father's best whiskey, well so be it. He turned to Moses. "Tomorrow it will be my turn to help you, so don't stay up too late with your Jemma."

"Forest," Moses corrected. Although he would always think of her as Jemma somehow. Realizing there was whiskey in the cider he declined to partake of it because he didn't want it on his breath when he visited Forest and her father later on.

Their task completed, Derek and Moses parted company, each going their own way to work on their land. Moses borrowed Derek's dowsing rods so that he could find water and dig a new well closer to his house. Water witching was what some called it, insisting that it worked every time. Moses was not so sure. He suspected that the dowsing rods did move but not in response to anything underground, just simply in answer to the random movements of the person holding the rods. Later in the day when he did find a source of water, he changed his mind.

Now leaning back in the wooden bathtub, he had filled with heated water from the stove, Moses thought to himself that at the moment nothing in the world felt as good as the water engulfing him. Closing his eyes, he luxuriated in the warmth, emitting a long husky sigh as it spread over his body. He felt contented. At peace. And damned pleased with himself for finding that water. Tomorrow, first thing, he would go to work on that well.

He envisioned it all now, saw himself with a fine house, a prosperous peanut farm, and enough money to impress Forest and her father. He daydreamed that his would be the easy life with nothing to do all day but give orders, make investments, and do what pleased him. He'd have the best cigars, drink the best whiskey and dress in nothing but tailored suits with matching vests. No more overalls and straw hats. Why he'd....

"Whoa! Hold on there." Cupping his hands, he splashed water over his face and hair, scolding himself for getting way ahead of the situation. His lofty dreams were out of proportion with reality. He had just started the work on his land, Forest hadn't given any indication that she saw him as anything but a friend, and he had a loan to pay back before he could even dream of being *hoighty toighty*, as he had heard Honora once call it.

Could he win Forest's heart, a pleasant endeavor seeing as how pretty she was? He wasn't certain, yet oh, how he wanted to. She had always made him feel as if he were special. And she *had* been glad to see him. It had been reflected in her eyes when she had looked at him.

Lathering the washcloth, he scrubbed his body vigorously, humming a tune all the while. It was a song he had made up in his head. A melodic song that put him in the mood for romance. He had it all planned out, knew just what he was going to do. And it appeared that Quentin was on his side and intending to do a bit of matchmaking. Tonight he was going to be all spruced up, wearing the suit that he had worn when he had gone to the bank to get a loan.

156

Lingering over his bath, Moses thought the matter out. "I'll take flowers to her," he said to himself, knowing how susceptible women always were to a bouquet. There were several on his land to choose from.

Moses stepped from the tub, wrapped himself in a large towel, dried himself off, and stared into the small oval mirror on the dresser as he combed his thick curly hair. Staring long and hard at his image in the mirror, he felt a stab of insecurity, perhaps because of his past. But even men who had once been slaves had a right to dream.

*But what do I really have to offer her?* He remembered the words he had heard Quentin speak and the way he was so sure of himself. But Moses knew he was just a man who worked the earth. Not an orator or politician. Forest was as pretty as a picture. She would have her choice of prominent men. And that thought sent a flash of jealousy through his brain. A jealousy he had no right to feel. Forest needed a friend, someone who cared for her, not a man thinking only of his own desires. Even so, he couldn't deny that he had a tender spot in his heart for Forest Faulkner, a warmth that radiated all through him as he envisioned those big hazel eyes.

Feeling inspired again, he hurried to dress in his blue suit with a white shirt and tie. He evaluated his appearance in the mirror, then with a grin, he hurried to pick a bouquet then rode out to the Faulkner cottage.

\*       \*       \*       \*

157

Amelia's hand trembled as she poured piping-hot tea from the small silver teapot into the delicate Wedgewood cups. It had been such a long time since she had been in the company of her aunt's friends that she was apprehensive. Still, she resolved to remain calm and levelheaded without raising her voice, no matter what was said. And above all she would not let anyone pry information from her about her friendship with Derek Cameron. What was blossoming between them was a secret she meant to keep for herself only.

"Your tea, Abigail." Amelia somehow managed a smile.

"Thank you, my dear." The cup swayed precariously on the saucer as the thin, sour-faced woman balanced it in her pudgy fingers.

"Lavinia." Lavinia Redwood glanced up nervously from the newspaper she was reading to take the proffered cup from Amelia's hand. "It's dreadful, just dreadful," she exclaimed, setting the teacup down and scanning the newspaper again. "Why didn't you tell me about the fire at the schoolhouse, Lucinda?"

"Because she probably didn't think it was any of your business," Abigail snapped peevishly.

"Everything that happens in this neck-of-the-woods is *my* business. My cousin twice removed owns one of the plantations and one of his sharecroppers sent his daughter to learn to read from Amelia." Lavinia took a sip of her tea, recoiling as she realized it was still too hot to drink.

"Well, I don't think the girl will be learning anything now that the school is nothing but cinders." Abigail snorted indignantly

Amelia had been happy all day just enjoying her time spent with Derek and looking forward to starting to teach the children again. But Abigail's reminder of the tragedy set her to thinking about the fire again and Jedidiah's tragic death. Oh, why couldn't these two bitter old widows talk about something pleasant for a change?

"So, tell me, Amelia, is anyone courting you lately?" Lavinia and Abigail exchanged knowing glances and for just a moment Amelia feared they knew about Derek. And if they did, they would soon tell her aunt and then the problems would begin. Aunt Lucinda would insist on calling on Honora Cameron and spoiling whatever happiness Amelia hoped for.

As it was Lucinda butted in. "Why yes someone is interested in her. A banker. An impressive man. Edward Cutler is his name."

*Edward Cutler.* Amelia nearly laughed out loud. Thank goodness her secret was safe, at least for the moment.

"A banker. Sounds as if he would be a good catch." Abigail sighed as she toyed with the spoon in her cup. "There was a banker interested in me once. But my father told him I was much too young to even think of marriage. I often wonder what happened to him. If he is still alive. If he fought in the war. If he ever thinks of me."

Lavinia interrupted her sister. "He wasn't a banker. He wasn't anything but a teller. And he had buck teeth. I never knew what you saw in him."

"Ha. You are just jealous because no one was smitten with you." Abigail set down the cup and stood up as if to confront her sister.

"Ladies!" As usual Aunt Lucinda was quick to intercede lest the argument get out of hand. Amelia meanwhile felt a bit of relief. As long as they were arguing with each other, they would be too preoccupied to bother with her.

"Forgive me, Lucinda!" The sisters' voices echoed each other in perfect harmony.

Amelia listened to the heated exchange with a shake of her head. There were so many things these two women did not understand, things that she had thought long and hard about since Jedidiah had died. There were so many things wrong in the world and she so wished that she could be the one to right them.

Amelia sighed, taking a sip of her tea. It was a bit too sweet and she realized she had been so intent on daydreaming about Derek that she had put in two spoonsful of sugar instead of one. She drank it anyway, however.

The conversation between the ladies and her aunt switched from talk of past beaus to politics—what the carpetbaggers were doing now was their favorite topic. Amelia thought how boring it all was and how small the world these women lived in really was. Her eyes darted to the doorway, wishing she could make her escape. Talk of the new political parties that were as numerous as feathers on a duck was far from enlightening.

A soft knock at the door interrupted Lavinia's prattling. As all eyes turned towards the sound. "Amelia!" Her aunt's shrill voice shattered Amelia's thoughts into splinters, and quickly she looked up into that so familiar scowling face. "The door, you ninny. Answer it. I declare, I don't know what to do with you. Always off somewhere else in your thoughts these days."

For just a moment Amelia feared that it might be Edward Cutler and that her aunt had invited him to tea. Slowly she walked to the door prepared to be annoyed. Opening it she was surprised to see Jedidiah's mother standing there. She tried to recall the woman's name. Like so many other Negro names it was biblical.

"Deliah!" It came to her in an instant.

"Who is it, Amelia? Invite them in." Aunt Lucinda's voice cut through the awkward silence.

"Yes of course. Come in, Deliah. How are you doing? I want to tell you again how sorry I am for what happened to your son."

Deliah shook her head. "You are very kind but no. I just came by to invite you to Jedidiah's funeral this evening at the church. I know he loved you. He would want you to be there."

Amelia was touched that Jedidiah's parents would think of her in their time of mourning. "Of course. I want to be there for you and for him. He was a special little boy."

Impatient to know who was at the door, Lucinda shuffled to the door, peering over Amelia's shoulders. Rudely she asked, "what on earth is *she* doing here?" She shook her head in the negative so fiercely that her hair came tumbling down from the security of its pins. "You don't want to be involved with *them*, Amelia. Whatever it is she wants tell her to go away."

Angered and embarrassed by her Aunt's rude manner, Amelia gestured for Deliah to come inside. "This is Jedidiah's mother, Auntie. Surely you want to offer her condolences. She lost her son." Clasping her hands together, she tried to regain her composure. "What time is the funeral?"

161

Deliah refused to set even a footstep into the house. "It will be starting in half an hour. I came purposefully to offer you a ride with us in our wagon. That is if you are not already occupied."

Amelia grabbed her hat from the rack by the door. Although it was evening it was so warm she didn't need a jacket or a shawl. "I would like very much to go with you."

"Amelia! You have company." Lucinda was horrified.

"No, they are your friends, not mine." Amelia felt defiant. "Jedidiah meant a great deal to me and there is nothing on this earth that would keep me from showing him the love and respect I have for his family and for him." Amelia had thought to keep a rein on her emotions, but it was impossible to talk about Jedidiah without crying. Life could be so unfair at times.

"Amelia. Amelia." Amelia could hear her aunt calling out her name, but she didn't turn back. Although she knew there would be a fierce argument when she returned, she felt a warm glow spread over her. What she was doing was right and no one, even her aunt, could tell her otherwise.

*    *    *    *

The small one room wooden church was painted white and had a steeple with a large bell that was ringing as Amelia walked up the path, following Delilah, her husband and four children. Jedidiah had been the only boy, his mother exclaimed. "He was my rose among four little thorns."

Inside, the church was packed to the brim with mourners. For just a moment Amelia felt like a fish out of water among so many people with dark skin and wondered how they would react to her presence. She soon found out that not only did everyone gathered greet her with hospitality, they were jovial and smiling. She was stunned. She had expected long faces and tears.

As if noticing her bewilderment Delilah explained. "This is going to be a *homegoing*. It's a Christian funeral tradition commending the going home of the deceased."

"Going home?" Amelia's eyes opened wide as she tried to understand.

"Home to the Lord.. It's a happy time because soon Jedidiah will be in heaven." Delilah explained that going home once meant the soul returning to Africa and that during the slave trade, slaves were not allowed to congregate to perform any kind of ceremony to bury the dead.

Amelia was horrified. "How dreadful."

"Slave owners were afraid the slaves would conspire to have an uprising if allowed to come together in a large group. But once the preachers came all that changed and we learned the glory of heaven and that death was freedom. That's why our rituals are jubilant.

As if reaffirming her words, an out of tune organ started playing a lively song. Then as Amelia took a seat on a bench in the front row a heavenly voice started singing. Amelia was surprised to see that the voice belonged to Jedidiah's oldest sister. She was so short that she was just barely visible beside the podium.

163

# ASHES AND AWAKENINGS

*"Draw a candle light. Etch it in the darkness of your mind," she sang. "So helpless and unhappy just like mankind."*

Amelia was intrigued by the words and the melody.

*"Sketch a tumbleweed. Racing off to nowhere, make a sign. So helpless and unhappy just like man kind."* The tune had minor notes that made it melancholy. Then just as suddenly it changed to lilting and joyful.

*"Faith is like that candle. Leading us to grace. And if we just have faith and try, we'll go to the righteous place....."*

Suddenly the little girl was joined by a chorus. *"Yes, if we just have faith and try, we'll go to the righteous place...."*

Everyone in the church began to clap their hands. Amelia did the same, realizing she was also tapping her foot to the rhythm of the song. Her good mood quickly evaporated, however, as the door of the church opened and the pall bearers brought in a small wooden casket.

"Jedidiah!" She couldn't help but mourn the fact that he had died before his time. As if sensing her emotions, Delilah reached over and squeezed Amelia's hand as if to say that Jedidiah would be all right.

After the song there was a prayer by an old, white bearded preacher whose voice was loud but strangely soothing. He reminded those assembled that death marked the return to the Lord and the end to the pain and suffering of mortal life. "Jedidiah is going to a much better place," he said, "where there is no hatred. No black. No white. Just sweet souls

164

rejoicing together." He painted such a rosy picture that for the first time in her life Amelia cast aside her fear of death. Closing her eyes, she could almost see Jedidiah walking up a pathway of clouds to a paradise of calm, peace, joy, and love.

Amelia had never realized just how musical Jedidiah's people were, but as the service continued, she not only heard the hymns but also felt them as the foot-stomping and hand-clapping accompanied the songs. Although she had a difficult time carrying a tune, she tried very hard to sing along.

At last the preacher returned and began to read the scriptures. "Tonight I will read Proverbs sixteen, sixteen," he announced. "How much better is it to get wisdom than gold! And to get understanding rather to be chosen than silver."

Amelia sat upright on the bench and leaned forward to hear every word. Surely Jedidiah had been wise beyond his years. That the preacher had chosen words that applied to the boy brought forth a myriad of emotions.

The preacher concluded by reading, "the wise in heart shall be called prudent; and the sweetness of the lips increaseth learning." With those words he looked directly at Amelia as if he could look right into her heart and she knew in that moment that the preacher understood how much she had truly cared about Jedidiah.

After the benediction as those gathered together said their final goodbye to Jedidiah, then formed a procession to leave the church, the preacher took her aside. What he asked of her was a surprise. "Would you be willing to set aside an hour or two on Sunday to teach the children, who just like Jedidiah want to be taught? Here at this church."

Amelia didn't even have to think about it. She was a teacher and that was what she would do. Teach.

## Chapter Twelve

Forest was more than just a bit nervous. Why? They were going to have a dinner guest tonight it was true, and they seldom if ever invited anyone to join them, and Moses was just a friend, so why did her hands tremble so as she tried to bring order to her unruly hair?

*What on earth will I talk to him about?* She thought anxiously, moving to her dresser mirror. She approved of the image that stared back at her. She had been able to put her dark hair atop her head in a classical style, parted in the middle with the mass of curls pinned up at the back. It was a style she had seen in a picture book. Forest decided she approved of this new coiffure. If here and there a curl escaped its restraint, well it would have to do for now.

It had been such a long time since she had worn a dress that it felt odd to feel the tightness of the bodice around her waist and to have to deal with skirts and a petticoat. Styles had changed since she and Quentin had lived in Philadelphia. Dresses were slimmer with skirts projected backwards and not as full as in the late sixties. She had heard that there were some women now who even wore a contraption called a *bustle*, but she was determined to never go that far. It was bad enough to have to negotiate all the fastenings on the bodice and the skirt.

Feeling more relaxed she looked at herself critically in the mirror and determined that she looked most fashionable and that the violet colored dress had

167

been a good choice. Its short sleeves were perfect for the warm weather and the oval décolletage, framing the unblemished skin of her throat was proper but interesting.

"Now for the shoes." Digging deep in her closet she could find only two pair. Both had low heels, were ankle high and in her opinion looked hideous. Casting them aside she decided to wear a pair of the boots she favored. Since the skirt was long, she thought of a surety that Moses would not even notice, although she made a mental note to be sure she didn't step on the hem of her dress.

Rustling as she walked across the floor to her jewelry box, she picked out a simple gold chain with a locket. It was a gift from Quentin. She was determined to one day find her mother and put her picture inside, but as of now it was empty.

"Forest. Your young man is here!" Quentin's announcement startled her and for just a moment she felt nervous again. *He's just a friend and nothing more*, she said to herself. *Just a friend. Just a friend.* Such a good friend that the meeting with him had totally distracted her from going to see Andrew Wyatt. But she would speak with Mr. Wyatt at another time.

Walking across the room she fought to regain her poise. She would think of Moses as he had been so long ago. A frightened boy who needed someone to care. A friend. Only that and nothing more. Taking a deep breath, she reached for the door knob and opened the door.

Moses was every bit as nervous as his *Jemma* was. He had never been a lady's man and had been so busy the past few years that women had been far from his mind. Now as he looked at the vision entering the living room, he couldn't help but gawk. Standing before him was a beautiful woman.

"You're wearing a dress!" It was the first thing that came to his mind and he felt foolish the moment his words were out.

Forest couldn't help but laugh. He was looking at her as if she were a sugar plum or a cinnamon stick. "Don't act so surprised, Moses. I don't dress like a boy all the time." She touched her tongue lightly to her lips to ease the dryness, unaware of the provocativeness of her action.

Moses' heart skipped a beat. If he had loved her when they were children, he loved her two-fold now. He had teased Derek for his infatuation with the teacher but now he was the one who had been shot with Cupid's arrow, a whole quiver full, he thought.

The flowers Moses held in his hand were not only lovely but fragrant, filling the room with their fragrance. Forest suspected that they were for her but since Moses hadn't offered them to her she didn't reach for them but merely complimented him on his choice of blossoms.

Feeling slightly foolish at having been so taken with her loveliness that he had forgotten about the flowers in his hand, Moses held them out to her. "I'm glad you like them. They are for you."

"Thank you. For just a moment I thought they were for Quentin," she whispered with a smile. Hurrying to find something to put them in and choosing the coffee pot to use as a vase temporarily, she took him by the hand. "Quentin's in the kitchen. He is the cook for tonight's dinner." Seeing the surprised look on his face she insisted that her father

169

was an excellent cook.

The kitchen was filled with the tantalizing smell that only food can bring. Standing by the small stove, holding a wooden spoon in his hand, Quentin looked just as comfortable cooking as he did standing before a podium.

"We are having possum stuffed with dressing and sweet potatoes," Quentin announced, looking apologetically at Forest. "I know Forest hates it when one of her little friends ends up in the cooking pot. She would rather stick to fish and vegetables, but I wanted to do something special to celebrate our crossing paths again."

The dish reminded Moses of his mother, who had decided to remain in the north with his father. "I remember my mother making baked possum. I was always annoyed when she called me away from my adventures with Derek to stuff the damned thing." Remembering that there was a lady present, Moses looked towards Forest and started to apologize but she shook her head.

Apples, plums, and pears completed the menu. Moses thought surely there was enough food to feed a small army, though the table was set just for the three of them.

Quentin gestured for Moses and Forest to take a seat, then brought forth a bottle of wine, pouring a glass for each of them. Raising his glass, he clinked his goblet against Forest's then against the one Moses held. "To the renewal of an old friendship and to the future," he said.

"I will most certainly drink to that," Moses declared, trying to focus on Quentin's face but finding himself captivated by Forest. He tried not to be too obvious as he glanced at her breasts then focused his attention on every detail of her loveliness, including her long, slim neck and the perfection of her features. The pretty child had turned into a beautiful woman.

Likewise, Forest's gaze centered on Moses and she liked what she saw. The lantern light emphasized the planes of his features, the mystifying depths of his brown eyes. In his blue frock coat, white shirt, and trousers he made a dashing figure. "I hope you are hungry."

"Famished." And indeed he was. He hadn't had a bite to eat since mid-morning.

"So am I, my boy. So am I, Quentin admitted.

Forest took three long gulps of her wine, letting it warm her. It gave her courage to flirt with their *guest* every once in awhile as they ate. She was even so bold as to let her knee touch his leg under the table.

"So once we parted ways and you went your way and Forest and I went ours, what happened?" Quentin asked, reaching for the sliced apples.

"Allegra Cameron had forged our papers and given us the name of a man working in the underground railroad. He found my mother a job as a maid, my father a job laying brick, and I worked in a factory." He shrugged. "Not anything exciting to tell. A few years later I put newspaper in my shoes so I would be taller and joined the Union army. It was a terrible experience to know that we were shooting at other men. I have to admit that I was still a kid so I stayed out of sight every chance I got. No heroics for me. And to tell the truth I spent more time helping with the cooking than hefting a gun. But one day when I *was* on the battlefield I ran across a soldier just as unnerved by the fighting as I was. A

171

Confederate soldier. Derek. The odds must have been at least a hundred to one that I would find him that day. The bond between us hadn't vanished with time so we started up our friendship again, walking, running, and sometimes crawling back to Richmond and then to Winding Oaks our home."

Moses realized his possum was getting cold so he started to eat again. It was Quentin's turn to talk. Although he strove to be polite, Moses could not keep from staring now and again at *Jemma*. Strange how her old name kept popping up in his brain.

"Forest and I headed for Philadelphia. I had written letters to several prominent gentlemen concerning employment and was fortunate that they had need of someone to advise them on issues. Forest was taken under the wing of their wives, daughters, and sisters. They watched her grow up as the war raged. We were comfortable, living in a nice but small house. Too comfortable. I should have known the financial bubble we all were in would burst but I didn't see the financial world crumbling until it fell flat on its face. Luckily I had the title to this property so we returned to the place we had run away from."

Although Moses nodded his head as if he heard every word, in truth it was as if a cocoon of enchantment enclosed Forest and himself, a magic as potent as any poet could have dreamed up. As if they moved in slow motion, they noted infinite details about each other. She noted the way his brown eyes twinkled, the way he gestured so expressively with his hands when he talked. He noticed the way her cheeks dimpled when she smiled, the inquisitive way she tilted her head.

"The food. It...it was delicious," he blurted,

172

feeling strangely tongue-tied for the first time in his life when he realized that Quentin had stopped speaking and was waiting for his reply.

Forest had hardly eaten a bite. "Yes, it was." Looking at her goblet she longed for another glass of wine. Anything to give her courage. "Quentin and I talked about you several times. And I thought about you…"

"Thought about me?" Dragging his fingers through his thick dark hair Moses frowned, wishing he had had more experience with women. Hoping for good luck he crossed his fingers behind his back. What would she do if she knew what he was thinking, that he wanted to hold her in his arms and never let her go?

"We worried about your fate. You were so frightened."

His manly ego was pricked to think she had thought of him as a scared little boy all these years. "Well, I would not be frightened now. I have learned to be strong the past few years."

"Impressively so," Quentin said, sensing the awkwardness of the moment. "Have you ever thought of going into politics. Our new party could use a man like you."

'Politics?" Moses frowned. "No. I am a man who likes to use his hands. A man of the earth. I don't think I would be good at telling fibs." Noticing Quentin's stern look and fearing he had insulted his host he added, "and I doubt that I could ever be as eloquent as you, Sir."

Quentin's frown morphed into a smile. "Well, if you ever change your mind, please let me know." Not finished with his matchmaking, Quentin shooed them out of the kitchen insisting that he would clean up and do the dishes. He would join them when he had finished, he told them.

Following Forest into the living room, Moses paused in front of the bookshelf and was surprised to see she still had the book she had read to him that time so long ago. Reaching for it he smiled as he thumbed through the pages.

"The Nutcracker and the Mouse King....."

"You remember." She had kept the book even though she had outgrown it. It had special meaning to her because of the boy.

"I remember that the nutcracker is a girl's favorite Christmas toy and that it comes alive. He defeats the evil mouse king and whisks the girl away to a magical kingdom populated by dolls. Oh, how I wanted to be the nutcracker." *So that I could take you away with me*, he thought but did not say.

"And I wanted to be Marie. I had dreams about the magical kingdom. It was a way to block out what was happening in the war. So many men killed. We heard about it over and over again."

"Jemma...." Realizing he had called her by her old name he put his finger to his lips. "Forest," he amended.

Moving towards him she touched the hand covering his mouth. "You can call me Jemma if you wish. I don't have any reason to hide away any longer." She was going to tell him about the night her parents were running away and about how Quentin had rescued her, but it was clear he had other things on his mind.

"I want to see you again and again and

174

again...." The words came from his heart. All this time he had been so lonely and he hadn't even realized it until he'd looked into her hazel eyes and envisioned how love was meant to be.

Forest laughed, feeling so lightheaded that she was certain she could float on air at that moment. "And I want to see you too."

Compulsively he took her hand, his fingers closing firmly around hers. Then, bending his head, he pressed his warm lips against the upturned palm of her hand. A simple show of affection that he had seen southern gentlemen bestow on women of culture all the time.

Forest drew him towards the sofa where they could sit together. Noticing that he was favoring his right arm she asked him if he had a sore muscle.

"I worked from before dawn until just before I came here. Derek needed some desks constructed for a teacher who will be holding classes at a house on his property. Then there was digging and planting to do, cutting down a tree....."

"I can help," she whispered. "I have massaged Quentin's shoulders and arms when he has over done." Reaching up she touched his arm with gentle hands, kneading the muscles in circular strokes. She felt him relax as she moved to his shoulders. The muscles on his arms and shoulders were so masculine that any memories of the boy gave way to her desire for the man he had become.

Moving to the strength of his neck, Forest was telling Moses about how happy she was at the cottage as she massaged his strength. Suddenly he slumped over, laying his head against the back of the sofa, his eyes closed, a peaceful smile upon his face. He had

175

worked so hard, had been so exhausted that he had fallen asleep.

For just a moment she thought she should awaken him but remembering that he had worked doubly hard that day, she thought better of it. Going to her room she took a blanket and a pillow off the bed and returning to the living room, made him as comfortable as she could. Then on impulse she kissed him on the cheek, slowly lowered the wick on the oil lamp to extinguish the flame and whispered a fond "good night....."

\*       \*       \*       \*

It was very late when Amelia arrived home from Jedidiah's funeral. She felt a sense of comfort and calm that she had not felt since the fire had taken the life of the child. Somehow in her heart she knew that Jedidiah was all right. He had gone home. Now it was time for her to do her part in keeping his memory alive. Jedidiah would be the inspiration for her to teach other children just like him, those boys and girls who would now be given a chance to learn.

Walking up the steps to her aunt's house she was relieved to see that all the lights were out. She wouldn't have to suffer her aunt's tirade of annoyance, animosity towards others, and her warnings of what Amelia's actions would bring. Aunt Lucinda's scolding always left her feeling guilty when there was no reason. Surely it was never bad to be concerned for others. Wasn't that one of the lessons that going to church each Sunday was supposed to bring?

Opening the door, she was careful not to bump

into anything in the dark or make any noise that might wake her aunt. She even bent down to unfasten her shoes and remove them so that the sound of her walking across the wooden floor would not give her arrival away. Tomorrow when she woke she would be better prepared to deal with her aunt's reprimand.

Ever so slowly Amelia walked towards her room, remembering in her mind's eye what the area looked like in the light. Holding out her arms she used them much like an insect's feelers to navigate her way, at last reaching the sanctity of her bedroom door.

"And just what took you so long, young lady!" The strident voice behind her startled Amelia and she bumped into the wall. "Do you have any idea just how late it is?"

Rubbing her injured elbow, Amelia was surprised that instead of feeling intimidated she felt resentment and ire. She wasn't a child. Indeed, she was well beyond the age when she should have been deferential and obedient to another's wishes.

"It is quite late," she answered defiantly. "But it was well worth it. It was a joyous funeral." She wanted to tell her aunt all about it and how the experience had healed her own soul, but immediately her aunt started a quarrel.

"Joyous. Ha. I've heard *those people* are as primitive as beasts. Pagan. Unrighteous."

Amelia felt her ire bubble up inside her. "To the contrary they are just as spiritual as any

other church goers. Maybe even more so."

Lucinda gasped. "Amelia, watch your tongue lest you be damned forever."

"Damned? I hardly think so." Oh, what was the use. Her aunt was one of those people who was blindsided by her own narrow views. She would never have been able to make her understand. "But I don't want to discuss this with you tonight. I'm tired." All she wanted to do was to change into her nightgown and tumble into bed.

"Rubbish. We'll talk about your nonsense right this minute." Like a sleepwalker Lucinda shuffled across the room and finding the oil lamp quickly lit it with a match she had tucked in the folds of her nightgown.

The sudden light was blinding and Amelia squinted against the glare. "There is nothing to discuss."

"We have neighbors. I will be humiliated beyond belief if any of them saw you riding off with those...those people." Lucinda's frown distorted the features on her face and Amelia thought how ugly her aunt appeared when she was outraged.

"So that is what this is all about. Not about how late the hour is but because you care more about your own bigotry than about the murder of a little boy. A child I cared about very deeply. A boy whose little finger was worth more than the whole lot of your precious neighbors." Realizing that she was shouting, Amelia tried to calm her emotions by taking several deep breaths.

Lucinda was strangely calm. "How dare you. I have taken you in, fed you, clothed you, and provided a roof over your head. And this is the thanks that I get. You insult the people I consider to be my friends."

For just a moment Amelia nearly allowed herself

to feel intimidated but remembering her newfound courage she shook her head. "You have provided for me and for that I thank you, but you have never for one moment let me forget what I owe. A debt that can never be repaid." She wondered what her aunt's reaction would be when she told her that she was committed to teach the Negro children at the church every Sunday.

Instead of being angry Lucinda reacted with shock, perhaps because it was the first time Amelia had ever spoken her mind. "We are both tired. It has been a long, tedious day. We will speak more about this tomorrow."

Tomorrow. Watching as her aunt made her way to her own bedroom Amelia made a decision that she knew should have been made long ago. It was time to go off on her own. She needed to be her own person. Make her own decisions. Think her own thoughts. Live life the way she wanted to live it. But where was she to go?

Immediately she thought about a pair of kind blue eyes and a smile that always made her heart sing. Derek Cameron. The Avery mansion had been vacant for several years. Perhaps it was possible to pay him money so that she could not only teach there but live there as well. It was a proposal she would discuss with him tomorrow.

# ASHES AND AWAKENINGS

## Chapter Thirteen

The sun was just peeking over the horizon. Twinkling rays of sunlight danced through the slit in the curtains. A sudden sound disturbed the quietude—a rooster crowing. "Cookadoodledoo" Moses thought he heard through the fog of his dreams. He wanted to shush the damn bird so that he could continue to dream but as he heard a repeat of the crowing he buried his head in the pillow to try and block out the sound.

Suddenly he lifted his head with a start. A rooster? He didn't have a rooster. Chickens yes but rooster no. disconcerted he looked around him. Where was he? And what was that appetizing smell wafting through the air.

"Jemma!" He remembered now. Quentin and Jemma, or Forest as she now called herself, had invited him for dinner. He remembered the delicious Possum that Quentin had cooked, remembered exchanging stories of their lives after they had parted at the train station, remembered sitting beside Forest. He had told her about his muscles aching and she had gently touched his shoulders then his arms as she gave him a massage. And then he must have fallen asleep. He could only hope that he hadn't snored.

Looking down he smiled as he saw that she had covered him with a blanket and given him a pillow. That was his Forest. Always thoughtful and kind. "My Jemma!" he whispered. If only that could be true—that she truly belonged to him-- he would have

180

been the happiest of men.

"You're awake." Dressed in a red and white checkered calico dress with an outdated full skirt and a white apron trimmed with red, she greeted him.

"That damned rooste," he mumbled, then remembering that a lady was present he shrugged.

She laughed, a melodious sound. "That is General Bragg."

"General Bragg?"

"The Confederate general famous for being a big loser and for sounding retreat before it was needed. All the chickens have names. There is Caroline, Camila, Charlotte, Cecilia, Chelsea, and Calliope."

The fact that she named her chickens amused him. "I never thought to name any of mine. Perhaps one day you can visit my place and help me pick out nicknames for them."

She didn't even have to think about an answer, it just popped out. "I'd like that." Her eyes met his and they both smiled simultaneously.

"Something smells delicious." He followed her to the small kitchen and was pleasantly surprised to see the table already set for two. He looked around but didn't see Quentin and supposed he was already at work around the grounds.

"I am very good with leftovers," she boasted. "I have blended small pieces of last night's possum with wild onions, green peppers from the garden, pieces of potato, and eggs. Scrambled. And there are fresh berries and of course coffee." He sat down and after she had dished out his portion, she sat down beside him.

The coffee was hot so Moses waited a moment

before he took a sip. "I apologize for falling asleep when I did. I fear I wasn't very good company."

"You had worked hard. I understand. Better for you to fall asleep where you had a comfortable couch than in the wagon while on your way home. Besides, I'm glad we had more time to spend together."

"So am I." Moses was famished so he didn't say much more as he concentrated on eating the tasty breakfast she had prepared. Forest on the other hand chatted on and on about Quentin's political escapades and his hopes for the future. "Now that Negroes like us have been given the vote he wants to make certain that we have a choice on who to vote for."

He looked up when she said the words "Negroes like us" because at the back of his mind he set her apart from himself. Forest looked as though she had more than just a little white blood in her veins, just like his mother who also had a lighter complexion.

"Your father is certainly good with words. I was intrigued by what he was saying. But I am not so certain that it will be easy to get one like us elected to a political office."

She popped a berry into her mouth then said, "I think it is entirely possible. Anyway, we have to try. Nothing ventured, nothing gained, as Ben Franklin said."

"Ah, good ole Ben. I hear tell that he only owned two slaves unlike some of the others who had dozens and dozens." He frowned as he thought about the hypocrisy of some of the other founding fathers such as Washington, Jefferson, and Madison who had talked about all men being free while they held other men in bondage.

"Quentin says that is all in the past and that there

is no need to hold grudges. Although I have a confession to make." She put down her fork. "I still hold a grudge against the man who tracked down my family and put my mother and father back in bondage."

"You know who it was?"

Her frown contorted her pretty face for just a moment then she lowered her voice. "I saw him the other day at the bank. I delivered a message from one of the men in Quentin's party and the sight of his face nearly made me panic. I can never forget running away from him that day."

"Did you confront him?"

She shook her head. "No, that's where I was going when we bumped into each other. But I am going to seek him out and ask him if he can help me find my mother and father. I pray every night that they are still alive." Seeing that Quentin had entered the room she quieted.

"Ah, I see Forest has fed you well this morning." Picking up a mug from a rack on the wall Quentin poured himself a cup of coffee and sweetened it with a peppermint stick, ignoring Moses' look of stunned surprise.

"Added to your dinner last night I fear I may become fat as a hog," Moses answered, eating the last bit of his eggs. "I don't know how to thank you for your hospitality."

Quentin had a coy look in his eye as he moved the peppermint stick back and forth, stirring his coffee. 'You can thank us by being our guest again. Soon." He looked at Forest. "We have a lot more to catch up on. So many years have gone by and all too quickly. I am afraid I am becoming an old man."

183

"Oh no. Not you." Forest was quick to reassure him. "You have the stamina and intellect of a much younger man."

"Sometimes," Quentin said chuckling. He quickly became serious. "But while we are on the subject of age and stamina, I want to present to you once again the idea of becoming politically involved in the changes this country is going through. Like the metamorphosis of a gigantic butterfly from a caterpillar. We need a young, vibrant man like you, Moses. A man to lead the people like the Moses in the Bible."

Wiping his mouth with the back of his hand since there were no napkins, Moses stood up. "No. That kind of life is just not for me. Besides, I am too busy with my peanuts and work on Winding Oaks to even think about such a thing. But I do appreciate your kind words."

"True words." Quentin shrugged in a gesture of defeat. "But don't think I won't mention this again. We need your kind of man."

Forest left her breakfast half-finished as she got to her feet to walk Moses to the door. "I'm so glad you could visit us. It means a lot to me to have your friendship."

Friendship. Moses thought to himself how he wished he was in a position to offer her something more. But she deserved the world and he just didn't have the world to offer her. He would have to settle for what they could have, at least for the moment.

*　　*　　*　　*

Guilt was a heavy burden to endure but as he opened the door to his father's room, Derek felt more than just a twinge of self-reproach. He had not visited his father since the O'Leary woman had begun helping his mother tend Charles. Derek had been swamped with responsibility, had been working until his hands were blistered and calloused, yet he knew there was another reason. Ever since he was little more than a child and his father had sold Moses, there had been a deep resentment that had begun to grow like a sapling. That bitterness was now as big as a tree.

Entering the room, he was more than a bit shaken to see that the once robust Charles Cameron was now a frail man, an old man, showing signs of his age. As Derek looked upon the figure propped up by several pillows, he felt a surge of sympathy and just a twinge of affection.

"How is he?" he asked Catriona O'Leary.

"Just as ornery as ever, or so Honora told me. He's sleeping now but when he is awake he is a handful." She got up from the chair by Charles' side. "I haven't seen any signs of pneumonia. But the apoplexy has left him unable to move his right arm or fingers. He wants to get out of bed but your mother is afraid he might fall. And that has infuriated him."

"He's stubborn."

"Aye, as stubborn as a mule."

Mrs. O'Leary's voice seemed to disturb Charles' sleep because his lips twitched and he moved his head. Then suddenly his eyes flew open. "Well, so my long-lost son decided to make an appearance," he scolded looking straight into Derek's eyes.

Derek was taken aback by his father's

antagonism. "I'm sorry, but I have been working my fingers to the bone so that we don't lose everything. But it appears that rather than show a thimble full of gratitude you would rather quarrel."

"That depends."

"Depends on what?" Derek had promised himself that he would not lose his temper.

"Never mind. You wouldn't understand like Bevin did." Just saying the name seemed to bring him the memory of pain his eldest son's death had brought him.

"I'm not Bevin."

"No, you are not." He paused, then gave into a fit of coughing. Charles tried to sit up but was restrained by Mrs. O'Leary.

"You need to reserve your strength," she said softly.

"And you need to mind your own business, you damned *mick*!"

"I'll be beggin' yer pardon!" Mrs. O'Leary snorted.

Charles tried to get up again and this time fell back because he was too weak. "You can beg my pardon all you want but I don't care. I don't want you here. You *potato eaters* aren't much better than the Nigrahs!"

"Well, is that so?" Her flushed face divulged her rising anger.

"Yes, it is so. I wish you would go back to Ireland and I wish that Lincoln had sent the Nigrah's back to Africa where they belong." His ranting took up too much energy and he fell back among the pillows, leaving Derek to sooth Mrs. O'Leary's ruffled feathers.

"He doesn't know what he is saying," Derek explained. "He is just ranting and raving. He didn't mean any insult."

"Ah, but he did." Catriona O'Leary wasn't that easily swayed.

"He's a fool!" Helping her move Charles to a more comfortable position in the bed, he said, "the Cameron's are Scottish. We're Celts too."

"Aye. Yer name would be *Cumarán* there. In Ireland I mean." She grinned, showing that any animosity was not transferred to him. "It means crooked nose."

Reaching up Derek touched his own nose. "Thank God I have not suffered *that* fate." He waited a little while longer just in case his father woke up but it looked like Charles Cameron was deep in sleep. His loud rumbling snores was proof of that.

Looking around the room Derek was reminded of all the times he had timidly tried to get his father's attention only to be set aside. To Charles Cameron his son Bevin was the moon and the stars. He just hadn't had time for his younger son. Derek's sister, Allegra, had suffered a like fate. Even when the Cameron mansion had been spared from being burned to the ground by Yankees because of the kindness she had shown to Union prisoners, Charles had not shown any gratitude.

"I'm sorry, Mrs. O'Leary. But upon my word he is harmless."

"Is he?" Her expression seemed to tell him she was just bursting at the seams with the desire to tell him something.

"What?"

Going to the small desk at the far side of the bedroom she pulled open a drawer and reached inside. Pulling out two pieces of paper she held them in front of his nose. He saw that the first one was an article from *The Daily Dispatch*, one of the Richmond Newspapers. The other was from a rival newspaper-- *The Daily State Journal*, published in Alexandria, Virginia. Looking closely, he could see that they were both articles about the Ku Klux Klan and their reign of terror.

The articles told about the Klan being formed the year after the war was over by a small band of Confederate veterans in Tennessee. How it had expanded from a localized membership to a nation-wide group that spread violence and terror across the South. It spoke about the white hoods, flowing sheets, fiery crosses, and the horror their vigilante violence brought forth.

Looking up Derek defended his father. "Just articles. I won't lie and tell you that my father isn't a hate-filled man, he is. But President Grant put a halt to this nonsense a couple of years ago and the Klan was stopped."

Was he trying to convince Mrs. O'Leary or himself? Derek scanned the two articles again, trying to remember anything at all that might have been a hint that his father was involved in such a terrible organization. There was nothing definite that came to mind, although he did remember his father laughing several times and referring to the Klansmen as being dressed up as Confederate ghosts. He had thought the gossip about the KKK wearing blackface to mock their victims a fine joke indeed.

"No!" It just wasn't possible. Striding over to the desk, he put the articles back in the drawer and chastised Mrs. O'Leary for snooping.

Realizing that it was getting late, ticking off all the things that had to get done that day, Derek took the stairs two at a time. He was surprised to see Amelia in the entranceway waiting for him. "You're early. School doesn't start until an hour from now."

Amelia put her hand up to her tousled hair. She hadn't slept a wink, had taken little time to do her hair, and worried that her garments were more than a bit wrinkled. "I know. But I had a terrible quarrel with my Aunt Lucinda because I attended Jedidiah's funeral and I didn't want to have to face her this morning."

"I see." Derek knew all about such things. "Do you want to talk about it?"

"Perhaps later. What I need to know now is if it would be possible to pay to stay at the Avery Mansion. I just can't abide living with my aunt any longer." She didn't want to break down in tears in front of him so she bit her lip to keep from crying.

"You mean live there?" The idea was intriguing because it would mean that she would be closer to him.

Amelia felt strangely timid as she waited for his answer, telling herself that she should have made other arrangements. Perhaps staying with one of her aunt's friends or looking for a cheap hotel in Richmond. She didn't want him to find her needy.

"I think it would be a fine idea," he blurted. "And I know mother would be most approving. She won't admit it, but I think she gets more than a bit lonely for another woman's company."

# ASHES AND AWAKENINGS

Amelia hurried to firm up the agreement. "And of course, I would be only too happy to help your mother if she needed me. I often helped Aunt Lucinda." She was so relieved that the matter was settled. Now the only thing that needed to be done was to inform her aunt that she was leaving.

*　　　*　　　*　　　*

Amelia thought that if life was a book, she was starting a whole new chapter. But just what kind of story would she encounter? The question was both exciting and vexing. One thing she knew, however, unlike the months and years she had spent with Aunt Lucinda, from now on what happened would be of her own making.

"Do you need any help unloading the rest of the wagon?"

Looking over at Derek she shook her head no as he helped her down from the high wooden seat. "I know how busy you are. You have already helped me more than anyone would dare ask for."

And indeed, he had given her assistance in every way imaginable. Since the buggy she always used to travel in was her aunt's, Amelia had found herself without transportation. Derek Cameron had come to her aid, however, not only driving a wagon to transport her belongings from her aunt's house to the Avery Mansion, but also giving her a shoulder to lean on. On top of that he had unloaded the heaviest of her clothes trunks and carried them upstairs to the room that would be hers.

"You needed someone to lend a hand. What

190

kind of man would I be if I hadn't volunteered to help out?" He couldn't stop thinking about the argument he had with his father. He would never understand how anger and hatred had ruled Charles' actions. "Besides, it did me a bit of good to get far away from here for a moment."

"Fresh air and pleasant scenery always help clear one's mind," she responded, feeling a sense of loss as she watched him walk away to return to his work.

"Remember, if you need help I will be working on a new well between this house and the main one. Just whistle and I will be at your disposal," he called out, breaking into a run as if to help make up for lost time.

Turning back towards the wagon, Amelia concentrated on gathering up two lighter boxes and the two flour sacks that contained the odds and ends that represented her life with Aunt Lucinda—books, knickknacks, a small box of mementoes of her mother and father, a doll she had as a child and couldn't seem to throw away, a wooden jewelry box her father had given her, and lastly the carving of the angel Jedidiah had made for her.

As she lugged the boxes and sacks up the stairs of the Avery House Amelia couldn't help but think about her confrontation with Aunt Lucinda. Her aunt had called her ungrateful, a stubborn fool, and had warned her that the path she was on would lead to trouble. She had also told Amelia that it would not be long before she would come crawling back and pleading with her aunt to take her back in. Only when she had followed Amelia outside and seen that she was not alone, had Lucinda softened her tirade. Looking first at Derek and then at Amelia, then at

Derek, and then at Amelia again she had clucked her tongue and jumped with both feet to the wrong conclusion.

"So that is the way it is," was all her aunt had said. There had been no show at all of regret for the harsh words spoken or even one sign of affection.

"She is wrong. I will never go back," Amelia mumbled to herself, trying to brush off the feeling of sorrow that threatened to engulf her. It was deeply troubling to realize that her aunt had never held much affection for her. All those years of trying to please her had all been for naught. But from here on out the only person she would seek to please would be herself.

## Chapter Fourteen

The air was fresh as it can only be after a cleansing rain. Moses breathed in deeply and walked briskly towards the Winding Oaks mansion. For the first time in a long while he felt light of heart. Happy. He felt as if he didn't have a care in the world. He was going to make a success of his farm and when he did he would have something besides just his heart to offer Forest.

"Moses!" Looking behind him, he saw that Derek was hurrying to catch up with him.

"You look happy this morning," Derek exclaimed as he matched him stride for stride. "Is that sparkle in your eye because of peanuts?"

Thrusting his hands in the pockets of his pants, Moses paused for a moment to gaze up at the sky. Strange, but it was as if he were looking at the world through different eyes, viewing it less critically and seeing only its calm and beauty.

"Moses?" Waving his hand in front of his friend's eyes Derek laughed. "Don't tell me. It's a woman. I have been actin' much the same."

"Hmmm?" Moses was immersed in his own thoughts, remembering the touch of Forest's hands as she had massaged his sore, aching muscles. And how she had put a pillow under his head and covered him with a blanket.

"I asked you if you were thinkin' about someone."

"Um hum." Moses knew that tonight he would

193

have very pleasant dreams of a dark-haired beauty with the most fascinating eyes. *Jemma*. Somehow, he would always think of her by that name.

"All right. If you want to keep secrets, I won't press you. I have spent some time in dreamland too. And as a matter of fact, the object of *my* dreams is now livin' in the old Avery house." As they walked Derek told his friend about Amelia quarreling with her aunt and asking if she could not only teach but live at the old mansion.

"How utterly convenient." Now it was Moses who was in the mood to tease. "You can sing her love ballads beneath the window."

"And have her throw rotten eggs down at me?" Derek warbled a few notes, trying not to be too off key.

Moses wrinkled up his nose. "You're right. Singing is not your specialty. Perhaps you should learn how to play the harp."

"Like an angel?" Derek pretended he was strumming the strings. "You know I can be all thumbs." He grew serious. "Father is recoverin'. Yesterday he insulted Catriona."

"Ah yes. Your father does that kind of thing very well," Moses grumbled, then softened his tone. "But I'm glad he is getting back to his grumpy old self." He could tell that something was bothering Derek. "What is it?"

Derek thought for a moment then decided to mention the articles on the Ku Klux Klan that Catriona had found in his father's desk drawer. "It's probably nothin'. Just a warped interest in the doin's of violent men, but I was troubled none the less. I thought about the fire at the schoolhouse and the

194

death of Amelia's student."

Moses hadn't told his friend about the incident with the red painted letters on his house but now he did so. "I don't know if the two incidents are related but they could be."

"A return of the *Invisible Empire of the South* as they were once called. Cowards is what I call them, hidin' beneath their robes and sheets." Once again, a thought crossed Derek's mind about his father being a part of that evil group but he brushed it aside.

"Burning schools and churches was their specialty as I remember." Moses hated to admit it but a few years ago when the group was active he had been more than a bit frightful. Men would do in crowds what they would not do alone. Like a vicious pack of rabid hounds. But Congress and prosecutors had put a stop to the madness.

"We will need to keep watch just to make certain such an incident doesn't happen again." Once again Derek's mind turned to the work that needed to be done. "I need your help this mornin'. I was diggin' a well and hit a rock that is so big I can't seem to remove it. It will take two to do the job."

Following Derek, Moses grabbed the shovel handed to him and started digging. And digging. And digging. But somehow they couldn't find where the rock ended. "I don't think it is a rock," he finally exclaimed.

Derek had come to the same conclusion. "Then what is it?"

After more digging and shoveling, the answer was at last revealed. Buried deep in the ground was a wooden coffin. Although whose casket it was Derek could not say.

195

# ASHES AND AWAKENINGS

*     *     *     *

One by one Amelia's students filed up the stairs, intrigued by their new surroundings. Some were glad to be attending school again but a few grumbled and acted as if learning was a drudgery. As they took their assigned seats at the make-shift desks Moses and Derek had made, she took a silent rollcall, noticing at once that one student was missing. Beauregard. Was she surprised by his absence? No. Somehow in her heart she had suspected that he had tattled to his father and brought down the wrath that had caused the death of an innocent boy.

"Good morning, class."

"Good morning Miss Seton."

There was a squeal from Mary as Jimmy pulled her long braid. Quickly Amelia reprimanded him, hiding a smile as she realized it was just like old times. She had missed the children, even the naughty ones.

"We'll begin with arithmetic today. I want you to add these numbers without counting on your fingers. Ten. Seven. Twelve. Nine and four." She waited to see who came up with the answer first.

"Is this old mansion haunted?" Travis Jeffries seemed frightened. "I don't cotton to no ghosts."

Amelia hurried to assure him. "Of course not. It was just abandoned after the new house was built, that's all. But the Camerons have been kind enough to let us use this room as a school."

"It's pretty. I wish my mother and father and all my brothers could live here," Maybelle said wistfully.

196

"I wouldn't want to live here," Spencer Adams shouted out. "Too much dust. "Ugh."

Amelia looked around at some of the cobwebs she seemed to have missed. "There won't be tomorrow." She forced a stern expression. "Now back to the numbers."

"Thirty-three." Jimmy called out."

"Fifty." Travis nodded his head as if counting.

"Boys don't know anything.    "Forty-two." Maybelle was proud of herself.

"Yes. Maybelle is correct."   Amelia presented several other numbers for subtraction and addition, then moved on to reading.  Usually each student had their own book but after the fire books had been scarce so the students had to share the books that Derek had provided.  Books he said he and his sister had read when they were children.

Maybelle read aloud from *Westward Ho*, a book about an unruly boy who sets sail with Sir Francis Drake, Sir Walter Raleigh, and other privateers to the New World.  Her reading was slow of pace and she stumbled over some of the words so her reading took up a lot of the morning.  Then it was Spencer's turn. He chose *The Gorilla Hunters*, a book set in Africa. The main characters were three boys.  As Amelia listened to the story, she quickly decided that its theme of animal killing and the hunt for a gorilla was not suitable for her students.   That decision was amplified as she saw Jimmy and Travis giggling and making comments about apes turning into men.

"Thank you, Spenser, but we will move on to a story Mary can read aloud." *Children of the New Forest* seemed a better choice.  As she listened to Mary read in her high-pitched voice about four children and their lives at the time of the English Civil War and Commonwealth, she relaxed.

Writing was the last subject of the day. Since there was only the large chalk board, Amelia had first the boys then the girls take their turn. As punishment for pulling Mary's hair, Jimmy was the one chosen to erase the board. Then it was time for the children to go help their parents, whether at home or in the fields. Amelia watched as they hopped, skipped, and jumped down the stairs.

Amelia had been so anxious to leave her aunt's house that instead of carefully folding her clothing and putting each garment in separately, she had jammed them in her suitcases. Now she had to pay the price by shaking each garment out and hanging it in the wardrobe armoire. Always one to be neat and orderly, she arranged each dress in the order she planned to wear them. When she was finished, she sat down in a rocking chair by the four-poster, canopied bed.

"Well, if this house is haunted I will certainly have plenty of company," she whispered to herself, remembering all the paintings of Camerons she had viewed on the wall down below.

Whether or not the house had ghosts, Amelia was certain she would feel very comfortable in her surroundings. In addition to the bed and the chair, there was a huge gilded mirror, a dressing table, a desk, and several chairs, all early Victorian, in a room that was twice the size of the one at her aunt's house. Downstairs there was a very big kitchen, much too large for her requirements, but which she could use to store her breakfast supplies and other staples. As for her personal needs, there was a

KATHRYN KRAMER

washstand in an alcove off the bedroom, with hand painted porcelain tiles and a porcelain bowl and jug. For bathing there was a bathroom with a big brass tub and a small stove where water could be heated.

"Please feel free to eat dinner at the main house. I want you to get to know my mother," Derek had said to her. It had been an invitation she had not wanted to turn down. Closing her eyes, she thought about Derek and how she felt a close connection to him in so many ways. She didn't mean to let her daydreaming about him lull her into sleep, but as she opened her eyes and saw that it was growing dark, she bolted out of the rocking chair. She would be late for dinner if she didn't hurry up.

Walking as fast as she could, Amelia arrived at Winding Oaks. Remembering that Derek had told her that his mother had to let the entire kitchen help go because of finances, she didn't go to the main entrance but went to the back of the house where the cooking area would be. Opening the door, she turned to the right and could feel the heat from the fire. A kettle was heating; she saw it from the corner of her eye.

Moving closer she gasped as she realized that she was not in the kitchen at all but in the bathing room. Standing beside the tub, as naked as the day he was born stood Derek with his back to her. She noticed right away that his legs were well formed and that he was muscular.

As he turned around, her eyes were drawn to his chest and the tuft of hair which trailed in a thin straight line down his navel, to that part of him that marked him as a male. For just a moment she was mesmerized by his power, strength, and the virile

199

good looks.

"Amelia!" Hurriedly he reached for a towel to wrap around the lower half of his body.

Amelia could feel the heat of her blush. "I....I....I was looking for...for the kitchen so that I could help your mother with dinner. B...but I......" She couldn't take her eyes off of him, remembering what she had seen. In her mind she imagined him completely undressed again. Would she ever be able to forget this moment? She doubted it.

"The kitchen is close by. If you had turned left and not right you would have found it." He couldn't help but notice how she was staring. Secretly it pleased his male ego. "I would escort you there except I am a bit indisposed." He tried to control his smile.

"Oh, no. No. No. I can find it on my own." Putting her hand to her throat, Amelia turned around and hurried in the direction of the kitchen.

*    *    *    *

Amelia soon learned that Honora Cameron was everything her Aunt Lucinda was not. She was kind, she was caring, and she knew how to make a person feel at home. Most important of all was all the love she carried in her heart for her family.

"I remember when Allegra, Derek, and Bevin were children. Oh, how they loved their fried chicken. Made just the way we are makin' it tonight," she was saying to Amelia as they dipped the wings, drumsticks, breasts, and thighs into buttermilk, then rolled the pieces in breadcrumbs.

200

"My aunt always boiled the chicken," Amelia replied, carefully plopping each piece into the frying pan atop the iron stove.

Honora laughed. "Oh, no, no, no. Chicken was meant to be fried, although I do admit that I was sorry to have to cook these two. But they had stopped layin' and things being as they are......" Her voice trailed off as if she remembered a grander time when money hadn't been as sparce.

Amelia tried to break the awkward silence that ensued. "I cannot thank you and your family for being so kind to me...."

"Oh poo!" Honora waved her hand as if brushing such a thought away. "Derek told me all about how you were teachin' that young boy, Jedidiah and about the fire and all. It is the very least we can do. In my mind you are a heroine."

"Not really. I just tried to help a child who loved books and wanted to read." For just a moment Amelia's mood turned melancholy as she thought about all that had happened. She concentrated on the chicken. When she looked up, she saw that Honora was looking intently at her.

"You remind me of my daughter Allegra. She had your spirit, your goodness, your capacity to love those who need it the most. Perhaps one day soon you will meet her."

"I hope so." Her words made Amelia feel light of heart. She was talking as if Amelia would be around for a while. Did she dare to hope?

There was an unspoken promise that dinner would be delicious. Not only was there chicken but Honora had made biscuits the prior day. And there would be carrots, gravy, and grits.

"Like you, I am from up north originally so I was used to eatin' potatoes not grits. I swear sometimes I thought the war with the north would be about which tasted better potatoes or grits." She winked at Amelia. "But I learned to like them." Once again, her thoughts were on the past and she told Amelia of how her parents had underhandedly broken up her first marriage to Allegra's father. "Charles was a widower, ten years older. He had a son a little older than Allegra. It was an arranged marriage. I didn't love him at first, but I learned to love him."

Amelia tried very hard not to even think about seeing Derek without a stich on, but the image kept dancing before her eyes. "My aunt was intent on arranging a marriage for me."

"But you wouldn't allow it. You seem to be the kind of young woman who will let your heart be your guide." Suddenly Honora was very blunt. "How do you feel about my son?"

Amelia dropped her long cooking spoon in the gravy. "Well, I.....I....I. He has been very kind to me."

'It is written in your eyes. You are fallin' in love with him." When Amelia started to say otherwise, Honora said quickly, "I couldn't be more pleased. He needs somethin' besides work in his life. He has paid dearly for his father's sins." What those sins were she didn't say.

Amelia enjoyed the rest of the conversation, feeling more and more at ease as the two of them finished cooking the food. When it was ready to be served Derek offered a hand in putting the serving dishes on the table. Amelia noticed he had also put plates, napkins, knives, forks, and spoons on the table.

202

During dinner it was Honora who did most of the talking, telling Derek about Charles and how he was getting much stronger. Although Amelia tried very hard to concentrate she couldn't help but focus her attention on Derek as she remembered how he had looked standing naked beside the bathtub. She wondered what it would be like to have him make love to her the way the men in the books she had read had made love to the heroines. Would he be a fierce lover or would he be gentle?

"And that is why I think we should have Amelia move into this house, Derek. She should not be livin' alone in that dreadful place."

"What?" Amelia was stunned. She had never thought that she would be living with the Camerons.

"Your thoughts are my thoughts exactly, mother." This time his eyes caught Amelia's as she looked his way. The look that passed between them said far more than words ever could. If it was true that Amelia was headed towards love then it was obvious that *they* were going there together.

## Chapter Fifteen

Standing as still as a statue, Forest stood at the front window of the cottage. Closing her eyes, she made a wish, that when she opened them again she would see Moses in his wagon coming to pay a call.

"You have been looking out that window every day at this time for seven days now, Forest. Are you watching for the sandman?"

Forest remembered that story. Quentin had told her about the sandman. It was said that he came at night to throw sand in the eyes of children to help them fall asleep. Hearing about the creature had frightened her so that she hadn't been able to sleep for at least a week after hearing about him. Instead she had locked the door to her room and watched the door to make sure the monster wasn't able to get in. She hated sand.

"I am not looking for the Sandman, I can assure you. The very idea used to give me nightmares." She turned around. "I was just looking out at the night."

"And that is why you have put on a dress every evening this week?" Quentin smiled knowingly. "You have to give him time. He'll come to call. Just be patient."

"Patience is not one of my virtues," she confessed.

"As I well know. But you will need at least a semblance of that virtue for the time being. The young man is busy. Farming isn't easy." He sat down

204

at his desk. "It is much like politics. You have to sow the seeds, wait for them to grow, and then reap what you sow." Reaching for a pen and paper he said, "I must write that down to use in one of my speeches. Let's see, there is a proverb that says those exact words. Future consequences are unavoidably shaped by present actions." Quentin was very pleased with himself for remembering.

"Maybe I should go to him," Forest whispered, knowing the moment the words were out that she had too much pride to throw herself at him.

"Mmmmm. What?" It was obvious that Quentin was now immersed in his own world.

"Never mind. I'll just go and read Jane Austen for the umpteenth time." She was anxious for the next political meeting for two reasons: to talk with Andrew Wyatt and to go to the library to pick up a few new books.

"Yes. Yes, that is good." He paused in his writing. "Wait. No. I have a copy of *The Conduct of Life* by Ralph Waldo Emerson, that is much better reading." He smiled when she nodded acquiesce.

Forest felt as if happiness was within her grasp, as if she could reach out and touch it. *Oh, I know he feels the same way. If only......* she thought. She couldn't even think of one thing she would change about him. He was handsome, honest, patient, kind and caring. Even when they were just children she had seen his good qualities.

As if reading her mind Quentin said, "he has something very special about him. I think it is the honesty that shouts out at those nearby. I tell you, Forest, he could have a bright future in politics. If I could only persuade him."

"No!" She felt fiercely protective. "From what I

have seen of those men who surround you they are like vultures. They would rip a man like Moses to pieces without even a care. You know what they are, but I would be afraid that he would be much too vulnerable to deal with them." She was going to tell him that she had recognized Andrew Wyatt but thought better of it. If she found out any information she would tell him then.

"He could help me change the world." Seeing her scowl, he shrugged. "As you wish, my dear."

Thinking about Andrew Wyatt caused Forest to think about her parents. "Do you think that I will find my mother and father someday?" she questioned.

He was startled. "Your mother? Your father?" He seemed just a bit flustered. "Well I....I just don't know. Anything could happen I suppose." He tapped the desk with his pen. "Why do you ask?"

"Moses was telling me about his mother and father when he was here," she fibbed, "it made me wonder about my own."

His tone of voice was soothing. "I am so sorry, Forest. It has been such a long time ago. So much has happened. You might never find out. It is a fact of life you must learn to live with."

Forest didn't answer. She remembered Quentin quoting Voltaire once about the truth. Voltaire had said, 'Cherish those who seek the truth but beware of those who find it.'

*　　*　　*　　*

It had been a hellish week! One of the field hands had just up and left with no explanation, leaving Moses and Derek shorthanded. There hadn't been even a drop of rain. Then one of the wells had

206

gone dry and the water level had dropped far below the pump intake. Since there wasn't even a cloud in the sky they both knew they couldn't count upon a storm to give any aid. And as if that wasn't, enough Moses' wagon had lost a wheel and needed to be fixed before he could go anywhere.

"It's a good thing I am not superstitious," he mumbled beneath his breath.

"What did you say?" Unlike Moses, Derek was in a good mood despite the setbacks the week had handed out. On Saturday he was going to help Amelia move her things into the main house and that made him smile. He sensed his mother was playing matchmaker and that pleased him a great deal.

"I was just cursing our bad luck. I'm not one for carrying around a rabbit's foot, a four-leaf clover, a horseshoe, or a lucky penny, but I just might have to start doing so." Lifting up the body of the wagon, he balanced it precariously as Derek attached the repaired wheel. "Try to hurry I'm not Samson. I can only hold it up so long."

Carefully turning the wheel to connect it to the axel via the hub, Derek completed the task as quickly as he could. "You seem just a bit cranky. I don't think it is just the wagon."

Moses felt relieved to let go of the wagon and set it back down on all of the wheels. "I have been listening to you and all your lovesick talk and I suppose I'm more than a bit jealous."

"Jealous?" Derek tried hard not to guffaw, but he couldn't hide his smile.

"I have wanted to go visit Forest but as I looked around at my small house and my broken down old wagon I lost my nerve. I don't have anything to offer her." He made a sweeping gesture with his arm towards his house. "I can't see her being happy here. She is much better off with Quentin or a man who can sweep her off her feet."

Moses expected sympathy but Derek didn't give him anything but ridicule. "If that is how you feel you are a damn fool!"

"A fool?"

"A *damned* fool!" Taking note of the expression of anger of his friend's face he added, "you are a good man. The best. You can not put a price on honor or love."

There was a long pause as the two friends just stood looking at each other. Finally, Moses said, "that's easy for you to say. You're not a former slave. You have always had everything." There, he had said it. He had expressed what he had always hidden inside. Although he treasured his friendship with Derek he had always felt the difference between them that went way beyond the color of their skin. And he had felt that way since the first time he had been forced to call Derek "master".

"Everything!" Now it was Derek who was getting peeved. "An overbearin' father who doesn't hide his vindictiveness, a father who is a drunk and was so careless with what money he had that he has impoverished not only himself but my mother. Hell, all of us. The responsibility of a once great plantation that is fallin' down around my shoulders no matter how hard I try....."

Moses regretted his words the moment they were spoken. "I'm sorry. I didn't mean what I said."

Once again there was an uncomfortable silence. "Yes, you did." Derek's frustration faded just as quickly as it had sparked. "And I can't really blame you. I didn't have to run away because I had been

208

sold. I didn't have to constantly look over my shoulder for fear that I would be dragged back to a place where I was treated like the livestock." He shook his head. "All I can say is that I am sorry for what my father did. For what they all did in the past. But what is past is past. At least for you." Derek wiped his grimy hands on the seat of his work pants.

"I hope so." Moses wasn't as certain as Derek was. The South was still like an open wound, slowly healing yet vulnerable to toxicity.

Putting a hand on Moses' shoulder Derek said, "and I meant what I said. Forest would be a very lucky woman to be loved by you."

It was so easy to become discouraged when times were so precarious and there were those who did everything in their power to make others feel inferior. But Moses took Derek's words to heart. He wanted to believe that perhaps he had a chance with Forest after all. "Then by all means I'll go calling tomorrow evening. What do I have to lose?"

Derek took a step closer to him and sniffed the air. "That's a fine idea, but I can tell you right now that if I were you I would take a bath first," he teased, his previous annoyance melting away.

"Very funny." Reaching down, Moses picked up a fistful of dirt and Threw it on Derek's trousers. "And now so should you!"

Derek immediately reacted, scooping up a dirt clod and throwing it at Moses, just as they had done in their boyhood.

Ordinarily such shenanigans would have brought forth a wrestling match, but it had been quite a long day and they were both tired. Not having the energy to walk back to the plantation lands, Moses gave Derek a ride in the wagon. Passing by the loose pile of dirt where they had tried to dig a well only to find a mysterious casket, Derek asked the question that puzzled them both.

"So, who do you think is buried there?" It was an interesting mystery.

"Who and when, I would ask." Moses pulled at the reins and halted the wagon so that Derek could slide down for another look.

"And why is a casket there and not in the family cemetery at the back of the orchard?" Kneeling down he tried to get a closer look to see if there was any kind of writing on the coffin. It was disappointing to see that there was not even one mark to give any kind of clue.

"You are the one who should answer that question since it is obviously one of your family members." Securing the horses and wagon Moses slid off the wagon and joined his friend.

"That casket looks as if it has been there for a long, long time. It wasn't put there recently. I'd be suspicious and think it had somethin' to do with the war, but that coffin is much, much older than that."

Derek looked at Moses and Moses returned the stare. They both were tempted to dig the casket up and look inside. "We could........" Moses suggested, then shook his head. "But it would be disrespectful and if one were superstitious….."

"It might bring bad luck upon our heads and make us no better than the body snatchers who go after cadavers to sell to medical institutions." The very idea was ghoulish and caused Derek to shudder. There was something about the dead that was deeply disturbing.

"Perhaps your father would be able to tell you…."

Derek was immediately against that idea. "I would ask my father but the last time I spoke with him he nearly bit my head off. I think tomorrow we should just fill the hole in and let whoever's remains are there rest in peace."

"Are you sure?" Moses had a morbid interest in solving the mystery. "I wonder if it could be your great, great, great grandfather who was the pirate."

Moses' words unleashed a torrent of boyhood memories and all the times they had tried to find the treasure. Blackbeard's treasure was said to have been buried on the property by a Cameron long ago.

Derek remembered all the tales he had heard from his father about Jared Cameron. It was whispered that Jared Cameron had been a pirate, had sailed with Blackbeard, married his daughter, and stolen a chest of treasure from the pirate known as "the Devil." Supposedly the treasure was hidden on Cameron land by Jared's son, Avery. For years, the Cameron heirs had searched for the buried coins. And once upon a time he and Moses had thought that they had found one. A golden coin.

"If you are hell bent on findin' out, *you* could dig up the casket and find out." Derek thought of it as a joke. "There might be a clue to the treasure. Maybe even a map."

The mischievous side to him wanted to do just that but as he thought about it Moses said, "Oh no. Trying to find that treasure is what got me in trouble in the first place." He couldn't help but remember that because of that coin he had brought the wrath of Charles Cameron down upon his head without even doing anything wrong.

For just a moment he and Derek shared that memory. "I remember bein' so excited that I ran to

Allegra. "I found the treasure, Allegra. Blackbeard's treasure!" I said. "I was certain that there were more coins in that old curing shed."

"I saw you both go in, but then that nasty friend of your sister's shut and locked the door out of pure malice."

"And we didn't notice until it was too late. And then the fire......" Like a nightmare from the past he remembered running to the door and struggling frantically to open it. But he and his sister were trapped.

"After you were saved from the fire and freed I told the truth about who had locked you in, that it was your sister's friend Daphne, and as punishment for the truth your father sold me to that bastard Jensen. But you and Allegra helped me escape and sent me and my family on a journey to a new life on the Underground Railroad." Moses thought of Forest. "And if not for that I never would have met Jemma."

"Perhaps some things are just meant to be. My mother says that God works in mysterious ways." Derek patted him on the back. "And my mother would tell you, that you were meant to be with Forest. Mrs. Cameron is, I fear, a hopeless romantic."

"Let's hope Honora is right. But we will see when I concede to your mother's wishes and pay Miss Forest a visit." The very idea made Moses feel much lighter of heart and gave him a renewed determination to be a success.

*    *    *    *

Should she or should she not? All during the buggy ride into Richmond Forest mulled the choice that was presented to her. She could forget about

212

Andrew Wyatt and the fact that she had recognized him and go about her life, or she could confront him and demand that he answer all the questions that had tormented her for so many years. Which was it to be?

I could be opening Pandora's box if I persist in confronting that man. The story of Pandora was from Greek mythology and one of the first tales Quentin had read to her when she was just a child. She remembered it well, even after so many years. Pandora was forbidden to open a box that was a gift from the gods. But despite trying to tame her own curiosity she disobeyed. She was just too tempted to find out what the box contained. When she opened the box, however, she set free all the illnesses and hardships that the gods had hidden in the box. As she saw all the evil spirits coming out she was scared and tried to close the box as fast as possible. What she did not realize was that she had trapped hope inside.

"And that is why evil exists in the world," she whispered, little realizing that she had spoken aloud.

"What did you say?" Quentin looked over at her as he held firmly to the reins.

"I was just pondering evil and remembering the story you once told me about Pandora." What if just like Pandora she unleashed a host of evil upon herself and Quentin by seeking out Andrew Wyatt. Pandora couldn't put the malevolent forces back into the box once they were free. What if the same was true for her?

"Ah, yes, Pandora. That colorful Greek story has caught the imagination of writers, artists, and men of all religious backgrounds. But what I want to know is this—was it inevitable that Pandora open that box?"

It was so like Quentin to pose such a question. "I suppose you could say that it was. Just as it must have

213

been for Eve to take a bite of the apple."

"Good correlation, my dear. I am proud of you."
As the wagon hit a bump, Quentin once again
concentrated on the road.

Forest was of a mind to forget her foolishness
and let the past be the past. She would go with
Quentin to the Capitol just as she usually did and that
would be that. She thought that her mind was made
up and yet as they approached their destination, she
suddenly had a change of mind.

*I owe it to my mother and father to find out the
truth*, she thought. To do otherwise would be the
epitome of selfishness.

"Quentin, can I borrow the buggy? I have an
errand in town."

"Another errand?" He was taken aback for the
moment but then he nodded. "You can't fool me. You
are hoping to see Moses. I understand. A walk with
that handsome young man certainly beats sitting
around a smoke-filled room listening to a bunch of
old men."

She hurried to assure him, "You're not old and I
like to listen to you." She grinned. "But I can't say
the same for Matthew Stewart. He is so full of
himself. I laugh every time you give him his
comeuppance."

Nothing more was said, then as they reached the
Capitol Quentin alighted from the buggy and handed
Forest the reins. "I hope you won't be so starry-eyed
that you forget about me and leave me stranded."

"That would be much too cruel a punishment."
She felt a stab of guilt that she was keeping something
from him. Watching him walk up the hill she almost
called him back, then realized that it was too late to
have second thoughts.

The road was strangely devoid of very many wagons or buggies and Forest felt that good luck was shining down on her as she parked the buggy and secured the horses. Thrusting her shoulders back and holding her head high she entered the bank, pausing to appraise her appearance in one of the bank's floor length mirrors.

The air buzzed with the voices of both customers and bank personnel. There was a flurry of activity. Cashiers from the farms were depositing the money that other customers would be borrowing. Would Andrew Wyatt be too busy to see her? She hadn't thought about that. She looked around anxiously but didn't see his face in the crowd. Had she been foolish to come? Probably. Nevertheless, she craned her neck in search of the offices beyond the main banking floor. Could he be there? She would never know if she did not investigate.

Forest walked down the hallway reading the names lettered in gold on the door. *Robert Hatcher, Charles Greenway, Jeremiah Harrington.* On the last door was the name she sought. *Andrew Wyatt.* Raising her hand, she started to knock when a voice from behind startled her.

"Can I be of some help?" Turning, she found herself being scrutinized by the very man she was seeking. His piercing eyes peered at her from above his large hawk-like nose.

"No...I...I...." She felt at a sudden loss for words, wondering how she was going to explain herself.

"Wait a minute, I recognize you."

For just a moment Forest's heart seemed to stop, then start to beat much faster than usual. It was as if she were running from him again. She wanted to flee

215

but fortitude kept her from giving in to her instincts.

"You recognize me?" she managed at last.

"You are the errand boy. You brought me a message the other day." He gave her a sudden smile. "Do you perchance have another missive?"

She shook her head, struggling to find the right words. Before she could even think to reply, he had taken her by the arm and led her into one of the other offices. "Sit down. Sit down, boy. I've been meaning to pay a visit, but this will save me a trip up that long, steep winding road." He pulled up a green velveteen upholstered chair the color of money, obviously for her.

Forest didn't take a seat but eyed him cautiously, remembering the havoc he had caused that fateful day. She searched his face for any sign of recognition, but he didn't act at all as though he had any idea who she was.

"Have they decided on a candidate yet?" he asked, taking a seat behind the desk.

"No." She decided to make a bold move. Reaching up she removed her hat, letting her hair flow down over her shoulders. She waited for him to respond.

"A girl. I should have known. You are much too pretty to be a boy." He laughed a bit nervously. "But why?"

She clasped her hands together tightly and swallowed hard. "Look at me…."

He leaned closer but shrugged. "I don't know what game you are playing but I am a busy man."

"Fourteen years ago. On the riverbank. You were following a boat. When you caught up with the man and the child, you killed the man with a knife."

216

"You are accusing me of murder?" He feigned annoyance, but by his expression he was beginning to remember.

"I am that child and I want some answers. How much were you paid to do your dirty work?"

He sat back in his chair, not at all phased by her accusation. "Ten dollars a slave. Three if you count the other two I had to divide it with." He openly leered at her. "Of course, I was robbed of the money I would have gotten for you. Damn that Quentin."

"Quentin?" So, he knew what Quentin had done. "He saved me. Like a guardian of the gods. I will never be able to repay him."

Forest could hardly believe her ears when Andrew Wyatt broke out in laughter. That laughter was unnerving and goaded her into anger.

"What are you laughing at?"

His laughter faltered perceptibly. "You don't know."

"Know what?" She had never expected to be met with hilarity.

"Why, that Quentin was working *with* me. We were both slave catchers. Patrollers. Paddy rollers." As if he perceived her to be a simpleton he explained. "Quentin and I were among an organized group of armed white men. We monitored and enforced discipline on Nigrahs. And when they tried to break free, we chased after them and brought them back to face their just punishment."

It was as if her heart stopped and moved up to her throat. She couldn't talk. For a moment she feared she wouldn't even be able to breathe, but at last she gained control of herself. "No. Quentin would never. He wasn't......" She didn't know why the man was lying but he was.

217

"He did and he *was*! If you don't believe me just ask him. Ask him how it is that he was conveniently on that shore at the same time as me." His voice rose in volume. "Ask him!"

She wouldn't listen to such a horrible falsehood. "No!" Forest turned to leave, but he detained her.

"Quentin Faulkner was a slave catcher. That is how he made his money."

She wanted to scream at him, rage and call him names, but somehow she maintained her composure, saying only, "you are a liar!"

"I have no reason to lie. According to the law I did nothing wrong. Quentin on the other hand interfered with the recapture of a fugitive. But that is water under the bridge since you were all freed by those damnable Yankees. Nigrah lovers that they be." He answered her frown with a benevolent smile. "Next time you see old Quentin tell him hello for me."

Andrew Wyatt took out a cigar, rolling it between two fingers as he looked at her. He started to speak but Forest didn't stay to listen. She felt as if the whole world was crumbling beneath her feet, felt nauseous, sick at heart. She left the office, slamming the door behind her. She had done it. She had opened Pandora's box and now her life was in limbo.

## Chapter Sixteen

Derek knew now what torture was. It was having a beautiful woman in the house whose bedroom was just across the hall. Whether by design or by accident Honora had insisted that Amelia take Allegra's vacant bedroom. Now it seemed that unless he was working outside, they were constantly in close proximity. Was it any surprise then that she preoccupied his thoughts during the day and haunted his dreams at night?

This morning had been particularly trying for some reason or other. Her bedroom door had been open just a crack but enough so that he could hear her washing her face and brushing her hair. He could hear the rustle of her garments as she gathered them together. He could hear her humming as she chose what dress to wear.

He was alone upstairs with a beautiful woman, a woman who was undressing just a few yards away, and yet he knew he couldn't touch her. It was a thought that plagued him as he had stripped off his nightshirt and pulled on his work trousers. He tried to keep from thinking of Amelia buttoning each one of her little pearl buttons, but it was nearly impossible. He wondered if the skin on her shoulders was as flawless as he imagined. Would her breasts be as soft to his stroking fingers as he supposed? The sensation of her nearness taunted him, teased him.

"Damn!" Realizing his train of thought, he had known that he had to get out of there and quickly. Gentleman though he thought himself to be, he was

219

also a man. Trying to get her out of his brain he had thrown himself into his work in the tobacco fields with a fury, causing his workers to look his way. With a snort of derision he realized he had been talking to himself.

*Hell, I'm a fine one to give Moses advice on women,* he thought. It seemed the deeper his feelings grew the more nervous and tongue-tied he became when he was around her. He longed to hold her in his arms and yet his gentlemanly protocol dictated he stay an arm's length away. She was pretty, as smart as a whip, kind, gentle as a kitten and as alluring as a siren song. That she was also eligible preyed on his mind.

"Just what do I do with Miss Amelia Seton?" With a curse he realized he was talking to himself-- out loud again. "Damn!"

He forced himself to concentrate on his tobacco crop and was pleased with the progress that had been made. The plants were sticking their *heads* out of the ground promising to make the plantation profitable if he tended them as carefully as if they were his children. He could not take the risk of being further indebted to the bank.

"Derek......"

Like a song on the wind he thought he heard his name. Turning around he saw that Amelia was standing just a few feet away from the tobacco plants. She was holding a bottle in her hands that Derek sensed was his mother's homemade cider. Dressed in a pale blue dress, her hair flowing free she was stunning—like the vision out of a dream. Wiping his hands on his pants, he hurried to greet her.

"Don't tell me. Mother sent you on this errand of mercy," he said, taking the bottle from her hands.

He tried his best not to guzzle the tart brew, but he was too thirsty.

"You look so hot and miserable. I wish......" She wished so many things.

"Most of the really hard work is completed. Now all that has to be done is to take care of the plants and hope there is not too much rain." Raising the bottle to his lips he drank until the bottle was dry.

"But I thought rain was good for crops?"

"Too much rain and too many days that are overcast can slow the plant's growth. Heavy rain leaches the nutrients in the soil and can affect plant growth." He was strangely aroused as he looked down at the ground and noticed her bare feet peeking from beneath her skirt.

"I felt like going without my shoes, just like I did when I was a child." Her shoes, which she held in her hand, were just too confining on such a lovely day. Besides, it gave her a perverse sense of pleasure to realize that her aunt would have been scandalized by such a show of rebellion.

Ankles and feet had always acted upon Derek as an aphrodisiac. Perhaps because they were the one part of a woman's body that was always covered. Although he fought against temptation, he found himself looking at her ankles and feet again and again. Perhaps that is why he said rather gruffly, "you had best put your shoes back on. Tobacco plants can sometimes make people who are not used to them quite ill."

"Oh!" In disappointment she hurried to comply. "I didn't know."

He regretted that he had been so harsh with her. "Most people don't realize. But I have been around tobacco plants since I was just a boy as you well know." He changed the subject. "How did school go today. Has young Beauregard ever come back to school?"

"No." Their eyes met and held and she sensed that he was thinking the same thing that she was. That somehow Beauregard figured in on the fire at the school. "How I wish I had been more careful and not let him see..."

"It wasn't your fault." He reached out and touched her shoulder, unleashing a current of feelings that he had tried hard to suppress. He was surprised when she reached up and put her hand on his. They stood there for several moments just looking into each other's eyes, but then he said, "Just think of all the good you have brought to the other children—both black and white."

"I hope that I have given them a chance to live better lives." She thought for a moment, wondering if she should make a request of him. "Derek, I.....", She decided that he looked so tired that now was not the time.

"You were going to say something. What?" He didn't want her to hold anything back.

"I know you are busy. And I appreciate all that you have done for me and the children, but...." She felt ungrateful but the children needed books. She couldn't teach them to read without them. "Books. After school I took the liberty of peeking in the attic at the Avery House and I saw quite a few of them all stacked up neatly in a pile. Perhaps some day you could give me a hand in retrieving them and....."

"Books. For the children." He started to laugh much to her dismay. He quickly explained. "You never cease to surprise me. So many women would be asking for something for themselves and yet as always you think about your students." He was tired as hell and yet he found himself saying, "Lead the way and we will take a look at these books you have found."

Stopping along the way Derek washed his face in hands in a bucket in the back of his wagon and dried them on an extra shirt that was flung on the seat. Hitching the horses, then helping her onto the high wooden bench he guided the horses to the old mansion.

"You and my mother have most certainly established a friendly relationship. I'm glad. You both need the camaraderie."

"She is an unusual woman. I admire her a great deal." She had made Amelia feel as if she truly was part of the family.

"I think the feeling is mutual." Glancing over at her he realized that all the qualities he admired in his mother could be found in Amelia as well. "I only wish she had ended up with a better man than my father."

"Derek. What a thing to say." Amelia was shocked, although she had noticed that Derek seldom if ever went into his father's room.

"It's true. He has never put anyone above himself. I don't think the word love is in his vocabulary." Arriving the short distance to the Avery mansion he secured the horses, then helped her down from the wagon, his hands around her waist lingering

223

for much longer than need be. Then he was following her up the stairs and into the Avery house.

"You have never said anything about your parents," he exclaimed, wanting to know more about her.

"My father died in the war. My mother took her own life." Her answer was blunt and to the point. "Aunt Lucinda reluctantly took me in. I was just a child who I fear got in her way."

"I'm sorry." He imagined that she would have been a very pretty little girl. "But you certainly grew to be a remarkable woman."

"I grew like a little weed without much tending." Arriving at the attic, Amelia reached up to pull down the ladder. "Did you ever play up in the attic when you were a boy?" Carefully she climbed rung after rung.

"No. There was a rumor that it was haunted. I believed it when I was a child but found out that the rumor was spread just to keep people from coming here. Besides, Moses and I spent most of our time outdoors."

The attic was filled with cobwebs, dust, a generous amount of old furniture and various odds and ends from another era. It was faintly illuminated from the light of a small, broken window so that Amelia and Derek could maneuver their way around. Amelia found a doll missing its head, a kite without a string and a toy boat. Derek located a wagon without wheels and a stuffed dog with a missing ear. Once treasured items but now just discarded memories.

"Here they are!" Amelia felt a surge of joy as she looked through the collection of old dusty books. "The *Legend of Sleepy Hollow*, Sonnets of

224

Shakespeare, *The Little Mermaid* by Hans Christian Anderson, and an assortment by Charles Dickens."

Derek was looking through old boxes as well but his discovery was of a different kind. Something unexpected. It was a trunk with a broken lock, shoved far off in the corner, hidden under debris. "What the devil?"

At first he thought that what he had found were just some old sheets and black wall hangings but as he took out one of the items and saw two holes he had a sick feeling in his gut. Putting one of the "sheets" over his head he knew in an instant.

Ripping the white hooded robe off of himself Derek felt a surge of outrage sweep over him. Digging deeper into the trunk he found several guns, ropes, knives, and handcuffs. His anger intensified as he saw an old book with scrawled names written in black ink.

Looking up from sorting the newly discovered books, Amelia was taken aback by the intensity of anger she saw on Derek's face. Setting down the books she was carrying, she moved closer to him. "What is it? What's wrong?"

"Maybe everything." One name caught his eye, but he didn't want to believe it. There in black and white was proof that his own father had been involved in the horrendous activities of the Ku Klux Klan. And not only a member but an officer, a leader. There could be no denying that name, one as familiar as his own. Grand Titan, the ledger read. Charles Cameron.

# PART TWO:  Secrets Revealed

## Richmond, Virginia

## 1873 - 1874

"There are no secrets that time does not reveal."

Jean Racine

## Chapter Seventeen

Trust is a fragile thing. Trust in someone meant having faith that they would always be truthful. It meant believing that if they said the sun would rise in the morning you knew that it would because they said so. It meant believing in them so that you shared their hope for the future. It meant that you had confidence that what they told you was real and sincere. It meant that you knew that what they did and said would be in your best interest because they cared. Forest had always had trust in Quentin, would have trusted him with her very life but after her confrontation with Andrew Wyatt the trust she had was now very fragile.

*"Quentin Faulkner was a slave catcher. That is how he made his money,"* Andrew Wyatt had said. *"If you don't believe me just ask him. Ask him how it is that he was conveniently on that shore at the same time as me."*

*No. It can't be true. Andrew Wyatt was lying,* she thought over and over again. She didn't really believe Wyatt's story and yet she found herself looking more critically at Quentin. What she knew about him before he rescued her would fill a thimble. It was as if his life began that day that he had whisked her away through the trees to safety. He never spoke about himself prior to that time. Never.

Forest thought about her altercation with Andrew Wyatt that fateful day. She had been so distraught, confused, and angry that she had walked up and down the streets of Richmond like a sleepwalker. Over and over again she relived that moment at the bank when her innocence had been shattered and doubts had crept into her brain. Only when she had heard the city clock striking three had she been shocked out of her soulful reverie.

Running as fast as she could she had gone back to the buggy, watered the horses, jumped onto the seat, grabbed the reins, and headed to the Capitol building. There she had found Quentin standing out front pacing up and down.

"I am so sorry I was late. I...I went to the dressmaker but somehow she had confused my appointment and so I had to wait while she measured another customer," she lied.

As usual Quentin was not one to scold. Instead he was relieved. "I was so worried about you. It isn't like you not to be punctual. But I must confess I had so wanted you to hear the debate I engaged in with Matthew."

Looking at him her doubts were set aside for the moment. His concern for her was authentic and not feigned. He cared about her. He always had and he showed it in so many ways. How could she even think for a moment that he had once gone after escaped slaves with whips and chains? Much less her parents.

"I'm sure you triumphed over him as you always do. Matthew has speaking skills, but you make him look like a beginner." For the first time since talking with Wyatt she smiled.

"Well, I'm afraid he gave me a whipping today," Quentin answered, taking a seat beside her in the buggy.

"A whipping!" The reminder of slavery dashed her good mood and she tried to find the words to ask him if he had ever chased after anybody. "Aren't you glad that there is no longer slavery," she whispered, "how terrifying it must have been to have men with guns and ropes and dogs chasing after you. Don't you think?"

Did she imagine it or did he tense at her words? For just a moment her scrutinizing gaze skewered him as she waited for his reply. Perhaps even a twitch or a blink of the eye would give him away if he was guilty.

As always, he was adamant. "Of course, it would have been terrifying. And cruel. And senseless. Thank the good Lord that those who engaged in such things have found just punishment."

"All of them?" She thought about Andrew Wyatt who didn't seem to have been disciplined or penalized.

"As far as I know." He thumped the briefcase he had tucked in the crook of his arm. "And once our political party comes to power there will never be such an atrocity again. No more slavery, no more unfair practices, no more violence. Never again. Never!"

His answers had seemed so genuine, so heartfelt that she had put Andrew Wyatt's chattering out of her mind, at least for the time being. Quentin could never hurt another human being. That was that.

Even so, a tiny seed had been planted in her mind. She found herself spending more time alone, knew that she didn't feel as unquestioning towards Quentin's actions as she did before, found herself paying closer attention to his words.

"Forest, are you feeling unwell?" Looking up from his journal Quentin adjusted his reading glasses as he looked in her direction.

"I feel fine," she answered, realizing now that she had been so deep in thought that she had been staring at the wall.

"Are you certain?" He ran his fingers through his hair and sighed. "You just don't act like yourself lately."

She tried to make light of it. "Well I am just me, myself, and I. Just the same Forest. Or maybe I feel more like Jemma today."

"Jemma?"

She tried to find the courage to ask him then and there if what Andrew Wyatt said was true. It was a perfect opening. "Yes Jemma. I was just thinking about the day you…you came upon me and saved me from being caught by the slave catchers."

"Slave catchers!"

Did she imagine it or did he seem to pale? "Yes. I have done some reading about what happened to runaway slaves. I hadn't realized that there were paid professionals who chased after them. Slave patrols who took them back to their owners to be mutilated or branded."

"A horrible profession." Shaking his head he averted her eyes.

"I was so naïve that I didn't know about them. But that must have been what those men chasing after me were. Do you suppose?" She walked over to where he sat. "Do you have any idea what happened to my mother or father?"

Putting his hands up to his face he seemed troubled. "No. No, I don't. Although I have thought about it many times. But sometimes it is best to let the past be just that---*the past*."

Her emotions were in turmoil. "But it is not easy to forget. Not when it was your family. Not when you remember having seen your mother abused and hurt." She couldn't help the tears that stung her eyes. "I can't let the past just die. I want some answers. I want to know."

Quentin did not answer or intrude on her prattling. Instead he put his hands to his chest and began gasping for breath. Horrified, Forest put her hands on his shoulders. What if he was having a heart attack?

"Father!" She hadn't called him that for a while. "Do you need a doctor?" She tried not to panic but the thought reverberated in her mind that if he was critically ill she couldn't leave him to get the doctor, nor would it be wise for him to walk to the buggy for a ride into Richmond. And the fact that there were no close neighbors made it all the more precarious.

The silence was only disturbed by Quentin's wheezing as he struggled to get his breath. Leaning his head against her he reminded her of a child. Perhaps such a thing brought out the boy in the man. In all men. Apprehensive about leaving him all Forest could do was unloosen his shirt and stroke his thick graying hair.

"You will be all right." He had to be. Like a mouse nibbling at a cheese the thought gnawed at her mind that her questions might have brought on the attack. She felt a twinge of guilt that grew the longer he struggled. "Oh, Quentin. I'm so sorry......"

Then just as quickly as it had come upon him, Quentin started to breath normally. She felt him relax against her. He shook his head as if to clear it, then said, "It must have been stress. That debate today was contentious. I must remember not to allow anyone to goad me from now on." He looked up at her and tried to smile. "Could I impose upon your good graces to fetch me a cool glass of water?"

"Water?" She laughed with relief. "Right now I would go out and catch a moonbeam if that is what you needed to feel better." And at that moment she knew that she would have at least tried.

Walking to the kitchen she made up her mind then and there not to even think of raising the matter again. And yet.......

\*     \*     \*     \*

Moses lay in bed, staring up at the moonlight dancing on his ceiling from the open window. Slowly his thoughts gained coherency as he sorted out his emotions. He couldn't keep putting off the inevitable. Derek had given him good advice that he had not acted upon. And why not? Every night since he'd first met Jemma he had fantasized about her, first as a boyhood crush then as a man. At night he dreamed about her, longing to hold her, warm and naked in his arms, giving vent to the hunger her nearness inspired.

Jemma. Forest. It didn't matter what her name was he only knew that she was a woman with whom he wanted to share his life, his soul, his heart without fear of betrayal Oh, how she drew his love. Not just that she was pretty. No, it was something much more. It was the kindness she had shown him right from the

232

first. It was as if his soul cried out to her. Just the thought of her gave purpose to his very existence.

Putting his hands behind his head, Moses reflected on his life. He was a man who seldom believed in dreams, who held few illusions, knew all too well mankind's faults and cruelty and so guarded himself accordingly. But if he were truthful with himself, he wanted someone to share his future with. Someone he could open up his heart to, who would love him in return. But how could she grow to love him too if he stubbornly kept to himself?

*Go to her*, said the voice in his head. *It is not too late for a walk in the moonlight. Or perhaps even a kiss.*

Determination overcame his exhaustion. Rising from the bed he washed his face and hands, combed his hair, and dressed as quickly as he could. Though it was too late to go picking flowers he knew of something else he could give to Forest as a gift, a gold coin that had quite a story attached to it. Once long ago he and Derek had searched for Blackbeard's treasure and found the coin buried in the dirt. Moses had kept the old coin as a memento of his boyhood days. Now he had a better use for it. He would give it to Forest as a token of his affection and hope that she would be patient and wait for him to improve his finances.

"Nothing ventured, nothing gained....." he said to himself, remembering that Forest had said that to him once. Pushing open the front door, Moses saddled up one of the wagon horses and was on his way.

*     *     *     *

One lone lamp shone in the window of the cottage when Moses arrived, silhouetting one figure sitting at the desk and the other standing nearby. Taking a deep breath, Moses gathered up his courage, moved to the door and knocked loudly. He could hear the steady thump of Quentin's feet as he came to answer the door.

"Moses, my boy! What a pleasant surprise." He opened the door wide and beckoned him inside, patting him on the back as fondly as if he were a son.

Quickly Forest came up behind them. Moses' couldn't help staring at the vision she made in a pink cotton night gown. His smoldering gaze ran lingeringly over her. She was even more beautiful than he remembered if that was possible

"I was thinking about you. I wanted to see you." If he had been conjured up by a magician she wouldn't have been any more grateful for her good fortune. She trusted him and there were so many things she wanted to say.

At another time he would have felt brazen to come here so boldly, but now she was so welcoming, so glad to see him, that he cursed himself for a fool because he hadn't come to visit much sooner.

Looking first from Moses, then to Forest, then to Moses again, Quentin feigned a yawn. "I am so very tired. I hope you two won't mind if I retire to bed early." He winked in Forest's direction. As old Ben Franklin said, "early to bed and early to rise, makes a man healthy, wealthy and wise." He shrugged, "lets hope he knew what he was talking about." Without even a backward glance he left the room.

"Oh, Moses!" Impetuously she reached out for him, her hand resting on the firm hardness of his

234

chest. Then she threw her arms around him and hugged him so tightly he could barely breath. For a long drawn out moment she held on to him, then stepped back.

"If I had known you would be so glad to see me I would have come here much sooner," he teased, then seeing the troubled look on her face, he asked, "what's wrong?"

"It's Quentin. Early this evening he had a spell of some kind. We were talking then suddenly he grabbed at his chest and had trouble breathing." She closed her eyes as if in pain. "I thought it was his heart."

Gently he took both of her hands in his. "And is he still feeling ill? If so, I can drive your buggy and take you both into Richmond to see a doctor."

Her breath came out in a long sigh of relief. "No, he quickly recovered no thanks to me and my harsh words."

"Harsh words?" Moses couldn't even imagine that she and Quentin would argue. "Tell me what happened."

In a rapid flow of words, she told him about her confrontation with Andrew Wyatt and his accusations against her foster father. "That disgusting man told me that Quentin was a slave catcher and that the reason he was there that day on the shore of the James River was because they were working together. That means that Quentin...that Quentin....."

"I can not believe that what he said is true. Quentin has always seemed to me to be the gentle giant type who would not knowingly swat at a fly unless forced to do so. I can not picture him holding a gun or a whip and running after fugitives."

She put her head on his shoulder, burying her face in the folds of his shirt. "Neither can I. But I asked him anyway and that is what led to his falling ill."

He stroked her hair, whispering words of comfort, telling her that what happened was in no way her fault. "You did the right thing. Quentin has a right to know about that man's accusations. He needs to allay any suspicions you might have or else what was said will be a wall between the two of you for a long, long time."

What he said made sense. "Of course, you are right. I must tell him about my meeting with that horrid man and what he blurted out. And then I want to find out some answers about what happened to my family. I have a right to know."

"Yes, you do. I would want to know if what had happened to your family had happened to me and mine." He was going to ask her to take a walk with him, but Forest had other ideas in mind. Standing on tiptoe, her eyes riveted on his mouth, she initiated a kiss.

"Mmm," he groaned, pulling her into his arms. A hungry desire that clamored for release, swept through his body as he caressed her lips. If she only knew how he'd longed to be with her. Now his mouth closed on hers, engulfing her in a maelstrom of delicious sensations.

Passionately Forest yielded to him as her lips and teeth parted to allow his exploration. Her hands slid up to lock around his neck, her fingers tangling in the thickness of his hair. She sighed against his mouth, trembling with pleasure. This, this was what she had wanted to experience, to be in his arms and have him

236

kiss her.

The feel of him, strong, warm, and loving was all Forest wanted in the world at that moment. She didn't fully understand everything that was happening to her--she only knew that he alone could arouse such an urgent need within her. He was the source of every comfort, every beautiful thing she could imagine.

Moses forgot everything but the sweet, soft lips beneath his. All caution fled as the hungry desire he had tried to put from his mind sprang free. He was aware of nothing but an intense driving need for her. He tightened his arms around her and his kiss deepened in intensity as he explored the moist sweetness of her mouth, craving her kiss as others might crave strong drink.

Moses inhaled of her fragrance. Violets. Her sweet yet heady aroma. Desire bubbled like a powerful tide, hot and sweet as he continued to kiss her. He was overwhelmed by his emotions. His hand crept up her rib cage to close over the shapely curve of her breast. Just as he'd supposed, her breasts were softly enticing.

Forest was stunned to feel warm seeking fingers on her breast, yet she didn't push his hands away. She thrilled to his touch, surprised that he could rouse in her such rapturous feelings. As his fingers stroked and caressed her, she moaned low in her throat and leaned against him. It was such an intimate act and yet she felt no shame. Somehow it didn't seem wrong for Moses to touch her like this.

"Whew!" Coming to his senses, Moses drew his mouth from hers and pulled away. "I guess I don't have to tell you how much I care about you."

"And I don't suppose I need to tell you that I feel

the same." She gestured towards the sofa but Moses shook his head.

"It is a beautiful moonlit night. The kind that I hear many poets write about." He held out his hand to her. "Shall we take a walk?"

"By all means." She took his hand but before he opened the door Moses reached in his pocket and held out the gold coin. "What is it?"

"Right before you met me, before I ended up in the trunk on the way to freedom, Derek and I found this coin. I kept it as a memento but today I realized that I wanted to give it to you. We can have the jeweler put a hole in it and I will buy a gold chain and you can wear it around your neck."

With a smile he told her about the rumor that the Cameron's' founder had sailed with Blackbeard and that there was a treasure buried somewhere on the plantation grounds. He talked about the day he and Derek had found the gold coin and that his friend had given it to him as a memento of the start of their adventures.

"But we didn't get a chance to look for gold. His father sold me and you know the rest of the story." He kissed her on the forehead. "Because of this coin I met an angel."

He held the door open for her and together they walked as a spray of silver moonlight shone down upon them. It was silent except for the hooting of an owl and the far-off high-pitched bark and yips of a pack coyotes.

Walking hand in hand they felt the innocence of the night, the calmness, the solitude. For a long drawn out moment it was as if they were alone in the world. Moses found himself wishing that they could somehow stop the earth from turning and stay just as they were forever.

The sound of a twig snapping and a rustle in the bushes interrupted their reverie. Feeling a protective instinct, Moses stepped in front of Forest, holding his hands out to guard her if it was a predatory animal. With alarm he saw the shadow of a dangerous two-legged animal. Someone had been spying on them and now that someone was running away. Moses thought of going after the intruder but not wanting to leave Forest alone he shook off that idea.

"We better hurry back to the cottage," he instructed. "Does Quentin have a gun?"

"Yes," she cried. "He has three and I know how to shoot, just in case there is trouble." They ran, not walked back to the cottage, closed the door, and locked it from the inside. Breathing heavily, they watched the small clock in the living room tick off the time. After a long time had passed, they sighed with relief.

"Perhaps it was a hunter." Moses wanted to think that was who it had been and that they had spooked him with their presence. Whoever it was, however, he decided to stay until morning.

## Chapter Eighteen

Tossing and turning on his bed, Derek could not keep his thoughts from the disturbing discovery he had made at the Avery mansion. His father, the head of the Cameron family, had been involved in threatening, terrorizing, bullying, beating, and possibly even murdering those he considered his enemies. Hiding his identity behind a hood and a robe, he had done the unforgivable. Banding together with others of his ilk he had allowed himself to do the kind of things that designated him as a monster.

*Damn him! Damn him all the way to hell*, he thought, clenching his teeth in anger. What he did had put a permanent stain on the Cameron name and honor. He had gone against every ethic or moral fiber he had preached to his sons and acted worse than a beast. He had taken justice into his own hands and acted much worse than any of the transgressors.

The very idea of his father even participating in such dark deeds made Derek feel nauseous. He remembered right after he had returned from the war hearing about the avenging southern men who it was said were dressing up in white as Confederate ghosts to spark fear in the hearts of the Negroes, carpetbaggers, northern politicians, and occupying soldiers. There were also those who put black makeup on their faces to mock the newly freed slaves as well as those who wore gigantic animal horns or pointed

240

wizard or dunce hats. At first it had seemed that they were merely farmers and former plantation owners rebelling and involving themselves in mischief, but as the attacks became more frequent and violent the danger of the Klansmen had become obvious to nearly everyone.

*Only a fool would not have realized the threat they presented to the efforts towards peace*, Derek thought. And yet there were many fools or perhaps fellow conspirators who had tried to defend what the Klan was doing.

*"Why sometimes mischievous boys who want to have some fun go on a masquerading frolic to scare the Negroes, but they don't hurt them in any way,"* one representative had said when explaining what was happening. "Stories are exaggerated and it keeps up the impression among the Negroes that the Klan is watching them and won't let them get away with anything."

"Mischievous boys. Ha!" Derek said aloud, remembering hearing about a young Negro who had witnessed two of his black neighbors being stripped, choked, and beaten. Another had a fireball thrown into his house by men in red calico capes, wearing coon-skin caps. Suddenly houses were put to the torch, crosses appeared on church grounds, and there was a rash of Negro men hanging from trees in what some insisted were suicides. Only the Federal government had been able to put a halt to the carnage. Or had they? Remembering the fire at the schoolhouse that had killed an innocent child, Derek suspected that some of the Klan had merely gone underground.

241

Beams of moonlight danced through the windows; casting figured shadows on the ceiling overhead. Silhouettes that were disturbing and demon-like. Turning his face away, Derek couldn't forget how domineering his father had been to both Bevin and him. He had to admit that he had always been intimidated by his father. It was a feeling that had turned to resentment and anger when his father had so callously sold Derek's friend because of an imagined slight. A part of Derek had never absolved his father for what he had done. He didn't really think he could ever forget or forgive.

Oh, how he wanted to confront his father now, to take the book, hoods, and robe to the bedroom and throw them in his face. But he couldn't do that while his father was recuperating. His mother would never forgive such an action no matter what his father had done. And so, he had to keep silent, all the while knowing the truth.

*Truth. Truth. Truth.* The word reverberated in his head. For several long, tormented hours, he lay awake trying to push the dark thoughts and memories from his brain, but sleep just wouldn't come. He tried to think of pleasant things, reminding himself of the pretty woman who lay so close to him. Just across the hall. Closing his eyes, he could see her face.

She was in a ballroom where dozens of crystal prisms glittered from the ceiling. Twirling and whirling, she came within an arm's reach of him. Stretching out his arms he took her into an embrace. They were laughing together as they danced. But the music grew faster. Louder. Other people joined them on the dance floor. Strange people.

Colors blended into each other until the features on the faces of the people were indistinguishable from one another. They all looked alike. But suddenly a face loomed like an ominous moon above them. A threatening masked face with a long nose, glittering eyes, and a frown that changed into a menacing smile. The figure had lips that moved but there wasn't any sound. And yet as if answering a signal, a group of white and red robed beings floated into the room. They pulled his dancing partner, Amelia, from his arms.

"No!" He tried to catch them, but it was as if he were on a treadmill. He wasn't going anywhere.

Torches appeared as if out of nowhere, floating to the hands of the robed creatures who brandished them in front of Amelia's eyes as if threatening her in some way. Opening her mouth, she screamed a silent shriek and although he wanted to save her his efforts were useless. Waving her arms frantically, trying to keep her balance, Amelia turned just as the floor dropped out from under her feet. She was falling downward into a great gaping hole. "No!"

His hands reached out to grasp her. "Amelia. Amelia. Amelia!"

Through a haze Derek heard a voice calling out his name.

"Derek?"

She reached out to him and he sought the safe shelter of her arms, thinking that his nightmare had morphed into a pleasant dream, a dream that was soft and fragrant.

"Derek!"

ASHES AND AWAKENINGS

Opening his eyes, he was pleasantly surprised that she was in his bedroom. "Amelia, what are you doin' here?"

"You were mumbling my name, so loudly that I could hear you across the hall and through my door. "I thought something had happened."

He remembered bits and pieces of the dream and shivered. "It was just a dream. A nightmare." He rubbed his eyes. "But so damn real."

"They sometimes are, particularly if there is something that troubles you. Today must have been quite a shock for you." She reached out and took his hand, clasping it tightly as their fingers entwined. They stayed hand in hand for a long moment in time then she said, "I had better go back to my own room."

"Don't go. Please."

He was mesmerized by her gentle voice, charmed by the vision she made in her white cotton nightgown. Her long strawberry blonde hair was hanging loose, framing a face with large eyes, high cheekbones, a well-shaped nose, and full lips. She was so utterly lovely.

She blushed at the boldness of his stare and at the sudden realization that he was completely naked beneath the covers. "Derek....."

"How I wish this was our weddin' night," he whispered, then said, "I've embarrassed you." But he didn't regret saying the words. What he said was true.

They looked steadily at each other for a long, long time. His eyes caressed her, embraced her as firmly as if he touched her with his hands. He imagined what it would be like to slowly slip the nightgown from her body, to bring her down to lay

244

beside him, to touch her breasts, her stomach, her thighs.

She had a confession to make. "I…I wish this was our wedding night too." Slowly she raised her chin, initiating a kiss.

Derek groaned, closing his arms about her as he pulled her into the curve of his hard body. Her hands reached out to touch him and the feel of those hands was his undoing. They swept all reason and caution from his mind. The pleasure he felt in the intimacy of their embrace and kiss was like an antidote to his anger and his emotional pain.

The tip of his tongue stroked her lips as deftly as his hands caressed her body. She moaned, turning her head so that his mouth slanted over hers and his tongue sought to part her lips. She mimicked the movement of his mouth, reveling in the sensations that flooded through her.

Derek's reaction to Amelia's nearness, to the soft mouth opening to him, trembling beneath the heated encroachment of his lips, was explosive. For one moment he nearly lost his head completely. His hands pushed her back slightly as his fingers fumbled at the front opening of her nightgown, searching for her soft flesh. Then just as suddenly he stopped. Pulling away from her he held her at arm's length.

"Go up to bed, Amelia." His tone of voice was stern.

"Derek…." She was trembling. Never in all her wildest dreams had she realized how primitive and powerful desire could be. Nor how fiercely and how quickly her emotions could get out of control.

He repeated what he had said, more forcefully this time. "Go to *bed*, Amelia."

Jedidiah's death had taught her how fragile life could be. Tomorrow wasn't guaranteed to anyone. She was here with Derek now. They cared about each other, desired each other and at the moment that took precedence over propriety.

"I don't want to go. I want to stay with you."

He brushed the hair back from her face with an aching tenderness, then lifted a strand of her hair that had tumbled over her breasts. His fingers were strokes of velvet as he caressed her. "I love you, Amelia."

She felt his breath ruffle her hair and experienced the sensation down the whole length of her spine. "I love you too."

Slowly his mouth came down on hers again. Time was suspended as they explored each other's lips. Pressing her body closer to his, she sought the passion of his embrace and gave herself up to the fierce sweetness. The world seemed to be only the touch of his lips, the haven of his arms. She couldn't think, couldn't breathe. It was as if she were poised on the edge of a precipice, in peril of plummeting endlessly.

Derek lifted his mouth from hers and held her close for just a moment. Dear God, what she did to him. Slowly, languorously, his hand traced the curve of her cheek, buried itself in the thick red-gold glory of her hair. She was playing havoc with his senses. He wanted to make love to her, so much so that it hurt, yet with a fire that was tempered with gentleness. He felt a warmth in his heart as well as his loins.

"I don't want to hurt you. Never that."

"I know you don't and I know you won't." Her

hand touched his, squeezing it tightly. "I have read about passion in my books but what I read didn't prepare me for the feelings you awaken in me.

The soft, rounded curves of her breasts and stomach pressed against him as they lay down together. Her head rested against his chest.

"Are you sure.....?" he asked. If not, then he would end this before it began.

Something warm and deep flowered instinctively at the sound of his voice. "Yes. Very sure." No matter what happened in the future she would have this night to remember.

Derek held her chin in his hand, kissing her eyelids, the curve of her cheek. He kissed her mouth with all the pent-up hunger he had tried to suppress for so long. His tongue gently traced the outline of her lips and slipped in between to stroke the edge of her teeth. "Your mouth tastes so sweet," he whispered against her mouth, "and you are so soft."

His hands explored her innocent beauty. He felt her tremble beneath him and opened his eyes, mesmerized by the potency of her gaze. He found himself trembling, too, with a nervousness that was unusual for him. Anticipation, he supposed. Eagerness. Desire. He would make it beautiful for her, this much he vowed.

Slowly, leisurely, Derek stripped Amelia's nightgown from her body. His fingers lingered as they wandered down her stomach to explore the texture of her skin. Like velvet, he thought. "You are so beautiful."

She glowed under the praise of his deep, throaty whisper. "Am I...?" The compliment pleased her, made her surer of herself in this quest to experience the unknown.

"Very..." He sought the indentation of her navel, then moved lower to tangle his fingers in the soft wisps of hair that joined at her legs. Amelia tingled with an arousing awareness of her body, as if she was discovering herself through Derek's exploration. The lightest touch of his hands sent a shudder of pure sensation rippling deep inside her.

Their lips touched and clung again, enjoying the sweetness of newly discovered love. As if it were the most natural thing in the world, Amelia moved her hands over him, too, caressing him. Exploring. He took her hand and pressed it to his arousal. She felt the strength of him as her eyes gazed into his. Then he bent to kiss her again, his mouth keeping hers a willing captive for a long, long time.

Twining her hands around his neck, she clutched him to her, pressing her body eagerly against his chest. She could feel the heat and strength and growing desire of him with every breath. "Derek..." Amelia tried to speak, to tell him all that was in her heart, but all she could say was his name, a groan deep in her throat as his mouth and hands worked unspeakable magic.

Raising himself up on his elbow, he looked down at her, and at that moment he knew he'd put his heart and soul in pawn. He pressed their naked bodies together, shivering at the vibrantly arousing sensation. "Amelia...." Her name was like a prayer on his lips.

The warmth and heat of his mouth, the memory of her fingers touching his manhood sent a sweet ache flaring through Amelia's whole body. Growing bold, she allowed her hands to explore, delighting at the touch of the firm flesh that covered his ribs, the broad

248

shoulders, the muscles of his arms, and the lean length of his back. He was so perfectly formed. With a soft sigh she curled her fingers in the springy hair that furred his chest.

His lips nuzzled against the side of her throat. He uttered a moan as her hands moved over the smoothly corded muscles of his shoulders. "I like you touching me."

It was if they were breathing one breath, living at that moment just for each other. She could feel his passion building, searing her with its heat. They shared a joy of touching and caressing, arms against arms, legs touching legs, fingers entwining in the joy of discovery. Mutual hunger brought their lips back together time after time. She craved his kisses and returned them with trembling pleasure, exploring the inner softness of his mouth.

His hands were doing wondrous things to her, making her writhe and groan. Every inch of her body caught fire as passion exploded between them with a wild oblivion. He moved against her, sending waves of pleasure exploding along every nerve in her body.

His hands caressed her, warming her with their heat. They took sheer delight in the texture and pressure of each other's body. He undulated his hips between her legs and every time their bodies caressed, each experienced a shock of raw desire that encompassed them in fiery, pulsating sensations. Then his hands were between their bodies, sliding down the velvety flesh of her belly, moving to that place between her thighs that ached for his entry.

The swollen length of him brushed across her thighs. Then he was covering her, his manhood at the entrance of her secret core. With as much care as was humanly possible, he slowly entered her. His gentle probing brought sweet fire, curling deep inside her with spirals of pulsating sensations.

She felt his maleness at the fragile entry way to her womanhood as he pierced that delicate membrane. Every inch of her tingled with an intense, arousing awareness of his body. There was only a brief moment of pain, but the other sensations pushed it away. Amelia was conscious only of the hard length of him creating unbearable sensations within her as he began to move within her.

Derek groaned softly, the blood pounding thickly in his head. His hold on her hips tightened as he possessed her again and again. She was so warm, so tight around him that he closed his eyes with agonized pleasure as he moved back and forth, initiating her fully into the depths of passion.

Instinctively Amelia tightened her legs around him; certain she could never withstand the ecstasy that was engulfing her body. It was as if the night shattered into a thousand stars, bursting within her. She was melting inside, merging with him into one being. As spasms overtook her, she dug her nails into the skin of his back whispering his name.

A sweet shaft of ecstasy shot through Derek and he closed his eyes. Even when the intensity of their passion was spent, they still clung to each other, unable to let this magical moment end. They touched each other gently, wonderingly.

"I knew that I loved you," he whispered, "But I didn't know how much." Far from quenching his desire, what passed between them had made him all the more aware of how much he cared for her.

Cradling her against his chest, he lay silent for a long, long time as he savored her presence beside him. His hands fondled her gently as she molded her body so trustingly to his. Derek realized that for the first time in his life he was truly content. Without someone who really cared, life was hollow and meaningless. Amelia made him feel alive! For the moment, the ghosts of the past had been exorcised and he looked forward to the future.

*    *    *    *

Warm rays of sunlight flickered on Amelia's eyelids, awakening her. Yawning and stretching, she thought for just a moment that she was in her own bed, but the sound of breathing reminded her of what had passed during the night. Derek!

A flush of color stained her cheeks as she recalled the words he had said, the things he had done and how she had responded so eagerly. Beneath his hands and mouth, her body had come alive and she had been lost in a heat of desire. His hands against her breasts had not only warmed her but also comforted her and she knew that she had given him solace as well and helped him forget the sins of his father. And what now? How would they feel in the light of day about what had happened? More importantly, where did they go from here? What would she and Derek be to each other now?

Lovers. Once Amelia might have thought the word to have a tawdry ring to it, but feeling as she did about him, she couldn't believe that the passion and joy they had found together last night was wrong. The world could be a much happier place when two

251

people were in love.

Friends. She definitely wanted that. Despite the fact that their relationship had taken on a new dimension Amelia didn't want to lose the camaraderie they had shared. There were other things besides passion that drew her to him. Derek was someone she could talk to, depend on, someone who could make her smile.

Turning over on her side, she stared into Derek's sleeping face. His features were in repose, yet she could nearly imagine the dimples that accompanied his laughter, could almost feel again the softness of his lips as they brushed against hers.

A stray flaxen curl had fallen across his wide brow and she brushed it back out of his eyes with tender concern. Certainly, he was handsome but that wasn't what had attracted her to him. It was his honesty, his strength, his gentlemanly manners, his kindness to her. Leaning forward, she touched his mouth lightly in a kiss. Her impulse was to awaken him, but he looked so peaceful that she had second thoughts. Let him sleep. They had all the time in the world to reenact the passion of last night.

Picking up her nightgown from the floor, she hurried to put it on, then quietly, so as not to awaken him, she tip-toed to her own chamber. There was a pitcher of water and a china basin on a table in her room. Picking up a small washcloth she dipped it in the water and quickly used the corner to clean her teeth. She used a larger cloth to give herself a sponge bath.

Dressing in a yellow calico frock and combing her hair Amelia looked at herself in the mirror wondering if lovemaking showed in a woman's face.

252

Did she still look the same? Her Aunt Lucinda had always said that you could tell if a woman was a harlot because of the hard look on their face and in their eyes. Had she lost her innocence? No, she looked just the same.

There was a lightness in her steps as she descended the stairs. She was happy and it radiated from every pore, or at least she thought it did. Looking around she didn't see Honora anywhere so she supposed that she was the first one up. Hearing a light rapping at the door she looked around and realized she was the only one available to answer it.

Catriona O'Leary grinned at her as she opened the door. With a nod she introduced herself. "I brought a big pot of oatmeal sweetened with cinnamon and other healing spices for the mister," she explained. She paused at the door and Amelia realized that the Irish woman wanted an escort to Charles Cameron's room. It was an area of the house Amelia had avoided since coming to live at the mansion but now, out of a morbid curiosity she walked a step ahead of Catriona and led the way.

The room was dimly lit but Catriona quickly lit the lantern on the table near the bed. The light illuminated the ashen and pale face of a thin man. An old man. A man who looked like an ancient version of Derek. A gravely ill man. A pitiable man. Not at all the ogre she had expected to see. Perhaps then even monsters had to experience their due punishment.

"How is he?"

"Mornings are the worst, but all in all he seems to be getting stronger. Keeps asking for his whiskey, says it will heal him right away, but of course I say no. It was his whiskey that put him in this bed, in a

253

manner of speaking."

"Whiskey!" Charles Cameron's eyes opened wide at the sound of the word. Though he had looked like a living cadaver he now was more like a raging banshee and Amelia could well imagine what he must have been like before he had taken ill. Was it any wonder that Derek was intimidated by the man? As he wrestled with his blanket and his sheet, she could almost imagine him as he must have looked, marauding with the Klan.

Quickly she took her leave, shuddering as she hurried back to the main hallway. There she was greeted by Honora. "There you are my dear. I was lookin' for you. I made apple cobbler with the apples that fell from the tree out back. We will have some for breakfast. It's Derek's favorite." Her gaze moved to the stairs. "That's odd. Derek is usually the first one to take a seat at the breakfast table. He always has so much work to do. It isn't like him to sleep in."

Amelia feared that the twinge of guilt she felt was written clearly on her face. "Well, he…he…was having trouble sleeping. Nightmares, you see." She looked down at her hands because she didn't want to look into Honora's eyes and give herself away.

"Nightmares? Hmmm." She laughed softly. "I certainly hope that you were able to take those nightmares away."

Amelia took a deep breath and nearly choked. "I…I…"

Honora gently touched he arm and winked. "When you get to be my age you recognize a look of love when you see it. And all I can say is that it is about time." She gave Amelia a gentle nudge towards the kitchen.

254

"I do love him!" Amelia didn't know how to put her feelings into words.

"I could read that in your eyes the moment I saw the two of you together. And it was obvious to me that he felt the same. That's why I wanted you to move in here. I wanted to give you two lovebirds a chance to try your wings."

Honora had a great deal to tell Amelia as they put the finishing touches on the morning meal of poached eggs, berries, cobbler, and biscuits. She told Amelia that because of his father's shortcomings, Derek had been responsible for keeping the family finances afloat in order to save the plantation. She also told her about her stepson, Bevin, and how Charles had coerced him into marrying the daughter of a wealthy planter to further his own interests. She said that it was marriage to the selfish woman that had goaded the young man to go off to war and to his death.

"I will not let such a thing happen to Derek. I want him to marry the woman he loves. And I know in my heart that woman is you."

How could Amelia not feel as if her heart had wings? Honora's words gave her hope for the future, a future with Derek. He loved her and she loved him. How could anything go wrong?

## Chapter Nineteen

A seed of doubt planted in a person's mind can grow quickly into a growing wedge of dark suspicion. That is what Forest soon learned as the days passed by. She also found out that deep roots of distrust strangle trust and affection. She remembered what Moses had said to her, "*Quentin has a right to know about that man's accusations. He needs to allay any suspicions you might have or else what was said will be a wall between the two of you for a long, long time.*" But although she knew that he was right she had yet to find the opportunity to discuss the allegation with Quentin. At the back of her mind was the fear that such a conversation might spark another bout of the sudden illness that had come over him. And so she stayed silent.

"Forest, there you are. Are you sulking again?" Quentin sounded annoyed and Forest supposed that the emotional barrier that she had built between them affected him as well as herself.

"I'm not sulking. Just thinking. About what happened to my family." It played on her mind like a melancholy melody. Was there any chance she would ever see them again?

Quentin's tone was gentle as he shook his head. "There are things that are within our power to change and things that are not within our grasp to do anything about. In time you will see."

"I will never forget them. My mother was the light in my world and then that light was extinguished

256

because she wanted for us all to be free. I won't give up until I know the truth."

"Truth can be a bitter pill at times," he said, more to himself than to her. "Much better not to take anything or anyone for granted because like a wisp in the wind it can all blow away....."

His words played heavily on her mind and she felt a twinge of guilt because of the way she had been acting. "I don't take things for granted, Quentin. I will always be thankful to you for all that you have done." She tried to lighten the mood. "Is there a political meeting again today?" She hoped with all her heart that there was because that would give her the opportunity to pay another visit to Andrew Wyatt. It appeared he was the only one who could give her even a hint of what had happened to her family.

He smiled at her enthusiasm. "Why, yes there is. It appears that many southerners are going to be barred from voting. That needs to change. This will be the year to give our new party wings. Matthew and I need to come up with a strategy for the coming election. And we have yet to find the right candidate."

"What about you?"

He shook his head. "I am not what they need. We need a much younger man. Like your Moses. If only we could convince him."

"I think he would be perfect too, but he has a farm to run." She laughed softly. "And he wants to make time to visit here."

"Seems he has found the time several days this week." He wagged a finger in the air teasingly. "Ah, but I don't think it is *me* he wants to see. There must be some other attraction." He scratched his head.

"Let's see. It must be the possum and how it is cooked to perfection."

She nodded in agreement, playing along with his humor. "Why yes, I do believe it is the possum."

The playful banter reminded her of old times. It was the closest they had come to the way their relationship had been prior to her first visit with Andrew Wyatt and she felt a sense of relief. Perhaps all was not lost after all.

Later that day she felt rejuvenated and hopeful for the future. Moses had brought a sense of stability to her life as well as his unbridled affection. Her relationship with Quentin seemed to be mending and there seemed to be a sense of tranquility in the air. They had the cottage, food for the table, the birds were singing, and life was good. Plopping her hat on her head she followed Quentin out the door and to the buggy.

"It is too bad that women can't run for office or I could be your candidate," she joked as they rode along.

"And you would bring a lot to this wounded country," Quentin answered without any sign that he was mocking her. "You have all the needed qualities and a fine mind. Perhaps one day women will get their chance just as we Negroes have gotten ours."

"Perhaps. But by then I will probably be old and gray." It was, however, a fantasy that amused her as they rode into Richmond. Her daydream was over, however, the moment they arrived in the city. She felt a twinge of guilt as she once again told Quentin a falsehood about visiting the dressmaker.

"Another new dress?" He seemed amused. "Well, I suppose I should be glad that you have suddenly taken a fancy to dressing up your beauty. A love in one's life can work wonders."

This time it was Quentin who kept the buggy. Stopping in front of the dressmakers he took his leave of her with a wave of his hand and a grin, telling her that it might be a couple of hours before he was back.

As soon as she saw the buggy disappear down the street, Forest wasted no time in walking to the bank. There was one thing for certain. She would not let Andrew Wyatt intimidate her today. That the bank was less crowded seemed to bode well, she thought as she pushed her way through the door.

"Well, well, well, what do we have here? You don't look affluent enough to have an account." The tall, skinny man looked as though he would block her way, but Forest hurried past him. She knew right where she was going and didn't need directions to find Andrew Wyatt this time.

She found him sitting at his desk going through a stack of papers. In order to get his attention, she cleared her throat. Though he looked up with a smile on his face, that smile soon vanished. "You again. What the hell do you want?"

"Answers." She pushed into the room and boldly sat in a chair across from Wyatt's desk.

"Well, you are a cheeky little thing, aren't you?" Deciding that she wasn't just going to go away, he put down his pen and leaned back in his black leather chair. "What's the matter? Didn't Quentin tell you what you wanted to know?"

"Quentin doesn't have anything to do with this. It is between you and me." Her eyes held steady as she stared him down. "What happened to my mother and father? Are they still alive? Where are they?"

"I have no idea. After the slaves were freed they were dispersed everywhere. There were even some who wanted to send them back to Africa so that this country wouldn't have to deal with them getting everything. Even the damned vote." He was angry now, almost forgetting that she was there. "Whites and blacks just can't live together equally in the same country. There has to be someone higher up to keep them Nigrah's in their place."

She ignored his tirade. "What happened to my parents after they were captured?" There was a part of Forest that didn't want to know for fear that the truth would be devastating. "Were they returned to their owners? Or punished?" She feared the worst. She knew that many runaway slaves were whipped, shackled, beaten, mutilated, imprisoned, or branded.

"Your parents." He snickered. "Your mother was returned to the plantation where she was branded to keep her from running again."

"Branded!" Forest could almost feel the pain that would have caused.

"With an "R" for runaway."

Forest bit her lip so hard that she nearly cried aloud, but she didn't want to show weakness. "And my father?" She feared the worst for him. If her mother had been branded then her father's punishment would have been twice as bad.

"Your father." He looked at her with just a thimbleful of sympathy. "You don't know."

"He's dead!" She nearly lost every ounce of self-control but managed to appear to be calm.

"To the contrary, my dear. Your *father* is very much alive." He hurried to explain. The slave who

260

was living in the same slave cabin as your mother was not your sire."

"What do you mean?" She tried very hard but couldn't really remember her father. But her mother she could never forget. Her mother had been very pretty. And gentle. And kind.

"I mean that your true father was the man who owned your mother, the plantation owner, *William Trenholm*. Ask Quentin. He can tell you the story."

"William Trenholm?"

Once again Forest was shaken by her altercation with Andrew Wyatt. And once again he had strongly implicated Quentin in what had happened that terrible day when she had been fleeing with her parents from the slave catchers. Was Andrew Wyatt telling the truth or was he toying with her and carrying out some twisted vendetta against Quentin Faulkner? In her heart she knew that she could no longer remain silent. She had to talk to Quentin even if he might be upset by her questioning.

*     *     *     *

Moses had never thought he had a "green thumb" but as he surveyed his garden, he had to give himself a pat on the back. Not only were the peanuts doing well but the other crops he had planted were also thriving. He had to give credit to Honora, however, because she was the one who suggested lettuce, snow peas, radish, and spinach to be planted alongside the peanut plants. He thought how surprised Quentin and Forest would be when he had harvested his salad and brought the vegetables for dinner. It

261

would be his contribution and thanks for all the times they had fed him supper.

*Now if only my crop is profitable*, he thought. But why wouldn't it be when each plant produced nearly fifty peanuts. They were sought after for oil, food and as a cocoa substitute. Even the plants that were of poor quality could be used to feed livestock. Hurriedly counting the plants and multiplying by the price he estimated to receive, he was certain that he could pay back his share of the loan. The rest was up to Derek.

Thinking about his friend, Moses smiled. Since Amelia Seton had entered the picture and was living at the mansion with the family, Derek's mood had improved significantly even on days when there were nearly impossible hurdles to face. He smiled more, laughed once in a while, and seemed more relaxed. There were even times when they seemed to go back to their boyhood days and played pranks on each other, harmless shenanigans like putting sugar in the salt container or hanging the horse's harness up in the tree. Derek had even planted another coin in the dirt, insisting that they should dig there for Blackbeard's treasure. They had both had a good laugh and talked about whether or not the treasure really did exist.

Moses liked to mark the days before Amelia had come into Derek's life as "BA" which stood for – Before Amelia, although he had to agree with Derek that Forest had put a bounce to his walk as well. They both had to concur that loving someone changed everything and gave a purpose to living.

Hurrying through the rest of his work, Moses couldn't keep Forest from his thoughts. She was more than just pretty, she was thoughtful, intelligent, and inspiring. She made him feel as though he could be king of the world someday if he only tried. And because she believed in him, he believed in himself.

Looking out at the horizon and seeing that it was nearly time for the sun to set, Moses thought to himself how he used to damn the end of the day because he had so much work to do and was running out of time. But now the dusk meant spending time with Forest and Quentin at their cottage in the woods. If it wasn't really enchanted, well sometimes it seemed to be.

Walking back to his house, Moses grabbed the bucket of water he had heated in the sun and washed the traces of his labor away. Changing into clean clothes and drying his hair he looked around for something to take with him tonight and found the perfect gift in a jar of cherry preserves Honora had given him. Whistling a tune, he saddled up his horse and headed off to his rendezvous in the woods, thinking to himself that by now he could find the way even if he was blindfolded.

Moses could see the lights of the cottage from a distance, beckoning him like a shining star. He looked forward to a pleasant evening of good food, conversation, and later a walk in the moonlight. When he arrived and was greeted by Forest at the door, however, he was unsettled by the tension that hung in the air. He noticed at once that neither Forest nor Quentin were smiling.

"I'm so relieved that you are here," Forest exclaimed, taking him by the hand and leading him inside. "I paid a visit to Andrew Wyatt again today," she whispered, so softly that she was certain Quentin could not hear. "The man I told you about. He said some things that I have to ask Quentin about. I want to know the truth."

"And you deserve to know the truth. I'll stand by you no matter what the truth is." In his heart Moses hoped that the Wyatt individual was lying. But they had no time to discuss the matter further. There was a smell of something burning in the air.

"The goose!" With a cry of alarm Forest ran into the kitchen with Moses and Quentin close behind. They were just in time to pull the smoking bird from the stove before it caught fire, but the apron Forest was wearing was singed. With a frustrated grumble she took it off and hung it on a hook near the kitchen door.

"Is everyone all right. No one got burned?" Quentin was concerned as he looked warily at both Forest and Moses.

"No harm done." Trying to lighten the mood Moses said, "I love roast goose. The only time my family ever had it was twice at Christmas time when we were living up north."

"The thighs and drumsticks need to be well done but the breast needs to be medium or even rare for the best flavor. But I fear the entire goose will be quite crispy," Forest exclaimed shaking her head. "I couldn't save the goose from the Bobcat that killed it and it looks like I couldn't save it from my paltry cooking skills."

"Hush. It will be all right. We'll just scrape off the skin." Quentin put a hand on her shoulder. "Perhaps it was the whisky that was to blame." He turned to Moses. "It was my recipe of bourbon, wild onions, garlic, salt and pepper. I think perhaps the bourbon caught fire."

Moses suddenly remembered the cherry preserves that he had put in his saddlebag. "I brought Honora's preserves for supper. I'll be right back."

"No, I'll get them for you. I need some fresh air." Now that the time had come to tell Quentin the entire story of her visits with Andrew Wyatt Forest felt sick at heart. She had the gnawing feeling in her stomach that once she told him what had been said, things would never be the same no matter what the outcome was.

Moses had the same premonition. He could tell that Quentin was troubled and he couldn't help but have sympathy for him. He knew that no matter what had happened, Quentin was a good man.

"Forest is troubled and I don't know how to soothe her anxiety," he said to Moses.

"Just talk to her. The two of you have a special bond. I don't think it can be broken."

"I hope not." But Quentin didn't act as if he was sure.

The table was set and the food was already in the plates when Forest came back from her walk. In addition to the goose there was apple stuffing. Okra, berries, and oat bread slathered with the preserves Moses had brought. Although the meals were usually filled with conversation and chatter, tonight everyone was silent, so still that only the sound of their chewing disturbed the quiet. Although Moses had been ravenous earlier, he somehow had lost much of his appetite and had to force each forkful into his mouth.

At last when supper was finished, and the dishes whisked from the table the hour of reckoning had come.

265

"Do you remember that day when I was given a message to deliver?" Quentin nodded. "Imagine my horrified surprise to come face to face with a nightmare from the past."

"A nightmare?"

"The man I gave the message to was the same man who tried to capture me when I was just a child. I could never forget that face." Closing her eyes, she revealed all that had happened that first day and that she had gone again to visit with Andrew Wyatt.

"We discussed his profession as a slave catcher, and he told me that…that you were working with him. He said that you were both in a group of armed white men who monitored and enforced discipline on slaves. And that you chased after them and brought them back to face their just punishment." She looked Quentin straight in the eye and asked, "is it true?" Oh, how she wanted him to tell her that what Andrew Wyatt had said was a lie.

"I have dreaded this moment for so long and now it is here." Quentin's eyes sparkled with unshed tears as he answered in a choked voice, "yes, it's true. And I have regretted what I did all these years with you."

*No. Quentin would never. He wasn't… But by his own admission he had been a slave catcher.* Forest felt as if a tight fist was squeezing her insides. She felt Moses reach for and squeeze her hand and only that gesture kept her from totally losing her self-control.

"I was young. It was the only way I could survive, or so I thought at the time. I was one of the lucky ones who had been freed by my master, but freedom had its own risks and liabilities. I had nowhere to go, nowhere to turn. I was poor, penniless, and hungry. And then I met Andrew who

266

took me into his gang of patrollers. He schooled me in the ways of survival."

"And so, you hunted, hounded, and betrayed poor tortured souls who were only running away because they had been so badly treated. How could you?" Suddenly it was as if she were staring into the face of someone else. Someone she didn't even know. Not really. "You were one of those terrible men who hurt my mother, did God knows what to the man I thought was my father, and chased after me." She thought about the man who had so diligently rowed her to shore and tried to save her from her fate. The poor man who had been killed right before her eyes.

"My duty was to keep watch, only that. I never laid a hand on any slave. You must believe me." Quentin wiped at his eyes.

She wanted to scream at him but somehow she managed her self-control. "And because you were one of them, that is how you conveniently were on that shore. It wasn't an accident. Were you supposed to grab me?"

He put his head in his hands, shaking his head as he spoke. "No! They hadn't planned on your getting off the boat. I was supposed to be on alert in case any of the others broke free. I hadn't been expecting to come across a child."

"But you did!" At the back of her mind she remembered how he had clamped his hand over her mouth and taken her to safety. Quentin Faulkner had saved her from capture that day, but she wasn't in the mood to be thankful.

Quentin's expression was pleading. "I took one look at your pretty little face, the fear in your eyes, saw your tears and I couldn't let any harm come to you. So, I swept you off to a safe place and hid you where they would never find you."

"But you didn't lift a finger to help my mother." She choked back the tears.

"There is no way I could have done so." He tried to take her hand, but she hurriedly pulled her hand away. "Give vent to your anger, I understand, but I want you to know this truth as well. Because of you I changed my life and became a much better man, a man who made a vow never to do harm to another human being and to do all that I could to help others like you and like me. It is a vow that I have kept. That is why I am spending my time at the Capitol."

"And you never thought to tell me the truth." He had been her hero, a man she had respected, admired, and loved and now she didn't know just how she felt about him.

"I did, so many times. But the thought of your hatred made me a coward. And for that I ask you to forgive me. Please. I beg of you." In a gesture of humbleness he got down on one knee. "Please."

"I don't know if I can." Forest didn't know how she felt about Quentin at the moment. She had been so hopeful that he would deny everything, but instead he had corroborated Andrew Wyatt's story.

Moses had been quiet, just watching the heart-rending scene before his eyes but he spoke up now. "Give her time, Quentin. Time can heal a great many wounds."

"Time......" Quentin echoed. "Ah, yes. I must at least do that for her. And hope within my heart that she comes to take pity on my stupidity and immoral behavior and try to mend our relationship. In the

268

meantime….."

Forest put her hands to her throat. She felt as if she were suffocating, as if she were going to fall in a heap on the floor. "Take me out of here, please, Moses. I just can't stand to be here one moment longer." All she knew was that just looking into Quentin's face brought her a deep sorrow.

"Are you certain?" Moses was worried about Forest yet also concerned for Quentin's well-being. He didn't want anything to happen to him and then have Forest regret her decision.

Forest's answer was to at last break down in a flood of tears, hardly even realizing that Moses swept her up in his arms and gently carried her outside. She felt him lift her up on his horse's back and then hoist himself up to ride behind her.

ASHES AND AWAKENINGS

## Chapter Twenty

The evening had not turned out at all like Moses had thought. And now he was riding to his small house with Forest riding with him. He couldn't help the feeling of nervousness he felt as he saw the roof come into view. Would she think that his home was little more than a hovel? He couldn't help the sense of shame. He had wanted to bring her here, it was true, but not before he had made it fit for someone he cared so deeply about. What would she think? It was a far cry from the charming cottage in the woods.

"Forest......."

She turned her head just a bit as she said, "Jemma. From now on my name is Jemma. Forest is gone forever."

"Jemma. I want to apologize for how littered and dusty my home is. You deserve much better." Riding up to the hitching post he dismounted then helped her down. "I'm afraid that this is it. This is where I sleep and eat. But most of the time I'm working."

"Apologize for what? Being there when I was so in need of someone to help me keep my sanity?" Hurrying to the door, she waited for him to open it.

Lighting a lantern by the door, Moses beckoned her to step inside. "Please excuse the mess. I was...."

"It's fine, Moses. It just needs a woman's touch."

270

He forced a smile and gestured for her to sit down on one of the chairs he had plucked from a peg on the wall. Then he pulled up a three-legged stool for himself. "You must be exhausted." He knew that he was.

"No, not really. I don't think I will be able to sleep a wink after what Quentin told me tonight. He shattered my world."

"And his own," Moses added.

She didn't seem to hear. "He lied to me all those years. I thought he had just come out of nowhere, like some hero. But all the while he was one of the villains. Because of him and the others my mother was branded. How can I ever look him in the face knowing what I know now?"

"I think he lied partly to protect you, Jemma, as much as to keep you from knowing the truth." Moses wanted so much to take off his boots and get comfortable but there was something inhibiting about her presence there. "You have to admit that he was very good to you. He could have turned you over to the other slave catchers but he didn't."

"Yes, I suppose that he could have." For just a moment her anger seemed to soften.

"Instead he made a home for you and kept you safe all these years." Seeing a pitcher of water on the kitchen table he asked. "Are you thirsty."

"Not for water. Do you have anything stronger?" She felt in the mood to do what men always did and get roaring drunk to ease her heartache.

He did have, but he was hesitant to offer it to her. "How about some cider?"

271

She shook her head no. Her eyes scanned the tiny house. There was a table and two mismatched chairs. A small settee made out of boards and padding was in the middle of the room. A small narrow bed stood at the far end. It was meagerly furnished yet it had a certain appeal. She thought of all the ways she could help him by cleaning it up and adding a woman's touch.

He noticed her looking about. "I made the furniture. What there is of it."

"I like it. It has character." Spying a bottle of whiskey on a shelf she bounded up and snatched it before he could tell her no. Drinking right from the bottle she choked on the fiery liquid.

"Be careful. You're not used to that." He tried to wrench it away from her, but she was belligerent.

"I will be after tonight," she retorted stubbornly. She took another swig and choked again. "I didn't realize that drinking took practice." She had told herself she wouldn't cry but now as the agony and heartache took its toll she succumbed to a full flood of tears, covering her face with her hands.

"Jemma. Jemma. Jemma." He put his arms around her, unnerved by her sobs, though he knew she had reason to cry. "I'll help in any way I can. I would go to hell and back for you. You know that."

She looked at him through her tears. "Yes, I do and you don't know how much that means to me." She looked up, all too acutely aware of the firmly muscled body so close to hers. His mouth was just inches from hers as he whispered words of comfort. Slowly, vibrantly, she was bound by a fragile silken thread that was woven about them. For just a moment

272

she allowed herself to forget the past and concentrate on him.

"Jemma," he whispered. She brought out a sense of protectiveness in him. He wanted to sweep her up in his arms, carry her off and never let go. He wanted to protect her from anyone who might try to harm her, even if that man was Quentin.

Moses heard the fabric of her gown rustle against her skin as she moved and felt a flash of desire surge through him. Just being near her fired his passions. No other woman had ever caused such a potent reaction. She was special. He had somehow felt that from the moment his eyes had touched upon her so many years ago. He had loved her when they were children and he loved her now.

Slowly he tightened his arms around her. Their gazes locked and she couldn't look away. An irresistible tide, the warmth of her attraction to him, drew her. Wordlessly she watched as he slowly lowered his mouth to hers. Then he kissed her with a surprising gentleness for someone with his strength. For a moment all she knew was the feel of his lips. Clinging to him, she relished the sensations the caress of his mouth evoked. She could feel his heart pounding against her breasts as his kiss deepened. She couldn't think, couldn't breathe.

Reaching up, she put her arms around his neck, pulling him closer as she opened her mouth to the caress of his lips. It was just a kiss, and yet it was so much more. It was a promise of what could be, a celebration of the feelings they shared.

The world seemed to be focused on the touch of his lips, the haven of his arms, the hardness of his body against hers. She couldn't think, couldn't breathe. She couldn't have said a word even if she'd had to. All she knew was that his arms were strong yet at the same time gentle, and that his mouth fit so perfectly against her own. Something deep within her burned, ached, and yearned. And she could tell that he felt the same. Even so, she felt him push away from her.

"What's wrong?" She wanted to be in his arms again.

"I am not going to take advantage of you when you are feeling such pain. You have been through hell tonight. I want to be your protector not your seducer." His mind was thinking like a gentleman, but his body had a mind of its' own. Still, he didn't want them both to have regrets come morning.

"But I want you," she blushed, not being used to being so forward. "I want you in all ways."

"And I want you too. So much it hurts." And indeed, it did hurt, far more than he had expected. "But we both need to get some sleep. We can talk more about where we go from here in the morning."

She had forgotten that he worked hard and that he would need to get his sleep. "Yes, in the morning."

Moses kissed her on the forehead and gave her a gentle push towards the small bed. "I have a shirt you can use as a nightgown," he whispered.

"Where are you going to sleep?" It didn't look as if the bed could hold two people.

"There." Moses gestured towards the settee, telling a white lie, "I often sleep there. It's very comfortable." He hoped she would not realize how hard and lumpy the settee could be.

274

"Are you sure? I hate to kick you out of your bed." She watched as he pulled a cotton shirt out of a wooden box that acted as his cloths closet. He handed it to her.

"Very sure. You are my guest. I want you to get a good night's rest and we will talk more in the morning, about many things." About Quentin of course, but also about where she fit in his life from now on. He doubted she would be in a hurry to go back to the cottage after what had happened.

"All right. I'll say goodnight then."

Moses turned his back as she undressed, knowing the greatest torture he had ever known. It took all his self-control not to turn around or sneak a peek, but he resisted all temptation. She deserved his respect.

"All right, you can turn around now." The sleeves of the shirt were much too long for her and it was much too short so it didn't cover her knees. Under different circumstances she might have laughed, but she was beginning to think about Quentin, wondering if he would be all right. In spite of what he had done she still cared about him.

"Do you want me to tuck you in?" Without waiting for her reply, he pulled back the sheets, and then covered her once she was in the bed. He said a final good night then extinguished the lamp. Fumbling around in the dark he collapsed on the settee without even bothering to get undressed. Still, as tired as he was, he couldn't get to sleep until he heard the soft, gentle sound of her snoring.

\*     \*     \*     \*

275

The lamp on the study desk was burning low and Derek reached over to turn up the wick, at the same time straining to keep his eyes on the papers scattered before him. He was going over a list of money owed and money paid out. The figures didn't coincide. Where some of the money had gone was a mystery. For a man who was tight with a dollar, Charles Cameron had spent extravagantly. The problem was he had dug a hole so deep that Derek wasn't certain that if he worked non-stop for a year and a half he could pay it back.

"Just what have you been up to, Father?" Leaning back in the chair, a plush red velvet that his father had picked out himself to go behind his new oak desk, Derek stretched his arms over his head as he stifled a yawn. It was late. He should go to bed. Amelia was most likely waiting for him.

"Amelia." He knew he would give her the world if he could. He knew that she was the woman he had been looking for all his life. He wanted to be with her until the day he died. But how could he think about his future when so much was at stake? Hell, he wouldn't even be able to take time for the wedding, if she said yes to his proposal.

*A wedding*, he thought sourly. *Would his father insist his Ku Klux Klan friends be included on the guest list?* At the reminder of what he had found in the Avery attic, Derek flipped through the papers on the desk until he found what he was looking for. *The old book!* His anger was renewed as he looked at the scrawled names written in black ink. He studied those names intently now. "Jefferson Jensen, Grand Dragon. Thomas Bedford, Grand Cyclops. Charles

276

Cameron, Grand Titan" And there were more who belonged to this invisible empire of the South, as the book called them.

He read aloud that although the Klan had started out as an amusement activity to frighten newly freed slaves, it had morphed into a military force serving the interests of the southern Democratic Party. The planter class like his father. Those who desired the restoration of the white race as rulers of sorts. Lords. Masters.

In disgust he read some of the names. *Travis James. Waylon Tucker. Walter Johnson. Edward Hadaway. William Trenholm.* He stiffened as he read a name he recognized, the name of his brother Bevin's father-in-law. *Uriah Van Diran.* He remembered what a real bastard the man was and his part in Moses being sold that terrible day.

"What are you doing?"

Amelia's voice behind him startled him for a moment, but as he saw her standing there, looking so lovely in the glow of the lamp light he smiled. "Playing the game of Pinkerton detective."

"Oh, and can I play?" Her voice was seductive.

There was a growing sense of intimacy as she sat beside Derek. She sensed his presence with every fiber of her being. The lamp sent a soft, golden glow over them as she took a seat in the chair he pulled up for her. Derek's knee was touching hers as they sat side by side and she was very much aware of him.

"Did you know your hair shines with red fire in the glow of the lamp light? Such lovely tresses. How I wish that I could run my fingers through it, just to see if it will set fire to my hands the way your love has set fire to my heart." Even his voice drew her, rumbling with its low-pitched masculinity each time he spoke.

She was aware that his attention was being focused on her, just as avidly as she had studied him, but she didn't answer. His eyes were caressing, moving from her head to her neck and lower, lingering on the rise and fall of her bosom.

"Are you coming to bed soon?" She wondered what had captured his attention, then seeing the book she understood. "Are you going to talk with your father about his activities in the Klan?"

"Not yet. I was just looking at some of these names."

She looked over his shoulder, tensing as she recognized one of the names. "Walter Johnson."

He turned his head, "yes do you know him?"

"Beauregard Johnson was the student I told you about. The one I suspected of having something to do with the fire at the school that day. You don't suppose….."

An alarm sounded in Derek's brain. "It is possible." He felt a twinge of fear surge through him. "Amelia, you must be careful from now on when you go to teach the young Negro children at the church. Make certain no one follows you. We don't want a repeat of what happened at the school, just because these crazy bastards have a vendetta in their craw."

Closing the book and securing it safely in the desk, Derek wanted to put the Klan out of his thoughts, at least for tonight. He was sitting beside a pretty woman, he loved her and she loved him, it was late, and he had amorous thoughts on his mind. For the moment at least everything seemed perfect.

ASHES AND AWAKENINGS

## Chapter Twenty-One

Turning over on her side, Forest stared into Moses' sleeping face. His features were in repose, yet she could nearly imagine the dimples that accompanied his laughter, could almost feel again the softness of his lips as they had brushed against hers. He was her only light in a world that had suddenly gone dark. He was the gentle breeze that had kept away a storm. He was the strength that had held her up when she was at her weakest point. He was a friend who had come to her aid when she had thought herself to be friendless and alone.

"I love you, Moses. More than you will ever know." She had known before that they had a special bond, but now she knew of a certainty that it was a bond that could never be broken.

Emotionally drained after her quarrel with Quentin, Forest was not surprised at all that she had not been able to sleep a wink. She was assailed by memories of how it had been during the happy times with Quentin. He had never been anything but kind to her in all the time she had known him. He had cared for her, taught her, and given her all the comforts of a home. Yet all the time he had known the truth and had hidden it from her. Was his kindness then only given because of a feeling of guilt?

Sitting up in bed, she sat for a long while just thinking things over, remembering that fateful day as if it were just yesterday. The boat, the river, the wind, her mother's cries, her own fear as she ran as fast are her legs would carry her. She thought about poor Joseph and how he had sacrificed himself for her. There had been no justice for him nor would there ever be.

"Emma!" She had lost her precious doll along with her innocence. She had never known fear before but she had learned it that day. She had never seen hatred revealed but she had glimpsed it in the eyes of the man she now knew to be Andrew Wyatt.

*Quentin.* Just where did he really fit in all of the tragedy of that day? All these years she had thought of him as her hero only to find out from his own lips that he had been a part of it all. He had not been her rescuer but her adversary. And yet as Moses had reminded her Quentin had said that because of her he had changed the course of his life.

*"I took one look at your pretty little face, the fear in your eyes, saw your tears and I couldn't let any harm come to you. So, I swept you off to a safe place and hid you where they would never find you."* he had told her. *"Give vent to your anger, I understand, but I want you to know this truth as well. Because of you I changed my life and became a much better man, a man who made a vow never to do harm to another human being and to do all that I could to help others like you and like me. It is a vow that I have kept. That is why I am spending my time at the Capitol."*

"Because of you I changed my life," she whispered, seeing the sorrow on his face as he said those words. Oh, how she wanted to forgive him, but could she?

Tormented by her deliberations, she rose from the bed, pacing up and down in her bare feet. She needed time. She wanted more answers. She required a special healing that was not just for her heart but also for her soul.

Seeking to push her thoughts from her mind, Forest carefully lit the lantern in the kitchen. Trying very hard not to disturb Moses' slumber she set out to put a few things in order. The floor was in desperate need of sweeping so she searched for a broom and found one in the corner. When she was finished, she took the time to organize what few food supplies he had in the kitchen—canned food, jellies and jams, bread, coffee, salt, sugar and honey. Now every item had its place. Seeing a basket on the table, she supposed that it might be for eggs and determined to check the small chicken house for eggs as soon as the sun came up.

Moses' clothes were next on her list. Picking up those that were scattered on the floor she separated those that were wearable from those that needed washing. The clean clothes she folded up and put in the wooden box he used for his "closet" and the laundry she put in an empty flour sack she found near the washstand.

Forest noticed that Moses only had a few books: Jules Verne's *Twenty Thousand Leagues Under the Sea*, Uncle *Tom's Cabin*, Charles Dickens' *Great Expectations,* a book of poems, and the *Bible*. She also found a book under the bed, a book of Hans Christian Andersen fairy tales. Picking it up she saw that two stories were dog-eared, stories she had read to him that time so long ago when he had been a frightened boy hiding out in a trunk in the baggage car of that train.

"The Steadfast Tin Soldier and The Ugly

282

Duckling," she read softly. The reminder brought tears to her eyes and she remembered the frightened boy. But Moses wasn't a boy any longer. Looking over at him as he stirred in his sleep, she felt a surge of emotion, a tide of affection.

Standing back, Forest surveyed her accomplishment and felt very proud of herself. She had taken chaos and transformed it into a well-organized household. And just in time. The sun was blinking on the horizon and she knew Moses was an early riser. Hurrying out to the yard she searched for and found the tiny henhouse. Luckily the hens had been generous and she plucked up five eggs.

"I must think up names for you all," she said with a laugh, but her mood sobered as she thought she saw two shadows pass hurriedly behind the henhouse door. "Hello......" She shrugged, thinking she had possibly imagined it. Moses lived far away from any neighbors. Had it been a pair of animals? She put the incident out of her thoughts as she walked quickly back to the house, passing by an apple tree that gifted her with three apples.

Back in the kitchen she searched for the tin containing lard for the eggs but there wasn't any. She knew she would have to make a list of items that needed to be purchased next time Moses went into Richmond. Instead she put all five eggs in a pan of water and lit the stove. Soft or hard-boiled eggs would have to be the choice this morning, along with toast from the bread on the table. Cleaning off the top of the stove she plopped the bread down, remembering to watch it carefully so it didn't burn. She thought about boiling the apples to make applesauce but knew there was not enough time.

Moses would have to eat them sliced this time.

"You're up!" The sound of Moses' voice startled her for just a moment and she turned around.

"I couldn't sleep so I made myself useful," she said in greeting.

"Useful?" With amazement he looked around. "Did a fairy godmother visit here during the night? Or am I in the wrong house?"

"Just me. I thought you needed a bit of help." The look on his face made her smile. He clearly appreciated what she had done. "I couldn't find the lard so I boiled the eggs. And there is toast. And apples. That's all I could find."

He remembered when she had made breakfast for him at the cottage. "I don't have much. I keep trying to find the time to go into town but time has a way of slipping past, it goes so quickly."

"Yes, it does."

Moses liked having her with him yet it felt awkward to be together in such small surroundings. Even so, Forest did everything she could to make him feel comfortable and soon he found himself sitting down to a tasty breakfast. "I can see that you are soon going to have me spoiled. And I like it."

They both tried to keep the mood light yet hovering over them was the question of how Quentin was faring this morning, the first morning since that fateful day that Forest had not been by his side.

At last Moses brought the subject up. "Have you thought about Quentin?"

"I thought about him until I thought I would go mad. I hope that he is doing well." She didn't have the heart to eat, although she had been hungry when

284

she first sat down. "No matter what happened I don't want him to be unhappy."

Moses broached a touchy subject. "The whole issue of slavery has hurt so many people. Charles Cameron put a dagger to my heart when he sold me that terrible day. And yet, somehow I found it in my heart to forgive him."

"Did you? Did you really?" She looked him straight in the eye.

He fidgeted, trying to come up with an honest answer. "I forgave him yes. But I can never forget what he did to me."

"Ah ha!" She emphasized with a nod of her head.

"Forgiving and forgetting are two different things. You can forgive someone and yet not forget what was done to you. It hovers at the back of your mind. But if you allow it to ferment it can tarnish your very soul."

Oh, yes, his words sounded so right, but Moses had to reflect on whether what he was telling her matched how he felt deep inside. Had he really forgiven or forgotten what Charles Cameron had done? The money he had loaned Derek had not been to help Charles but to help Derek. Had it been just Charles who was in debt he knew he wouldn't have lifted a finger to help. Now he realized perhaps he needed to follow his own advice and try and put the past behind him.

\*     \*     \*     \*

There was nothing in the world that could burst a man's bubble as quickly as talk about finances. Moses was walking up and down the rows of peanut plants when Derek pulled up in his wagon, motioning to him, telling him that they needed to talk. The look on his face did not give Moses hope that the news was good.

"You look as jovial as Lee did the day he surrendered to Grant. What's wrong?"

Getting out of the wagon, Derek picked up the ledgers on the wagon seat that were weighted down with a large rock and held them out for Moses to see. "Something is not right. The numbers don't add up. There is a large chunk of money missing."

Moses took a cursory glance at one of the sheets. "It looks OK to me."

"That is what I thought, too, until I did the arithmetic. And then going through my father's notes and letters I discovered that there is money missing because he has been making speculative investments in some railroads."

"Railroads?" Moses thought that was strange considering Charles' hatred towards the northerners even though there was a northern railroad boom earlier in the year.

"He probably thought that since there was a boom in railroad construction following the end of the war that his money would earn a big investment. I am not so sure." Even though the railroad industry was the largest employer aside from agriculture Derek feared there was a big risk involved.

"Have you talked with him?" Moses felt a flash of anxiety wondering if Charles' actions would hinder the ability to pay back the money he and Derek owed.

He had heard about other men losing everything because of poor investments. He didn't want them to be among those unfortunate men.

"I haven't done so because he has been so irrational lately. I am afraid sometimes that the drink and his illness have taken a toll on his mind." Derek remembered hearing his ravings as he passed by the door. "But I will talk with him any day now. I have to. There is another matter I want to ask him about."

"Another matter?" Derek looked so grim that Moses wondered if he really wanted to hear what was on his friend's mind.

"Follow me." Leading Moses to the back of the wagon, Derek pulled the tarp off a large box. "Look inside."

"Bed sheets?" He wondered if Derek was playing another prank on him. "If something is going to pop out at me, I don't think this is funny. We both have work to do."

"Take a closer look, my friend." Reaching in the box, Derek held up one of the robes. "I found this in the attic at Avery House." He held up another robe, this one the color red. "And this." He hefted a handful of hoods.

"No!" For a minute Moses didn't believe his eyes. He disliked Charles Cameron, but he had never thought the man would sink so low as to ride with the Klan. "Perhaps these things belong to someone else and they were just hiding them in that old house."

Derek's laugh was forced. "You are making excuses for my father. *You*!"

Moses wrinkled his nose as he frowned. "I'm only trying to be fair. Forest had a confrontation with

287

her father and is staying at my house. I gave her some valuable advice about forgiving and forgetting. I don't want to be a hypocrite."

"Forest stayed at your house?" Derek raised his eyebrows knowingly.

Moses was quick to explain. "No! It was not like that. She was here because of our friendship. Nothing happened. Nothing whats-so-ever!"

"Yet," Derek quipped. He forced himself to get back to the matter on hand. "I wanted to think my father was innocent just the same as you, but then I found this." He dug through the items in the box and found the notebook. Opening it up to the page with the names he held it right in front of Moses' face. "Here is a list of the Klan members in this area. My father's name is written just as clearly as can be."

Moses scanned the page and saw Charles' Cameron's name written very clearly at the top of the page. *Jefferson Jensen, Grand Dragon. Thomas Bedford, Grand Cyclops. Charles Cameron, Grand Titan.* With a scowl he read some of the additional names. *Travis James. Waylon Tucker. Walter Johnson. Edward Hadaway. William Trenholm. Uriah Van Diran.*

Uriah Van Diran, he remembered that name very well. "I'll be damned." He sensed his friend's pain. "I'm sorry, Derek."

"I don't even want to think of all the havoc he has caused or the people he has harmed. How can I live with this?" Taking the book from Moses' hands he threw it on the ground, scattering some of the pages. "Damn it!"

Kneeling down, Moses picked the papers off the ground, straightened them, and then handed the book back to Derek. "You don't have reason to feel guilty. You didn't do anything wrong."

"But I am the seed of that man. I grew up under his thumb. How could I have been so blind to his absences and secretive behavior?"

Moses still couldn't get over the fact that Charles Cameron was a man who had brought terror to others, but he tried hard to sooth Derek's self-reproach. "Just when were you given the responsibility of being your father's watchdog? Was it your job to notate his comings and goings?"

Derek shook his head. "No!"

"You were living your own life, working hard to keep the plantation going. Dodging all the carpetbaggers, northern soldiers, and squatters who wanted to stake out a claim on your land. Let it go, Derek. Don't torture yourself with imagined mistakes. It happened in the past."

"But I'm not so certain it hasn't continued. The fire at the schoolhouse. Remember that. Amelia recognized one of the names as belonging to the father of one of her students."

Moses stiffened, recalling the hateful red letters marked upon his house. And he thought about that night at the cottage when he and Forest were taking a moonlit walk and he had thought he had seen shadows. "Forest!" What if she was endangered because of her association with him? What if the same sick, twisted, individuals who had tried to intimidate him came back and Forest came to harm?

"What's wrong?" Derek knew Moses nearly as well as Moses knew himself. He recognized *that expression.* "You look as if you just swallowed a rock and can't breathe."

289

"I didn't mention it to you, but several weeks ago I came home and found red letters forming "nigger" scrawled in red pain on my house. No accident. Just a show of hatred. What if they come back again and Forest is harmed in some way?"

He didn't wait for Derek to answer. Hurrying back to the house he made an instant decision. As much as he liked having Forest in his house, he had to take her back home to the cottage. She would be much safer with Quentin than she was with him under the circumstances.

*　　*　　*　　*

Forest was so proud of herself that she nearly busted all the buttons off the shirt she had borrowed from Moses' closet. Not only had she gone into Richmond for much needed supplies – lard, turnips, beets, cabbage, dried beef, oatmeal, grits, coffee, flour, and a sack of beans, she had also found a large wooden tub, some soap, and a rope to use as a clothesline and done his laundry. Feeling very extravagant she had also purchased a quilt for the bed from a woman selling them at the marketplace, her gift to him for being so good to her.

"I am making this into a real home," she said to herself. All it needed was tender loving care, determination, elbow grease, and the right purchases. Checking through his dishes and utensils—Mason jars used for glasses, broken plates, cups and bowls, mismatched knives, forks, and spoons, she made a note to purchase replacements as soon as she could.

Looking in the direction of the bed she was tempted to plop down and get the rest that had

290

escaped her during the night, so she changed back into Moses' shirt. Sitting on the bed a thought came to her mind. There had to be some way to make the bed more hospitable to sleep on. Thinking perhaps the settee was more comfortable, she rose from the bed and gave it a try, only to find that it was hard as a rock. With a sigh of exasperation, she stood back up.

*Moses told me he often slept on this couch but he was just saying that so I wouldn't realize I was pushing him out of his bed*, she thought. Well tonight she would insist that they share the bed. Surely if the two of them were cuddled up together they wouldn't take up too much room. And perhaps if they were together, he would make love to her. Just the very thought caused her to feel a surge of emotions.

What would it be like to make love with Moses? To have him touch her, stroke her, to lie with her head against his chest? Closing her eyes, she was so immersed in her daydreaming that she didn't hear him come up behind her.

"You have been working more miracles, I see." He could hardly even recognize the place.

"Do you like what I have done?"

"I do!" With a cursory glance he could see that she had not only gotten necessary food stuffs but had also picked up his garments and washed those that needed cleaning. The focus of his gaze moved to her. She looked very alluring with her shapely bare legs showing from the knee down. "You look so much better in that shirt than I ever could."

"Do I?" She was flattered by the look of desire she saw in his eyes. Reaching out she clasped his hand and pulled him towards the bed. She wanted to finish what they had begun last night.

291

Moses pulled away.

"What's wrong?" Her disappointment showed in her eyes. "I thought. I hoped….."

He put his hands on her shoulders and drew her closer. "So did I. If you only knew how many times I dreamed of having you here, in my arms, in my bed. But….."

She could tell that something was troubling him. "What is it?"

He quickly told her about all that Derek had conveyed to him, and about the fire at the school. "And a few weeks back someone painted words in red on my house. Hateful words. Derek has warned me that there could be trouble in this area."

"If there is, we will stand together and fight them off," she exclaimed, putting her arms around his waist, and hugging him tight. "I'm not afraid."

"Well, *I* am. Very afraid. Not for myself but for you. You just don't understand what men in the Klan are capable of. I just couldn't bear it if something happened to you because of me." She smelled like the roses outside his front door and he wanted nothing more than to push caution aside and make love to her. But reason prevailed so he once again stepped away.

"Moses….." She knew before he told her what he was thinking. "You're going to take me back to the cottage."

"You will be safe there."

"But what about you?" She fought to keep the dark thoughts far from her mind.

"I'll be all right." He pointed to a rifle in the corner of the room and he had a pistol hidden under the bed. "Did you think about what I told you about

Quentin. Can you come to terms with what he did?"

She nodded. "I have forgiven him but not forgotten what transpired. We will need to talk things out." As she reached for her clothing he turned around, once again fighting the temptation to watch her. Then once she was dressed, they walked hand in hand to the wagon.

Moses helped her up on the seat then got up beside her. As they drove off Forest looked over her shoulder, fighting against the sadness that closed around her heart.

## Chapter Twenty-Two

The glare of the noonday sun beat down on Amelia's head as she guided the Cameron buggy down the rocky, pitted road towards the church. It was the third Sunday she had honored her commitment to teach the children and she found herself anxious to resume their lessons. Like Jedidiah they were eager to learn, bright and appreciative. They were also very creative and loved to sing. She looked forward to hearing them with each visit and wondered if she was teaching them or they were teaching her. One thing she had learned was how important music could be so she now set aside time for singing when she taught the children at the Avery mansion as well..

Humming a tune that she had heard the preacher call a "spiritual" she felt blissful and content. She had found a stack of children's Bible stories in the attic and had asked Derek if she could appropriate them for the children today. They were illustrated stories from the Old Testament, each about a different personage: Noah, Ruth, Samuel, Esther, Joseph, David, Samson, Jonah, Sarah, and Moses. Ten stories, one for each of her students.

*How I hope they don't ask me why all the pictures are of people who are white with light hair,* she thought, remembering when Jedidiah had asked such a question about the stories he had read. If they did, she was prepared to tell them that the pictures were representative of the people who lived very long ago and far, far away.

Amelia had been so immersed in her thoughts that she had forgotten Derek's insistence that she use caution in her visits to teach the children, but now that she was reminded, she looked behind her. Was she imagining it or was there a buggy on the same pathway? Nervously she flicked the reins, urging the two horses into a faster gait.

After traveling for several minutes, she looked back again. The intruder was still there, closing in on her no matter how fast her buggy went. Determined to confuse them so they didn't know where she was headed, she took a right turn instead of a left and headed in another direction.

It seemed that the sound of hoofbeats was pounding in her ears, matching the rhythm of her heartbeat. She didn't have anything but a buggy whip for protection. What if her pursuer was one of *them*? But that was foolish. They would have no reason to harm a hair on her head, or would they? For a moment she fantasized that her pursuer was dressed in hooded white robes.

"Faster! Faster!" She swore beneath her breath. Apparently the damn horses didn't understand English because they weren't obeying her command. Flicking the reins in a frenzy she felt the wheels hit a bump, felt her hands slip from the reins and realized too late that she had been thrown out of the buggy. Only a pile of hay kept her from serious injury, although as she lay on the ground she knew that she had not escaped unscathed.

Pausing to catch her breath before trying to stand, Amelia looked in the direction of the buggy pursuing her. It was a man in a blue suit and hat. Not a frightening sight at all. Shakily she got to her feet, knowing for a certainty that she would have at least one or two large bruises, but thankfully nothing broken.

"Amelia!"

The voice calling her name was only too familiar and she cringed as Edward Cutler pulled his buggy up beside her. Although she was relieved that he was not a white-hooded Klan member he was not a person she wanted to see.

"Amelia, are you all right? You took quite a tumble." He hurried out of his buggy and was quickly by her side.

Dusting herself off she mumbled, "I'm just fine Edward. Just fine. No harm done."

He grabbed her by the arm. "Are you sure?"

She shrugged off his hand. "Quite. Nothing injured but my pride." She was just going to ask him what he was doing way out there, but he answered her before she had the chance.

"Your aunt told me she had heard you were staying with the Camerons. I came by to see if you wanted to go to church but you seemed to be going in a different direction entirely." His beady eyes seemed to be prying into her very soul.

"I am just out for a buggy ride, that's all. I didn't have a destination really." Her explanation sounded strange, but she hoped he would believe her. "Is Aunt Lucinda doing well?"

"She misses you a great deal. I'm sure it is very lonely living there all by herself." Taking off his hat he ran his fingers through his curly red hair. "Very lonely."

For just a moment Amelia felt a twinge of guilt

296

thinking about her nights of passion with Derek while her aunt was all alone. "We had our differences but I will visit her soon," she explained. "But what about you? Did you come all this way just to see me?" Or was he here to take a look at the Cameron property in hopes that it would soon be his own? Remembering the ledgers Derek had shown her she felt a twinge of unease. Edward Cutler was a devious kind of man.

He seemed to read her mind. "My visit was two-fold. I have heard through the grapevine that there is a coming monetary crisis. It seems there has been just one thing after another. That fire in Chicago and then one in Boston, the equine influenza."

Amelia stiffened. His talk of fires put her on edge. "I can assure you that all the Cameron horses are doing just fine." She knew how important horses were to the stability of everyday life because nearly everything from wagons, buggies, equipment used horse power. It was no wonder that the epidemic would affect the country.

He laughed. "Certainly the horses drawing your buggy were in high spirits. But that isn't the only thing. Since the German Empire stopped minting silver there has been a drop in demand and the value has plummeted. I don't suppose the Camerons have any silver or silver coins hidden away?"

*If they did I wouldn't tell you*, she thought but didn't say. "I have no idea. Certainly they don't fill me in on any financial matters." It was getting late and she had a schedule to keep. She was in a hurry to get rid of Edward, round up the buggy, and head to the church.

"Hmmm, I hoped that they would."

For just a moment when she looked at him he

297

reminded her of a skunk. "Well, they do not and if you will excuse me, I don't have much more to say, Mr. Cutler."

He ignored her curt manner. "That is fine because I don't have much more to say either, except that my offer of marriage is still open."

"What?" Only by the greatest self-control did she keep from losing her temper.

His grin was ominous. "Your friends the Camerons are on a pathway to poverty. I learned through some banking friends of mine that some of the money the Camerons received in a loan came from the Freedman's Savings Bank. That Nigrah bank is losing money as quickly as a sinking ship loses passengers. When it fails and they call the loan in I will be right there to cash in."

Never in all her life had she wanted so desperately to slap someone silly, but she merely turned her back on him and walked away.

"Take care of yourself, Miss Amelia. I'll keep in contact for that rainy day I know is coming."

*Oh, the nerve of the man*, she thought. Yet at the back of her mind she was deeply worried. Men like Edward Cutler somehow always got their way. What if......? Climbing up in the buggy she watched and waited until he was out of sight, then she guided the horses back on the road that would take them to the church. She would remember, however, to tell Derek as soon as she could about her confrontation with a rat.

\*     \*     \*     \*

Forest had to admit that it felt good to put her anger aside and give Quentin a chance to redeem himself. Moses had been right about forgiving and forgetting. There was a difference. She forgave Quentin for his past wrongdoing but in her heart she knew she could never forget what had happened that fateful day.

"If it had been up to me, I would have stayed away, but Moses talked to me about putting what happened behind me and remembering that you have been very good to me. He brought me back here so that we can have a chance to mend our relationship and have hope for the future," she had said.

"He's a good man! I owe him a great deal. He brought you back to me," Quentin stated, blinking away impending tears. It was obvious by the dark circles under his eyes that he hadn't gotten much sleep.

"He is a great man and I love him," she replied, looking out the window wistfully as she watched him disappear down the road. Moses had promised to join them for supper that evening and she knew the hours would drag by until then.

"And it is obvious that he is quite fond of you too. I couldn't be happier." Moving to his desk, Quentin picked up his pen. He liked to call it his very best weapon. "The pen is mightier than the sword," he liked to say, quoting Edward Bulwer-Lytton. "And writing is our key to immortality."

"I want to spend my whole life with him," Forest said more to herself than to Quentin.

He looked up from his writing. "Ah, the love of the young. If only it were that simple. But love can fly out the window when life gets trying. Before you

299

commit yourself to a lifetime with anyone you need to make some plans."

Plans? "What do you mean exactly?" She had expected Quentin to be enthusiastic about the idea of Moses being part of the family.

"He needs to be able to support you without working his life away." In frustration he toyed with the pen. "If only I could get that boy interested in politics I know he could have a very bright future. Why just his name---Moses. What better name could a man have than that of a legend who parted the Red Sea and took his people to their promised land. I tell you he would be inundated with votes."

"If you are that impassioned why don't you talk with him at supper this evening? All he can tell you is no. No. A hundred times no." Or would he tell Quentin yes? Forest wondered just how well she really did know Moses. She had thought she knew Quentin and he had surprised her.

Nodding, Quentin changed the subject. "I thought we would have fried squirrel for supper."

"Squirrel?" For just a moment she was horrified, fearing that he meant to eat the cute little rodents that she had befriended in the yard behind the house. But then she saw that he was only teasing her.

"While you were gone, I wanted to clear my mind and heal my heart so I went fishing. I caught four fish. Moses told me to use grasshoppers as bait and his advice was perfect." That said, Quentin got back to his writing.

"Fish." Forest approved because it was an easy meal to fix. She would dip the fish in buttermilk then sprinkle it with flour and pepper before putting it in the frying pan. It would go well with carrots and squash. If she had time she could even bake a cake. Vanilla with chocolate frosting. She knew that Moses loved chocolate. Before she started cooking, however, there were questions that needed to be asked.

"Do you know what happened to my mother?"

Her question startled Quentin because he dropped his pen. "No!"

"Then you don't know whether or not she is still alive." The fear that her mother might be dead was like a shroud hovering over her emotions.

Quentin answered but didn't turn around or look up from his papers. "After I encountered you and took you to a hiding place where you would be safe, I cut all my ties with the others. I'm sorry, Forest. I would like to tell you that all is well and that your mother is living a contented life, but the truth is I don't know."

"I was told that William Trenholm is my real father. Did you know him?"

This time Quentin put down his pen and turned around to face her. "I didn't know him but I knew *of* him. He was not a very congenial or trustworthy man. It was said that he worked his slaves to near death. He was known to be a liar and a cheat. I'm sorry Forest. I wish I could tell you that he was worthy of your respect and love."

"Was he the one who sent the slave catchers after us?" There were so many questions whirling in her mind. She wanted to know everything that led up to the fateful day that had changed her life forever.

"I think he must have been, but I was not the one he contacted. I just did as I was told." For a long while Quentin remained silent, staring off into space as if reliving the events of that tragic day.

"Was Andrew Wyatt the one?" The seed of anger in her heart continued to grow.

"No, Andrew was nearly as unimportant as I. We all received our orders from Samuel."

"Samuel?"

"Samuel Ferrell."

Forest made a mental note of that name. "Somehow I will find him. Someday I will learn about my mother. And when I do there will be all hell to pay."

With that vow said, forest turned and walked to the kitchen. Gathering all the items that were needed for the evening meal, Forest put on her apron, heated the stove, and began preparations for her culinary feast.

*     *     *     *

It was late. Much later than Moses had realized. Hurrying back to his house he flung open the door and went inside, surprised by how empty it seemed without *her*. Although Forest had only been there one day, she had touched his house as if by magic and turned it into a home.

*Was I a fool to take her back home*? he asked himself. No. He knew in his heart that she belonged with Quentin and the safety he offered her, at least until things quieted down a bit. But oh, how he was anxious to hold her in his arms again.

Although he was dead tired, Moses somehow

302

found the strength to pull off his work clothes, wash himself, search through the newly folded garments in his makeshift closet for something to wear tonight. He settled on a tan pair of trousers, brown boots, and a white shirt with green and black trim. Although not usually vain he examined himself in the mirror and had to admit that he liked what he saw. He was a damned fine-looking Negro if he did say so himself. He only hoped that Forest thought the same thing.

Because he was already late for dinner, Moses didn't take the time to pick any flowers. Instead he saddled one of the horses and was just about to mount when he saw something alarming. Torches held aloft by a group of men coming his way on horseback. Fearfully he craned his neck and started to run back to the house to get his rifle but as if out of nowhere he saw that two men stood in front of his door, blocking it from entry.

The sound of hoof beats echoed in his ears as the men rode closer, dressed not in white but in black to help them blend into the darkness. Moses knew there was no chance of escape. His only hope was that he could reason with these men. They had no quarrel with him.

"Evening." Moses pretended that seeing armed men, garbed in black and wearing hoods, carrying rifles and riding on horseback, was the most normal thing in the world.

"You goin' someplace, Nigrah?" The man rode up alongside him. It was just the kind of man he wanted to protect Forest from. Now he was glad she wasn't here.

"Yes, I have an appointment with a friend, Sir," he answered, acting in a deferential matter he knew they expected from those with darker skin. Moses quickly counted the invaders. One, two, three, four, and five. More than he could overthrow and defeat.

"You the owner of this land?" the shortest of the five seemed to be even more brazen than his companions.

Ordinarily Moses would have told the truth, but knowing the anger that former slavers felt towards Negroes owning land he lied. "No, Sir. I am merely working dis land, I is," he said, talking as he once did when he was a slave. Men like this expected as much. "De owner, he is away, but he be coming back soon."

"He's a god damned liar. That young Nigrah lover Cameron, the son, gave him this land."

Moses tensed every muscle in his body.

The obvious leader of the gang asked in raspy tone, "You lyin' to me, Nigrah?" Before Moses even had time to blink, the man slid down from his horse and lunged at Moses. One of the men who had ridden with that man joined forces, making it a fist-flaying free-for-all. Moses winced as he felt the full force of a blow cut his lip, then another hit him in the eye. Then he was down.

"Just a little something to help you learn a lesson," the man chided. "We don't cotton to Nigrah's telling untruths."

Although Moses wanted nothing more than to get up and give these men as good as he was given, he stayed on the ground, hoping a drubbing would be the end of it.

"Well, I hear that telling lies isn't all this Nigrah has been doing." The man who had been blocking the door to Moses' house stepped forward. "I hear this black bastard has been having his way with a white woman."

Every nerve in Moses' body was on alert as he realized what the man was saying and that he meant Forest. He could have explained everything right then and there---told them that like him she was Negro, or at least partly so, but out of his love for her he kept his silence saying only, "I am sorry, Sir, but you are wrong. I haven't touched any woman at all."

"Liar. I saw you touching her when I looked through the window. You'll not be telling fibs when your tongue is hanging out and your face is purple." With a nod of his head, he brought three of the men running, their rifles pointed in Moses' direction.

Moses didn't want to die! He hadn't prepared himself to meet his maker just yet, but what could he do. If he ran they would shoot him, if he fought they would beat him into unconsciousness, if he cowered they would merely toy with him and then hang him anyway. Wasn't that what these cowardly masked renegades did?

"Lynch the lyin' black bastard. Do it!" The leader of the group seemed to be in a hurry to get his evil accomplished so he could make a hasty escape.

"Aw, that isn't a way to act Christian," Moses heard one of the men say. "Would you like me to say a prayer?"

"Or maybe he would like to kiss the good book before we send him on to God." "The man pulled out a Bible from beneath his shirt. Moses thought how odd it was that the man had come equipped with a bible in his belt, but he didn't say a word.

"Get up, Nigrah!" A jab to Moses' ribs brought

him to his feet and hastened him along.

"We gotta find a tree. Can't hang this darkie from thin air." The voice was from someone who hadn't spoken up yet. Who was he, Moses wondered?

"There's one over there."

With horror Moses looked towards a tree he had been meaning to cut down a few days ago. Now it was going to be the place of his execution by this bunch of bullies.

"Please. Don't do this. I haven't done anything to harm anybody. Please." He thought of Forest and how if he died they would never have a chance to make love. Closing his eyes, he could see her face and the true sense of his loss nearly brought him to tears.

"Hear that, boys. He's pleading for his life. What do you say? Shall we take a vote?"

The voices were beginning to sound alike. Moses felt a shiver of fear travel up his spine. Were they just toying with him or did they really mean to hang him?

"I say hang him. But first let's have a bit of fun." The man who had spoken nodded to two other men. Laughing those two men held Moses with his arms behind his back while the third man pulled Moses' pants down.

"I heard these Nigrah's were hung like horses. Let's see if it is true!"

Every bit of Moses' self respect withered as he helplessly stood there with his trousers around his ankles. He remembered seeing slaves being examined at slave markets and now truly understood how they must have felt. It was dehumanizing. Soul-

306

shattering. It turned a man into nothing better than an animal.

"Damn. Will you look at that! Twice the size of yours, Aubrey!"

"Is not! At least when I was much younger I was as big as that."

Laughter crackled in the air.

"Maybe instead of hanging him we should just geld him right here and now. Then turn him loose."

"We can't now that you spoke my name, you stupid fool." The man named "Aubrey" was obviously angry.

"Then let's move on to that tree."

They pushed and shoved Moses, snickering as he tried to walk with his trousers pulled down. At last after they had gone a short distance, they gave him time to pull his pants back up. Looking first to the right then to the left, Moses searched desperately for a way to escape. There was none. But perhaps it would be better to take a bullet in the back than to endure what they had planned for him.

"Do you have any last words?"

Any last words? Moses had a thousand words he wanted to say but once again he pleaded for his life. "Don't do this. You will have my death on your conscience." A rapid succession of emotions stormed through his brain.

"Conscience? Conscience? As if any of us have one."

"The rope."

Moses watched soundlessly as they reached the tree and flung the rope over one of the sturdiest

307

branches. One of the men secured it and when he was done, he stepped back. "Come on, let's get this over with."

It seemed they were in a hurry to hang him. Beads of perspiration trickled down Moses' brow as he was pushed forward. He felt the thick hemp go around his neck, so tightly that he felt as if he were going to choke.

*So, this is the way I'm going to meet my death.* Such a tragic fate. Senseless. Stupid. He wanted to scream, wanted to cry, wanted to beg again and again for them not to kill him. But that was what they wanted and he was determined that was not the satisfaction he would give them. Not him. Not now. Not ever.

## Chapter Twenty-Three

Derek was in a foul mood as he flicked the reins and guided the buggy over the rutted ground. Amelia had told him about her encounter with Edward Cutler and how she had found his words worrisome. Normally he wouldn't have been concerned had it not been for the convoluted bookkeeping of his father and the missing finances. But Cutler's mention of the Freedman bank and his reference to the devaluation of silver deeply troubled Derek. That was why right after dinner he had decided to go see Moses and discuss the matter.

*"It's late. Must you go alone?"* Amelia had asked him, volunteering to accompany him. In order to soothe her anxieties, he had agreed to take a rifle with him just in case there was any trouble. It was a Henry repeating rifle so he felt secure.

There were some questions he wanted to ask Moses. He knew that the bank had nineteen branches in twelve states and that the bank was under the direct authority of Congress and issued loans backed by real estate, but what else did they know about it? How secure was it? After all, he remembered how the Confederate currency had been reduced to worthless shreds of paper right after the war.

Looking up at the sky he could see the half moon overhead and the ions of twinkling stars. It was a clear and windless night. The kind of night for a romantic walk outside, but instead of enjoying Amelia's loveliness he was once again trying to guard the family's assets. Would his obligations ever cease?

Turning his attentions back on the road, Derek was certain that his eyes were playing tricks on him. It looked as if five stars had come down to earth and were twinkling in the distance. He shook his head, assuming that he was seeing some kind of reflection or imagined apparition, but the flickering light remained in his line of vision. Suddenly he realized what it was. Torches!

Remembering the fire at the school he urged the horses into a frantic gallop. The flickering flames were near Moses' property. He could see shadows. Could see five men in a circle around another man. A man with a rope around his neck. They were near a tree and as he came closer Derek knew he was witnessing a lynching.

"Moses!" Dear God, it appeared that he was too late. He could see that his friend was already dangling from a rope, his legs and arms twitching.

Derek knew he had to think fast if he had any chance of saving his friend's life. Driving the buggy at full speed he guided it to the spot Moses was hanging and rammed him in such a manner that Moses' body landed on the buggy's seat with a thud.

"Hey, what the hell are you doin'?"

"You're not wanted here."

Picking up the rifle Derek shouted out, "untie him or I swear I will kill you all." As he saw the men go for their own guns, he shot a warning bullet at the feet of the man who appeared to be the leader. "I mean it. Reach for your gun and I will put a bullet in your gut!" He motioned for the figure closest to the wagon to lend him a knife. Watching the men out of the corner of his eye he quickly cut the rope from around Moses' neck, nicking his flesh just enough to draw a trickle of blood.

Moses' eyes were closed, he was still. Derek assumed that he was dead. It was as if a hand gripped his heart. Why? It was senseless. Murder. At that moment he knew what hatred was.

"I know who you are," he taunted. I found my father's book that has your names and signatures. Before I am through with you bastards you will be just as dead as my friend."

"Book. What book?" The man sounded worried.

Derek knew the names of the Klansmen by heart. "*Jefferson Jensen, Grand Dragon. Thomas Bedford, Grand Cyclops.* Do those names ring a bell? If not, let me call out more, *Travis James. Waylon Tucker. Walter Johnson. Edward Hadaway. William Trenholm*" His anger knew no bounds.

"Damn. How the hell…..?"

"I'll see that they hunt you down and execute every last one of you." He hoped the men would be tried, convicted, hung by the neck, and then went straight to the realm of hell.

Wait! Out of the corner of his eye Derek thought he saw Moses' body twitch. Was it possible that he was alive or in the midst of a death throe? He thought he heard a cough and a gurgle, then to his amazement Moses started to sit up.

"My God, you're alive." He waited for Moses to answer but no sound came out of his mouth. Then he remembered hearing about men who had recovered from hanging from the neck. They often were hoarse and had trouble talking and swallowing.

"You wouldn't be coddling that Nigrah if you knew what he has done. He seduced a white woman," one of the men called out.

"He did no such thing. She......." Derek was just about to tell them that the woman they had seen was of mixed blood, but Moses reached out and grabbed his arm, shaking his head "no" as he did so. Despite what had happened he wanted to protect Forest.

"I saw him with my own eyes...."

Derek pointed the gun to that spot right between the man's eyes. "I said he didn't. And I say that you are trespassing on someone else's property. And I tell you that if I see any of you again within an inch of my land, with your foolish dark nightgowns and face coverings, I will take this rifle and cram it right up your ass!" He pointed the barrel of the gun at the man who seemed to be the leader. "Then I'll take that book that condemns you all, the book I have in my possession right to the authorities. Do I make myself clear?"

There was a silence that stretched out over several heartbeats in time. Then all five heads nodded.

"What happens on this land is none of your business." Oh, how Derek wished he could see the men's faces revealed. Which men were they? He didn't know for sure. What he did know, however, was that the book he had hidden back home was worth its weight in gold. "Now get the hell out of here before I change my mind and decide to shoot you one by one then announce to the world what you all have done."

Derek watched as the men rode away, only then did he turn his attention to Moses. "Are you OK? Nod if you are."

312

Moses nodded, but he was rubbing his throat and Derek could tell he was feeling more than a bit of pain.

"I'm taking you back to Winding Oaks. There is a woman taking care of my father there and of course mother has healing skills like no other." He ignored Moses' gestures and attempts to talk. He knew what was best for his friend. Not only did Moses need medical attention but Derek thought surely that it would be better if he stayed at the mansion. There was no guarantee that the men wouldn't come back and if they did, this time they might be successful in their attempt to hang him.

*    *    *    *

Where was Moses? Forest paced the floor—up and down, back and forth---then looked out the window a hundred times or more. But her fretting didn't bring him to the front door and the longer they waited the more concerned she became. Moses wouldn't just not show up. That wasn't like him at all. Something had happened. Something that didn't bode any good.

"Forest, you are going to wear a hole in the floor if you don't stop pacing. Your anxiety isn't going to bring him here by some kind of magic." Quentin meant to sooth her fears but as Forest looked into his eyes she could see that he was worried too.

"There has been Klan activity near his farm. A schoolhouse was burned to the ground and a young Negro boy burned to death. And Moses was vandalized. He wanted to protect me but I should have been there to protect *him*!"

313

"Nonsense! If anything serious happened to him you would most likely have been harmed as well. Fools rush in where angels fear to tread, Forest. Or so Alexander Pope has said."

Usually Forest didn't argue with Quentin but she did so now. "And Edmund Burke said 'the only thing necessary for the triumph of evil is for good men to do nothing.' And that includes women as well, or so I would assume." She waited for Quentin to contradict her but instead he laughed softly.

"Bravo.   Bravo!   I have taught you well." Plucking his suit coat from the rack he moved towards the door and looked back at her. "Make sure the fire on the stove is out then join me in the buggy. We are going to go see your young man and if there is anything amiss we will come to his aid."

Forest hurried to the kitchen and made certain the fire had died down in the stove. Looking at the table set with plates, forks and spoons, and the food she had prepared all in serving bowls, she fought against the melancholy and fear that threatened to overwhelm her. They were going to Moses' aid, that was the important matter. If he was in any kind of predicament, they were on their way. Grabbing a light shawl in case there was a chill in the night breeze she joined Quentin in the carriage and they were off.

"Do you know the way?" Quentin asked.

"Vaguely, she answered truthfully. She had been so troubled by what had happened with Quentin that she had not really kept watch on where Moses was going.

"Do I turn left or right on the road up ahead?"

"Right." She tried hard to remember. "Then turn left on the road following. Moses' farm is at the far

314

corner of the Winding Oaks Plantation lands."

"Ah, Winding Oaks. I know very well where that is located. I'm afraid the Camerons have a rather shady reputation. Charles that is."

"Do you have a gun with you?" Although Forest knew that Quentin had an aversion for weapons she knew that in this instance they might need to be armed.

"I did. A pistol. But I hope beyond hope that I will not have to use it."

Forest hoped so too, but as they approached the house it was obvious that something disastrous had happened. Approaching a tall tree with an overhanging branch they could see a severed rope swaying back and forth in the breeze. Jumping out of the buggy as soon as Quentin pulled it to a halt, Forest ran to that rope and examined it carefully. It was obvious that it had been a noose but that the fatal loop had been sliced in two.

"Looks like there was a lynching!"

Quentin's words sounded an alarm within Forest's soul.

"No!" Not wanting to believe the worst, she hurried to the house. There were no lights on inside and although she kept banging on the door no one answered.

"Forest!" Coming up behind her Quentin was prepared to deal with whatever had occurred. "You must stay calm…"

"Stay calm?" How could she when it appeared that the most important person in her life might have been taken from her. And for what reason?

Quentin looked in the window. "I don't see

anyone moving about inside. They might have taken him somewhere." He didn't want her to even guess what might have happened to Moses but he knew. It was not uncommon for those who perpetrated such violent acts to burn their victim's bodies or possibly dismember them to hide their atrocities.

"Where would they have taken him? Where?" She felt a rising tide of hysteria but bravely pushed it aside. Picking up an axe she hefted it like a lumberjack and broke the lock. Lighting the lamp inside she searched everywhere."

"He is not here, Forest." Quentin grasped her by the shoulders and forced her to go to the door. "I'm so sorry."

"Moses' friend is Derek Cameron. We must hurry to the plantation house and let him know what has happened. He might be able to help us." Extinguishing the lamp, she closed the door and hastened to the buggy with Quentin following close behind her.

*     *     *     *

The Cameron mansion was a huge two-stored white manor with six columns soaring into the air, a true symbol of the South. Forest gazed in wonder, thinking to herself that it would take eight cottages like Quentin's to equal it in size. Her eyes took in the broad porch, decorated with potted plants, flowers and carved wooden benches and the window shutters of forest green. The house was perfect in every detail, as if sculptured by a master's hand, or so she thought. The kind of house she had seen in her dreams.

Quentin walked towards the house with a bearing straight and proud, not overly impressed. Perhaps because he had seen mansions like this many times. "Come on, Forest. Don't be timid. That's not at all like you." He raised his hand to the big brass knob on the front door, but before he had the chance to touch it, the door was opened by a very pretty woman with red-blond hair, dressed in a pale green dress that highlighted her peaches and cream complexion.

"I have come to see Derek Cameron," Forest exclaimed, eager to get Derek's help in finding Moses.

"Derek?" For just a moment the woman faltered and looked a bit wary. Who was this stunning dark-haired woman who was asking to see him?

For a long drawn out moment both women assessed each other as women often do. Sizing each other up from head to toe and then back again they were a bit guarded, until Forest quickly explained the tragedy that had ensued that very evening.

"You're Forest!" As Forest nodded Amelia took her by the hand. "Moses is here. Mrs. O'Leary and Honora are tending to him. Come with me. After all that has happened he will be so glad that you are here."

"He's here? He's alive!" Forest felt her heart leap up in her throat. Moses hadn't been taken captive or killed then. Wordlessly she followed Amelia upstairs.

"I must warn you. He is having trouble talking because he is hoarse. The rope those Klansmen put around his neck caused a bit of damage to his throat. And he was beaten so he is bruised, bloodied, and battered. But he is alive."

317

"Alive!" It was as if her prayers were answered. As Amelia opened the door and Forest got a glimpse of Moses lying so still on the bed with two women hovering near him, she nearly cried. But Moses didn't need a show of emotions right now he needed good care which the women could give him-- and love, which Forest knew she had in abundance.

"Go on in. I know from experience how strong love can be. Seeing you will be the best medicine anyone could give him."

Watching him writhe in pain, Forest felt his suffering as if it were she who had been assaulted. A tremor of apprehension ran through her, a deep fear that he might not survive. The possibility struck her like a physical blow.

"Moses...."

At the sound of her voice he tried to lift his head. A strange sound came from his throat and she was saddened to realize he was trying to call out her name. Hurrying forward she came to his side and knelt beside him, reaching out to him. Despite his agony Moses clutched tightly to her hand, his face contorted with pain.

"Don't try to talk. When you didn't come to dinner Quentin and I went to your house. We saw evidence of what those terrible men did to you. I knew about your friendship with Derek so I came here to get his help and here you are." She nuzzled her check against his hand.

Honora took notice of the way the two were looking at each other and smiled. "He was very lucky that my son came by his house when he did. If he hadn't arrived in time the consequences would have been tragic."

"I know." As Forest looked around she at last saw Derek, sitting on a stuffed chair in the corner. She turned to look at him. "From the bottom of my heart I thank you. I would have died if I had lost him."

"So would I." Standing up, Derek came to Moses' side. "I shudder to think what his fate would have been tonight if I hadn't ridden out to talk with him about a financial matter. Or if I hadn't known some secrets that were more useful than ammunition." He looked towards Amelia, conveying a message that only the two of them could share.

It seemed that immediately Honora took Forest under her wing. "I know how much you care about him. Would you like to stay here, at least for tonight?"

Forest felt uncomfortable accepting hospitality from someone she didn't even know. She hesitated at first but longing to be by Moses' side she at last nodded. "Are the servant's quarters nearby?" She wanted to be close enough that she could look in on Moses.

"The servants' quarters? Oh, no, no, no. Moses is like a son to me. And if you are important to him then you also will be part of our family. There are two rooms on this floor that you and your father may call your own while you are here."

Forest was wary at first because most white women she had known in the past could be gossipy and cruel, but Honora Cameron emanated compassion and sincerity. "Thank you from me and from Quentin."

Watching the lovely newcomer in their midst, Amelia decided at once that she truly liked her. There

319

was something about Forest that reminded her of
herself. Despite the seriousness of the situation she
smiled at the thought that Honora was matchmaking
once again.

## Chapter Twenty-Four

The flickering flames of the oil lamp illuminated the face of the man lying on the bed. Honora had given him a dose of laudanum so he was at last sleeping soundly. As she watched him sleep, Forest gently wiped the perspiration from his face, feeling his plight tug on her heart. She could hardly imagine what it must have been like to be hung from a tree, not to mention the terror he must have felt to be surrounded by men who had declared themselves his enemies.

"You are alive. You were not taken from me. We have our whole lives together to look forward to. I knew that I loved you, but I didn't realize just how much until this moment."

Honora and Mrs. O'Leary had removed his shirt and trousers in order to tend his injuries and now she let her eyes roam over what she could see of his body. His arms and chest were well-muscled, and she remembered their strength when he had held her. A tuft of black hair lightly covered his broad chest and trailed in a thin straight line down to his navel. He was perfect in every way.

"Your skin is a few shades darker than mine and for this you nearly paid with your life!" It was so unimaginable that there were still men who hated other men for this ridiculous reason. She wondered if there was really any hope for mankind and decided that there had to be, or all was lost.

As if sensing her searching eyes, Moses stirred in his sleep, a soft groan escaping from his mouth.

"You are safe now. There is no one here who will harm you. Rest," she whispered. His pain tugged at her heart. In his defenseless slumber he brought out all the protective instincts within her and she vowed to do everything in her power to see that he would be safe from this moment on. Reaching for a linen sheet, she pulled it over his half-nude form.

"How is he?" She recognized the voice as Amelia's. How could she ever thank the women in the Cameron household for their help tonight?

Forest turned around to look into the kind eyes of a woman she knew understood her emotional pain. "He's in a deep slumber from the sleeping draft Honora gave him, but so far there is no sign of a fever or infection."

"I know that if Derek was lying in that bed right now I would be distraught, but like you I would stay by his side. Love will help in his healing. I really do believe that."

"I have your Derek to thank for Moses' life. If not for him......" Just thinking about the consequences of no one stepping in to save Moses caused Forest to put her hands up to her eyes to hide the tears sparkling there.

Amelia sat down on a chair by the bed. "They have been friends since they were born. They grew up together. I don't know if Moses related the story to you."

Forest looked up and nodded. "He did. They have been much more than just friends. I sometimes think Derek considers Moses his brother. They have been through so much with the war and the aftermath

322

and such."

Amelia reached out and touched Forest on the shoulder. "I heard about how kind you were to Moses when he was on the run, traveling on the Underground Railroad. You must be a very special kind of woman. I know I would like to be your friend."

Returning the pressure of Amelia's hand Forest said, "I would like that two. Moses told me that you are a teacher and that you aren't afraid to teach little children with dark skin despite the risk you run for yourself to do so. That makes you even more special than me."

The two women might have talked more but as Moses cried out Forest's name in his sleep, Amelia left the room so that the two could be alone.

Touching his face with her hand, Forest reassured Moses that he was all right. "I'm here. I won't leave you. I promise."

And she kept that vow, long into the night until the light from the oil lamp sputtered, then died. Exhaustion was starting to overcome her, the excitement and worry of the day taking a toll.

Lying down next to Moses on the large bed, Forest sought her own slumber, feeling serene in the comfort of the warmth of his male body. Despite the circumstances, the danger, and his condition, she felt giddy at his closeness, in much the same manner as when she had partaken of too much wine that day at his house. She drifted off to sleep with his head on her shoulder, his arms and legs carefully entwined with her own.

# ASHES AND AWAKENINGS

*   *   *   *

Moses was lost to his haze of dreams, frantic visions which tortured him as he twisted and turned in the throes of sleep. They were going to hang him. Mutilate him. But he wouldn't tell them about Jemma. No, he wouldn't. He couldn't. They would harm her as well. But he needed to warn her. But how? The rope was biting into his neck, it was keeping him prisoner. He couldn't run. Couldn't walk. Couldn't get to his horse. He was helpless! Again, he tried to cry out but his words were soundless. All he could manage was a moan. He reached out his hand, grasping, groping like a drowning man, wanting to escape, to get away from this madness.

His loud, raspy groans woke Forest. Fearing that his thrashing about would do harm to his injuries, she sought to quiet him, putting her hands on the center of his chest to hold him down.

In the haze of his dreams Moses felt the hands upon his chest and tried desperately to escape them. It was as if he were walking down a long tunnel, moving toward a light, but someone was holding him back, trying to keep him from his destination. But he couldn't see the villain's face. Reaching out to clutch at the throat of the faceless man he wanted to destroy him. He reached up to squeeze the neck of his enemy.

Forest fought wildly against the strength of the hands which held her. His fevered energy was nearly more than she could manage as she sought to tear his fingers from her slender neck. He was choking her; she couldn't breathe. He must have envisioned her as

324

his enemy.

She tried to call out for help, but no sound escaped her lips until at last she managed to gasp, "It is Jemma. Jemma. Forest."

He recognized her name and his hold upon her loosened. Forest's heart was still pounding wildly in her breast as she sought to calm her trembling. A nightmare had caused his violence and she wondered what demon he had been grappling with. Had he perhaps recognized one of the men?

"It's only a bad dream," she said softly, reaching out to touch his brow. There was no sign of a fever. The laudanum then? Her words soothed him, for he quieted.

Fearing that his thrashing about had reopened the cut on his throat, she gently examined it with her fingers. At her touch he stiffened and issued forth a moan, but the wound was dry and the rope burn on his neck didn't seem to be blistering. The bandages had held tight.

Her voice seemed to quell his nightmare and he relaxed and she imagined she saw him smile. He knew she was with him somehow. She felt the warm, soft touch of his fingers upon her breast, sending a shiver of desire coursing through her blood. His hand cupped the tender flesh, caressing the peak through the thin material of her dress with infinite tenderness. She moved her hand with the intent to remove the fingers, but the sensation was so stirring that she somehow could not bear to do so.

His exploring hand moved lower, sliding over her small waist to rest on the full curve of her hip. The shock of pleasure took her breath away and she shivered, making a vow that as soon as he was healed they would consummate the strong feelings of emotion they had for each other. Seeking his warmth, she nestled close to his body once again. His strength enveloped her and she raised her hand to touch his face. Somehow, she had the feeling that she was dreaming too. If that was true, then she never wanted to awaken. She wanted to be with him like this forever.

Moses awakened just briefly to the realization that he held the vision of loveliness tightly in his arms. He had dreamed about her so many times, and now she was with him. He brushed his fingers over her cheek, tracing the curves of her ear, tangling his fingers in her hair. For the moment, his memories were pleasant ones, chasing away his nightmares. Closing his eyes, he

entered a dream world of his own making and welcomed that blissful mist of slumber.

\*    \*    \*    \*

Amelia lay down upon the bed and snuggled into the warmth of Derek's arms, her head against his chest. If only she could remain in his arms forever, safe from the cruelty and ignorance of the world like what had happened to Moses tonight.

"What are you thinking?" His voice was barely more than a whisper.

"How happy I am here with you, that I wish it could always be this way. That I feel safe in your arms."

Reaching out, he caressed her. Her body was perfection. How he loved the smooth soft skin of her body, the peaks of her breasts, the taste of her skin, the fragrance of her hair.

"Are you hungry?" she asked innocently. "You missed dinner and haven't had a bite to eat all night."

"Hungry for you," he answered, opening his eyes to look at her lovely face. "I long to find myself nestled in your velvety softness." Feverishly he kissed her, his lips teasing hers until the assault left her breathless.

Reaching up to fasten her arms around his back, she clung to him, pulling him closer and she returned his kisses with wild abandon. His hands and mouth moved over her body, bringing forth a rippling fire of pleasure, and she in turn stroked his back, her soft hands at last sliding down to touch, to explore his male hardness.

Wrapping his fingers in her hair, he buried his face in the long silky strands, inhaling deeply of the sweet rose fragrance. "You are the one I love, more than anything else in this world," he mumbled against her hair.

Gently he pressed her down among the pillows, his mouth tracing a path of flame across the flat plain of her stomach. There was not an inch of her he did not know already, but he wanted to rediscover the glory of her, arouse her to the highest heights, bring her the greatest of pleasure.

Amelia felt the ripples of desire course through her blood like the sparks of a radiating fire consuming her as he probed gently between her legs. His manhood was sheathed within the moist softness of her body like a sword in a scabbard. Although they had made love several times before this, this time their joining was filled with a frenzy as they surged together. Amelia held on to him tightly as the world seemed to quake beneath them, arching to him, moving with him as powerful shudders swept through them both. Clinging to each other, they glided slowly back to earth to drift off into a contented slumber once again.

When Amelia awoke it was to find Derek sitting on the edge of the bed looking down at her. "Breakfast awaits you, my love," he said, gesturing toward the oak table. Spread out on a white linen cloth was a veritable feast.

"But I should have brought breakfast to you since you were the hero of the night," she answered. Getting out of bed she wrapped a sheet around her nakedness and walked towards the table. There was a small box wrapped in white tissue paper. On top of the box was a red rose.

"Open it," he said softly.

Amelia felt like a child again, waiting to see what Santa had brought. She remembered that after she went to live with Aunt Lucinda Santa Claus never came again. Aunt Lucinda had said it was because Santa didn't have her new address.

"It's been a long time since I received a gift," she said, her fingers trembling as she tore off the tissue and opened the box. Inside was the most beautiful sapphire ring she had ever seen. In addition to the gemstone it was embellished with filigree and delicate engravings. "It's beautiful!"

"It belonged to my grandmother, Victoria. I will tell you all about her as you eat. She was a very unique woman. It was her engagement ring."

"Engagement?" She didn't dare hope.

"I love you and I want you to marry me. Will you?" It was time they began a life together. Seeing the love Forest and Moses shared reminded him of his own feelings for Amelia.

She didn't play coy. "Yes! And I love you too." She held out her hand, smiling as he put the ring on the ring finger of her left hand. "You know the Ancient Romans believed that the ring finger had a vein that ran directly to the heart, the Vena Amoris, meaning the vein of love," she said softly.

Sitting down to eat, Amelia eyed the dishes before her: biscuits with sausage gravy, grits, baked beans left over from dinner two days before, and an assortment of fruits—apples, plums, and pears. He had also brought tea, knowing that she preferred it over coffee.

"Heavens," she exclaimed with a laugh. "If I eat all of this, I will grow fat as a pig and then you won't love me at all."

"Fat or thin, I would love you," he answered, taking a seat opposite her. The food was delicious and as they ate, he told her all about the woman whose ring she now wore.

"My grandmother, Victoria, was quite an interesting woman. Her family had made a fortune from tobacco and my grandfather's family also had a lucrative tobacco plantation. It was an arranged marriage." He took a bite of an apple, then after swallowing it he continued. "It was rumored that her new husband, Stephen, my grandfather, had trafficked in smuggled goods but she ignored the rumors and delighted in spending his money. In return she bore him two sons, Charles, my father, and Nathaniel who is my uncle. When my grandfather died she had to run the plantation on her own. Like you she was lovely, intelligent, and strong. And those are the traits I want in my wife."

She was also reflective. "Like you my father had a brave heart and a kind manner. I remember that he was never too busy to spend time with me, even if it meant drinking pretend tea from my miniature tea set or fixing my doll if it lost an arm or a leg. He was the one who encouraged me to learn and to become a teacher one day." Looking up from her plate, Amelia realized Derek was studying her. "What is it?"

His voice was soft. "I was just thinking that someday when we have children I hope they will speak as well of me as you do of your father."

Talk of children made her blush. "They will. I know you will be a good father."

They ate the rest of the meal in silence, each deep in their own thoughts. As usual Amelia hurried to dress after they were finished. It was early and she could sneak off to her own room before anyone noticed. Or so she hoped.

## Chapter Twenty-Five

Moses awoke as the first pale pink streaks of the dawn's light filtered through the small window of the bedroom. He opened his eyes slowly, expecting full well to be within the accustomed confines of his house, but instead he was in an unfamiliar bedroom. His heart quickened as he stiffened, eyes opening wide to take in his surroundings, recognizing it as a room in Derek's family plantation house. That familiarity was the catalyst that brought back his horrific memories of what had happened last night.

"A lynching. Me. Those bastards!" he croaked, putting his hand to his throat. Remembering the violence and threats of the evening he moved his hand down to his crotch, fearfully exploring but thankfully finding out they had not carried out their threat. *They* were still intact.

*Thank God for Derek*, he thought, though only remembering a few details of his friend's rescue of him. Everything was in a fog, his thoughts muggy and scattered. He remembered being set upon by those five dangerous men, remembered the threats, the physical assault, the rope going around his neck. He remembered feeling the rope tighten, choking life's breath from his lungs. He had begged for his life but they had laughed and spit in his face. They had tried to humiliate him and in that they had succeeded much to his regret.

331

He could hear the steady breathing of the young woman who lay beside him and he turned his head in that direction to stare into her sleeping face. Forest! She was with him. He seemed to remember her voice soothing him as he lay there in his dazed slumber.

"I was not dreaming," he breathed, assailed by the memory of being held close in her arms as she tried to bring him comfort. As he looked down at her he saw her eyes flutter open and he felt a sense of well-being and of love. Once again, she was by his side when he needed her. He started to reach out to her but the effort only brought forth pain. So, he had not gotten away totally unscathed.

Moses' face was etched with pain, yet still such a handsome face. His dark eyelashes cast a shadow on his cheekbones, and his full lips were parted as he drew in a shallow breath. "Move slowly when you move," Forest whispered. "You might have a rib or two cracked I heard Honora say."

*There is such a strength about him, even in his wounded state*," she thought. This time she could not resist the urge to caress him, and let her fingers touch his lips.

The heat of his body was arousing as they lay curled up together, his uninjured arm flung across her stomach, his leg resting between hers in a position of intimacy. They seemed to fit together with perfect unity as if made each for the other. She spread her hand over his chest and felt the light furring of hair there, heard the beat of his heart, and closed her eyes in contentment.

The sound of the household moving about – Amelia, Derek, Honora, and Mrs. O'Leary who had spent the night, awakened her and Forest realized they had fallen back asleep. Easing herself onto her elbow, slowly so as not to waken the man beside her, she let her eyes drift down his body once again. She could see that the bruises, cuts, and swelling seemed to be healing properly and felt relieved that Honora and Mrs. O'Leary were skilled at healing. Her gaze moved lower, lingering on his chest and hips in a manner that was quite familiar and very bold. Having slept alone all her life, she now wondered what it would be like to awaken to this man beside her, his arms about her possessively, his hands tangled in the long strands of her hair, for all the mornings of her life.

A rasp of air as Moses tried to speak startled her and she looked up to find the penetrating brown depths of his eyes staring at her. His efforts to make himself understood troubled her. Leaning closer to him she tried to comprehend what he was saying but it was a struggle for both of them to communicate.

He swore beneath his breath. His jaw tightened in anger as the memory of his near lynching came back to him full force. He tried to sit up in bed, but he was still much too weak. His vulnerability shattered him. He couldn't lounge around in bed, he had work to do.

"You will gain back your strength. Mrs. O'Leary says that she knows of healing herbs that will soon have you back on your feet. Trust me."

He nodded that he did trust her, trusted all of them. He knew he was safe here. She looked at him and saw in his eyes the depth of emotion that was overwhelming and spoke more clearly than words could ever have done.

Shaking his head, Moses seemed agitated that he

333

could not make his thoughts clear but Forest solved the problem by going to the desk in the bedroom and picking up a fountain pen, and a piece of paper.

"Use these," she exclaimed.

His voice was a croak, a whisper as he fought against the fatigue which threatened to engulf him. "Thank you," he managed to say.

Forest could sense his frustration at being struck down at a time when he so needed to be strong, yet she knew that were he to attempt to go back to his house it could mean collapse. There was also the added danger of the men coming back to finish what they had started. He would be no match for his enemies in his weakened state.

She tried to read his thoughts as she watched him scratching frantically on the paper. "Derek said he is going to go over to your fields and take care of your plants."

"Tell him thank you," he wrote. "I owe him my life. I want him to know I am aware of that."

She read what he had written and nodded. "I will."

Something else seemed to be troubling him. He gathered all his energy to sit up, his long legs dangling over the bed, his hand reaching out to steady himself on the bedpost. On shaky legs he sought to stand, to walk, only to sink in desperation to the hard-wooden floor.

Forest was at his side in an instant, offering her arms to him, pulling him to his feet, then pushing him back gently onto the bed.

"Damn! Damn!" he gasped. He seemed to be condemning himself.

334

"You didn't do anything at all to deserve this. You can't be blamed that there is hatred in this world."

He nodded and leaned against her, his breath stirring her hair. "Quentin."

"He's here with me. When you didn't show up for dinner we knew something had happened and went to your house."

That admission from her deeply troubled him. What if they had crossed paths with the Klansmen? They might have been harmed as well. He shook his head no, over and over again.

"You're troubled that we might have encountered those men. I promise you that Quentin and I will be very, very careful going forward. With monsters on the loose it is impossible to tell what could happen. I realize that." Reaching out she caressed his hair until he had settled down. They were so engaged with each other that they did not hear the door open until they heard a loud gasp.

"Who are you?"

Turning around Forest was sure that they were seeing some kind of poltergeist or wraith from hell. With his long gray hair flying in all directions, his eyes flashing fire, his white nightshirt clinging to his skinny body he looked unworldly.

"And you. Nigrah. What are you doing in that bed? This house isn't some brothel! Get out of here right now, Moses. Out. Out, I say."

In stunned awareness Forest looked Moses full in the face, asking him silently who the man was who called out his name. As her gaze met his she was alarmed by the anger she read in Moses' eyes. It was obvious that there were unpleasant memories attached to this marauding individual. She was just about to question the man when a shriek of anger sounded behind him.

"Charles, what are you doing out of bed?" Honora was both annoyed and concerned.

"I don't want him here. And I don't even know *her*. What has become of this household?" The man swayed on his feet and looked as harmless now as he had looked threatening a moment before.

"What you want is of no concern. You are not in any shape to be issuing orders, Charles. Come back to your bed or you will answer to me." Taking him by the arm like a naughty boy, she pushed him towards the door, turning to say to Forest and Moses, "I am sorry. Disregard what he said. You both are our guests. I will make sure he doesn't bother you again."

The intrusion left Forest shaken and Moses seething with anger. He was angry about having been hung from a tree like a criminal. He was tired of being treated worse than a dog. Sick at heart that no matter what a man accomplished he was ill-treated because he had darker skin. He was finished with being treated like a slave. He had been freed. Disgusted by all the promises that had been made and not fulfilled.

Forest watched as Moses furiously scribbled on the paper. She read what he wrote. "Tell Quentin I will run for public office and I will win!" The look of determination told Forest clearly that he meant what he wrote. Moses had just joined with Quentin in the fight against the hatred and injustice of the past. He was going to become a politician and try to make a better future so that what had happened to him would

336

never happen to anyone else.

*    *    *    *

Rising before dawn Derek threw himself into work with a fury, doing the chores of two men. He had promised himself that he would take Moses' place and take care of his peanut plants while he recuperated, plus he had his own tobacco crops to tend to. With that determination on his mind, he kept on going until he ached in every muscle and his eye lids were heavy with want of sleep. And all the while he tried to control the fury that gnawed at him, anger that men that he had known since the time he was a child, friends of his father, would do something so low, so vile , as to try and lynch another man just because of their prejudices.

*Hateful old men*! Trying to hang on to a time when they were living like kings and lording it over other human beings. Cowards, afraid to face their victims without hiding their faces. Soulless individuals setting themselves up as judge, jury, and executioner without giving a person a chance to plead their case.

"And my own father was just like them," he whispered, bending down to pick up a shovel that had been discarded out in the field. Things were beginning to shape up. A second well had been dug near the place where Moses had decided to build a tool shed and he had even built a makeshift bridge across the stream near the crops for hauling materials across. It would save a lot of time and make it easier to get water to the fields.

337

Derek noticed that Moses was quickly acquiring a collection of tools, including axes of every size, hatchets and hammers, a chisel, shovel, and hoe. It was too bad that he hadn't had a chance to use one of them to defend himself when he had been cornered. Instead, the Klansmen had taken him unaware and fallen upon him in the darkness.

Pausing in his labor Derek thought back to the confrontation, glad that he had taunted them and threatened them with the fact that he knew who they were. He hoped that they were sufficiently worried. How lucky it had been for him that he had discovered that book in the old attic of the Avery House when he did. Even so, there were still many questions that he wanted answered and he was resolved to have those questions answered. He needed to make certain that there wasn't going to be a repeat of what happened to Moses.

Finishing his work on both work sites, Derek washed his hands in a bucket of water and headed back to plantation house. Without even bothering to clean himself up, he took the front stairs two at a time and made his way to his father's room. It was time to have it out with his father. The attack on Moses had changed everything.

Opening the door to the bedroom, Derek was relieved to find that his father was all alone. At the sound of the door closing, Charles Cameron opened his eyes. "I'm hungry, I want my supper." Focusing his eyes on Derek, he was surprised to see him standing there instead of either Honora or Mrs. O'Leary.

"You'll get your food in due time but first I want you to be honest with me," Derek declared.

"Honest with you." The blue eyes squinted as he stared back at his son.

"Did you really think that what you did wouldn't be found out?" *Strange*, Derek thought, *but despite his feeble state I can't find it in my heart to have any pity.*

"Found out about what?" For a moment Charles Cameron looked like a gambler who had been caught cheating.

"I was going through some things in the old Avery mansion attic. I was surprised by what I found, Father, or should I call you *Grand Titan*?" Clenching and unclenching his fists, Derek tried to control his temper.

For just a moment it looked as if Charles Cameron would choke. His voice came out in a rasp. "What on earth are you talkin' about? You....you ungrateful....."

"I found the book. With all the names of your partners in crime. So don't pretend with me!" Derek paused, watching the myriad of expressions that were exhibited on his father's face. The truth had been revealed. "Did it make you feel important and powerful to terrorize helpless men? To burn and destroy everythin' they had worked hard for. To hear them beg for mercy that was not going to be given? Did it make you feel more like a man to put a rope around a man's neck? Did you laugh as you watched his feet dangle and his eyes bulge as you murdered him?"

"You're damned right it did! It gave me the satisfaction of vengeance. I lost everythin' I worked for and....."

"That *you* worked for? As I recall you had slaves toilin' out in the fields and servin' you your whiskey on the veranda. I don't remember you ever liftin' a finger to do much of anythin' except order others around like some king."

"You know nothin', you young pup. Those Nigrahs and carpetbaggers deserved everythin' that was handed to them." Charles paused, cleared his throat then continued. "They came down here from up north to rob us and make our slaves think they are our equals. But we roared like the lions of hell and….and…"

A fit of raspy breathing and then coughing interrupted his answer. Then Charles Cameron tried to get out of bed but collapsed in a heap on the floor. Seeing his father in such a helpless state quelled Derek's anger like a dash of cold water. Moving forward he meant to help his father back into bed but his father recoiled at his touch.

"Get away from me…."

It was a tragic scene that met Honora's eyes as she pushed open the door. "Derek, what on earth is going on?" Rushing to her husband she quickly helped him back into bed.

"I was merely confronting a monster." Derek wondered if his mother had any inkling of what her husband had done. Or had his father kept her completely in the dark. He wanted to ask her, but her attention was centered on her husband and so the opportunity was lost. In disappointment merged with disgust, Derek left the room. But he was determined to get the answers he wanted at another time.

\*   \*   \*   \*

It had been a long time since Derek had faced a reprimand from his mother. But as he approached her by the door to the dining room the expression on her face told him he was going to be rebuked because of the scene in his father's bedroom.

"Good Lord, your father is far from being a well man," she began. "He is slowly recoverin' and gettin' his strength back but an emotional upset like I witnessed will set him back. What on earth were you thinkin'?"

"I wanted to get some answers. After what happened to Moses I am tired of mollycoddlin' nasty old men, even if one of them is my father." Derek wondered if he should confide in his mother all that had happened and his father's connection to the perpetrators.

Honora Cameron put her hand up to her face, brushing several hairs that had escaped the security of her bun. "Your father is a complicated man. Like all of us he has his faults."

"Faults. Is that what you call it." He was so angry he was afraid he would explode. "I call it murderous behavior." Looking his mother right in the eye he knew he had to ask the question. "Did you know what he was involved in?"

"Smugglin'? Yes. But I blame your uncle Nathaniel. And I have to admit that if not for both of them we would have been roamin' the streets by now like a band of gypsies." Nervously she toyed with her hair, trying to put it neatly into place. "But that is all

341

behind us now. We survived and must now confront the oncomin' hurdles thrown in our paths."

"*Smugglin'*?" Derek was astounded by what his mother had just told him "Just one more sin added to his tattered soul."

"Unfortunately your father has never been a God-fearin' man." She sighed and reached out to him. "But come, it is almost time to eat."

"I've lost my appetite." For a moment he was uncertain if he should continue, but as she started to walk through the door, he gently touched her arm. "Don't go yet. There is another question I have for you."

"If you want to know if you can have your weddin' to Amelia here, the answer is yes." For the first time since they started to talk, Honora smiled.

"No, it's not about that." He motioned with his head toward the alcove where they could have some privacy and she followed as he led her there. "I found somethin' in the attic at the Avery house that is quite disturbin'. Were you aware that father was the Grand Titan of the Ku Klux Klan a few years ago?"

He stared into her eyes, expecting to see a look of horror or surprise, but she was expressionless. "I *was*." Seeing his look of disgust, she hurried to explain. "One night when he thought I was asleep I caught him sneakin' out of the house. I followed, thinkin' he might be havin' an affair. I saw him remove a trunk and several other objects from a hidin' place."

"Robes, hoods, and their ceremonial book that includes names and the offices his friends held. And their signatures," Derek exclaimed.

342

"Yes. I watched as he put the robe on and started to slip the hood over his head. He was on his way to meet up with his cronies so that they could terrorize a judge who didn't see things their way." For just a moment she seemed to be reliving that scene. "I stepped out of the shadows and I told him that if he went to his rendezvous I would leave him."

"And did he go?" As long as he could remember it had been his father who dominated the family and didn't care what anyone said or did.

"No. He agreed to stop maraudin'. He took off those hideous garments and handed them to me. Later he brought the other items to me and told me they had all agreed to disband their Klan."

"Because they knew you could turn them in!" Derek wasn't impressed by his father's gesture of submission.

"I am the one who hid the items in the attic where I thought no one would find them. And that was the end of it all......"

"But it was not the end, Mother. I think they might have been the ones to burn down the schoolhouse with a young boy inside. And when I came upon those hooded men who had attacked Moses, I remembered the names in the book. I challenged them and called out those names one by one. They ran like frightened rabbits. So, the Klan has been rejuvenated. But of course, Father was here so he wasn't in any way involved. But the others were."

"I see."

Derek could tell that despite her lack of response his mother was deep in thought. He could almost read her mind. Even though the men were friends of

Charles Cameron they could be dangerous, as any
cornered animal could be. They could retaliate if their
activities were revealed yet if nothing was done, they
would no doubt continue to harm others. The question
was, where did they go from here?

\*    \*    \*    \*

Was it possible for life to return to normal?
Moses was healing quickly thanks to Honora and
Forest's care and yet at the back of his mind was the
fear-provoking memory of armed men putting a noose
around his neck and trying to lynch him. Derek was
living with the knowledge that his father had once
done horrific things as a member of the Klan, that he
had been a smuggler, and that they would
undoubtedly always be at conflict with each other.
Amelia felt that Derek truly loved her but lately he
was unusually quiet and withdrawn and she worried
that his feelings for her might be ebbing away.

Forest felt frustrated in her efforts to calm
Moses' fear and resentment over the way he and
others were treated. Though usually very kind and
loving his determination to seek retaliation for his
years of emotional pain was tarnishing the affection
they had for each other. And all the while Charles
Cameron stayed to his room but was getting stronger
and stronger.

## Chapter Twenty-Six

It seemed that Forest was becoming nearly as familiar with Moses' body as she was with her own. Insisting on taking over for Honora and Mrs. O'Leary, it was now her hands that tended his wounds, her fingers that gently massaged the healing herbal salve into his wounds, her arms that helped him out of bed, and her shoulder that he leaned on whenever he felt dizzy. When he moaned in his sleep, she reached out to him, her hand and gentle words soothing his tortured murmurings.

Forest's eyes swept over him now as she gently wiped his arms, shoulders, and neck with a cloth moistened with healing herbs. Would she ever get tired of looking at his manly beauty? She knew for a fact that she would not. He was now and always had been a strikingly handsome man. Even the bruises, welts, and wounds couldn't destroy his good looks. His smooth skin was the color of coffee, his arms well-muscled, his waist thin, his legs straight and strong, and his manhood—that part of him that marked him as male—was well defined. Just looking at him was strangely exciting, stirring her blood with languid heat, bringing forth a longing that she wanted very much to fulfill.

As if sensing her searching eyes, Moses stirred in his sleep and for a long while it was peaceful, so tranquil that she nearly nodded off to sleep once or twice. Then unexpectedly, she found herself looking into the deep, dark depths of his eyes as his eyelids fluttered open

"Jemma," he whispered, reaching up his hand to entwine the soft silken strands of her hair, pulling her closer. I was having a dream about you." His voice was still hoarse and it added a seductive tone whenever he spoke.

"A pleasant dream I hope." She was relieved that he hadn't been dreaming about that night he had met violence at the hands of the Klan.

"We were together again on that train but instead of being children we were grown. Like we are now. You were reaching out, trying to unlock that trunk I was in to set me free." His hold on her hair kept her captive. "You told me that you loved me."

"I do. So much."

His eyes were penetrating, looking deep into her very soul, then he smiled. "I can feel it. It's as if we are two beings who share a soul." Loosening his hand from her hair, he closed his eyes. Thinking that he had fallen asleep she started to get up from the bed, but his hand reached out to take her hand. "Thinking about you that night was the only thing that gave me courage."

"And loving you gave my life new meaning. When you didn't show up at the cottage I knew something was wrong and my heart nearly stopped. And then when I saw you and what had been done to you I almost died. But I knew I had to be strong for you. For us. For our future."

"You gave me hope. You always have."

She was his lovely guardian angel. He could fully appreciate her loveliness, could see the outline of her tantalizing breasts. Round, high, firm, they

346

seemed to invite his touch. He found himself wanting to see the rest of her, to strip away those full skirts and view what lay beneath. The hot ache of desire sparked within him and it was all he could do to fight the urge to reach out for her. Tearing his gaze from her, he sought to control his baser urge.

"Just as soon as I get my strength back I need to get back to work. The sooner I can make my farm profitable the sooner we can be together. Until then I have nothing to give you but myself."

"That's all that is important. I want *you*."

He sat up quickly, too quickly. Reaching up a hand to his head, he fought off the dizziness which consumed him. Forest offered her arms to steady him, assailing him with the beguiling scent of flowers which came from her hair. Her hands reached out to touch him, to caress him, and that touch was his undoing.

His eyes seemed to devour her, hypnotize her. As she stared into his eyes, Forest's heart began to hammer at the glitter of desire she read there. She found herself remembering the firm gentleness and pressure of those warm lips against her own. Without any awareness of what she was doing, she leaned toward him, the soft material of her gown tightening across her breasts as she did so, making him aware of their tempting allure. As if reading his mind, she took his hand and put it on the soft swell of her breast.

"I've wanted to touch you like that for so long….."

They moved together into an embrace as he kissed her, her mouth opening under the pressure of his as the kiss deepened in intensity. The kiss had the pleasant taste of the herbal tea and honey she had given him earlier.

He pulled her with him to the bed, ignoring the pain that blazed in his neck. For a man who had faced death, desire had given him sudden strength. He was completely ruled by his emotions, as all his resolve, his vow not to touch her, was swept away in the tide of his passion. He only knew that Forest was beside him and that he wanted her as he had never wanted any other woman. She was lovely and tempting and warm.

He clasped her in his arms, and they lay side by side, he tugging at the hem of her nightgown, she hurrying to remove it and toss it aside. His muscles strained against the softness of her curves as they continued to drink of each other's kisses. Forest gave herself up to him, feeling as dizzy as Moses had only a moment before.

"Forest," he breathed, stroking, and teasing the peaks of her breasts until she moaned low and whispered his name just as he had whispered hers. She yielded to his hands, those hands that searched out the secrets of her woman's body.

Forest's pulse quickened at the passion that burned in his eyes. Knowing that she had to be careful not to touch his neck, she bent forward as his mouth descended upon hers. It all seemed so unreal, as if they moved in a dream.

Wrapped in each other's arms, they kissed, his mouth moving upon hers, pressing her lips apart, hers responding, exploring gently the sweet firmness of his. She gave herself up to the fierce emotions which raced through her, answering his kisses eagerly.

"Forest!" he groaned, his mouth roaming freely, stopping briefly at the hollow of her throat, lingering there, then moving slowly downward to the skin of her bare shoulder. He felt a fire in the blood, a raging inferno. His lips caught hers, molding his mouth to hers as his fingers slid down her stomach, to explore the softness there again.

Forest was lost in the flush of sensations which swept over her. Holding him tightly against her, she felt wanton, aware of her body as she had never been before. His mouth flamed on hers, plundering the softness. Like a bolt of lightning, passion passed between them.

You are beautiful," he whispered. "I love to touch you." She was a vision of perfection as she lay there before him, her body illuminated by the soft sunlight seeping through a slit in the drapes. Looking down at their bare bodies joined together he thought that they looked like chocolate and caramel. Blended together in sweet perfection.

"And I love to feel you touch me." She could feel his hot breath stir the veil of her hair, could feel the brush of his lips against her temple. His pulse began to pound as his eyes took in her long legs, the slim waist, the firm, rose-tipped breasts Continuing to admire her body, running his fingers over her soft skin with adoration, he whispered words of love to her. Tracing a path of fire, his lips moved across her stomach and she trembled at his caress.

Passion exploded between them with a wild oblivion. Moses molded her against him, the fire released in him finding its match in her own passions, her own desire. She melted with his every touch, tangling her fingers in his thick black hair as he slid his fingers down to explore the center of her being.

"Make love to me," she cried, her body

responding with a will of its own, writhing as his fingers touched the opening petals of her womanhood. She had no fear, though she was a virgin and had heard that the first time brought forth pain. He would be gentle with her—this she knew.

The probing length of his manhood slipped hotly between her thighs, and he came to her with a slow but strong thrust, entering her softness as their bodies met in that most intimate of embraces. He heard her cry out softly at the pain as he broke the membrane of her maidenhead and hurried to assure her. "No more hurt. No more. Only pleasure from now on, I promise you."

Burying his long length deeply within her, he let her adjust to this sudden invasion of her softness. She found he spoke the truth: there was no more hurt, only ecstasy, like the currents of the deep sea as his body drew hers. She was consumed by his warmth, his hardness. Tightening her thighs around his waist, she arched up to him, wanting him to move within her. He did so, slowly at first, then with a sensual urgency.

His lovemaking was like nothing she could ever have imagined, filling her, flooding her, nearly drowning her in sensual stirrings that shattered her world. Clinging to him, she called out his name not once, not twice, but several times.

Moses gazed down upon her face, gently brushing back the tangled hair from her eyes. From this moment on she was his. He would never share her with anyone. She would be his wife in fact if not in name.

"Sleep now," he whispered, still holding her close. With a sigh she snuggled up against him, burying her face in the warmth of his chest, breathing in the manly scent of him. She didn't want to sleep, not now; she wanted to savor this moment of joy, but as he caressed her back, tracing his fingers along her spine, she drifted off.

\*    \*    \*    \*

Moses awoke to find Forest cradled in his arms. Her thick lashes fanned out over her cheeks and her mane of curly hair was spread out like a fur cloak over his chest and shoulders. As he looked at her he felt an aching tenderness. She looked much younger, snuggling up against him in her sleep. The passion they had shared passed before his eyes and he felt a tightening inside, an inward anger at himself that he could have so easily forgotten his vow not to claim her, and yet, were he to live forever he would remember this first time they made love.

"I love you, Forest Faulkner. Never doubt it."

As if hearing his words in her sleep, she shivered and he gathered her into his arms, the heat of his body warming hers. He stroked her hair and closed his eyes, remembering. Never had he realized that love could be like this, such shattering ecstasy as to be almost pain. Were anything to happen to her, were anyone to harm her.... It was a thought he dared not even imagine.

*If only I could protect her from the world, this world which can often be cruel*, he thought. He felt her stir and looked down into her eyes.

"Moses," she breathed, reaching up to touch his cheek as if to confirm that he was real and not some fabrication of her dreams.

351

He cupped her face with his hand, bending to kiss her soft open lips. Like a flower opening to sunshine, she moved her mouth upon his, feeling again the wondrous enchantment.

Moses' hand reached out to caress her, sliding his fingers over the soft mounds of her breasts. How could he fight these feelings he had for her? Her body, pressed against his, drove him beyond all thought, all reasoning. He shuddered, burying his face in the silk cloud of her hair as their bodies touched and blended into each other.

They did not hear the sound of footsteps as Derek entered the room. Only his "ahem." He looked sheepish as they looked up at him. Reaching for the sheet, Forest covered herself. Moses didn't bother to conceal himself.

"Don't you ever knock?" Moses couldn't hide the annoyance from his raspy voice.

Derek was hiding a piece of paper in his hands and now he held it up for Moses to see. "This was nailed to the door and I would imagine there is a twin note nailed to your door at your house. The Freedman bank is calling in the funds for their loan early."

"What?" Moses grabbed the notice from Derek's hand and hastily scanned it. "I'm being lynched again but this time in a different way. And you are being lynched right along with me."

The notice stated that a series of speculative investments had caused the bank to take on bad debt and that a decision to build a new building in Washington, D.C. had added to the bank's money troubles. It was declared that unsecured loans and the fact that some debtors could not repay debts had undermined the bank and that they needed to call on reserves from others who had taken out loans.

"So, we are to pay early because they went into debt?" Derek was furious. "We need to get you a lawyer, Moses. There is no way that either you or I can get our hands on the needed monies, at least not now."

"Neither of our crops will be ready for harvest until next month. This is a ridiculous request." Moses' throat was dry and the unfairness of the bank infuriated him. A fit of coughing wracked his body. Forgetting about her modesty, Forest hurried to the night table and brought him a glass of water from the pitcher.

"I didn't mean to upset you." Derek was regretful. "I just thought you would want to know as soon as possible."

Moses looked at Derek and it was as if all his dreams had blown away in the wind. He was also concerned for his friend. What would be the fate of Winding Oaks if the loan was called in and Derek could not pay his field hands or buy necessary supplies?

"What in hell are we supposed to do?" A cloud of gloom seemed to hang in the air, consuming them both.

Forest had kept silent but now she spoke up. "Quentin knows a great deal about the law. He even acted as a lawyer when we were living up north. You should talk with him and see what suggestions he has."

"Quentin." Moses nodded, agreeing with her suggestion. "Where is he now?"

"In Richmond. At the Capitol, but he will be back at the cottage later in the day." Realizing that she didn't have transportation she looked at Derek.

He seemed to read her mind. "We can take the buggy and bring him back here to talk things over. Is that agreeable to you?" As she nodded Derek felt a wave of relief sweep over him. Everything would be all right. Quentin would find a way. He had to.

*    *    *    *

There was not even one smile visible as Derek, Moses, Honora, Amelia, Forest and Quentin sat around the dining room table after supper, discussing the options for paying back the loan Moses had received from the Freedman Bank. If Derek had been a gambler, he would have said that the odds were against them.

Quentin adjusted his glasses as he scrutinized the documents before him. "Congress voted to permanently close the Freedman's Bureau a couple of years ago, but the bank has remained operational. Frederick Douglass has been asked to run the bank as one of its trustees and we all know how brilliant he is and that he can be trusted. Problem is that there are scoundrels as well who aren't honest individuals. Matthew Stewart told me that Douglass found rampant corruption with the bank and that risky investments were being made with depositor's savings."

Moses balanced against the table to keep from falling forward but he forgot everything else as he concentrated on the problem at hand. "I was always afraid that it was just too good to be true."

"Lincoln meant well when he established the system for newly freed slaves but then he was assassinated five weeks later and I don't think those who took over were as visionary as he. Many were in it for themselves," Quentin proclaimed. "I have heard that Douglass invested ten thousand dollars of his personal funds, however."

"It's called Freedman's Savings and Trust Company," Derek scoffed. "But it seems they should take the "trust" out of the name."

Quentin held up his hand. "Don't be put off by what has happened, Derek. Like so many things that came out of the war, the bank began with a sense of high moral purpose. Not only to help in the transition from slave to free but also as a safe place to keep money."

"Safe?" Moses was trying hard to control his temper. "When I run for office I am going to remember what happened. There needs to be more protection against fraud and risky investments."

"But what do we do in the meantime?" Derek didn't want to bring up the subject of his father having spent all of the money they had in reserve, but it was on his mind.

Quentin stood up and began pacing up and down as he thought the matter over. Then he asked, "is there any way you could pay a percentage of what is owed just to keep them off your backs?"

The silence was deafening. But slowly Amelia got to her feet. "My father set some money aside for me when I was born. A dowry of sorts, although it isn't really called that anymore. I had thought to wait until..."

Derek's pride took hold of him. "No! Absolutely

not. I won't have you paying my debts for me. There has to be another solution."

Again, there was silence. "How long do we have before this matter is critical?" Moses asked.

"Three weeks." Quentin shook his head. "Perhaps four if I find a way to get you some more time."

"Four weeks. We will have to make do with that," Honora said softly.

"As Abraham Lincoln said, 'the best thing about the future is that it comes one day at a time….."

## Chapter Twenty-Seven

How quickly things can go from bad to worse. As if struggling financially was not difficult enough it seemed that the entire country was in the grip of a financial downturn. Through the "grapevine" Derek learned that the banking firm of Jay Cooke and Company had closed its doors. A major economic panic was sweeping the nation. A panic that was mirrored in the faces of Derek, Honora, and Moses.

Moses received a letter from his father in the north telling him that factories had been producing more goods than people could afford to purchase and as a result prices had been lowered. England also had been hit and was not purchasing products in large quantities as before. Like a domino effect it caused factories to close and workers to be let go. Luckily for now Moses' father still had his job. But it seemed only the number of bankruptcies was flourishing.

"It's as if the ground is collapsin' under my feet," Derek complained. "What else can go wrong?"

Unfortunately, he was soon to find out. As if perched on a steep hill, agricultural prices had started to go down, down, down---falling rapidly. The price Derek could get for his tobacco crops was devastatingly lower than it had been at the start of the planting. The same was true for Moses' peanut crop.

"We'll have to work twice as hard to make half as much," Moses bemoaned. "And we will have to insist on being paid in gold not in silver or greenbacks for our crops. Paper currency is risky."

"How are we going to pay our field hands?" Derek was calculating the sums in his head, scowling as he said, "we can't cut their pay in half. They have families."

"What then?" Moses put his hands up to his face, rubbing his eyes with the palms of his hands. "We can't sell our souls to the devil, although at this point I find myself tempted."

There was a long silence before Derek spoke. "Sell our souls to the devil. Perhaps that is just what we might have to do."

"What?" Moses took his hands from his face and stared at Derek as if he had lost his mind.

"No, no. I know what you are thinkin'. I'm talkin' about my Uncle Nathaniel Cameron. The black sheep of the family. The devil himself accordin' to my father."

Moses shook his head. "I don't remember him."

"That's because he made himself scarce. He wasn't welcome here. He was the black sheep of the family. A smuggler durin' and after the war. A real son of a bitch for sure. But by all accounts a rich one."

"But what good will that do you?"

"I don't know. But I do know I have to do everythin' in my power to keep things goin'." Slipping on his boots Derek looked with concern at Moses who was ready to go to work for the first time since he had been lynched and beaten. "Are you sure that you are ready to go back to work?"

"I have to be ready. I can't let you do it all by yourself. Particularly not now when everything is collapsing around us." Although his ribs were still

358

sore, Moses was somehow able to hide his pain as he followed Derek down the stairs and out the front door of the Mansion.

Neither Derek nor Moses saw Edward Cutler until he came around the corner of the veranda and accosted them. "Good morning, gentleman."

Derek said good morning and Moses echoed. Both of them looked the red-haired man up and down, wondering what he wanted.

Edward Cutler was far from shy. He came right to the point. "I understand that like some of the others around here you are having financial trouble. Well, I've come to save the day."

"Save the day. Indeed." Derek took an immediate dislike to the grinning man.

"I would like to take this property off your hands."

"Sell it?" Derek tensed every muscle in his body.

The red-haired man was belligerent. "Yes, sell it."

"No!" Derek was not surprised at his emphatic answer. He had been working this land, giving his blood, tears, and sweat for too long to give in to someone like this. Someone who would never appreciate all that the property meant to the Cameron family. Money just wasn't everything. "This land is not for sale, to you or anybody."

That should have been the end of the matter, but it wasn't. Like an auctioneer, Cutler started rattling off amounts of money he would give for the plantation

Derek took a step closer to the man, standing nose to nose with him. "No means no." Now, get off of this land before I count to three," he threatened. "One….."

Watching the cloud of dust Cutler stirred up as he ran towards his horse, Derek felt triumphant. Even so, he knew he had made an enemy today. He also knew something else: that this wasn't the end of it.

\*　　\*　　\*　　\*

The Bible said that money was the root of all evil. Was it? As he walked slowly towards the door of his father's room, Derek was inclined to think so. Certainly greed was the foundation of immoral and malevolent behavior. Just look at his father. The pursuit of riches and affluence had been the dominating force of his life. How ironic that everything his father had worked for, cheated for, stolen for, and bartered his honor for was now hanging preciously by a thread.

Opening the door Derek expected his father to be in bed but found him pacing the floor as if somehow he knew what was happening. "I heard from Mother that you were still havin' dizzy spells. Shouldn't you be back in bed?"

Turning towards him Charles snorted. "I just pretended. If I can't have my whiskey that special blend of herbs she puts in my tea is a good substitute. Makes me feel like I'm twenty again."

"You've been lyin'?" Derek's anger was sparked as he thought of his mother waiting on this deceitful man day and night.

"A white lie and nothin' more. I've certainly told much bolder fibs." He squinted his eyes as he looked at Derek. "I suppose you will waste no time in tattlin'."

"Mother has a right to know." He wondered what other lies his father had told. "And I have a right to know when you will be strong enough to help me out in the fields."

361

Charles wrinkled up his nose as if he smelled something offensive. "Not for an awfully long time. You are the one who will have to keep crackin' the whip."

His reference to the days of slavery repulsed Derek. "If we lose Windin' Oaks there won't be even a whip to crack."

Stopping in midstride, Charles just stood staring. "What do you mean?"

"The economy is in turmoil and the bank is threatenin' to call in the loan payment early. In addition to that there is a red-haired rat trying to steal Windin' Oaks out from under us. We need money and your dipping' into the till has done us no good."

"I had my reasons."

Derek didn't take the time to ask just what those reasons were. He came right to the point. "I know you and Uncle Nathaniel were involved in smugglin'. What were you smugglin'?"

"Tobacco. To keep from payin' the import duties on foreign cigars." Charles explained that because of extensive trade and transportation ties between Florida and Cuba there was ample opportunity for clever men to earn a profit by smuggling both in and out varying quantities of both liquor and cigars to be sold on the black market. "With Nathaniel's help tobacco from this plantation made its way to Cuba. The enterprise made him a rich devil."

Ordinarily Derek would never consider asking his uncle for help, but these were desperate times. "Is there any way you can get in touch with him and see if he can give us the money we need?"

"Your uncle is in Florida." Charles was in thoughtful silence for several minutes. "But I think I know how I can locate him."

\*　　\*　　\*　　\*

The pathway leading to the cottage hadn't changed. The bushes still brushed against the windowpanes. The flowers were still in bloom in the garden. The front door was in the same place it always had been. The birds still sang. And yet as Forest returned to the cottage after staying at the Cameron home to take care of Moses, she felt as if everything was altered and strangely unfamiliar. She felt out of place as if the cottage was not where she belonged.

"It's so good to have you back home. I have missed you." Quentin greeted her at the door with a bouquet of freshly picked flowers.

She had missed him too and yet as she walked through the door and into the living room, she felt a deep sense of loss. Oh, how she would miss snuggling with Moses at night in his bed, and making love whenever they wanted to, and hearing his raspy voice say her name. But life had to return to normal after all. Moses had gone back to work on his land and she needed to help Quentin with his speeches and the upcoming campaign.

Quentin eyed her, sensing there was something missing. Her smile of course. "You look as if something has gone wrong. What is it?"

Forest forced a smile. "I'm just overwhelmed, that's all. It seems that I have been away much longer than I realized. But the world has to keep turning and life must keep ticking on."

"You miss your young man already." Quentin's expression showed his empathy. "But you will see him again." For just a moment a frown curved his mouth. "He hasn't changed his mind about becoming a candidate, has he?"

"No." It was the only thing that made her feel optimistic about all that was happening. "He has told me how dedicated he is to helping others like him. Like us."

"Good. Good." As he helped her bring in the belongings she had taken to the Cameron's, Quentin gave her a concise briefing on all that had happened during the meetings. "Adam Peterson has dropped out of the group. Seems he has been receiving threatening letters. Bartholomew Jackson has moved up north to pursue a career in law. Samson Waters will not be able to help us financially any longer as he has lost his position at the railroad. But the rest of us are determined to win and make a difference."

His exuberance spurred her on. "And I know that you will. I have faith in all of you and in what Moses can bring to the campaign. The Bible's Moses parted the Red Sea but our Moses will bring together all those who have suffered from inequity."

Quentin set down her suitcase on her bed and paused. "Say that again."

"The Bible's Moses parted the Red Sea but this Moses will bring together those who have suffered inequity." She could envision Moses so handsome in his suit, tie, and white shirt being introduced by those words to speak before a crowd of his peers.

364

"Good. Very good." Giving her a gentle nudge, he guided her to his desk. It was scattered with papers as usual. "I have written several speeches for him to memorize and…."

"No!" Forest touched his arm. "Moses wants to talk from the heart and tell all that he has experienced. He told me he doesn't want anyone to put words in his mouth. Not even you, despite his admiration."

Quentin stiffened, then relaxed. "Well, I guess I will have to let him have his way if it means counting him as one of us. And perhaps what he says will make an impression on voters. It is not everyone who is lynched, beaten, and yet survives to talk about it."

"Thank God!" As she remembered first seeing Moses bruised, beaten, and feeling pain in every muscle she cringed.

'He showed courage, that one. And proved beyond a doubt how much he loves you." He paused at the door. "When you think that even when he was facing death he protected you that is all I need to admire the man."

"Protected me?" Forest paused her unpacking, confused by Quentin's words. "How did he protect me that night? I wasn't even there."

"Then you don't know." Putting his fingers to his lips, Quentin looked as if he regretted saying too much.

'Know what?' When he didn't answer, her voice grew louder. "Tell me. What do you mean?"

Realizing there was no turning back now, Quentin blurted it out. "The reason Moses was set upon and lynched was because those Klansmen thought he had, as I heard they called it, 'sullied a white woman'."

"A white woman? But I'm not......." As realization swept over her, Forest felt as if a fist had punched her in the chest.

"They thought you *were* and Moses didn't say otherwise because he didn't want them to know that you are of mixed blood. He feared for you and wanted to make sure no harm came to you. *Now that is a man.*"

"Oh no! No." The realization that Moses had suffered and nearly died and not said one word was nearly more than she could endure. Looking towards Quentin she fought the tears that threatened to flow saying, "please leave me alone for just a moment."

"Of course. I'm sorry...."

Forest looked down at the nightgown she held in her hands, remembering the times she had worn it when they had made love. How his fingers had been so gentle when he had removed it to celebrate her naked body. He had been so gentle with her. So caring. And because of her he had nearly died. It was a sacrifice she could never make up to him for. A sacrifice that made her emotions crumble. Putting the nightgown up to her face, Forest tried to hide the sobs that came to her throat as she cried.

*     *     *     *

Amelia was certain that she moved through the children's lessons at the Avery House like a sleepwalker. There were so many things on her mind that she hardly heard the children as they read aloud their assignments, nor was she clear thinking enough to notice if their multiplication tables were correct or in error. She only knew that Derek and his family were perilously close to losing everything they had worked for generations to acquire and that there had to be some way she could help them.

There was another concern that plagued her as well. Although he had been absent in class for the past few weeks, Beauregard Johnson had returned out of the blue giving her a vague explanation for his absence. Amelia suspected that the reason the boy had turned up was to spy on her and cause more trouble if it was necessary. She knew that she had to be careful not to let it be known that she was teaching at the church on the seventh day of each week. She could not take a chance on some hate-mongering person setting fire to the church.

"Thirty-five."

"Beauregard's shout out of the answer shook Amelia out of her daydreams. For a moment she just stood there, looking at him, then remembered. "And what is nine times nine?"

"That's a hard one." The boy paused then shouted out. "Ninety-three."

"No, the answer is eighty-one." The smile she gave Beauregard was forced. "Everyone's assignment for tomorrow is to be able to recite the entire multiplication table with all the numbers from one to nine."

"Aw, numbers are boring." Sally made a face that expressed her disdain. "I wish the assignment was reading instead."

"Reading will be the next assignment. I'll find some interesting books." Amelia watched as the children filed out, taking particular interest in where Beauregard was going. It seemed that for today at least his actions were innocent enough.

At last when the children had left and she was all alone, Amelia's thoughts returned to Derek and the turmoil unfolding right before their eyes. *I have to find a way to help them*, she thought. Time was running out. Already two weeks of the four had passed and that left only two weeks to come up with at least some of the money.

*The money my father set aside for me is the answer.* But Derek had been against the idea because of his pride. However, if she were clever enough she could find a way to get him the money without his even knowing the source.

Tidying up the schoolroom, Amelia hurried down the stairs and hitched the horses to the Cameron buggy for the short journey to Aunt Lucinda's. Feeling more than a bit guilty for not having contacted her aunt more than once or twice since she had come to live in the Cameron Mansion, she prepared herself for the ordeal that was to come.

By the time she reached her aunt's house Amelia had convinced herself that there was a chance of helping the Camerons. But many of her plans hinged on whether or not Aunt Lucinda would give her the money set aside by her father. She had to, didn't she? Knowing her aunt as she did, she told herself that the answer was precarious.

"Ha, she wanted me to marry Edward Cutler, but Derek Camron is heads and tails above that money grabbing banker," she said to herself. Alighting from the buggy and hastening up the steps she was surprised to see her aunt sitting in her rocking chair on the front porch with a needle and embroidery hoop."

"Well, have you come to your senses?" Lucinda's fingers tapped a rhythm on the embroidery hoop, a sign she was highly agitated.

"Come to my senses. What do you mean?" Amelia leaned against the support posts of the veranda, wanting nothing more than to turn around and go back to Winding Oaks.

"You need to be married, girl, not whoring with some washed up wannabe tobacco farmer who doesn't have two pennies to rub together that aren't owed to someone else."

A shocked intake of breath from Amelia answered Lucinda's bold words, yet she was well past the point of caring. She loved Derek with all her heart and she didn't give a fig what her aunt thought. "So, Edward Cutler has been chattering in your ear."

"I can't imagine why but he still seems to be interested in you."

"Ha. Well I am not interested in *him*. I wouldn't give him the time of day if he were the last man on earth. Besides, I am engaged to Derek Cameron." Defiantly she showed her aunt the sapphire ring Derek had given her.

"Hmph. You think there will be a wedding. I'll believe it when I see you walk down the aisle. The Camerons have always been philanderers."

"Philanderers! Not Derek!"

Lucinda dropped her embroidery on the ground and her eyes bulged out with anger over the top of her silver-rimmed spectacles. "What fairy tale have you been reading? I thought you were smarter than that.

Men are all alike. You can't believe a word they say. What happened to your common sense? You are not the young woman who left this house. That young woman had at least a thimbleful of intelligence."

Amelia faced her aunt's fire with a spark of her own. "No, that foolish girl didn't have the sense to reach out for happiness because she didn't think she was worthy of love. Because you did nothing but criticize me. But Derek loves me and we will be man and wife and there is nothing you can say to make me think otherwise!"

"And you are proud of being that man's mistress, for mistress is just what you are."

Amelia spoke from the heart. "I would rather be Derek's mistress than be Edward Cutler's wife." Her words were quiet, but they carried conviction.

Lucinda shook her head. "All these years I've tried to take the place of your mother, God rest her soul, but I can see now how miserably I've failed. Your father would be mortified. You have come to a sorry end."

"My father would want me to be happy, and I am. Can't you even try to understand how I feel?"

"You think I've never been in love, child? How little you know. I know what loving means, I have carried that feeling deep within me for years. I know the happiness and I know the pain."

"I'm sorry." Amelia had never heard all the details of her aunt's life with her husband, but although she waited to hear more, Lucinda had said all that she intended to say.

"So, you have not come home to stay."

"No." It was the opening Amelia needed. "I came to ask you to put in motion the wheels that will allow me to obtain the savings that my father set aside before he went to war."

"The money your father left you."

The fact that her aunt didn't look her in the eye should have triggered alarm bells in Amelia's head, but it didn't. That was why she was unprepared for what her aunt would say.

"There is no money."

Amelia stared at her aunt in stunned silence then sputtered, "but…but my father's letter. It said in the letter that he had put aside sufficient monies for me for that time when I was to be wed and….."

Lucinda stood up abruptly, dropping her stitchery to the ground. "That is why I wanted you to marry Edward Cutler. He will take you without an exchange of monies. He wants to marry you even though you haven't got a penny to your name except for the paltry amount you get for your teaching."

"No savings!" It was as if the very earth had been pulled from beneath Amelia's feet. All her life she had thought that there had been money set aside. It had been her security. "Was the letter a lie?"

"No. No. You must understand what it is like to be a widow and then have a child thrust upon you to provide for."

"Thrust upon you?" Amelia thought that she had finally insulated herself against her aunt's unfeeling behavior, but the words cut her to the quick.

It seemed to be the time for confessions. Lucinda clenched her hands together as she revealed her perfidy. "Times were hard. I meant to just borrow a few dollars here and there and then pay it back but as time went on we needed the money to survive."

Amelia knew she had been betrayed. "You were using the money my father put aside for me yet you made me feel indebted to you. As if I were a burden. A little orphan girl with no money and no one to take her in. I thought I owed you the world."

"Amelia!"

Amelia couldn't endure hearing another word. Turning her back on her aunt without even a wave of 'goodbye' she hurried back to buggy.

KATHRYN KRAMER

## Chapter Twenty-Eight

The portraits on the wall seemed to come alive as Derek slowly moved down the hallway scrutinizing each one. All of their eyes were focused on him as if blaming him for the mighty Cameron empire crashing to the ground. What would they say to him if they suddenly came alive and could talk? Would they curse him? Damn him? Blame him? Or would they give him advice on how to pick up the pieces and put everything back together no matter what had to be done?

"Dear old Avery." He stared at the first painting of a dark-haired man with laughing eyes, lace fronted shirt, and three-cornered hat atop his head. Avery who had started it all. He remembered his grandmother telling him that Avery had settled in Virginia and married a girl he literally bought, an indentured servant. And there was her portrait beside him, a woman with flaming red hair, an upturned nose, and provocative pout, a lady dressed in emerald green holding a fan. He remembered that they had two sons, Simon and Owen. Owen murdered his own brother just like Cain, for the property and the treasure.

"Blackbeard's treasure," he murmured. Rumor had it that Jared Cameron, the first Camron, had married Blackbeard's daughter and acquired a treasure chest of gold coins. Coins that he and Moses had searched for when they were young. If only….."

He moved on to Stephen who was nearly fifty when the painting had been done. Next to him was

Victoria his grandmother, a feisty old woman as he recalled. He could almost hear her prodding him on, telling him that Camerons always won. That they never gave in or gave up.

Then there was Merlin Cameron, Megan Cameron, Stephen Cameron, Elizabeth Cameron, and lastly his father Charles Cameron sandwiched between the portraits of two lovely women, Honora and Bevin's mother, another lovely blonde. So many portraits and each and every one of them seemed to be telling him that he must do anything and everything to keep Winding Oaks or be damned. But what would Nathaniel Cameron say?

"Good ole Uncle Nathaniel!" He smiled for the first time that day as he left the gallery of portraits and walked down the long hallway to a room where the portrait of the black sheep of the family was hung. Out of sight of any guests who once might have been curious.

"And here you are." The portrait of a dark-haired young man with piercing blue eyes, a high forehead, and thin unsmiling lips, seemed to be challenging anyone who would gaze upon it. *I am my own man and I will do as I please*, the expression seemed to say. Derek had gone into Richmond three days in a row and sent his uncle several telegrams to his hotel in Florida requesting a meeting, but so far there had been no reply. Derek could only wonder at his uncle's fate. Had Nathaniel at last been penalized for his penchant for going outside the law? Or was he merely shunning the family that had rejected him so long ago?

"Ah, Uncle, you were my last hope." The clock was ticking. The days were passing by. Something

374

had to happen soon or all was lost.

"Derek."

Turning around he saw his mother standing behind him and he wondered again how she could have ever chosen to be married to his father. She was everything kind, good, and gentle while his father was just the opposite.

"Amelia told me you had come over here. Your father is asking for you." The look of concern on her face let him know that it was urgent.

He wanted to tell her that he had no interest in speaking with the hateful man but out of respect for her he left the Avery House and walked to the main house. Opening the door, he made his way to his father's room. His father was out of bed, sitting at his writing desk.

"Close the door and don't just stand there gawking," he heard his father say.

Trying to hide his frustration Derek said, "I have sent several telegrams to the hotel you told me Uncle Nathaniel was stayin' at but there has not been any reply."

"Not surprised. He has always been an elusive and stubborn bastard." He waved his hand in the air as if brushing the matter aside. "But no hindrance. We don't need his money after all. I have another plan."

"Are we goin' to rob a bank?" Derek asked sarcastically.

"Oh, that we could. That would certainly be the answer to our prayers." Standing up, Charles came towards his son in a shuffling manner. "It seems we are in luck. I received a letter from my good friend

Thomas Jamison, perhaps the only northerner I can stand. Anyway, he has a daughter just about your age."

"No!" Derek knew immediately what his father was planning, the devious old codger. "Don't get anything in your head."

Charles ignored Derek's outburst. "The girl is quite a beauty I am told. A red head like him. Her name is Angelique."

"I told you no!"

Shrugging off Derek's rejection he continued. "She has quite a large inheritance that would give us enough to pay a large portion of our debts and…."

"I don't care if she is as rich as the queen of England." That his father could even suggest such a thing was infuriating. "My heart is already taken."

"Bah!" Charles was so irate that he tipped over a chair nearby. "You need to think with your brain and not with your cock! Besides, women are all alike in bed. You just haven't sampled enough of them to realize that."

"I know that I love Amelia and she loves me." Derek wondered why he was even discussing the matter.

Charles tone of voice was like a growl. "Then keep her as your mistress. You would not be the first to do that nor the last." As if feeling a bit weak Charles sat down on the bed.

"Mistress? I would never insult her so." Was there anything in the world his father valued except money? He doubted it. "Besides, I have asked Amelia to be my wife.'

"Then *unask* her!" Charles grappled with his

376

anger. "If she cares anythin' at all about this family she will be the first to see that she gains nothin' by standing in the way. Besides, I doubt that she would want to marry a pauper with nowhere to live."

Derek could feel the heat radiating up his face from his mounting anger. It was no use arguing with his father. Charles Cameron always got his way. But not this time. Everyone else gave in to the tyrant but Derek refused to do so. Not now. Not tomorrow. Not ever. There had to be another way to save the Cameron estate and he would do everything in his power to do so.

*　　*　　*　　*

It was unsettling to feel the need to always look over your shoulder just to make certain that you weren't going to be taken unaware but since that night when he had been lynched and nearly died, that was what Moses felt compelled to do. In addition, he took his Colt model 1860 rifle and Starr revolver with him everywhere he went and even slept with a veritable arsenal under the bed. And just in case he slept too soundly he had booby trapped his house, secured his door with two locks, boarded up his two windows and just for extra precautions while he slept balanced a chair on two legs in front of the door.

It had been a very exhausting and extremely hot day with only two field hands to help him now. So tonight Moses had hurried with his dinner, eating directly out of tin cans, all the while thinking to himself how much he missed the cooking at the Cameron house. After dinner he had not even taken the time to remove more than his boots, shirt, and trousers, sleeping in his cotton drawers on top of the covers. Willing himself to think of Forest so that his dreams wouldn't turn into nightmares he fell into a heavy slumber.

Moses didn't know how long he had slept; he only knew that he heard the rattling of the tin cans he had strung up with a tripwire. Then he heard a loud thump, a bump, and a string of swear words that would have made any soldier blush. His instincts told him to reach for his rifle until he realized he was familiar with the swearer. It was Derek.

"Damn it all to hell, Moses. Let me in!" The banging on the door rattled the chair.

Dismantling his booby trap at the front door took more time than Moses had realized that it would but at last he was able to unlock and open the door to see Derek rubbing the top of his head. Although he knew it wasn't funny, there was something about his friend's expression that made him laugh. Derek, however, wasn't laughing, he was irate.

"What do you think you are doin'?"

"Protecting myself by any means necessary. And before you say another word let me just tell you that I am not a coward." He motioned for Derek to come inside.

"I wouldn't think that you were. I just think you are very smart. But I wish you would have warned me." Derek was slurring his words and seemed unsteady on his feet enough to signal Moses that he had been drinking.

"What's wrong? Did Amelia kick you out of bed?" Moses started to tease Derek but as he looked at Derek's face he knew in an instant that something was wrong. "Tell me......"

"What is wrong?" Derek took a step and nearly fell on his face. Only Moses' quick reaction saved him from a tumble. Quickly Moses pulled up a chair.

"Make yourself comfortable and prepare to spend the night." He aided Derek's hands in removing his shirt and boots. "You can take the sofa I'm too tired to offer you my bed."

Derek crossed his arms across his chest and frowned. "Why am I so unlucky that I have a total bastard for a father?"

"Just fortunate I guess."

"Very funny." Derek started to fall forward on the chair but caught himself. "He is so unreasonable and only cares about himself. Why?"

Moses shrugged. "I have no idea so why don't you tell me what happened that set you off like dynamite. Then I can answer your question."

Closing his eyes, Derek repeated all that had happened. "He actually had the nerve to tell me I should marry some carpetbagger's daughter just to get access to the money to repay the loan and keep the plantation runnin'."

"Using you as the sacrificial lamb! I hope you told him to go straight to hell!"

"Not exactly. But I did tell him I wouldn't marry anyone but Amelia. And that I love her." Moses helped him get up from the chair and together they moved towards the sofa. "He didn't care what I feel, or think, or want. Only that I do his biddin' on those damn tobacco plants."

"And you don't even smoke a pipe....." Moses was trying to lighten the mood but he had failed.

"No one in the Cameron family has ever

379

partaken of tobacco. Only cigars upon the birth of a baby." Collapsing on the sofa, Derek sighed. "How ironic. But Avery didn't want to plant cotton so......" He closed his eyes.

"Tobacco was a good choice then and now. One of the sharecroppers told me that he had heard through the grape vine in Richmond that P.H. Mayo and Brothers tobacco company is going to be manufacturing cigarettes."

"He is such a selfish bastard." Derek paused in his tirade. "Wait. What did you just say?"

"P.H. Mayo and Brothers tobacco company is gearing up to manufacture cigarettes," Moses repeated, louder this time.

And cigarettes used tobacco. "Men have been rollin' their own, particularly out west. But this is revolutionary." Derek's eyes opened wide. "And it will mean that there is every possibility that the price of tobacco will be goin' up."

"And up."

"And up! It will be worth a lot of gold." For the first time that day Derek felt a ray of hope.

*    *    *    *

It was surprising how quickly one person could get used to another person. They became part of your heart, your soul, your very life. For Amelia, Derek was an important part of her existence; the reason she smiled when she woke up in the morning, the object of her thoughts during the day, her incentive for being the best teacher that she could be, the reason she looked forward to the night, the cause of the ache in

380

her heart when he suddenly was missing, if only for a day.

All during dinner tonight she had kept looking at the empty seat at the table where Derek should have been and she felt a deep sense of loneliness consume her. Where was he? When was he going to come home? Was he safe? It wasn't like him to be late for supper. Honora had also been concerned, thinking at first that because there were now only four field hands Derek was still working. After taking Charles' dinner to him, however, she now suspected that they had a quarrel, the subject of which she did not want to discuss with Amelia. Had it been over money? Amelia thought surely that had been the cause. It was as if a large weight had been put on all of their shoulders.

*If only*, she thought, remembering her visit with her Aunt Lucinda. Her anger had tempered a bit now and she realized that instead of holding a grudge she must realize that if not for her aunt she might have spent her childhood in an orphanage like poor Jane Eyre. Even so, any respect or trust she had in the woman had died.

Now sitting in the drawing room with Honora who was busy with her embroidery, Amelia opened a book she had found in the attic of the Avery house. It was titled *A General History of the Pyrates* by Captain Charles Johnson, a book that had been published in England in 1724. Thumbing through it she saw that it contained the biographies of Anne Bonny, Calico Jack Rackham, Stede Bonnet, Mary Read, Bartholomew Black Bart Roberts and Blackbeard.

"Blackbeard," she said aloud.

"What did you say, dear?" Honora glanced up from her stitchery.

"This book. It tells all about pirates and gives an account of several of the most famous, including Blackbeard. I remembered when Derek showed me the portraits on the wall he mentioned that one of his ancestors, Jason? Jonas?"

"Jared Avery Cameron," Honora exclaimed. "It is a well-known fact that he married Quintana Marie Teach who was Blackbeard's daughter."

"Jared Avery Cameron and Quintana Marie Teach. Then it is true that he sailed with that pirate captain."

"So I have been told." Honora put down her embroidery, laughing softly. "It is quite a love story; one I doubt you will find in that book."

"Tell me. It will give me something special to tell the children."

"Quintana was called "the devil's daughter" because her father was the notorious pirate, Blackbeard. She was raised on a pirate ship, amidst dangerous men and there were those who said she was as fierce and as wild as the sea. She met Jared Cameron when her father captured his ship and held him captive. Yet something drew her to Jared Avery Cameron, the handsome and daring ship's captain her father and his crew had taken prisoner."

"Prisoner?" Amelia's face turned pale. "That must have been an ordeal. He was lucky they didn't make him walk the plank or leave him on a desert isle."

"That might have been his fate if Quinn hadn't taken a fancy to him." Honora laughed again. "It

382

seems that Jared was very handsome."

"Of course." Amelia closed the book. "All heroes of stories are."

"It is said that he was blond and blue-eyed like Derek."

"Then no wonder she fell in love with him." As she looked over at Honora, Amelia blushed. "But go on."

"Jared was hell bent on revenge at first. The pirates had taken everything from him that he valued, including his ship, which Blackbeard gave to Quinn and named her the ship's captain. But she showed him how to survive in a cut-throat and brutal world, their destinies became intertwined, they ended up with a treasure and that is as much of the story as I know."

"What about the treasure? Derek told me that it was a rumor that some of the treasure was buried somewhere on this plantation. By Avery, I think he said."

Honora leaned forward. "I don't know if that story is true. Moses and Derek searched high and low for any sign of it when they were boys and they did find a coin or two but in all these years no one has found even a hint as to where the treasure might be."

"But just think what would happen if that treasure was to be found. It would mean paying back the loan and bringing this plantation back to the way it was before the war." As soon as her words were out Amelia felt foolish. "But of course, it is most likely just a story. Things like that never happen in real life. Just in stories. I guess I read too much."

Honora was thoughtful. "No, stranger things have happened. And you are right, it would take pressure off of my son. It has been so hard for him since Charles has been in decline." She sighed wistfully and picked up her embroidery, concentrating on her remaining stiches.

Amelia returned to reading the book, fascinated by the information she found about peg legs, patches over missing eyes, a description of the pirate flag the Jolly Roger and the stories about pirates burying their treasure. Realizing that there was a pirate in Derek's family made it all the more interesting. So interesting that she didn't realize how late it was until Honora excused herself to go up to her bedroom.

Stubbornly Amelia waited, and waited, and waited for Derek to return but at last she gave up hope that he was going to come home tonight. Although she was deeply concerned, fearing the worst, there was nothing she could do. Only a fool would go out in the dark to look for him and the fact that Honora had not been alarmed gave her at least a shred of calm. It was a tranquility that was shattered as she passed his room and saw the empty bottle of whiskey discarded on a table by his bed. He had been drinking, and not just a little, he had been drinking a lot.

"That is not like Derek." Unlike his father, Derek was not a man who drank beyond his limit. Something was wrong. Hurrying into his room she looked around for a note to see if he had written an explanation of where he was going or why he wasn't coming home, but there was none.

Stripping off her skirt, petticoat, blouse, and shoes, Amelia decided to spend the night in Derek's room in the hope that he still might come home. Setting the book on the nightstand she lowered the wick on the oil lamp and climbed into bed.

\*    \*    \*    \*

Derek did not return to the Cameron house until the early hour of the morning. His head ached from the liquor he had partaken of the night before, his back was sore from lying on Moses' ungodly hard sofa, and his stomach was more than a bit queasy. Opening the door, he took off his boots so as not to make too much noise and alert the household that he had just returned. Then slowly he made the agonizing trek up the stairs, his head throbbing with each step he took.

Passing by Amelia's room he opened the door just an inch and saw that she was not within the room. Her bed had been made so he assumed she must be downstairs in the kitchen with his mother preparing the morning meal. He wondered if she had missed him last night and realized just how much he had missed her fragrant softness curled up beside him when he woke up this morning.

*My father just doesn't understand*, he thought. Love wasn't something that could be bought and sold like a commodity. Love was something precious, something that many people never found in their lives, a gift that two people gave to each other. He had that with Amelia and no matter what happened he vowed he would not let anyone wreak havoc on what they shared. With a silent promise he walked down the hallway to his room.

Opening the door Derek didn't see Amelia lying on his bed at first but as he came near the bed, he saw her half-clad form lying on top of the coves. She was

385

sound asleep, her breathing in and out a gentle snore. Stripping off his clothes and putting them in a chair he joined her on the bed. Reaching out he stroked her hair and felt a sense of peace wash over him. This was where he belonged – here with her.

## Chapter Twenty-Nine

The sun was shining through the clouds yet there was just a hint of an early fall chill in the air as Moses rode in the buggy with Forest and Quentin. They were headed for Richmond and what would be Moses' first time speaking at the podium. He tried to pretend that he wasn't at all nervous but the slight tremor to his hands and the way he kept clearing his throat gave his anxiety away. To put it simply, he didn't want to make a fool of himself.

"You look very dignified in your suit, but aren't you going to fix your tie?" Quentin asked as he looked over his shoulder at the backseat where Moses was seated.

"As a matter of fact, no," Moses answered. "I want the mark on my neck where the rope was tied to be visible. I want the men to know that what I am going to tell them really did happen. Otherwise they will think I am only telling them a story as politicians often do."

Quentin smiled at Moses' rebuke of those in politics. "Hm. That makes sense. I'll let you make the decisions on how you present yourself. I think it just might be about time that truth entered the game." He looked sideways at Forest, who was dressed in shirt and trousers. "Don't you, my dear?"

"Um hum."

Forest was usually talkative but today she was unusually quiet and Moses wondered why. She seemed melancholy and aloof, not at all as attentive and loving as she had been when they had both been staying at the Cameron house. She hadn't run into his arms when he arrived at the cottage nor impishly kissed him on the mouth the moment he walked through the door. Nor did she seek a place beside him in the buggy but kept her distance. It was almost as if she didn't want to be close to him and that deeply disturbed him. Once this ordeal of his speech was over he knew they had to have a talk to see what was troubling her.

"I've talked with the others in the party and with the exception of two or three they are in agreement that you are the perfect candidate. And once you reveal yourself to be honest, able, intelligent and willing I think the others will be on board as well."

"I hope so. But all I can do is try."

The rest of the journey into Richmond was made in silence with the exception of Moses softly practicing some of the lines from his speech that he wanted to be certain to remember. When at last they arrived at the Capitol, Quentin stopped the buggy so that Moses and Forest could alight, then drove off to find a spot to park the buggy and tend to the horses.

Moses fully expected Forest to take his hand to reassure him that all was well but as they made their way up the pathway, she walked ahead of him, her long, dark curly hair blowing in the breeze. At last he caught up with her and put his thoughts into words.

"Have I done something wrong? Something that has disturbed you?"

He looked so forlorn that she couldn't help but feel a tug at her heart. But how was she going to tell him that her aloofness was caused by her fear for him and that she wanted to protect him? That when she found out that she was the reason he had almost been killed it had broken her heart? How was she going to let him see into her soul and know the love that was there? No matter what happened a part of her would always love him.

"You haven't done anything amiss, Moses. It's *me*. I just need some time to think about a great many things."

She sounded so unhappy that it alarmed him and he tried to remember if anyone at the Cameron house had said anything to bring about her self-reflection, Charles Cameron perhaps. "If anyone has offended you or caused you harm I want you to tell me and I will….."

She put her fingers on his lips to silence him. "It's not that. It is just that I need to know where I belong."

'You belong with me."

His answer was so heartfelt, so poignant that on impulse she threw her arms around him and hugged him so tightly he could hardly breathe. But as two white men, walking up the steps stopped to stare at them with unbridled hostility, Forest quickly moved back and put on her hat.

"We need to hurry so that we can find a good place to sit. As near the podium as possible so you don't have to weave through the crowd in order to speak." Once again Forest hurried on ahead of Moses but he quickly caught up with her.

"I couldn't have done this on my own. I owe you and Quentin a great deal for believing in me. And I am grateful to Honora for having the patience to teach me how to talk proper English so I don't sound as if I am still a slave."

"We all might have helped a bit, but we only polished a diamond in the rough." Looking behind them and seeing no one was looking, she grasped his hand and squeezed it affectionately. "You can do this. I know that you can."

"Then let's go!" This time it was Moses who enthusiastically led the way.

Reaching the front doors Forest and Moses had to elbow their way through the crowd but were fortunate enough to find three vacant seats in the fourth row. Moses sat as near to the aisle as he could so he didn't have to squeeze past onlookers to walk up to the small stage at the front of the room.

Looking around Forest immediately noticed the grim expression on several faces. Tapping the shoulder of the man in front of her she quickly learned the reason, that a group called the White League had attacked potential Negro voters at the primary polls in Eufaula and Spring Hill, Alabama with seven Negroes killed and seventy others wounded. There had also been more than one thousand Negroes driven away from the polls due to the violence and fear that ensued.

"But we here in Richmond are far more civilized than Alabamians," the man boasted. Remembering what had happened to Moses, Forest attuned her ears to any further gossip.

Leaning back in her chair Forest's expression mirrored those of some of the others in the room. It was as if the white people had declared war on the black people and she being of mixed blood was in the middle of that war. To the Negroes she was considered white because of the color of her skin but to the Caucasians she was deemed to be black

390

because of the drops of Negro blood that flowed through her veins. Perhaps then people like her weren't meant to have a place in this world and were destined to be alone. It was a distressing thought.

"Excuse me. Excuse me. So sorry!" Quentin apologized as he stepped on the toes of a very heavy man who took up two seats.

Whispering in his ear Forest told him about the incident in Alabama.

"Not an isolated incident I am afraid," he informed her. "There were similar happenings in Georgia, South Carolina, Mississippi, and North Carolina. I suppose you could call it a "coup" of sorts." He knew what she was thinking because the focus of her eyes was on Moses. "Don't worry. I will make sure that he is safe. It can't happen here."

Forest wasn't so certain. Had she been wrong to encourage Moses to run for office considering the resentment that was rampant against the freed slaves, carpetbaggers, and Federal officials there in the South? With the guilt of being disloyal she found herself hoping that those present would pass Moses over and not want him as their candidate.

Unaware of what thoughts were whirling in Forest's mind, Moses thought her woeful expression was due to her being nervous for him. But he was determined that she would be proud. His mother had always told him that if you were going to do anything at all you must do it to the best of your ability.

The large room resonated with the buzz of the men's voices in a myriad of conversations. Moses laughed softly at the thought that these politicians sounded like a hive full of angry bees. The noise quickly silenced, however, as the man he knew to be

391

Matthew Stewart hit the podium with his gavel and asked for silence.  In a loud voice he announced the order of the speakers and Moses was relieved that he was number three.  It would give him a bit of time to compose himself.

The first speaker was a tall, frail-looking man with skin the color of Forest's and sandy blonde hair.  He spoke in platitudes assuring those assembled that their northern brothers wanted everyone in the country to be equal and that if they decided to put him on their ticket he would unite the party's white and black members.  His speech was met with grumbles and only light applause.

The second speaker was the antithesis of the first.  He was of mixed blood, dark of skin, short, and plump with a voice that sounded angry no matter what he was talking about.  Raising his fist several times in defiance he painted a picture of the war that was continuing and cautioned his listeners to be on alert at all times going forward. He emphasized the unrest that had settled in the South like a fog and warned that unless he was their candidate the state of Virginia would descend into a chaos matching hell's.  At the end of his talk the hall was quiet then broke into a smattering of hands clapping in accordance with his views.

"It's your turn."  Quentin gave him a not-so-gentle nudge.

Moses felt as if he were moving in slow motion as he made his way to the podium. He tried not to be aware of all the eyes staring at him, nor the few snickers as his notes fell on the ground and he bent over to pick them up. Quickly noticing that the pages were woefully out of order, however, he succumbed to the panic that swept over him. A panic that was wiped away as he looked at Forest's face and knew that she was rooting for him.

"I came here today to read the speech I hold in my hand but I have had a change of heart," he announced, tearing the paper into pieces and rolling them into a ball. "I am not going to make promises I can not keep or try to convince you of truths that are actually lies. I am going to talk to all of you man to man. We are humans, all of us, who share the same desires—to love and be loved, to provide for our families, to look forward to a future without fear, and to heal the sickness of hatred that has too long been part of our lives."

Moses swallowed then continued. "Over two hundred and fifty-five years ago the first slaves were brought to this land from far across the seas, chained together at the bottom of a ship with little hope for a better life. Their blood, tears, and sweat helped to build this land, a land that made us forget our original homeland. Some were lucky to have kind masters, others were mistreated. There were those who braved harsh punishment and even death to escape to freedom. And they were not alone. My family braved the dangers of the Underground Railroad. That opportunity was granted to us by a beautiful blonde-haired woman who went against her own to help us. She didn't judge us by the color of our skin nor did we judge her on the color of hers. Up north I worked among Negroes and whites alike in my new northern home."

"While still just a boy I ran off to join the Union army and learned once again that a man should not be judged by anything except what is in his heart and soul. I found out that we can work together for a common goal. One nation under God."

There were a few hostile comments made from the audience but Moses took them in his stride as he continued. "That is not to say that I have not suffered by the hands of those who are cruel and prejudiced." He tugged at his shirt to reveal the scars from his near lynching. "This is the mark that was left to remind me that there are those who are ruled by cruelty and violence."

There was a loud intake of breath as the onlookers realized he had nearly met his death. "But my life was saved by a man with skin the color of my attackers. A friend with whom I have worked together to build a better future for myself. Just as we can work together—black and white, yellow and brown—to build a better future for Virginia. We must fight ignorance with intelligence. Prejudice with tolerance. Hatred with strength. But where there is kindness we should reciprocate in like manner. I rest my case."

The room echoed with shouts of agreement and with applause. Moses didn't have to ask Quentin if he was to be the candidate, the answer was obvious by the way he was grinning. Later in the day it was formally announced. Moses Abraham Douglass was going to be the first black candidate to run for congressman in Richmond's history.

*     *     *     *

*P.H. Mayo and Brothers Tobacco Company* the sign read. All gussied up in his best tan suit, shoes, and a red tie, Derek hurriedly walked towards the huge red brick building on South Seventh street that was the key to his future. In the brown leather brief case that he carried was a written proposal that he and Moses had worked out a week before and he could only hope that it would stir up at least a small measure of interest.

*If only I can solidify this honey of a deal things will be looking up,* Derek thought, remembering that this particular tobacco company was one of the largest in America. They employed at least a quarter of a million dollars capital in their business, had four to five hundred hands at work, and had the capacity to produce nearly four hundred thousand pounds of the numerous superior brands that would be as Charles put it, "a real money-maker." The building covered about a third of a block and across the street were two large leaf factories.

The offices were on the top floor, right above the shipping rooms. Although the Camerons had never done business with this tobacco company before and had instead sold their tobacco to rival companies, Nathaniel Cameron had friends at the company for whom he had done quite a bit of smuggling during the war. When it came to money Derek's uncle hadn't cared if he was taking it from Union or Confederate officers. As a favor Nathaniel had finagled a meeting for Derek with Peter H. Mayo himself. Now it was up to Derek to strike a deal that would be mutually beneficial to them both.

Pushing through the front doors Derek made his way to the stairs and hurried to the floor that housed the offices. Reading the names above the doors he found Mayo's office at the end of the hallway. Knocking on the door he heard a gruff voice tell him to come on in.

A man with white hair, mustache and beard sat behind a large oak desk. "You must be Nathaniel's nephew," Peter Mayo rasped, eyeing Derek up and down as men do when judging another.

"I am." Derek stepped inside and closed the door behind him.

"Your uncle is as crooked as a dog's hind leg," Peter Mayo said with a sneer. "I hope you don't take after him."

Derek was taken aback. "I consider myself an honest man," he answered.

"Too bad, because honest men aren't any fun." Leaning back in his chair Peter Mayo roared with laughter. "Why you should have seen the look on your face when I challenged you. It was priceless." As he stood up it was revealed that he was short and stocky, quite a lot shorter than Derek.

"I know my uncle has quite a reputation for being a scoundrel, but he is a man who knows how to get things done that most men shy away from. In that way I take after my uncle." Derek noticed the cigar that rested in a saucer on the desk top. Although he didn't smoke, he took the cigar that Peter Mayo offered *him* but he didn't light it with a match.

"Why do you want to do business with us?" Peter Mayo asked.

"Because you are as good at marketing tobacco as we Camerons are at growing it." Reaching in the briefcase Derek grabbed the proposal and handed it to Peter Mayo to review. "I know that you have many brands that you both export and keep for domestic trade. Eglantine, Ivy, Mayo's Cut Plug, Holly,

Banquet Sweet Chewing, and Mayo's Genuine TJ. S. Navy, the first navy plug ever made in this country."

"Impressive. You have done your research."

"There are five men on the road as well as agents in Liverpool and Bristol, England. I can honestly tell you that with Cameron tobacco added to your stock pile you will need to double the men that you have."

Although Peter Mayo pulled up a chair for Derek to sit in, he preferred to stand. Looking down at Peter Mayo gave him a sense of power that he would not have felt if he were sitting.

"I know all about the Camerons. There was a time when they were synonymous with tobacco." Retrieving his cigar, he took a puff. "You have to admit your ancestors were quite colorful. Nearly as colorful as mine. The name Mayo is historic in Richmond." And another puff. "Why it was a Mayo who laid out the city with Byrd. And the great Indian chief, Powhatan, is buried on the old Mayo homestead."

"I don't think the Camerons can top that." Derek was anxious to come right to the point. "I heard through the grapevine that your company is going to mass produce cigarettes for sale and I would like Cameron tobacco to be a part of that."

"Well, you don't mince words. I admire that." Quickly Peter Mayo looked over the paper on his desk. "It seems fair enough to me. Most importantly, I need your tobacco. Shall we say that we have a deal?" Holding out his hand, Peter Mayo shook on it.

\*　　\*　　\*　　\*

It had started out to be an ordinary day. Amelia had helped Honora fix breakfast and then do the dishes, she had then hurried off to the Avery House to give the lessons she had planned the night before to her students, and then she had returned to the Cameron House to spend the rest of the afternoon reading while Honora worked on her stitchery. As it was, however, the day was not ordinary after all.

"I think it is time that I helped you plan your wedding," Honora announced suddenly, putting down her embroidery. "I know two people in love when I see them and I know you are perfect for my son."

Putting down her book, Amelia felt more than a little giddy at the thought. "I know I love Derek and I hope that he loves me even half as much as I love him. But….." She was going to confess that she had little to bring to the marriage, at least monetarily, but Honora shook her head.

"There are no *buts* about it. You are already a part of the family. It's time your portrait was up on the wall next to the others. And time for Derek's image to hang there as well." Honora smiled mischievously, "and time for me to be able to cradle a grandchild or two in my arms before I'm too old."

"You will never be old," Amelia answered, and she meant that. Honora was the kind of person who was young at heart, youthful in spirit, and had an ageless beauty.

"How I wish that was true." Thinking about the portraits, it seemed that Honora was momentarily transported to the past. "The years just seem to fly by at times."

Amelia couldn't help but wonder why Honora had married Charles Cameron. To her he definitely

398

seemed unlovable. But many times people changed and not for the best. She thought about her Aunt Lucinda who had once been the bell of the ball but who now was resentful and closeminded. Amelia was determined that she would never let such a thing happen to her.

"Of course, we will have the wedding here," Honora said softly. "You can make quite an entrance walking down the stairs. And we will have a reception in the garden. Of course, we will include your students and their families. And there will be my daughter Allegra and her husband, Reeve and their children."

"I would like that." Amelia wished with all her heart that Delilah, Jedidiah's mother, could be one of the guests but knowing how cranky and prejudice Charles Cameron could be she didn't pose that suggestion. Delilah was still recovering from the death of her son and didn't need to be confronted by a hateful old man.

"You can help me bake the bridal cake. I think it should be angel food, don't you?" Honora was ticking off a list of what needed to be done in her mind.

"Forest can be my bridesmaid." Amelia thought how sad it was that she didn't have any friends but her aunt had wanted it that way. The better to manipulate her she supposed.

"And of course, Moses will be Derek's best man. It will work out perfectly." Taking Amelia by the hand, Honora led her to the stairs. "And that leaves the wedding dress."

Amelia stiffened. "I don't have…."

"There is a perfect dress for you in a box in the attic. My stepson's wife, Daphne, wore it several years ago. If I am right, I think it will be just your size."

Together they climbed the stairs and then pulled down the ladder that took them up to the attic. Honora lit a lantern and knew right where the box with the dress was stored. Like a present it was tied with a bow and as she handed it to Amelia it was like opening up a gift at Christmas time.

"Oh, how beautiful!" It was a gown fit for a princess.

"Try it on. I can make any adjustments that need to be done. The good Lord knows I have had to become quite the dressmaker since the war ended." Politely turning her back while Amelia undressed, Honora waited until Amelia told her to turn around.

The white satin was cool on Amelia's skin and rustled when she moved. It was a dress the likes of which Amelia had never seen before. Best of all it was nearly a perfect fit except that Amelia's waist was smaller than Daphne's had been. But that would be easy for Honora to take in.

"And here is the veil and circlet."

Amelia felt as if she were putting a crown upon her head. The dress was magical, the kind that storybooks told about.

"There's an old mirror over here. Let me dust it off and you can take a look."

The diadem, lace and pearls gave Amelia the air of a queen; the veil hanging down her back looked like wings. The full-skirted white satin dress, that Honora told her had been made by a French dressmaker in New Orleans, was embroidered with seed pearls, the skirt billowing with its yards and yards of material as she moved.

"You will make a most beautiful bride," Honora said in praise. "Derek will be very proud."

"I hope so." It troubled Amelia that it was Honora and not Derek who had instigated a wedding, but she supposed it was because he had been so busy trying to find a way to pay back that cursed loan and tend to the tobacco plants.

"Stay right there. I need to go downstairs and get some pins so that I can mark the places where the dress needs to be taken in." Honora was humming a cheerful song as she climbed down from the attic.

The first time Amelia had visited this attic she had been looking for books but now she let her eyes wander. It was like being in a little museum, with items divided into sections. Each section was marked with a name and her eyes were drawn to the name Avery. She decided that as soon as she had extra time she would come back up and explore.

"I'm back."

There were only two places that needed a nip and a tuck. Honora had them marked very quickly. Amelia felt a strange sense of regret as she removed the dress and veil. It was as if she had been in a dream and now had to wake up. Putting on her own dress of blue cotton she was instantly transported back to reality. But thanks to Honora she now had a lovely dream of what it would be like to stand beside Derek and take the vows that would bind them together.

Amelia was so immersed in her imaginings that she didn't hear a knock at the door at first but as the knock became louder she hurried to the front door. It was strange because no one in the family ever used the bronze knocker. A fear that it might be Edward Cutler swept over her. The man was like a vulture waiting to strip his prey bare.

"Shall I answer it?" she called out to Honora, thinking to herself that if it was the greedy banker she would give him a piece of her mind.

"Yes, please, do, dear."

All kinds of retorts ran through her mind as she opened the door. But it was not Edward Cutler. Standing at the door was the most beautiful woman that Amelia had ever seen. Her hair was a fiery red, her eyes were hazel surrounded by long, thick lashes, her nose was just the right shape and size, thrust up at a haughty angle. Her mouth was full and pouty. Her body was shaped like an hourglass. She was in fact perfect in every way.

"May I help you?" Amelia asked, looking down at the three suitcases that were all of a different size.

"I certainly hope so." The woman gestured to a man standing behind her. "Franklin, get my bags."

Amelia was confused. Just who was this woman? A relative no doubt. "I beg your pardon. Were the Camerons expecting you?" she asked.

"Yes, of course." The woman eyed Amelia up and down just as Amelia had assessed her—woman to woman. "Charles Cameron sent a telegram to my father. I'm to be his invited guest."

"His guest." Amelia was taken by surprise.

With all the dignity of someone of royal blood the woman said haughtily. "My name is Angelique. Angelique Jamison."

\*    \*    \*    \*

402

To say that Angelique Jamison's presence in the Cameron household seemed to be problematic was an understatement! She was the kind of woman who knew how to wind any male in her sphere around her little finger. As for those of the female gender, it was obvious that coexisting with the self-centered woman was going to be grueling. Worst of all she did not even try to hide the fact that she was stalking Derek Cameron like a cat pursues a mouse.

"What on earth was Charles thinkin' to invite that creature here?" Honora whispered to Amelia as they were putting the finishing touches on supper.

"She said that her father was one of your husband's best friends."

Amelia had been confident in her relationship with Derek, but her self-assurance withered just a bit as she saw the way the newcomer in their midst flirted coquettishly with Derek every chance she got. Touching him intimately whenever she could—on the arm, face, or shoulder—she made no secret of the fact that she had him in her sights.

"Friend of Charles? Oh pooh! She didn't set foot on this doorstep because of daughterly duty. She is huntin'." Honora took out her frustration on the pudding she was stirring. "But don't worry, my dear. My son is not stupid. I raised him better than that!"

"But she is so lovely." Amelia felt like a dull pigeon in the presence of a peacock.

"Beauty is as beauty does. Besides, she is wastin' her time. Derek's heart is already taken." Honora scowled as she looked over her shoulder and saw that the newcomer had wasted no time in

403

procuring a seat right next to Derek at the dinner table.

Amelia saw the deliberate move also. "I hope you are right. But Derek is only human." Nervously she touched the sapphire ring on her finger. It was Derek's promise that they would have a life together.

"And so is she. Human. Not the princess that she supposes herself to be." Her words were drowned out by the sound of Angelique's laughter and her comment to Derek that he said the cutest things.

Amelia fought against the little demon of jealousy that threatened to overtake her but it was difficult to watch as another woman threw herself at the man she loved.

"There is so much about her that reminds me of Daphne, my stepson's wife. They could be twins." She patted Amelia on the arm. "I should have saved Bevin from Daphne's clutches, but I didn't. But I won't just stand by and watch this time." She laughed softly and the sound was ominous. "Our little houseguest doesn't know what she is in for but in the weeks to come she will soon find out."

# PART THREE :  Full Circle

## Virginia

## 1874

"The wheel has come full circle."

William Shakespeare

## Chapter Thirty

Time was elusive, or so it seemed. For some it moved too quickly, for others it moved much too slowly. One thing was true; however, no one could control the tick tick ticking of time as the hands of the clock moved from minute to minute, hour to hour, and one day followed another.

As far as Derek was concerned there were not enough hours in the day and he feared he was running out of time to complete the tobacco harvest and make certain that Peter H. Mayo received the tobacco that had been promised for the manufacture of his cigarettes. Trying to keep to a schedule meant getting up before the crack of dawn and working until he thought he would fall on his face. Adding to his stress was the presence of the houseguest his father had instilled in the household, a brazen woman who seemed to just pop up at the worst possible times to try and seduce him.

"Damn my father!" As usual Charles Cameron was determined to have his way no matter what he had to do or who would get hurt in the meantime. And all the while Derek was put in an awkward situation. If it had been up to him, he would have told Angelique Jamison to pack her bags and leave immediately. But his father was head of the household, the patriarch and so all that he could do was to skillfully avoid the traps the irritating woman set for him while at the same time assuring Amelia that she was his only love.

Added to the quandary he was in was the matter of the wedding. Understandably under the circumstances, with a rival dangling right before her eyes, Amelia was anxious to be married. Although that was what Derek longed for too, there were several things that made that difficult, at least for the moment--a lack of money and the threat of losing Winding Oaks if the money owed to the bank wasn't paid back soon, the gruesome schedule that had to be maintained in order to secure the future, and worst of all the threat from his father that if Derek dared to pursue a union with Miss Amelia Seton he would disinherit him and leave Winding Oaks to his brother, Nathaniel.

"You will marry Angelique Jamison and no other," were words Charles Cameron had declared the last time they had a confrontation. Not even Derek's threats to reveal his father's past in the Ku Klux Klan could sway him. Derek was trapped and as the days passed, he grew more and more resentful because of it.

To Amelia time seemed to be her enemy and not her friend. With Derek so busy in the tobacco fields the days were long and even teaching the children didn't fill the void in her days. Her only solace was lying in Derek's arms at night, even those nights when he was just too tired to make love.

*He loves me, not that Jamison woman*, she told herself over and over again. Derek was with *her*, she was in his bed, their hearts were in alignment, and that was all that mattered. Even Derek's father didn't have the power to pull them apart. Penniless she might be, but she was rich because she knew that love was really the most important thing in life. For the time being all was well.

Balancing his time was the major hurdle in Moses' life. The days were swift in duration and he soon found out that he had bitten off a little more than he could handle. There were political meetings he was obligated to attend, influential people he was scheduled to meet, information that he needed to decipher, books to be read, and all this on top of caring for a peanut crop that looked as if it would soon be able to be harvested. The plants had matured, the soil was not too wet or dry and conditions were right to go up and down the green rows of peanut plants and dig them up.

"I'll do it tomorrow." he said to himself, little realizing that he was saying that same thing over and over. For the moment the election came first in his mind because if he won the election, he felt he could help bring unity and fairness to the area. Only Forest was more important. It was, however, a cause of disappointment that although Forest was attentive and supportive, she was treating him more like a friend than a lover, especially when anyone was around. Although he had asked her several times if there was anything wrong, she consistently denied that there *was* a problem.

"We all must concentrate on your campaign so that you will be the winner," she had said when he had insisted that she explain what had cooled her ardor.

As for Forest, she treasured the time she spent with Moses although she was careful not to let him know how much she loved him. To her time moved too swiftly and the days were so short that she found herself mourning the sight of the setting sun each time it appeared in the sky. She was torn between her feelings and her need to protect him, but she sensed that time was running out and that Moses would soon coerce her into telling him what was troubling her.

*I have to make a choice between loving Moses in every way and revealing to the world that I, like him, have the blood of slaves running through my veins,* she thought again and again. Openly flaunting their love for each other might lead to another disaster and the last thing she wanted was for Moses to be dangling from a tree.

Forest felt a twinge of guilt that she had so far not pursued information that would help her find her mother. She was so close to finding out the truth and perhaps being reunited but so far, she had done nothing that could have helped her find out the truth. But she knew in her heart that had to change and that the man named William Trenholm had to be reckoned with soon.

*       *       *       *

Charles Cameron was getting stronger by the day. And with that strength came his need to wield more and more power over the ill-fated people in his path, much to their misfortune. Not content to wither away in his room he now made his presence known in the household, ruling over his domain with all the stern audacity of a king.

Whenever she saw that Charles was anywhere near, Amelia made it a point to avoid him. His cold stare, rude comments, and overall manner of disrespect towards her had left her in tears several times. Even Honora's calm assurances hadn't made her feel any better.

"His bark is much worse than his bite. Don't let him bother you, Amelia dear," Honora insisted as they retreated to the laundry room to do a load of wash.

"I'm trying to ignore his barbed tongue, but I can't overlook the fact that he doesn't like me," Amelia answered, using a large wooden paddle to stir the garments that had been soaking overnight.

"It's not that he doesn't like you. It's just that he is perturbed that you are thwartin' his plans." She reached over and affectionately patted Amelia's hand. "Derek has refused to give in to his father's demands because of his love for you. You should be complimented."

"You mean that he wants Derek to marry Angelique Jamison and not me." Although she had not meant to eavesdrop, Amelia had heard one of Derek's arguments with his father as she had walked down the hall.

Honora shook her head and sighed. "I'm afraid my husband is a bit old fashioned. In days gone by there were arranged marriages between the various prominent southern families but those days are as outdated as hoopskirts." Taking out her aggravation on the laundry she vigorously poked at the clothes in the wooden tub.

Washing clothes was a laborious process – first soaking the clothes overnight then putting them in soapy water. Then came the rinse in clean water either one or two times until all the soap was out. The garments would be wrung out and put on a rope strung between two trees in the courtyard to dry until

410

they could be ironed. Since Derek had been increasing his hours out in the field it seemed that the loads of laundry were endless.

"My Aunt Lucinda tried to play matchmaker for me," Amelia confided, "with a banker of all people. So, your husband is not alone in trying to forgo matters of the heart." She couldn't help but wonder how her aunt was doing and if she missed her in any way.

"Well as I have told you Charles pushed, prodded, and got his way with my stepson and the outcome was disastrous. I made a vow that he would never do the same to Derek, so you definitely have an ally in me. And to tell the truth, Amelia, isn't love sometimes as intricate a thing to win as a war?"

Amelia didn't have time to answer before they heard swearing, shouting, and grumbling from the other room. Fearing that Charles might have fallen or done something to hurt himself they both hurried to the drawing room.

"What is it, Charles. Are you all right?" Honora was at his side in an instant.

"All right?" Holding out the newspaper—the Daily Dispatch—for Honora to see, he sputtered like an old teakettle. "It says right there in black and white that *my* Nigrah is runnin' for Congress."

"*Your* Nigrah?" Honora mocked, scanning the article. "Moses isn't *your* anythin'"

"You know what I mean! He was mine. I owned him!" He ripped off his spectacles and threw them on the nearby table. "Why don't these black bastards learn to keep their place and not go pokin' their noses into the business of their betters?"

411

Honora tried to calm him. "It is their business now just as it is yours. By law, Charles. By law."

"By coercion you mean. We ought to hang every last one of them!" He punctuated his declaration by banging his hand on the arm of his chair.

"Has your brain been muddled by Mrs. O'Leary's tea?" Yanking the newspaper from his hands Honora swore a word that ladies never said. "Damn it, Charles. You should be proud of Moses not critical. You sound like an old, disgruntled bear."

"I have a right to be disgruntled! And those damnable Yankees are to blame! Interferin' in our way of life down here. They are tryin' to turn monkeys into men just to rub it in our faces that we lost that God-awful war." He tried to grab the newspaper, but Honora held it just out of his reach.

"That's the way it is, Charles. Winners take all. You are goin' to have to live with that." With those words spoken Honora gave Amelia a little nudge and they left the room. But when they reached the door and Amelia turned her head to look back, she had the unsettling feeling that Charles Cameron was not going to admit defeat.

\*　　\*　　\*　　\*

In all his wildest imaginings Moses had never foreseen what being in the public eye could do to a man's life. Suddenly he had been plucked from obscurity and shoved into the limelight. Photographers wanted to take his picture, reporters waited in line to ask him questions for their newspapers, the story of his near-lynching and escape from slavery on the Underground Railroad seemed to be everywhere. It was as if he couldn't walk down the streets of Richmond without being recognized.

*Richmond's Moses* was the name that had been given to him now that he had thrown his "hat in the ring" as Quentin called it. They called him handsome, exciting, and a new hope for Congress. It was said that he was going to part the "white sea" and give black people a chance to be represented. There were so many people that wanted to know every detail about him that when he received a letter from his father up north, he learned that the newspaper people had even interviewed his mother and father.

"I told you that you would be a good candidate," Quentin said to him now as they walked up the steps of the Capitol. "But I had no idea you would be quite this polarizing. *Charismatic authority* I call it."

"Moses is magical. Too bad women can't vote because I do believe that from the looks he receives they think of him as the prince of all their dreams." Forest tried to hide the twinge of jealousy she felt every time another woman openly flirted with him.

"I just hope that I don't disappoint those who have been so good to me and given me their support," Moses exclaimed, pausing to shake the hands of a few of his followers who were lined up on the stairs just to see him.

"You won't. You are a natural when it comes to politics and I ought to know." Reaching in his pocket Quentin pulled out a long list of men who were endorsing Moses for congress. "Even ole Gilbert Walker, the governor, has spoken kindly of you."

"The governor?" The very thought was intimidating to Moses and put a weight on his shoulders to live up to all the expectations.

Seeing the worried look on Moses' face, Forest felt a surge of compassion. There was so much expected of him lately that she could not help wishing he had never agreed to take politics seriously. Quentin was sometimes cynical about politics and knew not to be too trusting but Moses was so honest and anxious to help others that she was concerned about all the attention he was receiving. What if it sparked resentment in the minds of others like the Ku Klux Klan and he was made the target of violence again? What then? Bigotry was an ailment, and it could spread quickly.

Reaching the top of the stairs Forest, Moses, and Quentin paused for just a moment. Moses noticed the frown on Forest's face and tried to make light of the moment. "Well, at least I won't have to give another speech today," he teased.

"I suppose that is a good thing," she whispered. "I was afraid that you were running out of words."

Quentin joined in the merriment. "Not like me. I can talk all day and if I can't think of the right words, I just make some up."

For a moment they were distracted and did not notice the short, balding man until he bumped into Moses. Forest thought at first that it was an accident until the man shoved a card into Moses' pocket then took off running.

"Let's hope that was an admirer of yours," Quentin exclaimed.

"Or a photographer giving you his business card," Forest added, trying to ignore the shiver that

414

crept up her spine, an eerie feeling that she tried to shake off.

Moses turned the card over wondering just what it was and stiffened as he saw the picture of a white man with sandy-colored hair dressed in medieval garments. The image was hanging upside down from a tree by one ankle. At the bottom of the card were the words *"The Hanged Man."* It reminded him of the night of his lynching, but he wouldn't allow himself to feel any fear.

"What is it, Moses?" When he didn't answer she grabbed the card from his hand and looked at the picture. "A hanged man?" Was it meant to intimidate him or was it a warning of some kind?

"Let me see it." Quentin studied the card for several minutes before he said, "I've only seen a card like this once before, but I believe it is a Tarot card."

"Tarot?" Moses had never heard that word.

Quentin traced the drawing of the man with the tip of his finger. "The man is hanging upside down to view the world. It is used by fortune tellers."

"But what does it mean?" Moses wanted to know if it was meant to give him a message. He doubted that the card was meant as a gesture of friendship. Not the way the man had run away.

Quentin answered honestly, "I don't know."

All of Forest's protective instincts prompted her to take charge of the situation. "I have passed by a little shop by the dressmakers. An old woman there sells trinkets, good luck charms, and so-called love potions. She might be able to tell me."

Fortune telling had been immensely popular in Philadelphia, as she remembered. Some of the ladies she had known there had made a game of divination games, enlisting practitioners of the occult to entertain them. It was decided that Quentin and Moses would attend their political meeting and Forest would seek out the woman who had the shop to see if she could tell her what the card meant.

Walking at a fast pace, Forest hurried down the steps and made her way down Grace Street, being careful not to get in the path of any buggies or carriages as she crossed the road. The streets she moved down reminded her of the times she had gone to see Andrew Wyatt and she made a mental note to go and see him again in the upcoming days to learn more about her father, William Trenholm so as to locate her mother.

At last she reached the tiny shop that was wedged in between a cobbler's workshop and a pawn shop. Pushing open the door she was disappointed to see that instead of the old woman she had seen many times before a girl of about her own age stood behind the counter.

"Is the older woman here?" Forest asked, hoping she might be in the back room.

"Not today. But I can be of help." The girl smiled pleasantly.

Desperate for information, Forest showed the young woman the card. "I was told it was a Tarot Card. The Hanged Man. Can you tell me what it means?"

"Do you believe in the supernatural?"

"Certainly not!" Crystal gazing, palmistry, and other means to contact the dead was foolish. She remembered one of the ladies in Philadelphia talking about all the fraudsters, charlatans, and unethical

416

rogues they had encountered in the world of the occult.

"Then you don't want to speak with a dead relative or friend?" The young woman laughed. "I don't believe in that nonsense either but working here has netted me a dollar or two." At Forest's look of disappointment, she added, "but I know about the cards and I can tell you that this one suggests a man viewing the world from a different perspective than others. If you look at the card, the facial expression is calm and serene. His red hose represents human passion and the blue vest is knowledge."

"Then it doesn't signify death or anything like that?" Forest's sigh of relief was audible.

"The Messenger of Death card is a skeleton dressed in black armor, riding a white horse. This card can mean several other things. Self-sacrifice., martyrdom, surrender, or being suspended in time."

Forest pressed on. "If someone came up to you and handed you this card what would you think?"

"It would depend on who gave me the card, but it could possibly indicate a period of indecision or a need to suspend certain action." The young woman shrugged. "I'm sorry I can't give you more information."

Remembering her manners, Forest thanked her for her help. Turning towards the door she felt confusion and frustration. Although she knew more about the card than she had when she had entered the shop, she still didn't understand why the man had thrust it into Moses' hands. Whatever the reason it didn't bode well. But only time would tell.

# ASHES AND AWAKENINGS

## Chapter Thirty-One

The sound of the church organ accompanying the choir voices was like a balm soothing Amelia's heart and soul. She remembered a quote by Thomas Carlyle that she had read, "music is well said to be the speech of angels" and in that moment she realized how true it was. There was so much emotion in both the lively tunes and those of a more somber tone that it was as if she was lifted up to a higher place. A place where there was no cruelty and strife, and people were free to live in peace and love one another. Music "brings us near to the infinite,"

Closing her eyes, she listened as the choir sang the refrain: "*Go down, Moses. Way down in Eqypt's land. Tell ole Pharaoh. Let my people go.*" The music was so moving, so heartfelt that she felt tears sting her eyes. Putting her hands to her face she felt those tears and wiped them away.

"Don't cry, Miss Amelia......"

Amelia felt the gentle hand of one of her students caress her shoulder. Turning her head, she saw that it was Ruth, the young sister of Jedidiah, a pretty girl with big brown eyes and pigtails.

"I don't want you to be sad." The little girl's mouth curved downward into a frown.

Amelia smiled through her tears. "I'm not sad, Ruthie. It's just that the music touches my heart." She reached out and tickled the little girl under her chin. "Like *you* touch my heart."

"You touch my heart too." Ruth's mouth lifted into a grin. "All of us love you."

And it was that love that helped give Amelia the strength and courage to carry on despite all the hatred in the world, particularly that anger and loathing that she heard expressed by Charles Cameron on a daily basis. The children and the church had become her haven, the place she could come to regain her sanity and to heal her emotional wounds.

Amelia patted the seat beside her on the pew. "Come, sit beside me. Elijah is going to play."

Elijah was a gentle, shy, smart, and talented student of Amelia's, a cousin of Jedidiah's, who had learned how to play the violin from his grandfather. Listening to the notes that he generated from the violin was like listening to a human voice singing. Putting her arm around Ruth to embrace her they closed their eyes and listened, mesmerized for that moment in time by the echoing beauty that surrounded them.

Amelia imagined herself walking down a bright green pathway with sunflowers on each side. At the end of the pathway was Derek and beside him were her students, both black and white. They were all smiling and in their tiny hands were books, the key to the future, she had told them. As she walked forward, the children reached out to each other and held the hand of the little boy or little girl who stood near them.

The music was all-enveloping, erasing all the heartache she had felt during the week. When Elijah had finished his song and there was silence again, she felt a sense of loss and wished with all her heart that the music could go on forever. "Nothing among the

420

utterances allowed to man is felt to be so divine," Carlyle had written. She knew now that it was true.

As the reverend began his closing prayer, Amelia joined in. "Our prayer for mankind is this, that we can begin to truly love one another and forgive our brothers so that we can all live together in this world and in the next."

Amelia watched as the church members stood up and hugged each other as if they didn't have a care in the world. There were smiles and she heard the sound of laughter. The camaraderie was extended to her as each of her student's parents took hold of her hand to thank her for the positive difference she was making in their children's lives. Amelia felt her face flush as she was assailed by their praise.

"How did I do, Miss Amelia?" Still holding his violin Elijah waited hopefully for her opinion of his playing.

"I have never heard anything so beautiful," she exclaimed, putting her hand on his shoulder. "Your music took me to heaven. I had no idea that you were so talented."

The boy was all smiles. "I practice by playing to the animals, the lonely ones whose parents have been taken from them. I like to think that it makes them feel less abandoned."

"I'm sure that it does. I know that I was very sad and your song lifted my spirits." She looked over at Ruth. "Shall we begin to include songs in our classes?"

Both children agreed that they would look forward to taking time out for music. Elijah volunteered to play his violin any time Amelia asked him. Ruth confided to Amelia that she loved to sing and that Esther could play the piano and Samson the harmonica.

"Why don't we slip our music session between reading and arithmetic?" Both children nodded their heads in agreement.

"It's all set then. Next week we will start the new schedule." With Ruth on one side and Elijah on the other Amelia walked towards the church door and it was only in that moment that she noticed that there was a raging storm outside. The music had distracted her but now she could hear the thunder and see the large drops of rain.

"Oh, no!" She remembered Derek telling her that severe rainstorms could have an adverse effect on tobacco plants. And what about Moses' peanuts? She hoped that it was not raining as heavily at the plantation.

Taking a look outside Amelia could see that there was no way for her to drive the buggy with the rain beating down on the dirt roads. She would have to stay at the church until the storm broke.

"I'll stay with you Miss Amelia!" Ruth was delighted that she would have Amelia's company for at least a little while longer.

"Me too!" Elijah as usual was also concerned for the welfare of the animals. Running outside he herded two dogs, three cats, and a goat inside the church where it was warm.

"Is it all right ifen I stay here too?" Samson, a young boy so named because of his large size joined the small group. "Will you tell us a story?"

Realizing that she could use this moment to teach, Amelia suggested that they take turns reading a story from one of the books she had brought from the Cameron home. "Which story do you want?" She shouldn't have been surprised that the children suggested Noah's Ark considering the storm outside.

Going to the cupboard, Amelia pulled out *The Book of Bible Stories*, settled down on one of the benches and started to read. "The Lord saw how utterly wicked people on earth had become; every thought was only evil all the time. So, God said, "I will destroy from the earth the people I have created. And with them, the animals, birds, and creeping things."

"Not the animals!" Elijah shook his head, distressed at the thought of animals dying.

"Hush, Elijah. Let Miss Amelia read," Ruth chastised.

Amelia read on. "But Noah found favor with God who told him to build an ark for his family and for the animals. That should please you, Elijah."

"It does."

Amelia read a little further, then handed the book to Samson who read about the building of the ark. To Elijah she gave the part of the story where the animals were loaded on the ark two by two. Ruth read the last part of the story, adding a few of her own twists and turns.

"It's still raining," Samson said softly. "Can we read another story?"

Amelia had a better idea. "I think it would be nice if Elijah played his violin. Will you, Elijah?"

Accompanied by the thunder, Elijah picked up his violin and started to play...

423

\*     \*     \*     \*

"Rain! Damn the rain." There were times when Derek hated storms and this was one of those times because the rain was accompanied by wind.

It seemed there had been one thing after another: insects such as hornworms and aphids, fungus, not enough water, and now the drenching rain. Derek had tended the plants  fervently, fending off problems before they became serious. Now there was this.

Although harvesting had begun and there were plants in curing sheds. there was still a lot of topping to do. Using tents, pieces of canvas, blankets and anything he could get his hands on, he labored with his workers to cover the exposed plants, hoping that at least seventy percent of the crop would make it through the storm and the excessive moisture in the air.

"Easy....easy....."   Make sure that tarp is secure," Derek instructed two of the field hands, stepping forward to lend them a hand.

Soaked to the skin, chilled to the bone Derek persisted in the desperate effort to protect his valuable crop. He supposed that Moses was likewise facing problems with too much rain on his crop in too short a time. He was determined to go help him as soon as the tobacco was safe.

Thinking about his friend, Derek was reminded of Amelia telling him about his father's outburst because of all the attention Moses was getting. He couldn't help but smile. It was good for his father to get his comeuppance once in a while.

"I think we're good. Everything is tied up and secure," one of the field hands assured him.

"Thanks, Walter." It was good to have a young, strong man at the plantation to help in times such as these. "Rain is startin' to let up a bit."

"Are we done then?"

Derek nodded. "Go on home to your wife, dry yourself off and have a good, stiff drink. That will warm you up."

Wiping his wet face and hair with his hands, he watched his workers leave and was anxious to take his own advice. It would be good to snuggle in bed with Amelia tonight after the episode with the storm.

Saddling up his horse he rode to Moses' small farm to see if he needed any help and was relieved to see that Moses had covered his peanut crop with canvas as well. He would have stopped by just to chat, but the lights were off inside and he figured Moses had a rough day and was most likely curled up in his bed asleep. It was another reminder that it was where he should be.

Riding back to the Cameron house he stopped by the bathhouse, not to take a bath but just to towel himself off. Stripping off his pants, boots, and shirt he made do with just his underwear as he checked in the kitchen to see if there was anything left from dinner.

"Bless my mother and Amelia" he whispered in thanks, gorging himself on cold fried chicken and baked sweet potatoes. Finding a bottle of whiskey that his mother had hidden from his father, he poured himself a glass to wash down the food and to warm himself up. Taking the bottle of whiskey with him, he climbed the stairs, not at all surprised that the other household members had already sought their beds.

Not bothering to light the lantern, Derek stripped off his underwear and pulled back the covers. He was pleasantly surprised to see that Amelia was already in bed. He could hear the soft intake and outtake of her breathing. Trying not to awaken her, he slipped into bed beside her, fluffing the pillow then putting it under his head.

Suddenly Derek realized that Amelia had rolled over and that her naked body was pressed against his. Her soft warmth was especially stirring after toiling so hard against the rain. Closing his eyes, he gave in to the erotic feelings her nearness inspired, gasping as her warm fingers reached for his maleness. If he had thought himself too exhausted for lovemaking there was that part of him that had clearly been awakened.

Turning over so that they were face to face, their bodies caressing he reached for her breasts, cupping them as he moved seductively against her. Despite his aroused passions, however, there was a part of his brain that knew something wasn't right. Although Amelia had perfectly shaped breasts that were just the right size for his hands, these breasts were much larger.

"What in the hell?" Tracing the contours of the body next to his with his fingers, relying on his other senses as those without sight must do, he realized that the woman next to him was definitely not Amelia.

Bounding out of bed, hurrying to light the lantern, Derek was infuriated as he was greeted with the sight of a woman with long tousled red hair and a seductive smile. "Come back to bed, Derek."

426

Angelique's deception was, as Honora might have said, 'the straw that broke the camel's back' and Derek saw no reason to mince words. "Get out of the bed, out of this room and tomorrow I want you out of this house!"

Any other woman would have been embarrassed by his tirade but not Angelique. "Oh, don't be a fool. Our fathers want to see our two houses joined together so we might as well get better acquainted." Lying on her side she struck a seductive pose that exposed every inch of her to his gaze.

Derek's responded in a gruff but whispered voice, "I am just as acquainted with you as I want to be." Nervously he glanced towards the door. He was not so tired that he didn't realize what would happen if Amelia witnessed another woman in the bed they often shared.

Angelique made no attempt to get out of bed. "Oh, I don't think so. I'm sure I could do things to you that would be very surprising. Things that we would both enjoy."

Seeing her nightgown on the floor beside the bed, Derek picked it up and unceremoniously threw it at her. He was in a hurry to get rid of her before his worst nightmare came true. "Put this on and get out or I swear I will throw you bodily out of my room."

Something about his expression or the tone of his voice seemed to unnerve her because she did as he told her. Watching as she strode down the hall to her own room he sighed with relief, but sleep was a long time coming to him.

Derek was awakened by the pressure of another body next to him, hugging him tightly against her. Thinking for a minute that it was Angelique returning with more shenanigans he angrily pulled away. "What did I tell you?"

"I don't remember." Amelia's soft voice was a godsend and restored Derek's serenity. "I'm so sorry that I am so late, but the rain made it impossible to travel on the roads. I stayed at the church with some of the children until the rain stopped and it was safe to come home."

Reaching out to her he could feel the chill in her body and held her close. "I know all about the rain."

"Then you are not annoyed with me?" She was curious about why he had pushed her away.

"Annoyed? Hell no. Having you here beside me is the answer to my prayers." And he knew at that moment that he wanted her beside him for eternity. To hell with what his father wanted. It was time he stopped being intimidated by a hate-filled, overbearing old man. He intended to make Amelia his wife and if that meant losing his inheritance to Winding Oaks, so be it.

\*　　\*　　\*　　\*

There was a chill in the air from the recent rain that permeated Moses' house. Half asleep he reached down and pulled a blanket over his shivering body, but it was not enough. He was still cold. Groggily he got out of bed to start a fire in the stove, huddling near its warmth as soon as the flames flickered and sparked. Seeing the Tarot card of the hanged man lying on the floor nearby he was tempted to throw it in the fire and be done with it, but something held him back.

428

"What message were you supposed to give me?" he asked, admonishing himself for acting as if he expected the card to answer him.

He doubted that the card was meant to show him support because the man who had pushed it towards him was white and he had run through the crowd as if his pants were on fire. And why that card? Was it coincidence or a well thought of plan meant to intimidate him so that he would drop out of the race. A reminder of that night when he had been lynched.

"Drop out? Ha. Never!" The very thought angered him. "If anything, the card was a reminder of just why he had to find the courage to continue with his candidacy even in the face of danger. It was time that someone stood up to the bullies, thugs, and evil men who had been terrorizing those with dark skin since the first slaver had reached the shores of Africa.

Moses felt emboldened to know that there were others like him as well as those with white skin who were backing him. Not every white man was blind to the injustice of the past. There were others like Derek who wanted to see justice done so that all men could live in peace without the threat of more violence and killings.

Reaching down to pick the card up he turned it over and over again in his hands to see if there were any other clues as to its origin. But the card had no writing or symbols on it except what had been imprinted on the card. There was just the picture of the blonde man with his hands behind his back hanging from one foot, a foot wearing a yellow shoe that was tied to a tree limb. That and the number twelve.

Moses wished that he knew more about Tarot cards so that he might know what was to come. Forest had told him that there were twenty-two cards in a deck. Would there be more cards? Threats? Violence?

Quentin had told him about terror groups that had sprung to life with the upcoming elections in southern states. They were boldly making themselves more visible and threatening both freedmen and whites to try and force them to vote for candidates that would help the old southern aristocrats hold onto power. They wanted to undermine the reconstruction efforts. Each group had some symbol or emblem to identify them. Moses suspected that there was a group in Richmond and that the Tarot cards were their symbol.

"Well at least I wasn't given the Fools card," he said to himself. "Or the death card." At least not yet. No, whoever was behind this plot to use intimidation chose the one part of his life where he was vulnerable. But it wouldn't work. Whatever happened next, he would be ready for them.

## Chapter Thirty-Two

It was time. Forest couldn't keep putting it off. She needed to locate the man who had planted the seed in her mother that had given her life. He was a violent and abusive man, or so she supposed. He was the person who had done something so loathsome that it had caused her mother and husband to flee to freedom taking their little daughter with them. He must certainly be a monster. *William Trenholm.* The name would be forever implanted in her brain.

Forest had visited Andrew Wyatt at the bank while Quentin and Moses were at the Capitol hoping to find out the first piece in the puzzle of her identity as William Trenholm's progeny. She still had hopes that somehow she would be able to find out what had happened to her mother and her mother's husband. For some reason she could not understand, Wyatt had been reluctant at first to tell her how she could locate Trenholm. At last after her pleading, however, he had given her the name of a man he said might be able to give her that information.

"Peter Hawthorne," she whispered, looking at the piece of paper Andrew Wyatt had given her. Andrew had also provided Peter's address which turned out to be a suite of rooms right above a barber's shop. Her hands shook as she knocked at the door.

It took several attempts at knocking before the door was opened by a tall, bald, black man the color of ebony. "What do you want?" he asked gruffly.

"Are you Peter?" She couldn't help noticing the scars on his forehead, neck, and hands and she suspected he had once been a slave.

"I am. Who are you?" He looked her up and down suspiciously.

"My name is…..was….Jemma," she stammered. What a sad irony that she didn't even know her mother's name. Had it been Pearl? "I'm trying to contact William Trenholm," she blurted.

"Trenholm!" At the mention of the name the man named Peter tried to shut the door in her face but Forest had her foot in the doorway to keep it from closing. "Why are you lookin' for him?"

She could have made up a story, but Forest decided to be honest with this man. What did she have to lose? "My mother was a slave on William Trenholm's plantation. Although I believe she had a husband, William Trenholm sired a child with her. That child is me."

He was insolent. "So?"

'I want to speak with him to find out what happened to my mother," she exclaimed. "Please help me. Andrew Wyatt at the bank gave me your name and said you could help me."

"Andrew Wyatt," he scoffed. "How do I know you tellin' me de truth?"

"You don't but please hear my story." Forest took off her hat.

She could see that her being a girl seemed to soften Peter's attitude. "Go on," he said.

She took a deep breath. "My mother and the slave she was living with took me with them when they tried to escape from Trenholm. They were on a

432

boat. But somehow he tracked them down. A man named Joseph picked me up and tried to get away from the slave catchers by rowboat. But he was killed once we set foot on land. I ran away and was saved by a man who kept me hidden so that I wouldn't be taken by the trackers. The last I saw of my mother she was being beaten. I can still hear her screams in my nightmares." The memory of that day caused Forest to shudder.

The man surprised her by reaching out and patting her shoulder. "I heard about what happened. Trenholm was my master too. As mean a man as God ever created. But he got his punishment."

"Punishment?" She hadn't expected this information.

"He was such an ornery bastard that after de war when us slaves were freed nobody wanted to stay at his plantation no more. All the slaves runned away like mice from a badger's den. The lazy fool lost everythin' cause not one of his freed slaves would work for him for pay, no not for nothun'. Even his wife left him."

"He lost his plantation?" The man nodded and although William Trenholm had been the reason for the loss of her family, she couldn't help but feel a bit sorry for him. "But what about my mother and her husband?"

"I don't know. After they tried to escape, I never saw them again. I heard through de grapevine that Trenholm had strung that black man up as a lesson to any who might want to do de same."

"Strung him up!" Remembering what had happened to Moses she frowned. "But you never heard about the woman he escaped with?"

433

"I don't know what happened to Pearl. Oh, but she was a mighty fine-lookin' woman she was. So sad."

So she was right. Her mother's name had been Pearl. "You never heard anything at all about her?" Somehow deep in her soul Forest had always thought of her mother as having died. Was that what had happened?

"Nope. Not a word. So sorry, missy." Once again, he patted her on the shoulder in a show of condolence. "You will have to ask him. Trenholm."

"And just where can I find *him*?" she asked. "Is he still near Richmond?"

"Uh huh. He lives like a hermit in rooms above the pawn shop on East Main Street." He wrote down the address on an old envelope he had. "But you be careful now, you hear. There are those who don't think he is in his right mind. Don't let him harm you in any way."

She felt a great affection for Peter even though she had just met him. "I'll be careful. And thank you. From the bottom of my heart."

It didn't take long for Forest to locate the pawn shop in that part of town that had not yet been fully restored back to the way it was before the war. There were several buildings needing repair with missing bricks, broken windows, and faded painting. Like many shop buildings with upper floors she found that there was a separate entrance that was not connected to the pawn shop. Opening the rickety door, she climbed the steep stairs to a row of entrances.

"Room 203," she whispered, finding that now that she was here, she was quickly losing her nerve.

She turned around with the thought of leaving but had a renewal of courage and knocked at the door.

The door was answered by a gray-haired man who looked as if he might have been handsome in his youth, a man whose facial features were eerily like her own. The eyes, the shape of the nose, the mouth, the chin were replicas of Forest's. There was no denying that this man was her sire. It was shocking and unsettling to see the resemblance.

"Who are you?" The way the man squinted at her she could see that his eyesight was not good at all. Perhaps that was for the best.

Forest decided right then and there not to tell him her identity. What good would it do? And besides, as she looked at this man who was little more than a stranger, she knew in her heart that Quentin was her real father in all the important ways. She hadn't come here for a reconciliation.

"I am a relative of one of your former slaves. I seem to remember that her name was Pearl. I am trying to locate her."

"Pearl? Pearl?" Was she imagining it or was there a look of remorse on his hollow face? "I haven't heard that name for years."

"Yes. Pearl." She was relieved that he recognized the name. Perhaps she could find out the information she needed.

"Why are you askin' about her now?" He was menacing as he took a step forward, but she held her ground, thankful that she had kept her hat off. She suspected that William Trenholm would have been more hostile if he thought her to be a boy.

"I would like to know if it is possible to find her." She braced herself for the truth no matter how hard it might be to hear.

"Find her?" He shook his head. "No."

Without thinking she grabbed him by the arm, her voice strong and authoritative. "Then tell me what happened to her." Once when he was young and strong he might have been formidable, but he wasn't now. He was just a bitter, hateful, aging man.

He seemed to welcome her company because he invited her inside to sit on his settee. "She was a runner. An escaped slave. When they brought her back to me, I had to have her branded so that everybody would know." For a moment it appeared that he was immersed in an unpleasant memory of the past.

"She was branded." That her mother had been treated no better than a cow sparked an anger in Forest that was overwhelming. Even though it had happened long ago it took all of her self-control not to show her disgust. Taking a deep breath she was somehow able to ask cordially, "and then what?"

His entire body stiffened. "She was my slave, and I had every right. I don't see as how it is any of your business," he snarled.

"I have made it my business," she replied in a tone just as nasty as his. There were some people who only reacted to a show of strength. She sensed he was one of them. "What happened to her after she was branded?

"She tried to escape again so I had to sell her," he stated matter-of-factly.

436

Forest tried to keep the quiver out of her voice. "She was sold but to whom?" Perhaps it was not too late to find her mother after all.

"I sold her to a brothel." He sat down next to her, inching closer and closer.

Forest moved farther away on the settee. "A brothel." It was even worse than she had feared.

"She was a *Jezebel.*" He sounded angry. "Nigrah women always are. They have an insatiable appetite for sex. A brothel is a good place for them all."

"A Jezebel."

Forest remembered hearing the same name on the lips of the women in Philadelphia who twittered behind their hands that white men didn't have to rape black women because those women desired relations with men with light skin. When she had asked Quentin, he had told her that such a lie was a rationalization for what was happening between slave owners and their female slaves. The truth was, he had told her, that the female slave was at the mercy of the fathers, sons, or brothers of her master as well as of the master himself.

"Where...where is she now?" Closing her eyes, she said a silent prayer that her mother had somehow been able to escape from such a tawdry fate.

"Dead! The word reverberated in the air.

"Dead?" Had she screamed the word or was it only her imagination. "How did she die?"

He shrugged. "From what I was told, she got the great pox. Syphilis. I heard that she was given arsenic, mercury, or sulphur, maybe all three." He shrugged. "But the treatment poisoned her."

437

"She died from poisoning." Forest had to pause for a moment to calm her turbulent emotions. Taking a deep breath, hoping to keep from gagging, she said, "it must have been an agonizing death."

"It took her several days to die."

"Several days." Forest felt a sudden chill wash over her. Her voice cracked but somehow she was able to whisper, "how tragic." She wondered if her mother had died alone or if there had been someone by her side.

"She was very pretty with a great pair of tits. It was a waste of a good piece of...."

Anger took control of Forest as she reached over and slapped him across the face. "You bastard!"

The look of surprise on his face was almost comical. "What the hell!" Suddenly he stood up, pointing a finger at her. "I know who you are now."

"You know?" Forest quickly sprang to her feet, anxious to leave. She had gotten what she came for. Now she knew the tragic truth and this horrid man's part in it.

"You're that little girl. Pearl's child. You're the reason she ran away."

Forest could have told him the truth but knowing what he had done to her mother caused her loathing. She wanted to keep him out of her life. "No, I am not that girl. That girl is dead."

"Dead?"

"Yes. Dead!" In that moment she knew that Jemma was just part of her past, a chapter in her life, a door that was permanently closed. Leaving William Trenholm behind she knew now where her future was going to be and who she wanted to share it with.

\*    \*    \*    \*

The thunder that Derek had heard during the night's rainstorm was nothing compared to the rumble of anger he was greeted with as he walked down the stairs and confronted his furious father. "What the hell do you think you are doin'?"

Seeing Angelique Jamison standing beside Charles, her trunks and suitcases beside her, Derek knew that she had told his father about his declaration that she was to pack up and get out. "I'm doin' just what I should have done several weeks ago! Takin' control of my life."

"By bein' rude to an invited guest?" Charles raised his fist in anger and Derek was reminded of all the times he had been throttled by his father when he had defied him. But he wasn't a little boy now.

"Guest? After last night I would call her by another name," Derek retorted, glaring at Angelique. "But it won't work. I will not go along with your plans. I would not marry that woman if she were the last female on earth."

"The hell you say!" He turned towards Angelique. "Go unpack your bags. You are stayin'"

"If she stays then I will go." Sweeping into the room with a grand entrance, Honora came to Derek's side.

"What are you sayin'?" Charles looked first at Honora and then at his son then back to Honora again.

"I think you know." Putting her hands on her hips Honora's look was stern. "And I mean it, Charles. Derek has a right to marry whomever he

439

pleases, and all your foolishness is just that—foolishness!"

Charles turned his attention to Derek. "I told you. I don't have to leave this plantation to you."

Derek shrugged. "No, Sir, you don't. And I in turn don't have to work those damnable tobacco fields without one word of thanks. Nathaniel is welcome to this place. Or better yet you can let the bank take it."

"What did you say?" It was obvious to see that Charles Cameron was not used to not having his way.

Derek repeated, "I said let the bank take it for all I care. I will no longer live this way....under your thumb like some ninny. I have worked hard to keep this place goin' so that we could hang on to this land. I even made a lucrative deal to sell Cameron tobacco to the cigarette factory, but I am not goin' to give up everythin' just to please you."

"You mean *that* woman."

"I mean my future, my happiness. And yes, that woman. I love her and I want to spend my life with her. If that means leavin' here, I will do just that." Derek felt such a surge of relief standing up to his father that he nearly laughed aloud. In his heart he knew that whether or not Charles would admit it, he needed Derek in order for the plantation to survive. His threats concerning his brother Nathaniel were ridiculous.

Losing whatever patience she had, Angelique made her opinion known. "I'm gonna take my bags back up to my room, Charles and I do declare that my papa will not hear about this little embarrassment from my lips."

440

"What?" Scowling all the while Charles thought the matter through. Turning to Angelique he said softly, "I'm sorry, my dear, but your invitation here has been rescinded. Give your father my best."

"You can not mean that!" Putting her hand up to her throat, Angelique affected her 'southern belle' impression despite being from the north. "Why, I do declare."

Charles was no fool. "If it comes to a choice between you and my son...." He nodded with his head towards the front door.

With an indignant snort, Angelique turned her back on father and son, struggling to secure her luggage. Being at heart a gentleman, Derek gave her a hand getting her luggage outside. He promised to have one of the field hands give her a ride into Richmond. He could not keep from joking, "try not to seduce him. I have work for him to do when he gets back."

"Very funny." She refused to let him help her into the buggy. True to her nature she immediately started to flirt with Thomas, the man Derek had enlisted to take her away from Winding Oaks.

"Goodbye, trouble," Derek whispered as he watched the buggy ride down the road. He felt as if a great weight had been lifted off his shoulders. More importantly he now knew that from now on his fate was in his own hands.

*   *   *   *

The men walking out of the Capitol building were a hodge-podge of heights, weights, skin colors,

441

and style of suit coats. Some had smiles on their faces, others wore frowns, some were solemn and silent, others were chattering excitedly, and a few could be seen shaking hands. Anxiously scanning the crowd, Forest at last saw Moses and Quentin walking side by side down the stairs. She knew that these two men were not only part of her past but her future as well.

Waving to get their attention, she thought about how different her life had been from her mother's and about how tragic the slave system had been—far more terrible for women than for men in so many ways. To be totally helpless and at the mercy of others was the greatest of indignities. To be owned. To be considered nothing more than property was the greatest of all injustices.

"*You're that little girl. Pearl's child.* You're the reason she ran away," she remembered William Trenholm saying.

Forest knew now beyond a doubt that the reason that her mother had made the choice to be a runaway slave was so that her daughter would not suffer the same kind of life that she had been forced to endure. And in the end the woman named Pearl had made the ultimate sacrifice of her life. It was altogether possible that she had run away a second time to go in search of her little girl. In her heart Forest knew this was the case.

"Forest!" The sound of Moses' calling out her name was the sweetest sound she could ever hope to hear.

"Your timing is impeccable," Quentin exclaimed.

442

Both were smiling, giving her hope that it had been a good day for the two men she loved. She was so fortunate to have both men in her life. The moment that Moses was close she impulsively threw her arms around him and nuzzled his cheek.

"Mmm." He was pleasantly surprised by her show of affection and held her tightly to him, ignoring the stares of passersby. "I don't know what I did to deserve such a greeting but if you tell me what it was I will gladly do it again and again."

"I'm glad that you are the man that you are," she whispered in his ear. "And I love you."

"I love you too. More than you can ever know." Wrapped in their embrace they stood together for a long, long time. Only Quentin clearing his throat brought them back to reality.

"I hate to disturb you two lovebirds, but I am afraid we are blocking the sidewalk," he advised with a grin.

"Then I guess the three of us will just have to move along." Giving Quentin a quick kiss on the cheek, she put one hand on his elbow and the other on Moses' arm and walked with them back to the buggy.

"How was your trip to the dressmaker?" Quentin asked as he helped her into the buggy.

The time for telling fibs was over. "I didn't go to the dressmakers."

Instead of chastising her he laughed. "That's good to hear. I was wondering just where you were going to put all those new dresses."

Fighting to suppress her tears Forest explained, "I found out where the man who owned my mother

443

lived and I went to talk with him to see if I could find out what happened to her."

"Your mother!" Sensing her sense of sorrow Moses reached out and grasped her hand, squeezing her fingers to give her reassurance that he was there for her.

"What did you find out?" Quentin handed the reins to Moses and took a seat in the back so that the two young people could sit together.

"I found out that what I felt in my gut for so long was true. My mother is dead and has been deceased for a long time….."

Moses could feel her pain as acutely as if it was being transferred to him by the touch of her fingers. "Do you want to talk about it?"

There was a part of her that wanted to keep it buried inside her. Another part of her, however, needed to share the truth thus she told them both the story of her visit with William Trenholm and what he had told her about a woman named Pearl.

"When I think of all she suffered because she wanted to make certain I wouldn't be in danger from the man who owned us both, I want to rage at the world," she sobbed.

"I have no doubt that this William forced himself on her and the sad thing about it is legally he was well within his rights. A white man was free to do what he wanted with his property. The only time he could be brought to court was if it was considered to be a trespass on another man's property. Your mother wanted to get you away from that vulnerability."

"How can anyone be so cruel as to treat other human beings like chattel?"

"Ignorance," Moses exclaimed, remembering his own experiences with prejudice and hatred. "But at least we are out of bondage now." He hoped with all his heart that what he said was true. There were many different kinds of oppression.

"Are we?" Forest wasn't so sure. It wasn't that long ago that Moses had nearly been killed by the Klan.

"We are in for a fight; this I know well. The status of our people as being non-human is so ingrained in white people's minds that it is going to be a rough fight going forward. But we can do it through legislation. That is why Moses has got to win this election."

She leaned her head on Moses' shoulder. "I think he just might. And after what I found out today, I want to do everything in my power to help him win."

"That you have faith in me is enough," Moses said softly. "Your love and your faith give me wings."

"Then let us make the commitment to fly!" Taking the reins from Moses' hands, Forest flicked the leather straps sending the buggy gliding down the road so fast that it almost took to the air.

## Chapter Thirty-Three

Finally, it was happening. Amelia felt as if she were walking on air. Derek had proposed with an ardor that had totally won her heart and best of all he had been the one to want to hurry up the wedding.

"We have waited long enough. I want you to be my wife." He lowered his voice to a whisper. "Before my father reverts to his stubborn, grumpy ole self."

As if to monitor her husband's behavior, Honora Cameron stood beside him. Amelia could see her give Charles a poke in the ribs when he raised his fist and started to shout out something to Moses. It was obvious to see the contention between the two men without needing to hear any word spoken.

The ceremony was to be held in the large drawing room of Winding Oaks just as Honora had suggested. Quentin and Forest had volunteered to bring flowers to add to the flowers from the Cameron garden. Amelia's Aunt Lucinda had insisted on bringing the bridal bouquet as a peace offering of sorts.

"I may have been wrong, Amelia dear. It seems that you might just have gotten yourself a good catch after all," she had said. "And he certainly is handsome."

There were few people in attendance at the ceremony, only a few friends and a few of the

446

workers, unlike days past when such a wedding would have been the social event of the year because of the Cameron prominence in the area. But Amelia didn't care. Her only regret was that Delilah, Ruth, Elijah, and the others from the church were not in attendance. Despite the progress that had been made after the war there were still walls that had not yet come down.

Standing at the top of the stairs, Amelia could not help but feel like a beautiful bride. Her strawberry hair hung loosely about her shoulders, framing her face, and making her look like a fashion plate, Honora had said. Her headdress of lace and pearls gave her the air of a queen; the veil hanging down her back looked like wings. The full-skirted white satin dress embroidered with seed pearls, the skirt billowing with its yards and yards of material, floated like a cloud as she descended the stairs.

Dressed in red satin Forest glided down the stairs just a few feet ahead of Amelia to the music of piano and flute, a rendition of *Here Comes the Bride*. When they reached the bottom step, Forest smiled at her as Quentin came forward and offered Amelia his arm. Of the necessary old, new, borrowed, and blue, he was 'borrowed' to give Amelia away because she didn't have a living father. He escorted her to where Derek stood with Moses by his side.

"Will you, Derek Cameron, have Amelia Seton to be your wife? Will you love, comfort and keep her, and forsaking all others remain true to her as long as you both shall live?"

"Yes, to all of it," Derek answered, causing a ripple of laughter.

"Will you, Amelia Seton, have Derek Cameron

to be your husband? Will you love, comfort and keep him, and forsaking all others remain true to him as long as you both shall live?"

"With all my heart I will," she said softly.

The ceremony was over rather quickly as the minister mumbled his words over the couple, then pronounced Amelia and Derek to be man and wife. Amelia couldn't help comparing him to the bishop from the Negro church who was always so filled with vivacity and spirit. "You may kiss her now," the minister said with a smile. Derek bent down towards Amelia, removed her veil, and kissed his new bride.

"Mrs. Derek Cameron," Derek whispered. "How does that sound?" He looked over at Moses and winked as if saying it was his turn to marry Forest now.

Mrs. O'Leary had helped Honora prepare a veritable feast for the newly married couple, including a traditional wedding pie. Amelia tried not to think about how hungry she was as they made their way through the small crowd of well-wishers, including some of her students and their parents. She nearly laughed as she heard several of the children call out her name and wave to her. She noticed that even Beauregard was standing nearby.

The men gathered about the groom and the rum punch, pumping Derek's hand up and down so vigorously that he nearly felt like a waterspout. The women tugged at Amelia's hand taking her to their corner where they were chattering away with each other and expounding on their own wedding day stories. Forest stood in the corner with her valued prize, the bouquet of flowers that Amelia had thrown her way.

Amelia eyed the table that was covered with food— ham and freshly caught catfish. There were also assorted vegetables and fruits while the last held the wedding pie—apple she supposed. Whiskey, wine, and other such refreshments flowed freely, and out of the corner of her eye Amelia could see that Honora was carefully monitoring Charles to see that he didn't drink too much. Derek smiled across the room at her in amusement at how quickly all the food seemed to be disappearing. It seemed that most of the guests were both starved and unquenchably thirsty.

"Looks like we have a heap of starvin' people on our hands," she heard Charles say to Honora. Reaching for a glass he poured himself another glass of whiskey despite Honora's frown.

There was a buzz going on in the room in more ways than just one. Guests drank, chattered, and laughed and there was merriment all around. There had been so many dark days since the war that it was good to have something good to celebrate. The noise in the huge room was so loud that no one noticed the outcry at first, but as one of Derek's field hands barged into the room, the clamor quieted down.

"Fire! Fire in the tobacco fields," the young man cried out. Before long, those words were being echoed.

"Fire!"

"Tobacco fields!"

"Good God, a fire."

"Hurry!"

Amelia watched in shock, trying not to panic as she saw Derek and Moses strip off their jackets, and tear off their ties. She didn't have time to even say a

449

word to him as he and Moses ran towards the front door. Oh, how she hated fires. She was reminded of that day Jedidiah had lost his life in the school fire.

"No, Charles. No!" Honora's cry of alarm was ignored as Charles Cameron followed the example of his son, stripped off his jacket and tie and moved towards the door. All of the men and boys followed. Even a few of the women moved with the flow of those going to fight the fire.

Looking down at her fancy wedding dress, Amelia cursed the sense of helplessness she felt. But now was no time to be prissy. Picking up her full skirts she was determined not to trip as she ran up to her bedroom to change her garments. Derek needed her help. She wasn't going to hang back and wait to hear what was happening. The future of the entire family was going up in smoke.

*　　*　　*　　*

The pungent smell of burning tobacco leaves permeated the air like the smoke of a gigantic cigar. The smoke was visible like a huge cloud. As they came closer Moses, Derek, and three of the sharecroppers—Michael, Richard, and David, could see the orange and bright yellow as the fire crackled and sparked. They saw something else as well. Men on horseback carrying torches. The men were dressed in white hoods and robes like the cowards that they were.

"Damn the bastards! It wasn't enough that they tried to kill you, Moses. Now they are tryin' to take away everythin' we have worked so hard to build up."

450

The smoke stung Moses eyes, leaving them burning and watery yet he could still see enough to realize that this was not the mob that had attacked him that night. "It's not them. Look closer."

Squinting his eyes for a better look, Derek made the same determination. This was not the Ku Klux Klan that had once been led by his father. These men on horseback were another pack of rats. "Who then?"

"I don't know. And we don't have time to follow them and find out. We need to get that fire out as soon as we can."

Together, with Charles Cameron trying to keep up, they headed for the tobacco fields, stopping only to grab the canvas tarps they had used to cover the plants that day of the fierce rain.

"At least they didn't set fire to the curin' sheds," Charles croaked out. "That would have ruined us for sure."

"It's obvious they aren't tobacco planters or they would have known," Derek called out. The smoke caught in his throat and choked him.

"For that at least we can be grateful," Moses yelled out.

Flames leaped in all directions, licking hungrily at the dry hay and straw scattered on the ground to accelerate the fire. At least whoever the assailants were they knew how to create sabotage.

Derek looked for his father and saw him watching, transfixed in horror as the fire spread rapidly throughout the fields devouring everything in its path. He thought that as bad as it was for him this must be even harder for his father to experience. It was as if with each puff of smoke a Cameron

451

ancestor's ghost was making its presence known.

"Wet the tarps. We'll have to beat out the flames," Derek ordered.

Using the nearby water pump to draw the water, each of the men did as Derek instructed. Even Charles was busy beating at the flames, holding the fires at bay.

The instinct for survival and the determination to save the tobacco crops were the driving forces that led him on. Somehow they would put out the fire, save the tobacco, and thwart the villains who had purposefully started the fires.

Thick smoke billowed through the air stealing their breaths away but as they worked the brightness of the fire rescinded leaving only the smoke behind. They had hope. They had courage. They could do it!

Amelia had hurriedly changed into her oldest yellow calico dress and was hurrying to catch up with the men to see what was happening when she heard the sound of horse's hooves pounding the ground. Ducking behind one of the stone wells she gasped as she saw the white-garbed horsemen ride by. Unaware that she was watching they removed their hoods, mumbling as they did so.

"That should have done it. They can't work miracles," shouted out a voice she recognized only too well. As she saw the red curly hair she knew she was correct in her assumption.

"Edward Cutler!" So, he was the one behind this sabotage. An evil plot to steal the Cameron land. As she watched the men ride away she wondered it these were the same men who had set fire to the school. If so, they were Jedidiah's murderers.

452

Cautiously waiting until they were far down the road before she left her hiding place, Amelia was filled with rage. For the first time in her life she knew what it was to hate. Somehow Edward Cutler had to get his come-uppance so that Jedidiah could rest easily in his grave.

\*     \*     \*     \*

Fighting the fire in the tobacco fields had been a nerve-wracking ordeal but as Derek and Moses assessed the damage done, they could see that it wasn't as bad as they had first supposed. None of the tobacco in the curing sheds had been harmed. Only a portion of the tobacco plants had been burned and the area could be replanted the next year.

"The damn fools who did this weren't aware that smoke is a by-product of the tobacco curing process," Moses joked. "They did some of our work for us."

"Mayhap we might have stumbled on a new tobacco flavor," Derek stated in jest. "We could call it 'mellow arson'."

All of the men were covered in ash and soot, their clothes were torn. Reaching out Moses wiped Derek's face with the handkerchief he had in his pocket. "All that soot has made you as dark as me. Best get you cleaned up before they come back and try to lynch you. Believe me it isn't any fun."

Derek scowled at the reminder. "But at least we know it wasn't those asses who were in cahoots with my father like the last time." He looked around. "By the way, where *is* my father?"

They had been so busy fighting the fire that they

453

had lost track of where Charles had gone. The last thing Derek remembered was that his father had been using one of the tarps to swat at the flames alongside Richard, one of the sharecroppers but he could see Richard up ahead and his father was not with him.

"Richard, where is my father?" he called out.

"Haven't seen him," came the answer.

Derek shouted out his father's name over and over again but there was no response. For the moment it appeared as if Charles had just disappeared.

"I know my father. He wouldn't have gone back to the house. He cares too much about the tobacco plants to just leave." A strange sense of foreboding swept over Derek. He remembered that it had taken a long time for his father to get back his strength after his illness.

Together Derek and Moses searched for Charles, but it was Michael who found him. "He's over here!"

Lying on the ground near an area of charred tobacco plants, Charles was unresponsive as Derek knelt down and called out his name. Putting his head down to his father's chest Derek was relieved to hear a heartbeat. But his father's breathing was shallow which he knew was not a good sign.

"We need to take him back to the house," Derek declared. Mrs. O'Leary knows healing. She will know what to do."

Forgetting the animosity between Charles and himself, Moses didn't hesitate to help Derek get his father up and to his feet. But there was no way Charles had the strength to walk and they didn't want to drag him.

454

"Here. We can use one of the unused tarps as a stretcher and you and I can carry him," The journey back to the house had never seemed as great a distance as it did now. Forming a caravan all the men were silent as they retraced their steps to Winding Oaks.

"Derek!" Meeting up with the parade of men, Amelia gasped as she saw Charles' inert form lying on the make-shift stretcher.

"He collapsed while helping to fight the fires. Hopefully, Mrs. O'Leary will be able to rouse him. This whole thing was just too much for him. I should have insisted he go back. Or at the very least watched over him."

"Nonsense. You had your hands full with the fire." Amelia hurried to reassure him as they all walked back to the house. From time to time Amelia bent over to check on Charles. "This is in no way your fault, Derek. The ones to blame are those men who set the fires."

"And the frustrating part of that is that we don't know who they were. Moses and I both remember the culprits from Moses' lynching." He shook his head. "These men weren't the same ones."

"I know." The image of Edward Cutler astride a horse leading the others away from the scene of the treachery was emblazoned on her brain.

"What do you mean?"

"The men thought they were out of sight. I saw them riding back and hid. A few of them took off their hoods but I didn't recognize them."

Derek groaned. "Damn!"

"But I did know the identity of their leader." It

was so hard to believe. For just a moment her confidence in what she had seen faltered. Closing her eyes, however, she could envision the scene again and the face of the perpetrator. "Edward Cutler. I saw. I know it was him."

"Edward Cutler. The evil, devious, greedy bastard." The thirst for revenge was nearly as fierce as his thirst for a drink of water. "I ought to beat him senseless."

"I'll help you. I think he and his followers were the same ones who set fire to the schoolhouse." It seemed logical that Edward Cutler's motives in both instances had been the same—to send a message and cause such havoc that Derek and Moses would not be able to keep financially afloat.

*    *    *    *

The tobacco plants had not been harmed as critically as had been feared but the same could not be said of Charles Cameron. Although Mrs. O'Leary tried everything she could—every healing potion, every maneuver to help Charles' breathing and heartbeat, every incantation, he didn't show any signs of regaining consciousness.

"I'll ride into Richmond for the doctor," Moses volunteered, feeling Derek's emotional pain as if it were his own. He hadn't liked Charles Cameron in the least, but he feared that his death would devastate Derek because in so many ways and for so long they had been estranged.

"Thank you," Honora exclaimed, taking Moses' hand in hers. "I don't know what he was thinking.

Men can be so stubborn sometimes."

"He wanted to help us save the tobacco plants."
For the first time in his life Moses felt a twinge of
respect. He thought to himself that it must be hell to
get old. "Guess he didn't realize he wasn't young
enough or strong enough. I'm so sorry." Without
another word Moses hurried out the door for his ride
into the city.

Circling Charles, Honora, Derek, Emelia, Mrs.
O'Leary, Quentin, and Forest held vigil as he lay on
the settee. Honora had a wet cloth that she used to
wipe his face and neck from time to time, all the
while watching his chest move up and down to make
sure he was still breathing. Derek knelt by his father's
side, talking to him in hopes that a miracle would
occur and he would open his eyes.

"Even if he sat up and cursed at me I would be
glad." He moved closer so his father could hear him.
"We didn't always get along; we said some hateful
words to each other, but you have to know that
despite everything I tried my best to please you. I
knew how important Winding Oaks is to you and so it
became important to me as well."

"He knew, Derek." Honora whispered.
"Although he didn't say it, he was proud of all that
you accomplished. He knew that without *you* we all
would have been lost."

"Then why didn't he ever tell me? He never said
any kind or encouraging words." Derek fought to
control his emotions.

"Your father was afraid of showing his feelings."
Honora wiped the tears that stung her eyes. "He never
once told me he loves me, but I know in my heart that
he does."

Looking at his mother's face Derek could only imagine how hard this was on her. She had done everything in her power to take care of his father, understand him, and have affection for him. That must not have been easy considering his father's temperament. He had always wondered how his two parents had ever managed to live together but now as he saw the concern on Honora's face, he realized that she really did love this impossible man.

"I wish he would open his eyes." Derek felt gentle hands on his shoulders and realized that Amelia was conveying her strength to him by her presence.

The room grew silent. Time seemed to be standing still as they waited impatiently for Moses to bring the doctor. They heard the grandfather clock strike four, then toll the half hour. At last Moses barged into the room followed by the doctor.

"This young man told me what happened. Has he coughed up any blood? Cried out in pain? Gasped for air? No?" Walking over the Charles' side he took his wrist in his hand.

"Is there something you can give him?" Quentin inquired, moving closer.

"He's so pale." Amelia had a foreboding feeling.

Bending down the doctor pushed the folds of Charles' shirt aside and used his stethoscope, scowling all the while. The silence in the room was deafening as everyone stared at the doctor to see if they could read the diagnosis by his expression. Suddenly he said the words that everyone dreaded. "I'm sorry."

"Sorry?" Derek and Honora said the word at the

same time.

"It appears that Charles suffered a massive heart attack. Too much excitement. The smoke. The exertion." He shook his head.

"What can you do for him?" Honora's voice was shaking.

"There is nothing I can do." He put a hand on her shoulder. "He's gone. Dead."

"Dead!" Derek's voice was so loud that it startled everyone.

"Oh no!" Amelia put her hand to her mouth to keep from saying more. It was all like some ghastly bad dream.

They were all in a state of shock. It was as if they were watching a stage play, not liking the ending or the dialogue. But it wasn't a nightmare or a play. It was all too real and Charles Cameron, the patriarch of Winding Oaks Plantation, a man that had sometimes seemed to be interminable had succumbed to his mortality. The responsibility of the Cameron family and Winding Oaks would now fully be on Derek's shoulders.

## Chapter Thirty-Four

The funeral was going to be quite simple. The cloudy day added to the bleakness of the moment. Honora moved as if in a daze, the reality had not yet struck her. Derek was silent and brooding, trying to remain calm. He knew he must be strong, a pillar on which his mother could lean. Amelia was determined to be sympathetic and understanding of what her new husband was going through. Moses was thoughtful, surprised that despite all that Charles Cameron had done to him he still felt a strange sense of loss at the man's death. He remembered how he had once idolized his friend's father before that horrible time he had been betrayed and sold.

"Well, I'll be damned!"

Derek's outburst startled Amelia and she looked in the direction of his angry gaze, only to see five men about the age that Charles had been joining the mourners at the grave site. "What is it, Derek?"

"Those bastards have the nerve after all that they have done." Clenching and unclenching his fists he growled beneath his breath, "that's Jefferson Jenson, Thomas Bedford, Edward Hadaway, Travis James and Waylon Tucker. The clansmen who rode with my father and tried to hang Moses."

"What are you going to do?" Amelia whispered.

Bowing their heads and showing their sorrow they looked at Derek and took several steps back to avoid a confrontation.

460

"I'd like nothin' better than to call them out right here and now, but my mother would never forgive me. This is my father's time. But I swear."

Nervously Amelia looked over at Moses as he stood beside Forest, wondering what Moses would do if he knew the men who had nearly killed him were standing so close. "Are you going to say anything to Moses?"

"No. He would want to kick their asses and that would cause a scene." He frowned as he realized Quentin was within speaking distance to the Klansmen.

"I would imagine they wouldn't be as brave without their white hoods to shield them," Amelia scoffed. "Just like Edward Cutler."

Derek bristled at the name. "Another son of a bitch who needs to be brought to justice."

Taking his hand Amelia whispered, "in due time, my love. In due time."

They both grew silent as the plain oak coffin was lowered into the grave. Charles had not believed in expensive coffins. He was not a religious man and had not believed in an afterlife. He had once told Derek that all he wanted when he died was to be put in a plain wooden box and put in a hole and that all the rituals that accompanied burials was falderal. "When you are dead you are dead," he had said.

"From ashes to ashes and dust to dust..." intoned the minister.

The minister's words were accompanied by the soft sound of Honora sobbing and Amelia's heart went out to her. She supposed that you could not live so many years with a man, even a man like Charles

461

Cameron, without having at least a little affection for him.

"We brought nothing into this world, and it is certain that we will carry nothing out. The Lord gave, and the Lord hath taken away." the minister concluded. "Blessed be the name of the Lord."

Derek watched in grief as dirt was scattered over the coffin. There was such a finality in death. Thinking about the portraits on the wall he was reminded that his father would now join the Cameron forefathers in the afterlife, or so he supposed, although whether that would be in heaven or in hell he didn't know.

*   *   *   *

Anger was corrosive. Amelia could see that Derek's rage at what Edward Cutler had done was eating at him night and day. Knowing that the banker had been responsible for the fires set in the tobacco fields, which ultimately resulted in his father's death, yet not being able to see justice done was destructive to his very being. He had lost his appetite, he had trouble sleeping, his temper could be fueled by the slightest occurrence.

"You are not acting like the man that I married. You are turning into a stranger," she told him now as he paced up and down the room instead of coming back to bed.

"I'm sorry, but I just can't help it. I spoke to the police in Richmond and the sheriff of Henrico County and they were loath to go up against a wealthy, influential northern banker, cowards that they be. I was told to get in line because they had more important issues, such as dealing with all the people beaten, mutilated, and murdered in the area. I can't tell you the details because it would shock you to know the barbarity goin' on."

Amelia had heard whisperings among the parents of the black children she taught. She hoped that they weren't true. "Tell me. I want to know."

"It goes way beyond burnin' tobacco fields or tryin' to lynch a man. Or even burnin' down a schoolhouse even though there was a fatality." Derek put his hands up to his face. "My God, what is happenin' in this country? How have we tumbled into such barbarity and depravity? Or have I just been blind for all these years? I thought there was at least some code of honor."

Getting out of bed, Amelia came to his side, comforting him in the same way she did her students when they were in a state of despair. "If you tell me it will be helpful. And trust me, I am not one to be shocked. Not after the murder of my innocent Jedidiah."

He paused, then revealed what he had been told. "The police captain divulged that they were havin' difficulty comin' to terms with the savagery of lynchin's, burnin's, forced drownin's, severed ears, mutilations, and even open displays of skulls as trophies. Of both black and white people."

"Dear God!" Amelia thought she had heard everything because the war had been brutal but what Derek told her made her blood run cold. "Is Moses safe or is he putting a target on his back by running for office?"

"I suspect he is in a whole heap of danger, but he won't listen. It's as if a whole other war has been declared. And we are helpless. I'm just a tobacco farmer without much credibility." He wrapped his arms around Amelia and held her tight. "If not for you I would be going mad right now."

They were both silent for a long time just listening to the sound of their hearts beating in rhythm to each other's, then Amelia said, "So Edward Cutler is not going to be taken to task for what he did and he will continue to terrorize other former plantation owners until he is king of the carpetbaggers. Is that what you are telling me?"

"It is. And I fear he isn't done with Windin' Oaks just yet." Pulling away from Amelia's arms and running a hand through his hair he said, "a man like that is just waitin' for another opportunity. And so, we are just sittin' ducks. And that makes me madder than a puffed toad!"

Now it was Amelia who was pacing up and down. "No. There has to be something we can do. Edward Cutler thinks he is clever, but we can thwart him if we use our heads." Walking over to the small table in the bedroom Amelia reached for the pirate book and thumbed through it. "Ah, here it is. Blackbeard!"

"You mean my great, great, great, great grandfather?" He thought she was trying to take his mind off of the predicament they were in, but she looked so serious that he knew she had an idea. "What?"

"We need to think like pirates," she exclaimed.

"You mean make Edward Cutler walk the plank?" For just a moment it seemed he might smile but the expression on his face remained solemn.

"Oh, that we could." She put down the book. "You need to bury your gentlemanly ways, at least for a while, just as Jared Cameron did." Amelia had read so many books and had toyed with the idea of even writing one thus it was easy to come up with a plan. "You recognized the men who had ridden with your father in the Klan. They were at the funeral."

"That's right." He wondered what she was getting at.

"And they were there because they had strong ties of friendship with your father. Doesn't it make sense that they would likewise loath Edward Cutler and his band of copycats. Add that to the fact that Cutler and his gang were partly responsible for Charles' heart attack." She added, "and he *is* a carpetbagger….."

Derek smiled at last. "I had no idea that you could be so devious. I must teach you to play chess."

"Let's just say that I want to get some kind of justice for Jedidiah." Now it was Amelia who was frowning. "Edward Cutler set fire to the school as part of his plan to ruin you and get your property. He might not have meant to kill Jedidiah, but he did. And for that I can never forgive him. So, I have my reasons just as you do for revenge."

Sitting together on the edge of the bed they formed a plan wherein Derek would make a bargain with the old Klansmen not to reveal what they had done in the past if they would promise to cease any Klan activity and not to ever harm Moses again. Derek would ask them to help avenge Charles' death,

465

however, in one last late-night raid to frighten Edward Cutler out of his wits.

"Where will this take place?" Derek wanted to make certain that Winding Oaks would not be involved just in case there were repercussions.

"The charred remains of the schoolhouse come to my mind. As I recall there is a perfect tree there where the school bell once hung."

"Seems fittin' but how will we get him there?" That seemed to be a big problem. Derek didn't want Amelia involved.

"It has to be me who sends him a message. There is no other way." Remembering that her aunt was often in contact with the banker it was decided that Amelia would have her Aunt Lucinda give Edward a message that her niece wanted to meet with him at the site of the charred ruins of the old school. It was there that the plot would enfold.

"Does Edward know you saw him that night?" Derek wanted to protect Amelia at all costs.

"No. I was hidden behind the well nearby. He won't suspect anything out of the ordinary and his bloated ego will most likely goad him into thinking I have amorous intentions." Amelia laughed softly at the idea.

"We'll give it a try then. But I want you to stay far away. Is that a promise?"

Amelia didn't want Derek to see, but she had her fingers crossed behind her back as she said, "I promise."

"Then I'll speak with *the boys* tomorrow," he quipped. "It will be like a nursery of angry old racoons confronting a devious possum,"

466

\*   \*   \*   \*

It was late. Dark. The moon illuminated the night as it shown down upon the earth. Some called it a 'lover's moon. As he hid in the shadows near the ruins of the schoolhouse, Derek thought how ironic it was that the night was so perfect for those seeking a late-night tryst.

"You think you are meeting with my wife for a seduction, you son of a bitch," he said to himself. "But the surprise will be on you."

Dressed in one of the KKK robes he had found in the Avery attic, he intended to be an observer and not a participant in the events that were to enfold, despite the urge he felt deep inside that goaded him to join in.

The soft thud of horses' hooves alerted him to the fact that the others had joined him. Getting his father's old friends to stage this *event* had been much easier than he could have possibly imagined. It seemed that Edward Cutler was quite notorious among the struggling ole plantation owners, or so Thomas Bedford, once the Grand Cyclops, had told him.

"He nearly got his greedy Yankee hands on my Longwood Hills," he had said. "And by the same means as with Charles' lands. Bad loans. Fires. I just saved my lands by the skin of my ass."

"He completely destroyed William Trenholm," Edward Hadaway had replied. "Course now ole Will was his own worst enemy, the way he treated his Nigrahs and all. Getting his females knocked up.

Always sending the slave catchers after them. They couldn't wait to leave Sedgewood Plantation in the dust."

"Because of him Walter Johnson is a tenant farmer. He lost Laurel Hill," Travis James explained. "That's why he dropped out of our little organization here."

Derek counted the robed and hooded horsemen. There were four. He knew them to be Thomas Bedford, Edward Hadaway, Travis James, and Waylon Tucker. All of them had promised under the southern oath of brotherhood they had shared with Charles Cameron, that this would be the last time they would ride.

As they gathered around Derek, he gave his instructions, adding "remember, we don't want to kill him just scare the livin' daylights out of him. Send him runnin' back to his mama up north."

The men had arrived just in time and didn't have to wait very long before Edward Cutler's buggy pulled up in front of the burned-out ruins of the schoolhouse. Derek grimaced as he saw that the would-be Romeo was carrying a bouquet of flowers as he got out of the buggy and meandered up the pathway to the school. Taking out his pocket watch he looked very impatient as he looked around.

"Amelia!" he called out, as if he worried he might have somehow missed seeing her.

"Like a mongrel dog in heat," Travis James guffawed.

"Quiet." Edward Hadaway's warning came too late. Edward Cutler was startled by the sound of the voices. Running back to his buggy he started to get in.

468

"Now!" Derek gave the signal.

Like ghosts out of hades the four robed and hooded men rode towards Edward. Travis James reached down from his perch atop his horse and caught Edward by the shirt front to drag him out. Edward Hadaway, also on horseback kicked his foot out to send the banker toppling to the ground.

"Who are you?" Edward's voice was quivering and his fingers were shaking.

"Custodians of your conscience," Thomas Bedford proclaimed.

"You must have made a mistake," Edward Cutler put his arms up to shield his face as if worried they might strike him. The bouquet of flowers was forgotten and lay on the ground at his feet.

"No mistake. We have the right weasel. Don't we Mister banker?" Waylon Tucker was snickering as he yelled.

"Edward Cutler, be prepared to answer for your sins!" Thomas Bedford blurted out.

"No. No. I haven't done anything wrong." It was too late for Edward to get away because he was now surrounded by all four horsemen.

Like the *Four Horsemen of the Apocalypse*, Derek thought surprised that he felt a twinge of sympathy for the pathetic man. It was an emotion he quickly swept away as he remembered all that this man had done. Not just to him, Moses and the Camerons but to others as well.

"What do you want with me?" Moving to a kneeling position Edward looked as if he were going to pray.

"You have stolen, lied, deceived and destroyed. For that you must pay," Travis James shouted out.

"Take off your clothes," Thomas Bedford ordered.

"My clothes? No!" Once again Edward Cutler struggled to get away. His eyes darted again and again in the direction of his buggy.

In spite of his resolve to just be an observer Derek couldn't help himself and joined in. "Take them off or we will do it for you and we won't be gentle."

Slowly in a grotesque striptease, Edward Cutler took off his suit jacket, trousers, shoes, tie, and shirt. Standing in just his underwear he looked nearly comical and Derek nearly laughed out loud to see that this *lothario* wore long johns.

"There. Are you satisfied?"

"Not yet." In a gesture meant to intimidate, the four Klansmen lit torches and waved them around yelling and screaming—like male banshees, Derek thought.

"Get a rope and tie it to that tree," Thomas Bedford ordered, pointing to that tree from which a school bell had once hung.

"A rope?" It didn't seem that Edward Cutler could be more terrified than he already was, but the mention of a rope unhinged him. "No! No! No! Please....... I'll do anything you ask of me."

"Anything?" Derek called out.

"Yes. Yes."

Edward Hadaway ignored Edward Cutler's promise and as Waylon Tucker held on to the shaking

470

man, he looped a noose around his neck. "Hang him up!"

"Justice is served for the young boy who was killed because you ordered this very school to be burned to the ground," Derek called out.

"I didn't mean to kill anybody." It was obvious to everyone looking on that Edward Cutler had peed himself.

"And you have cheated, bribed, committed arson, and stole that which wasn't meant for a cheating northern scum like you." Thomas Bedord threw the other end of the rope over the tree limb.

Sobbing hysterically Edward Cutler got down on his knees begging for mercy, promising that he would never do anything to anybody ever again. Looking over at Derek for the signal and seeing Derek nod, the men untied the rope from around Cutler's neck.

"Swear to God that you will remember this night and obey your own words," Travis James shouted out.

"I swear to God!"

"If you ever go against your word you will be hung. Remember that." Waylon Tucker growled. Reaching down he gathered up Cutler's garments and flung them in his face. "Now get dressed and get the hell out of here before we change our minds."

Slipping on his pants, shoes, and shirt, holding his tie and jacket in his hands, Edward Cutler ran to this buggy as fast as his legs could carry him. Without looking at the men he urged his horses into a fast gallop and headed down the road without once looking back.

Derek watched him go but what should have made him feel victorious caused a far different

471

emotion. He felt disgust at himself. Disgust because he was a man of principles and yet he had thoroughly enjoyed the bullying of another man. He had given in to hate. Was he truly then any different from his father after all?

# KATHRYN KRAMER

## Chapter Thirty-Five

Tarot cards were becoming so prevalent at the Capitol Building that Forest quipped that she had access to nearly enough of them to become a fortune teller. They were multiplying as quickly as rabbits. Not only did Moses keep receiving them but other black candidates for offices were getting them as well, no matter what political party they adhered to. It was obvious that they were meant to deter those with dark skin from pursing their candidacy.

"I'm not afraid. Really," Moses kept saying again and again and always Quentin had the same answer.

"You should be!"

Quentin had warned Moses once before about the white paramilitary terrorist and hate groups that had been organized to intimidate the freedmen from voting and politically organizing. The most prominent were the Red Shirts and the White League that were made up of many Confederate veterans. They were committing violent acts and were therefore dangerous. Unlike the Ku Klux Klan and Knights of the White Camelia they didn't operate in secret but worked openly in communities and even solicited coverage from newspapers.

"As I have said, I think there is a similar group operating in Richmond and the surrounding area and they have the Tarot cards as their emblem," Quentin said now as he, Moses, and Forest sat in the hall at the Capitol assessing the latest card received. This one

473

had been slipped into Quentin's satchel a few days ago when he was not looking.

"The Magician. Well, at least they didn't give me the Fool!"

Forest looked at the card critically. It was an image of a medieval man who was standing in front of an altar with tools that seemed to represent all four directions. She had gone back to speak to the fortune teller and had been lucky this time to obtain the meanings of all of the cards in the Tarot deck.

"According to this list the card can stand for trickery and illusions or willpower, desire, creation and manifestation," she read. "Whatever that means." Seeing a notation scrawled in red ink she added, "generally associated with intelligent and skillful communicators. Hardly an insult unless there is a meaning we can't decipher."

"I think we must put them together and see what story we are supposed to read. Although this particular card is not threatening that doesn't mean anything at this point." Quentin looked over Forest's shoulder at the card. "Whoever is handing out these Tarots has an ulterior motive up their sleeve."

"All we can do is to watch and wait and be on alert," Moses declared. He was still on edge from having to fight the tobacco fields fire, worrying that his peanut crops could be next. The campaign was taking him away from the responsibilities on his farm. He was going to be glad when this was all over and the votes were counted.

Forest was absorbed in trying to guess the meaning of the cards so far. "We have been presented with the Hangman, The Chariot which signals hard work ahead, The Hermit which means to step back and make a careful examination of situations and decisions, and now the Magician. Clearly all of them have a significance to the upcoming election. The cards seem to be cautioning us to move slow."

Realizing that more men were shuffling into the large room, Forest put the cards away. There was no way to tell at this point who could be trusted. All she wanted was to sit back in her boy's disguise and act as a spy for Moses' campaign. Following Moses and Quentin to the front of the room she was alarmed by the worried look on Matthew Stewart's face as he banged a gavel on the podium to silence all the chatter.

"We are going to forego the usual bickering and speeches today because we have a most serious matter at hand. There has been a shooting of a congressional candidate in the sixth district. And I do not mean that it was accidental."

Moses remembered that the man was a mulatto who was a candidate for the Republican party. Like him, the man named Rupert Samson had been a soldier in the Union Army.

"And one of our Negro brothers in our party was beaten to within an inch of his life in district seven. The perpetrators want to undermine all that we have accomplished and in fact overthrow the Reconstruction government. Intimidation of northern and black candidates and officeholders is on their agenda and they will use force if necessary. They also want to keep black men from the polls."

The room erupted in chatter, everyone talking at once. It was obvious to see that all assembled had been rattled. Forest felt a shiver of fear streak up her

475

spine. Moses had survived once but would he be as lucky the next time?

"Silence. I am not finished!" Matthew Stewart rapped so hard with his gavel that the handle came flying off. Taking off his shoe he pounded that on the podium instead until the hall returned to order. "Backers of these violent organizations are helping to finance the purchases of guns and ammunition— Winchester rifles, Colt revolvers and others and they aren't to go squirrel hunting."

Forest felt the touch of Moses' hand as he reached over to reassure her. He whispered to her not to worry but he might just as well have told her not to breathe.

"I don't need to remind you of the Colfax Massacre last year when Christopher Columbus Nash, a Confederate veteran and former prisoner of war, led companies of white militias and killed nearly one hundred fifty Negroes whose only transgression was to try and defend the courthouse. We must do everything in our power not to be taken unaware were the same thing to happen here. That is why I am instructing all of you never to travel alone and when you do travel to be armed to the teeth. You can never have enough guns. If we need to defend this Capitol we will do so."

Once again, the hall deteriorated into jabbering, worried men. There were even a few who had heard enough and left the hall swearing loudly enough for all to hear that they weren't going to die for any cause. Forest couldn't really blame them. There was a part of her that wanted Moses and Quentin to do the same, but she knew that was something they would never do. Call it courage or call it stubbornness.

"We need to get some more guns," Moses declared as soon as the meeting was called to a close.

"And more ammunition," Quentin added. "We need to start thinking of this as a war."

"And I need to booby trap your cottage just as I did at my house so that you don't have to sleep with one eye open. If anyone tries to break in, they will be in for a big surprise." Moses worried particularly about Forest. The groups causing havoc didn't respect women. A seventeen-year-old black teacher by the name of Julia Hayden had been murdered in Louisiana by the White League.

"Quentin taught me how to shoot a gun several years ago, so I am not some helpless female. I can be of help," In truth Forest worried more about Quentin. He was getting older and it just wasn't in his nature to harm anyone.

"No more traveling alone late at night," Quentin decided aloud. "Once the sun goes down, we stay put."

It was decided that until safety precautions were put in place Moses would spend the nights at the cottage, an idea he was all in favor of. He hadn't given up hope of an amorous relationship with Forest being renewed.

"You will be a welcome guest not because we are afraid but because we like your company," she teased, eyeing Moses up and down. Oh, how she had missed being with him.

Following the men Forest was suddenly shoved against the door jam by two young men she had never seen before. The rudeness infuriated her and she started to follow them but her path was blocked by one of the party members, a man of great girth. By the time he stepped away the two men were out of sight and she remembered that day when a similar incident had happened to Moses. And just like that day she was gifted with a Tarot card stuck in her jacket pocket. She turned the card over and was unnerved to see that it was the Lover's card

*   *   *   *

Like a ribbon of bronze, the James River wound through the very heart of Richmond. Nearly every structure or place of importance had been constructed to be within sight of the river and any restaurant or hotel with even a thimble's full of importance had an upper floor with a view of the river. As Quentin, Moses, and Forest rode in the buggy they searched for a hotel that would be comfortable but not so expensive that they would be impoverished after paying the bill.

"Try to find a hotel that will have good food, I'm starved," Moses insisted.

It had been a long, tedious day filled with anxiety over Matthew Stewart's warning and the Tarot card that had ended up in Forest's possession. Because of Matthew's warning and the late hour of the day they had decided to spend the night in Richmond rather than driving back to the cottage on the long, lonely road.

"Anything would taste good to me at this point," Forest said with a sigh, scanning the buildings as they drove past.

At last they came to a three-storied hotel of brick that was not too ritzy and yet not too plain. It looked to be just right.  A sign overhead read *The Red Clover* with the picture of a four-leaf clover which seemed in Forest's mind to be a sign of good luck.

"This looks to be suitable," Quentin said, guiding the horses and buggy to a spot near the front door.  "It even has a stable for the horses."

It was decided that Moses and Forest would go on ahead while he got the buggy and the horses situated.  He would then join them in the hotel dining room.  If perchance there was no room at the hotel Moses would quickly inform him of such.

Helping Forest out of the buggy, Moses held on to her hand as they walked up the pathway to the hotel.  As they stepped inside, he knew just a moment of uncertainty wondering if the hotel was one of those that would take one look at the color of his skin and say there weren't any rooms.

Forest guessed the reason for his reticent behavior and prodded him forward.  "You are a candidate for congress. They won't dare refuse you a stay here. Just act as if you are king of the world."

Moses laughed.  "Well perhaps not the king but maybe a duke or prince."

There was a tall bespectacled man with a mustache behind the counter. Although he looked inquiringly at Moses and Forest with her boys' attire but long flowing hair, he was amiable to their request. "Three rooms?"

"Three adjoining rooms. There will be another man joining us as well," Moses informed him.

The man shrugged.  "Well you're in luck. There are three adjoining rooms on the third floor with a view of the James. Do you need help with your luggage?"

"No. No, we can handle it," Forest said sweetly."

"As you wish. Just sign the register," the man said stiffly, pushing it forward.

Moses picked up a pen and scrawled all three names.

"I'll show you and your companion to your rooms and when your companion comes along, I'll bring him right up." He handed Forest all three keys.

Moses and Forest followed the man up the stairs to rooms at the end of the hall - numbers thirty-five, thirty-six, and thirty-seven. Together they unlocked the door of the first room and went inside.

It was a pleasant room. Bright and sunny with white walls and red decor. There was a big double bed in the middle of the floor covered with a red, white, and green flowered quilt.

Forest eyed the red drapes and bedspread, the tiny vanity, the two chairs and table, and nodded with approval. "It will be just fine."

"There's a bathroom down the hall, next to room thirty-seven," the man explained pointing that direction."

"Thank you."

"Have a pleasant stay in Richmond."

"Thank you." Forest closed the door just as soon as the man stepped away. "See, he was very polite. Things have changed for the better. And you and Quentin will make it even better." It seemed the natural thing to do to throw her arms around his neck and hold him tightly against her. Moses put his check against her soft hair and was just going to kiss her when Quentin opened the door.

"Are you two kids as hungry as I am?" He impatiently gave each of them a shove towards the door. "First we eat and then we plan our war."

Moses and Forest followed Quentin down the stairs. He led them through the high-ceilinged entrance hall of the hotel's dining room, escorting them past the gold framed mirrors, to a room full of crystal chandeliers.

"It didn't look this fancy from outside," Forest said in surprise. "But you can't judge a restaurant by its décor. Let's see what the menu has."

"Fried oysters, mutton chop, pork steak, fried fish, terrapin stew, friend chicken, beef steak, and stuffed partridge." Forest couldn't help herself. "I wonder if the partridge comes with a pear tree with Christmas soon to be upon us." Moses and Quentin laughed, lightening the mood of the evening.

"Hmm, it says 'segars of the choicest brands' on the menu," Quentin read. "I wonder if the tobacco comes from the Camerons' fields."

Forest chose the mutton chop, Moses the fried oysters and Quentin decided to partake of the terrapin stew. All the meals came with squash, grits, and pumpkin pie. As they waited for the waiter who had taken their order to bring the food they talked about the matter at hand.

"We have been presented with the Hangman, The Chariot, the Hermit, the Magician, and now the Lovers, whatever that means," Quentin whispered, looking over his shoulder to make certain no one could hear.

"Why was Forest chosen for that particular

card?" As usual Moses was concerned for her safety.

"It can mean choosing a partner or it can represent a crossroads with a cautioning that one cannot take both paths," Forest stated, reading from the notes she had taken.

"Someone knows about us," Moses whispered in her ear. "That makes you vulnerable. Quentin and I will have to protect you."

"We all have to protect each other," she replied.

"Like the three Musketeers," Quentin added.

There was no further discussion as the waiter brought the food and they each concentrated on the cuisine before them. The room was strangely silent as the meal commenced. Both Forest and Moses were suddenly ill-at ease, floundering for something to say, vitally aware of each other in the dimly lit room. Although there was danger in someone possibly knowing they had been intimate the very memory of their days at the Cameron house came quickly to mind and was like an aphrodisiac. It was as if a cocoon of enchantment enclosed them, as though they moved in slow motion. They noted infinite details about each other that they had put out of their minds. Gestures, tone of voice, expressions, the way the other one smiled. She wanted to tell him that she wanted to be with him forever, wanted to be his lover again.

"Am I a third wheel?" Quentin asked suddenly.

"What?" Forest blushed as she realized how obvious her attraction to Moses was.

In answer Quentin threw back his head and laughed out loud. "Never mind. I was losing hope, but it seems that everything works out for the best in the end."

The evening continued on amidst delicious food and a bit of wine. Moses and Forest could not help the intimacy of their heated looks towards each other. Moses couldn't remember when he had been so happy. He was with Forest in a place with soothing atmosphere, there was a magic in the night, and he had a feeling everything was going to work out just the way he had always wanted. He could not take his eyes from her. He watched with hungry intentness the way her smile played upon her lips, the way her brown eyes widened when she was listening to him. He was absolutely mesmerized by her in the same way he had been the first time they had met. Reality, however, had an unfortunate way of intruding.

"Who is that man across the room?" Quentin's voice was like a dash of cold water.

"What man? Where?" Moses looked in the direction Quentin was looking and noticed a gray-haired man dressed in a black suit and black-tie staring in their direction. Nor did his gaze waver when he realized that Moses was looking right back at him.

"Do you know him?" It was obvious that Quentin's suspicions had been aroused by Matthew Stewart's warning.

"No. I have never seen him before." Moses was concerned that the reason the man was staring was because of the way he and Forest had been looking at each other. He didn't want her to come under undue scrutiny that might harm her.

"I wonder if he is in one of those groups that are targeting black candidates," Forest whispered. She felt more than a little anxiety when she noticed that he was getting up from his chair and coming their way. "Don't look now but....."

The man was all smiles as he held out his hand for a handshake. "I recognize you. You are Moses Douglass, the candidate for this district. I just wanted to tell you how much I admire your honesty and ideas for bringing this state back together." Reaching into his coat pocket he brought forth a stiff piece of paper and Moses and Forest braced themselves waiting for another Tarot card.

Looking down, Moses sighed with relief as he saw that it was the man's calling card. "Richard M. Vickery. Harper's Weekly."

"I am writing an article on all of the candidates running for office here in Virginia and I would like to get a quote from you on what is going on now between the political parties and why violence is erupting seemingly everywhere down South."

Moses didn't have to think about the answer he spoke from the heart. "There are those stoking anger for their own gains. They want to not only turn brother against brother, but they want to keep the fires of hatred going. The truth is it is not about differences of opinion but about a difference in values. It is about hate versus kindness, life versus death, bringing our country together or ripping it apart. All of us can either join together to build this country up or we can declare war on democracy and be responsible for the destruction of this country and the ideals on which it was founded."

"Spoken like a true patriot." The man patted Moses on the back. "The article will be out next week in time to help you with the election. Good luck!"

"Thank you, sir." Moses watched the man go

back to his own table and he sighed with relief.

"Your ideas are sparking notice," Quentin exclaimed. "Bravo! Harper's Weekly is a prestigious magazine. It will definitely help you get votes from the elite."

Forest was in a more somber mood. "When Mister Vickery came over to our table I was unnerved. If he had been one of our enemies, we would have been sitting ducks. That is when it came to me that if we are involved in warfare we need to go on the offense and not wait until our adversaries attack."

"What are you suggesting?" Quentin was intrigued.

Forest laid out her plan. "We need to contact the other black candidates and urge them to let it be known that Tarot cards are being used as a tactic of intimidation towards Negro politicians. Get the truth out in the open. Treat it like a badge of honor not something to be ashamed of. With all that is happening with the White League and the Red Shirts only a fool would not take the cards seriously."

"Unfortunately, those in law enforcement are acting like fools and poo-pooing the matter as a prank or a joke. I am afraid that they won't act on anything until someone gets killed," Quentin complained. "But I will work with Matthew to see if he can do anything to work with the authorities to prevent violence before it is perpetrated."

"In the meantime, we need to have eyes in the back of our heads," Moses added. "And be ready at all times for whatever may come."

\*　　\*　　\*　　\*

Quentin didn't even try to hide the fact that he was a sentimental matchmaker who wanted to see Moses and Forest together. Using the excuse that he was exhausted he hurried to his room—number thirty-seven, leaving them behind.

Standing at the top step of the flight of stairs, Moses and Forest looked into each other's eyes. Then suddenly he took her hand. Well, since we're on the top floor and our rooms are so close, I guess I should say good night."

"No. Please." Forest was quick to protest. "Don't...don't go just yet."

"Then I'll escort you to your room...."

Forest reached in her pocket for the key. She wasn't tired at all, nor did she want to say good night. "Moses, would you like to come inside?"

"Yes," was all he said. He could feel the magnetism that always seemed to be pull them together, even more so as they stepped inside the room.

Moses tried to keep his eyes from looking in the direction of the bed but as hard as he tried, he looked in that direction again and again. From the moment they had entered the room, he had been strangely nervous. He didn't want anything to go wrong. She was just too important to him.

"Make yourself comfortable."

He did, taking off his jacket and tie and slowly lowering himself down on the chair. He let his eyes scan the room, imagining that the one next door that was his would be much the same.

486

Moses cleared his throat. "Well, here we are," he said leaning back, feeling suddenly tongue-tied.

"Yes, here we are…"

He was aware of her nearness in every nerve, every sinew in his body. He was absolutely mesmerized by her. She was absolutely lovely, he mused, his eyes moving tenderly over her thick lashes, the sculpted planes of her face, her generous mouth, her neck and what lay below. Oh, how he wanted to feel her nestled in his arms. His gaze slid slowly, lingeringly over her body, touching on her breasts, and he felt his desire stir.

Everything within her was responding to him. Totally. Uncontrollably. Her senses were spinning as she pulled him to his feet and molded her body against his. She could feel the strength of him, relished the wide expanse of his chest, could feel the rhythm of his heartbeat.

"It feels to me as if we should always be together," he whispered in her ear. "You know how much I love you. I couldn't hide it if I tried."

"I wouldn't want you to." He made her burningly aware of how tightly her breasts had flattened against the hard planes of his chest.

"So, what are we going to do about it?" He stared at her for a long, taut moment. At that moment she was all he wanted, all that he desired. He nuzzled her ear, her throat. He was on fire. Nothing could stop him now.

She glanced towards the bed then back at him. Their eyes met, and her heart began to hammer wildly. Slowly, intimately his hand traced the curve of her cheek, the shape of her chin then moved leisurely down to the nape of her neck.

"You have the softest skin." Touching her had become an obsession. He wanted to slide his fingers over every inch of her body, know every intimate part of her again. He brought his head down, touching his lips to hers. It was a gentle kiss at first, but as his desires were fiercely ignited, the caress of his mouth upon hers became more heated. All the passion in his soul was revealed in the way his lips moved upon hers, then leaning down he lifted her into his arms, carrying her towards the bed.

Moonlight streamed through the open curtains, casting a shadow on the wall as he made his way across the room with Forest cradled in his arms. Poised by the bed, he looked into her eyes, searching for, and finding the answer to his unspoken question. She knew, they both knew, that their making love was inevitable.

With infinite care, Moses brought his mouth down to hers, his lips gently exploring her mouth's sweetness. Then his kiss deepened, became more urgent, caressing, plundering. The kiss drained her very soul, pouring it back again, filling her to overflowing. She returned his kiss, her defenses devastatingly demolished by the cravings of her own body. There was nothing in the world for her but Moses and the vibrant sensations that spread through her. Twining her hands around his neck, she clutched him to her, pressing her body eagerly against his chest. She could feel the heat and strength and growing desire of him with every breath.

Time seemed to stand still. Then with a sigh, he pulled his mouth away, looking deep into her eyes again. Everything about her was softness, tempered with the strength of determination. She inspired a maelstrom of emotions within him. Passion mixed with tenderness and respect. Slowly lowering her onto the bed, he slid down beside her, worshipping her beauty in silence. She heard the soft rhythm of his breath as he spread her hair in a dark cloak about her shoulders.

"You'll never know how much I have missed being with you like this," he whispered.

With questing fingers, he unfastened her shirt and pulled the material away from her shoulders, then he aided her hands as she slid her trousers and cotton drawers down around her hips. With a tug he pulled them off and tossed them to the floor. The coverlet beneath her was warm and soft.

Removing his shirt, he pressed their naked chests together, shivering at the arousing sensation that sent a flash of quicksilver through his veins. Forest tangled her hands in his hair, closing her eyes as his fingers lingered, wandering down her stomach to explore the texture of her skin. Like velvet. He sought the indention of her navel, and then moved lower to tangle his fingers in the soft wisps of hair that joined at her legs.

"In case you don't already know it, I think you are beautiful…" he whispered.

Feeling encumbered by his clothes, Moses pulled them off and flung them aside.

"You're beautiful too." Forest felt an aching longing to touch him the way he was touching her, but for the moment she contented herself by just looking at him.

She loved the color of his skin. It was the perfect shade of brown. She let her gaze roam over him. His arms were well muscled, his waist thin, his legs straight and strong. She thought about all the flabby, puff-faced men with milky white skin who insisted that men like him were inferior and she knew their arrogant talk for what it was—jealousy.

For a long time they were content to just lie on the bed together, kissing again and again, caressing each other, rolling over and over on the soft bed. His hands were doing wondrous things to her, making her writhe and groan. Every inch of her body caught fire as passion exploded between them, but as the heat of the moment increased Moses took her hand and pressed it to the firm flesh of his arousal. She felt the throbbing strength of him as her eyes gazed into his. Then he bent to kiss her, his mouth keeping hers a willing captive for a long, long time.

Their bodies touched in an intimate embrace and yet he took his time, lost in this world of sensual delight. She was in his arms and in his bed. She was his, if only for the moment. When dawn came, he could step back into reality if he must.

The swollen length of him brushed across her thighs. Then he was covering her, his manhood probing at the entrance of her secret core. She felt his maleness at the entryway to her womanhood and wanting to relish the feeling, she pushed upward. His body nourished her heart and soul like a feast and she fully realized what she had been missing. A man and woman in love were meant to be together.

She was so warm, so tight around him that Moses closed his eyes with agonized pleasure as he buried his length within her. He moved with infinite care, not wanting to hurt her, instead initiating her fully into the depths of passion.

Tightening her thighs around his waist, Forest

arched up to him with sensual urgency. She was melting inside, merging with him into one being. Clinging to him, she called out his name.

Moses groaned as he felt the exquisite sensation of her warm flesh sheathing the long length of him. He possessed her again and again. He didn't want it to end, didn't want the real world to intrude into this warm wonderful haven they had all too briefly created. She was silken fire beneath him. A fragile flower, blossoming at his touch. Think about reality later, he thought. Let your heart rule now. A tenderness welled inside him that for the moment pushed his bitterness of the past into the dark recesses of his mind.

*     *     *     *

The moon had shifted position in the sky, taking away its light as Moses and Forest lay entwined. It was dark in the room. Quiet. So quiet she could hear her heart beating. They did not speak, for neither really knew what to say. They had been swept away on a tide of longing for each other that neither could deny. Where were they to go from here?

Moses' arm lay heavy across her stomach, the heat of his body warming hers as she lay entangled with his legs and arms. It gave her a deep sense of peace and intimacy to be with him like this, but somehow it also made her feel a strange sense of fear. She couldn't forget that Moses had nearly been killed because of hateful men seeing them together and jumping to conclusions.

*I love him*, she thought. But did she love him enough to step into his world and let it be known that

491

once her mother had been owned? Pearl had been a slave. And yet her mother had been worth so much more than the white man who had forced himself upon her. Was she proud that William Trenholm had been her father? No! He had not been worth her mother's little finger. Her mother had been everything good in the world while her father had been all that was evil—the villain. White. Black. Mulatto. Quadroon. She was still the person that she was no matter what anyone wanted to call her.

Turning slightly, she looked over at Moses, smiling at how boyish he looked asleep. He needed her just as much as she needed him. Was she prepared to live without him because of other people's bigotry?

She had been living between two worlds, the world of pretending to be white and the reality world of having been born of a Mulatto mother thus, not having enough white blood to be completely white. Was she brave enough to admit to the fact of the black blood that ran in her veins? Or did she want to live forever in deception, condemned to remain alone for fear of discovery that she was not who she proclaimed to be?

Turning slightly, she looked over at him, smiling at how boyish he looked asleep. Moses was not only handsome he was also a good man. A kind man. An honest man. A man who loved her. She would never find a man like him again. She would never feel the love in her heart for any other man that she felt for him. Being with him had made her life have meaning. She wanted to be with him forever. To walk beside him, share in his dreams.

A deep yearning rose in her heart. Like all women, she eventually wanted a vine covered cottage and children. She didn't want to just be his friend, his lover, his mistress. She wanted to be his wife. If that was her greatest wish, she knew that she would have to be honest about who and what she was. If it was assumed that she was white but that he was of black blood, despite the white blood of his mulatto mother, any union between them would be against the law of the land. It was an irrational and bigoted law but the law none-the-less.

*Quentin.* She thought about his part in all of this. It was also thought that he was white, but Forest suspected that he had taken on that façade because of her. But Quentin knew the law and yet he had unashamedly fostered a relationship between Moses and herself. Why? Because he knew in his heart that living a lie had consequences and that it threatened a person's self-worth by preventing them from accepting the good in themselves without the need for a masquerade.

"What are you thinking about?"

Moses' voice startled her for just a moment but turning her head she smiled at him. "About you and about me and how I want to be with you for the rest of my life," she whispered.

"If only, but......." He was silenced by the touch of her fingers on his lips.

"I know what you are going to say, but don't. I know what is in my heart. I long to wake up to you lying beside me, I want to have your children, I want to share in your dreams, I want to grow old with you. If that means that I have to share in your pain as well," she shrugged, "that is the choice I am making."

Reaching out he tangled his fingers in her hair, forcing her to look into his eyes. "You don't completely understand. Once you cross that line between being thought of as white and entering *my* world you will cease to be fully human in some people's eyes. Without doing anything amiss you will be the subject of scorn. There might even be those who will hate you for no good reason. Here in Virginia, despite all the talk of people being equal you will be less equal just because of those whose blood you share. I love you more than life itself, but I can't ask you to risk so much."

Forest was defiant. "Should I instead spend my life without love, or perhaps take a chance outside the law to marry into the white world? Shall I sell my soul to make certain my lie is not found out? And what about children? Will I have to pray that my child will not have the same dark skin as their grandmother, my mother had?"

He crushed her to him, holding her to his chest for a long moment. At last he drew away, looking deep into her eyes. "Are you willing to gamble your future and spend your life with me?"

She didn't have a moment's hesitation. "Yes! We have our whole lives ahead of us, a lifetime of being together."

"I want to make you happy."

"You already have."

They shared a long and gentle kiss, a kiss that spoke of their love for each other and their hope for the days ahead.

## Chapter Thirty-Six

The sun dipped below the horizon announcing the end of the day and creating a painter's palette at the bottom edge of the sky. The evening sunset. Derek's eyes widened as he caught the last thread of twilight that was spreading out on the horizon, touching the land, and highlighting the panorama of tobacco fields before him. All of this was now his responsibility since the death of his father. It was a burden he didn't want and yet what else could he do? This land, the two mansions--indeed, every tree, well, garden, barn, and even the graveyard behind the main house, had been in the family for over a hundred years. Tobacco was his destiny.

"Oh, Father. Why?" His father was dead. Now he would never have a chance to calm the anger between them or make amends. All the things that he had wanted to say would be left unsaid. Even so, he knew his father would be proud of all that he had done and how he had managed to once again make Winding Oaks profitable. Thank God for cigars and cigarettes.

There was something else that he was thankful for as well. Since the Incident with Edward Cutler that cheat of a banker had not set foot on Cameron land again, nor had he carried through with his threat to collect the money due on the loan early. Intimidation had worked wonders even if Derek's conscience had troubled him now and again.

*So, I am master of Winding Oaks*, he thought. As if to emphasize that fact his mother had enlisted

495

the services of an artist to paint portraits of both Derek and Amelia to hang with the other Cameron portraits. Amelia, on her part, had decided to move those portraits from the Avery house to the mansion. Derek wondered if that gesture would mean that their ghosts would now haunt the Cameron mansion. Only time would tell.

Seeking out his horse grazing nearby, he mounted and headed back to the house with a strange sense of melancholy for those days of his boyhood when he had been so carefree. He and Moses had thought that the world was theirs to conquer. They had laughed together, fished together, gotten in trouble together, searched for Blackbeard's treasure together, gone swimming in the old lake together, and thought that they had all the time in the world to grow up and face responsibility.

"But the world caught up with us and we realized we did not have the key to eternity," he whispered.

Passing by the mound of dirt where he and Moses had tried to dig a well only to find a misplaced coffin, he paused. The day after tomorrow he would seek out Moses and have him help dig that hole again, this time to put whoever was buried there with the rest of the coffins in the plot in back of the house. It seemed the right and proper thing to do. It would also give him a permanent place to bury all the Klan paraphernalia and book he had found in the Avery attic. His father's friends had kept their part of the bargain and he intended to keep his. The past would be buried and stay buried. Like many other secrets that had touched the Cameron family that too would be suppressed.

The short journey back to the Cameron house

496

was a pleasant one and as always, he felt a warm glow in his heart as he spotted the white columns reaching up to the sky. *Home is where the heart is,* he thought, remembering Amelia quoting that old saying to him. Surely that saying was true, or at least it was for him. He had been born in that house, grown up in that house, and it seemed that it would always be the place that held his heart, especially now that he had Amelia to share his life with.

Taking his horse to the barn and unsaddling her, he hurried to the house before all the light left the sky. Even from a distance he could smell the enticing aroma of what was cooking for dinner and he hoped that Amelia would be up to joining them for dinner tonight. For the last week or two her stomach had been more than a bit queasy and he had missed her lovely face sitting across from him at the table.

Opening the door, nearly colliding with the doctor, he was unpleasantly reminded of the last time that good man had made an appearance. "Why are you here?" he blurted out without regard to good manners."

That Doctor Adams was smiling seemed to be a good sign. "I will let the ladies talk to you all about that," he said, patting Derek on the back then heading in the direction of his buggy.

"Tell me what?" Derek shouted out.

"You'll see….."

More than just a bit peeved by the doctor's sense of mystery, Derek pushed inside the door. He was met by his mother who likewise held on to her air of secrecy, insisting that Amelia had some exciting news for him.

"You look like the cat that swallowed the

497

parakeet, mother," he quipped, relieved that whatever the news was it was not something unpleasant. "Can you give me just a hint."

Honora's smile was mischievous, "Only that we had best stock up on napkins and maybe even consider getting a goat or two."

"Goats?" He was just going to pursue the matter when the soft rustle of skirts announced Amelia's arrival in the drawing room. Just as his mother had been smiling, so was she. He also noticed that her face had a warm glow as she took his hand.

"What is all this talk of napkins and goats?" he asked, much to her amusement.

In answer she drew him towards the settee and pulled him down to sit beside her. "Let me just say, my love, that you had best get caught up on your sleep."

The two women laughed and Honora exclaimed, "men really don't understand."

Putting her arms around his neck and holding him close Amelia whispered the news in his ear. "We are going to have a baby."

"A baby?" He was surprised, happily so. "A baby!" He started to sweep her up in his arms, then pulled away. "I don't want to hurt...."

Amelia snuggled into his arms. "I won't break, Derek. I promise."

"A baby." Now he knew what they meant by napkins and goats. He joined in their laughter. "A baby."

Honora's laugh faltered as she said, "one Cameron has passed out of this world, but another is going to be born. That is the way of life."

Derek thought about what it would mean to have a daughter or a son playing in the house and the yard. A replica of Amelia or himself. Or perhaps the baby would be a blending of both of them, a representation of their love. He wasn't certain what the future held but one thing he did know. From now on his life was not going to be the same.

*   *   *   *

Caution. Candidates. Chaos. Calamity. Those four words represented what was happening in the world of the congressional election. Rebellions against the "damn Yankees" and their "monkeys" were increasing. Anger towards those Yankees who were usurping the southern society was growing hotter by the minute. Inspired by defeat, loss, and ex-Confederate rage there were those who believed that there was no point in participating in the political process and that there was only one way to react--with guns and violence.

Quentin explained the open outpouring of anger to Forest and Moses as they sat in the hotel dining room waiting for their breakfast. While the violence was going on the hotel had become their fortress. "Fear can be a catalyst of violence. No one likes change even if change will bring improvement. Both the old aristocracy and the poor farmers who were suffering under the slave system believe that this country is solely for people with white skin. They don't think black people have a place in Richmond, or anywhere else for that matter, unless it has something to do with subservience. Thus the anger inside them flares up over the simplest things like a Negro not lowering his gaze when he meets a white man on the street, or a black man walking into an all-white church by mistake, not to mention Negroes running for office."

Moses' voice held a tone of resentment as he said, "yes, massah,  no massah, anything you say, massah. I know what you mean. It was well-defined how a slave was supposed to behave.  But now that they are free no one really knows how an ex-slave is supposed to act."

"Precisely!" Quentin continued, "suddenly the rules are different and the white people feel threatened. They are losing power so they want to stop blacks from doing things that they can do, especially voting. Voting gives a man a voice in what happens to him. So, what better way can they hold other men at bay than to dehumanize them because they have different color skin."

"Well, I wish this whole thing was over so that we could go back home," Forest grumbled, taking a platter of scrambled eggs from the waiter. The eggs reminded her of the chickens at the cottage. "There is no one to feed Caroline, Camila, Charlotte, Cecilia, Chelsea, and Calliope, not to mention all the eggs that must be accruing. Much fresher eggs than these I would wager." Scooping a portion of eggs on her plate she quickly salt and peppered them, something she did not need to do at home.

"I don't think it will be long before we can return," Quentin answered, taking a goodly portion of grits.  "Matthew says that President Grant is well aware of what has been going on down here and has sent several agents to investigate.  Matthew says that it appears the group perpetrating all of this is a copy of the Red Shirts and that they call themselves the *Arcana Alliance*."

"Arcana?" Moses had never heard that word before.

"It means secrets," Forest remembered. "The Tarot cards are divided into the Major Arcana and Minor Arcana. Thus they are a secret society."

"Thankfully, not so secret now," Quentin answered. "Just as we supposed the only candidates that have received the cards are black men, but exactly what the meaning can be is still a mystery. But so far no one has been killed."

"So far!" Moses exclaimed, watching as Forest heaped collard greens on her plate next to the scrambled eggs. His expression of distaste did not go unnoticed.

"They go very well together. You should try it," she challenged, handing him the bowl of greens.

"For supper yes, for breakfast no." Moses chose ham and hushpuppies to go with his eggs.

"Ah, a lover's quarrel I see," Quentin teased. "But at least you both like sweet potato pie." They all laughed, glad to change the subject to something that wasn't ominous. "Which reminds me. When are you two going to get married? It would definitely help in the campaign if Moses had a pretty wife."

Moses was quick to answer, "just as soon as she will have me, that is if you are agreeable, sir."

Grinning like the Cheshire Cat Quentin insisted that he would like nothing better than to see the two lovebirds married. "Forest needs a bit of taming," he said with a wink.

"I like her just the way she is," Moses answered,

501

"but I'm afraid she will have her hands full breaking me of my bad habits."

The discussion at the table turned to the matter of the wedding. Forest insisted she didn't want to make a fuss and that a wedding before a justice of the peace would be her preference. She wanted to keep it simple with only Derek, Honora, and Amelia in attendance. As to the dress, she would wear a pale blue silk taffeta that was only a few months old.

"You could get married right here in Richmond," Quentin suggested. "That way the justice of the peace won't have to travel." Forest was agreeable to that because it made sense.

"I wish I had a diamond to give you."

"I don't need a diamond. I have you, a diamond in the rough." Forest suggested that the gold coin Moses had given her would be melted down for the ring.

"And so, what started out to be a stark day of talk about violence and anger has taken a decidedly more pleasant turn," Quentin intoned, taking Forest's hand. "I couldn't be happier. My matching making worked out splendidly." Finishing their breakfast, the three people made their way up the stairs to their rooms.

It was Moses who spotted the small white object tacked to the door of his room. "Damn!"

Coming up behind him Forest knew what it was before she pulled it from the door. It was a Tarot card, this card more ominous than the rest. The picture was a skeleton in black robes holding a scythe—the messenger of Death. Written on the card in black ink were the words, "death spares no one."

502

# KATHRYN KRAMER

\*    \*    \*    \*

Moses was totally unnerved, fearful not for himself but for Forest and Quentin. "We need to get out of here now! Whoever our enemies are they know we are here and that puts us in danger."

Forest tried to calm the situation. "Tarot cards have several meanings. This card doesn't necessarily mean death. It could mean change or transformation."

"Under the circumstances I would think it means a dire threat of what is to come," Quentin argued. "Moses is right. We are not safe here. We must leave at once."

"Now I'm glad we didn't have any baggage with us," Forest whispered, "so we won't need to pack. We can slip down the stairs and…"

"I have to settle the bill," Quentin reached in his pocket for his money pouch, but Moses shook his head no. "Then I will leave the money on the bed."

"Shhh!" Taking a pistol, he had concealed under his jacket, Moses brandished it as he pushed open the door. Satisfied that there was no one hiding inside to ambush them, he gestured for the others to follow.

Moses' room faced the front of the hotel and from the window he could see the entrance to the hotel. Opening the curtains just enough to see down below he scanned the area.

"Is it clear?" Quentin inquired, more than a little rattled that their sanctity had been invaded.

"No!" What Moses saw down below was chilling. "There are about ten armed men dressed in

503

black and white garments that are similar to military uniforms. They are blocking all the exits down below. At least for the time being we are trapped."

Forest felt a flash of fear shoot up her back, but she fought to keep a level head. "The card was meant to force our hand. They expected that we would try and escape."

"And when we did, we would either be shot or taken captive," Quentin joined Moses at the window. "When we don't come out, they will no doubt storm in and forcibly take us."

"How many guns did you bring with you?" Moses took out another pistol that he had concealed in the waistband of his trousers.

"Only one," Quentin lamented. "I was a fool. I thought we would be safe here, so I left the rifles hidden under the seat of the buggy."

Moses swore under his breath. "Then there is no way we can hold our own or fight our way out of here. We will have to search for a place to conceal ourselves. Meanwhile I will try and find a way to get past those men and bring back at least a few more guns and some ammunition."

"And get yourself killed!" Forest was adamant. "I am the one who should go. They are targeting you and perhaps Quentin but most likely not me. Cowards like those wouldn't dare shoot a woman in broad daylight when there are witnesses."

"Don't be so sure. There have been women killed by the White League. Besides, you aren't dressed like a woman," Quentin exclaimed. "And there are undoubtedly some who would recognize you as having been with Moses and with me at the Capitol." As Forest started to leave the room,

504

Quentin blocked the way.

Forest was insistent. "We have to take a chance. Besides, I am smaller than either one of you and I weigh less. If we tie the bedsheets together, I think I can shimmy down without being noticed. They will be guarding those areas where there is an exit from the building." Forest sounded much braver than she felt. "I'll go out the window in my room since it is around the corner from Moses' room. It should be clear on that side of the building since they are only guarding the front and back exits."

"No!" Moses didn't want to take a chance of losing her even if it meant his own life was in danger.

Quentin on the other hand was contemplating the idea. "But how will you get the guns up to us without being noticed? It's not like you can hide them under your hat."

It seemed there was a hitch to every plan, but Forest had an idea. "Once I have my feet on the ground below you will pull the sheets back up. Then once I have the guns I'll signal you and you can throw the bedsheets down. I'll tie the guns in the sheets and you can pull them up."

"Then what?" Moses was not at all in favor of the idea. "You will be in danger if you try to come back upstairs."

"Which is why she should remain down below. She can hitch up the horses to the buggy after we have the guns and wait for us." Quentin was getting more confident about the plan. "We'll meet her at the back of the hotel and make our escape."

Moses still didn't like the idea. Taking her hand, he pulled her into an embrace. "I don't want anything to happen to you. You mean too much to me."

"I'll be careful. I promise." Putting her arms around his neck she pulled his face down so that she could kiss him. As usual their mouths fit perfectly together but this kiss had a fierceness, a passion that only danger can bring. At the back of their minds was the threat that if something went wrong they might never be together again.

Moses touched her face, tangled his fingers in her hair, breathed in the sweet smell of her skin as the kiss went on and on. At last as they heard Quentin clearing his throat, they parted. "Don't ever forget that I love you," Moses breathed in her ear.

Forest peered out the door to make sure the coast was clear then she signaled for them to follow. Pushing into her room they stripped the quilt and blanket off the bed and tore the sheets into strips.

"We are going to need more sheets," Forest exclaimed, looking out the window and estimating the distance to the ground below. "If only we had taken rooms on the second floor."

Quentin hurried to his room and returned with his bedsheets, tearing them into pieces as Moses and Forest hurriedly tied them together and twisted them into a makeshift rope. Doing the same with Quentin's sheet pieces they completed their task.

"Hopefully, it will hold," Forest whispered. "Now I wish I hadn't eaten breakfast."

Looking out the window to make certain no one was down below, she opened the window then threw the rope over the window sill, then before she could lose her nerve she climbed out the window, clinging to the rope for dear life.

Hand over hand, Forest climbed down the makeshift rope thinking to herself *don't look down!*

*Careful. You can do it.* As the "rope" began to sway precariously, however, she hesitated. Maybe she had spoken too soon.

Muffling the scream that was welling up inside her, she continued on. She wouldn't fall! She must not. There was too much at stake. When she felt dizzy, she put her head down on the rope until the swirling stopped. Taking a deep breath, trying not to look down at the ground which seemed to be so far away she moved downward

Suddenly she slipped. Her hands burned as she slid a few feet, then managed to catch herself in mid-fall. Only by sheer determination was she able to avoid plunging to the ground.

"Forest!"

Looking up she reassured Moses that she was all right. Though her whole body quivered, she took control of her fear. "It's all right." Clinging to the bedsheet, she took a deep breath and tried to steady herself again, then she continued despite the pain in her hands and arms. At last her feet touched the ground and she was running towards the buggy as if the very devil himself was after her. And for all she knew he was.

\*     \*     \*     \*

Quentin stared at his pocket watch as if he could somehow control the time and yet the minutes dragged by as the situation grew more dire. "Our enemies must be getting suspicious. If Forest doesn't return soon we just might have to think of another plan." Going to the window Quentin looked at the

507

distance to the ground and shook his head. "We would have to be touched in the head to even think of trying to emulate Forest's exit out of here."

Moses paced up and down the small room, going to the window every now and then as if he could somehow make Forest appear. "We should have never let her go. What if she was caught and they are holding her somewhere? What if...?" Moses quieted as the sound of a whistle could be heard from down below.

"She's here! That's my daughter. As brave as any man I know." Quentin threw the bedsheet rope over the sill. "It looks like she was able to carry three rifles, two pistols, and several cartridge boxes. "I'm no expert with weapons but it seems to me those guns should hold us for a while."

Leaning over the windowsill, Moses cherished the sight of Forest standing unharmed beneath the window tying the first rifle securely with the cloth rope. He knew if he lived to be one hundred years old, he would remember today and how she had bravely come to their rescue.

Hauling the rifle up was much harder than anyone could have supposed and there were more than a few times Moses feared the gun would slide out and fall to the ground, but at last he was able to haul it in through the window. Quickly untying it, he handed it to Quentin. "This one is yours."

Another rifle followed but this one was not tied as securely and started to slide out just as it reached a foot below the windowsill. Leaning over, Moses just barely had time to grab it before it would have dropped to the ground.

Forest started to tie up another rifle, but Moses

signaled that they needed the ammunition next. In order to get as many bullets as possible to Moses and Quentin, Forest took off her hat and packed it full of ammunition cartridges, then tied the bundle as securely as she could. Surprisingly, it was much heavier than she would have imagined but Moses was able to heft it up and pull it through the window.

As Forest started to tie up the third rifle she heard a sound coming from around the corner and barely managed to seek a hiding place behind a large rain barrel in time, watching as two armed men walked by. As soon as they were gone, she returned to her task, thankful that the two men had been so engrossed in conversation that they hadn't noticed the torn sheets dangling in the air.

As quickly as she could, Forest tied up the third rifle, holding on to it to guide it as long as she could, even standing on tip toes until the gun was out of reach. Her hands were shaking from nervousness and the exertion of climbing down the rope and she knew they were running out of time, yet she managed to tie up one of the pistols before she heard an ominous voice behind her.

"What are you doing?"

Carefully Forest reached for the pistol that was left, holding it securely as she slowly turned around. "Why I'm just out for a morning stroll. I ate far too much at breakfast."

"What the hell?" Noticing the pistol sliding up the side of the building the militia man wasn't fooled for a second. "You're with them."

Forest reacted quickly, fearing he would sound an alarm or worse yet, shoot her. Aiming for the hand that held his rifle she fired a shot, hitting her target.

509

The man's wail alerted her to the fact that her aim had been true.

"You bitch!" His rifle made a thud as it dropped on the ground but holding his wounded hand he started to run.

For a fleeting moment in time it was as if someone else had control of Forest's body as she acted intuitively and shot him first in one leg and then the other. Killing was not in her nature but she had hope that at least she had helped give Quentin and Moses a bit more time.

Hearing the shots, Moses and Quentin were horrified, fearing that Forest had been the victim, but as they looked out the window, they could see her fleeing down the pathway towards the stables. They heard another sound as well—the trod of booted feet climbing up the stairs.

"Quick. Secure the door. That will give us a bit more time and enable us to pick them off as they push their way inside." Moses watched as Quentin hurried forward. He had just enough time to lock the door before a shot rang out, splintering through the wood and striking him in the shoulder.

"Damn it, you've been hit!" Moses had just enough time to push Quentin to the ground before another shot rang out. Stripping Quentin's tie from his neck, Moses tied it tightly around Quentin's shoulder to stop the flow of blood.

"I don't think I can shoot my hunting rifle but I have one hand left to pull the trigger on your pistol," Quentin breathed, taking the gun from Moses' hand.

"They think this is going to be like hunting but this time the quarry is armed and ready," Moses exclaimed, waiting in expectation as the door was

510

kicked and battered in.

*    *    *    *

Forest had never run so fast in all her life, but it was as if her feet had wings now. Although she didn't look back, she knew instinctively that she was being pursued so she altered the direction she was running several times. And all the while she was thinking the best way to get the two horses and lead them to the buggy without being seen. Alas, it was not going to be possible because there were four men near the buggy. There would have to be a change in plans. They would need to leave the buggy here and come back for it later. Riding on horseback would have to be their mode of escape.

Glancing hurriedly from side to side, Forest kept to the shadows as she hurried to the stables.

Slipping through the opening, she pulled the door shut and caught her breath while waiting for her eyes to adjust to the semi-darkness.

It was quiet, only the nickering and pawing hooves of the horses disturbed the stillness. Although her ears did not perceive any human sounds, she was doubly cautious none-the-less. The stable was deserted. So much the better.

Locating the buggy horses, she lifted a bridle from a peg on the wall, quickly untangling the straps of the reins. Calming the horse with soft words, she slipped the headstall over the ears, then pressed the bit against the animal's mouth.

"Quiet, Lucretia, don't give me away," she crooned, adjusting the straps and buckles with a deft hand. She fumbled around for a saddle for a long agonizing moment, then at last locating its bulk, swung it upon the horse's back. Bending down she fastened and tightened the saddle girth with a horsewoman's competent skill. She then moved on to the horse named Delphinia and saddled that horse also. She reasoned they weren't really stealing the saddles because they would return them when they came for the buggy.

Opening the stable door, Forest led the horses through the opening, pausing for just a moment as she heard a loud cacophony of gunfire. Putting her hand to her mouth she tried to muffle her outcry of alarm. Moses. Quentin. What was happening? Were they going to be able to hold off the army of terror and get free or were they going to be killed? Fearing the worst, she urged the horses forward.

Moses and Quentin, meanwhile, were proving to be more formidable adversaries than their attackers had counted on. It was proof that guns could be equalizers in a fight. Together they had wounded four men and frightened off two more but had paid the price themselves. In addition to Quentin's shoulder wound Moses was hit in the forearm. Although he assumed that it was little more than a flesh wound it made aiming and firing a rifle much harder. Added to that was the fear that they would run out of ammunition.

"I don't know how much longer we can hold them off," Quentin gasped, obviously feeling a great deal of pain.

"And we need to get you to a doctor." Moses tried to ignore his own discomfort.

"Listen." Quentin remained totally still, not even

512

moving a muscle.

"What?" Moses didn't hear anything. "It's quiet."

"Precisely. Either they are regrouping, or they have pulled back. I'm no military leader but I would say now is the time to force ourselves down the stairs and out the front door." Quentin rose from his crouching position and moved towards the doorway, stepping over the broken wood and splintered panels.

"Let's go then!" Moses moved past Quentin in an effort to protect him. Seeing that it looked all-clear the two men cautiously moved out into the hallway. Taking a chance that they would not be shot at from the stairway, they hurried down the stairs. Since there were only two armed men in the lobby, they made a run towards the front door just as shots rang out.

"Quentin, are you hit?" Moses was relieved to see that Quentin had remained unscathed but as he felt a pain in his leg, he realized that he had not been as lucky. Hobbling after Quentin they were just about to lose hope of escape when they saw Forest pulling two saddled horses behind her.

"Hurry!" she yelled out.

It was quickly decided that Forest should ride with Quentin and Moses would ride alone. Since there was no time for Moses to tie a tourniquet around his leg, he could feel blood trickling down to his ankle. Even so, he knew that they had to make it. They could make it. They had made it in relative safety so far.

# ASHES AND AWAKENINGS

## Chapter Thirty-Seven

The first rays of the sun warmed the room through the large glass window in the master bedroom, the room Charles had once occupied. Opening her eyes, Amelia was a bit disoriented at first, not yet familiar with their new room and the larger bed. Turning over on her side she expected Derek to be curled up next to her, but the bed was empty. Sitting up, she was just about to put her feet on the ground when she heard his voice.

"Breakfast awaits you, my dear mother-to-be," he said with a grin, balancing a tray loaded with food. He set it down on the table near the bed, smiling so earnestly that she hated to tell him that lately she didn't have an appetite.

"What a nice surprise." Aware of her disarray, she combed her fingers through her thick mass of tangles.

Derek was aware of her needs and going to the dresser grabbed a brush and a mirror. "I love your hair when it is flyin' freely and not restrained. You look like a nymph or a naughty angel."

She laughed at his description. "One who is getting a bit rotund, I fear." She patted her stomach. "Your mother tells me that she thinks we are going to have a boy because I am starting to show so soon. She said that one could hardly tell she was with child when Allegra was born but that with you, she was plump after three months."

"Hmm. Well, boy or girl I will be elated to

welcome the bundle into the family." Instead of handing her the brush, he sat down on the edge of the bed and ran the bristles lovingly through the tangles. "I love the color of your hair. It was the first thing I noticed about you. That, and your smile."

The feel of his hands and the brush on her hair was so relaxing that she was afraid to close her eyes lest she fall asleep. "I noticed your broad shoulders, your eyes and the light color of your hair. And I was not blind to the fact that you are quite handsome."

"And I thought to myself that you were very, very pretty so it seems we had an instant attraction to each other." He finished brushing her hair and kissed her on the cheek.

"Just like in the books I love to read. Let's hope we have as happy an ending as most of my favorite stories do. Not like those the Brontë sisters wrote."

"Brontë sisters?"

She shuddered. "Never mind." The thought of her ghost haunting the moors was too distressing. She rose from the bed and put on her robe; a bit sensitive about her slightly protruding belly.

"I brought grits with milk and sugar. Soft boiled eggs. Fresh biscuits mother baked this mornin'. Apple cobbler. I even sliced off a bit of ham from last night's dinner. And I know how you love to keep up on what's happenin' in Richmond, so I brought up a copy of the *Daily Dispatch* and the *Daily State Journal.*"

"You know me so well." She smiled, remembering how she once told him she was as hungry for knowledge as she was for food.

"Oh, and I brought you tea instead of coffee."

Sitting down to eat, Amelia eyed the dishes before her and wondered how she was going to get any of it past her lips without feeling nauseous. Even the apple cobbler didn't seem appetizing. Hoping that she could tolerate the grits, she sprinkled sugar and milk on top and stirred it up. "I think I will have some of the tea." Perhaps it would calm her churning stomach.

Derek took a seat across from her. "Mother found my old cradle up in the attic. With a fresh coat of paint and a little cleanin' it will be as good as new. And I know she is busy knittin' a baby blanket. She told me it will be yellow since she doesn't know if the baby will be a boy or a girl." Derek couldn't remember when he had been so excited for an event to happen.

Derek's enthusiasm made Amelia smile. She had no doubt in her mind but that Derek would be a great father. "You and your mother are spoiling me. But I love every minute."

Seeing that she couldn't possibly eat all of the biscuits, Derek helped himself, eating not one but two. "I noticed that you haven't been eatin' very much at supper, so I wanted to do somethin' special to whet your appetite."

Somehow Amelia managed to eat all the grits in her bowl, drink half a cup of tea, and pick at the cobbler. "Looking at all the food it seems you think I am having twins," she joked.

Derek laughed. "I'll go lighter on the food from now on."

Amelia sighed. "I should go downstairs for breakfast I suppose. I'll make a note to myself to do just that."

Eating as much as she could without feeling sick, Amelia picked up the *Daily Dispatch*, scanning it for any important news. Some of the information didn't pertain to the family but suddenly one headline jumped out at her—*Candidate for Congress Wounded in Ambush at The Red Clover*, it read. Scanning the article, she was stunned to see that the candidate in question was Moses. He and two others had been set upon by armed members of a white vigilante hate group and had been forced to fight their way out in a gunfight, the kind one read about happening in the wild west. The article compared the group, called the Arcana Alliance, to the White League and Red Shirts who had been harassing and even murdering black candidates and potential black voters in Louisiana and Mississippi.

"Derek!" Amelia's hands were trembling as she handed the newspaper to Derek. "It's about Moses."

"Moses?" Derek had visited his friend's house several times and had been disgruntled when he had been absent for so many days. Reading the article, he understood why. "It says here that he and Quentin were wounded. Damn it all to hell, he could have been killed!"

"What is wrong with this country? Can't we live in peace even for a few minutes? What kind of world are we going to bring this baby into?" Amelia was understandably upset, particularly after all that had already happened.

Despite the seriousness of the story, Derek grinned. "It says that Moses and Quentin gave as good as they got. I guess those bastards learned a thing or two."

"Did they learn? Do they ever. Or is hatred

going to continue to rule the South?" She thought about her students, both black and white. She had hoped for a better future for them than a country ruled by anger, hatred, prejudice, and violence.

Putting down the newspaper, Derek rose from the chair and put his arms around his wife. "I have to believe that with time we can all learn to live together. That's why Moses wanted to run for congress. To help heal the wounds. He and Quentin are good men. If they can't make a positive difference then no one can."

"I hope so. But Amelia wasn't as hopeful as Derek. "If only we could see into the future. I wonder what the world will be like then. She hoped with all her heart that it would be more civilized."

\*　　\*　　\*　　\*

Life could certainly have some strange twists and turns, or so Forest thought as she sat between Quentin and Moses in the waiting area of the Richmond Court House. In order for Forest and Moses to get married she had to prove that she was not white. It might have been humorous if it hadn't been so peculiar.

"Interracial marriages are not allowed in Virginia," she remembered the judge saying. He had looked her up and down adding, "you don't look black to me."

"Excuse me, your Honor, but according to the one drop rule that is exactly what I am," she had countered.

"Then you are telling me that looks can be deceiving?" He had adjusted his spectacles to get a better look at her.

"Yes! Things are not always as they appear. Me, for example. My mother was a slave, her name was Pearl, and my father was the plantation owner. He was as white as a ghost and she was a mulatto, the color of light chocolate and beautiful." And the most heroic person she had ever known, a woman who had suffered in order to protect her child.

He had looked at Moses suspiciously as if he thought there was some plot afoot, then had turned back to her. "I can not proceed until I have proof that what you say is true. If you are really the daughter of a slave owner then you will need to provide some kind of record or affidavit to prove that what you are saying is true."

Reaching over now she affectionately squeezed Moses' hand, careful not to touch the wound on his forearm. They had been through a lot together but now the ambush at the hotel, the gunfights, the harrowing ride to find a doctor to care for Quentin's and Moses's wounds, all seemed like just an unpleasant dream. A nightmare that had a happy ending.

Word of the ambush had spread like wildfire and Moses and Quentin were viewed as heroes. If Moses Abraham Douglass did not win the upcoming election the entire county would have been surprised, or so Quentin insisted. Forest was both happy and a bit fearful for what that would mean for the future. They had experienced bigotry and violence and now she knew firsthand that it was contagious. Groups like the Ku Klux Klan, White League, Red Shirts, and Arcana Alliance were not the only groups to try and spread terror. Unfortunately, there would certainly be others.

520

Sadly, mankind had a history of such things.

"Don't look so glum. It will all work out and soon you will be my wife," Moses whispered in her ear. "That is, if you haven't changed your mind. You may find out that you don't like being considered black."

"According to the law that is really what I am. I just need to find a way to prove it so that they will allow us to be together."

It was a problem that kept getting increasingly more difficult as Forest was told by the record keeper that there was nothing in the files about her birth, but if she were to get a document signed by witnesses or a relative, or to find the notation written in a family Bible they could continue.

"It is as if I don't exist. There isn't anything that states that I was born. I feel as if I am invisible." It was a shocking setback and ironic when Forest thought about all the times she had been apprehensive that her black blood would be found out.

"I'm truly sorry, Forest." Quentin was sympathetic but was not a man to give up. "We will find a way."

"William Trenholm." She said the name like a curse. "He was the man who sired me and sold my mother to a brothel. Somehow I will have to get him to sign an affidavit about my birth." It was the only chance, yet remembering their last meeting, Forest wondered if he would be cooperative.

*    *    *    *

521

Walking up the stairs to Room 203 was like reliving a bad dream, Forest thought, but at least this time Quentin and Moses were with her. "If only there was another way," she whispered, finding that now that she was here again she was quickly losing her nerve.

Coming up behind her, still limping because of the wound in his leg, Moses was right behind her. "I'll make certain he signs the letter Quentin wrote if I have to grab him by the seat of his pants."

Imagining such a scene in her mind, Forest laughed. "That might be more difficult than you think. He may be getting old, but he is not a small man. I imagine there was a time when he was very formidable, particularly to his slaves." She waited for Quentin to catch up with them before she knocked at the door, not once, not twice, but three times.

At last the door opened. "You again? What do you want?" He started to close the door, but Moses' strategically placed foot kept the door open.

"She needs a favor," Moses exclaimed. He was taken aback by the resemblance Forest had to the man, but he disliked the man anyway. From all that he had heard William Trenholm was quite a bastard.

"And just who the hell are you, Nigrah?" William Trenholm displayed the superior attitude that Moses had been subject to for most of his life.

"He is going to be my husband," Forest announced proudly.

"Oh, is that so. And just why should I care?" William Trenholm was obviously looking for an argument.

Protectively stepping between the two, Quentin said curtly, "let's not beat around the bush, Trenholm. I know all about you and what you have done. If you don't want your name splashed in every newspaper in town with a list of your wrong doings and where you can be found, I would suggest that you cooperate. I know where all your skeletons are buried, so to speak. I think you get my meaning."

Forest expected William Trenholm to be belligerent but strangely enough he asked gruffly, "what do you want of me?"

"For legal purposes this young woman needs documentation of her date of birth and who her parents were." He dangled a piece of paper in front of Trenholm's eyes. "If you sign this, you will see no more of any of us. Bygones can be bygones. Am I clear on what I need?"

It was obvious that despite the fact that Forest didn't quite understand what Quentin was threatening, William Trenholm did. Taking the piece of paper, he went to a small writing desk, pulled out a pen, and signed the affidavit right then and there. With a snort he handed it back to Quentin.

Forest read the sworn statement over Quentin's shoulder. It read, *I, William R. Trenholm, do solemnly swear that on the sixth day of September, eighteen hundred and fifty three, Jemma, nka, Forest Faulkner, was born on the Belle Stone Plantation to William R. Trenholm and the female slave known as Pearl, a mulatto.*

"Will that do?" He turned towards Forest and snarled, "but that doesn't give you the right to start calling me Papa!"

Once his words might have hurt her but instead she felt such a loathing for the man that she was able to say, "I would never want to do that. You are merely a disgusting pig who forced yourself on my mother because she was unfortunate enough to be near you." She compelled herself to remain calm. "You may have owned her body, but you never controlled her heart or owned her soul. And for what you did to her, I hope you rot in hell!"

"I think we should go, Forest." Moses gently touched her shoulder, pushing her towards the door. "We have what we came for."

Trying to control the flood of emotions that threatened to engulf her like a tide, Forest walked down the stairs arm in arm with Moses, with Quentin following close behind. The past was dead and buried at last and the future loomed ahead, a promise of joy, love, and hope.

## Chapter Thirty-Eight

It was a perfect day for a wedding. The sun was shining but it was not too hot, there wasn't a cloud in the sky to threaten rain, and just a hint of a breeze was blowing. More importantly, although it had been a tedious task just to get a marriage license, it appeared that from here on in the wedding would go on as planned without a hitch.

"You haven't changed your mind, have you?" Moses teased, helping her alight from the buggy.

"Most definitely not. I read in the newspaper's society page that you are considered quite an eligible bachelor, being a candidate for congress and all," she answered with a smile. She put out of her thoughts the prejudice they both had experienced trying to arrange and document all the paperwork needed for their marriage.

The ceremony was going to be a simple one preformed by a Justice of the Peace in an office at the Capitol. Moses looked exceedingly handsome in his dark brown suit with a white lace cravat replacing his usual tie. Forest had visited the dressmaker in Richmond and was now dressed in a white embroidered cotton dress with a stiff bodice, fitted jacket supported with whalebone, tight sleeves, skirt and overskirt that was heavy with the copious amount of fabric that had been used. She wore a white hat over her upswept hairdo. It was similar to the one she used to wear, but this one had a white lace veil.

"Quentin tells me that now that we are going to

be married I have to start dressing like a lady, but I must say that I miss the freedom of wearing trousers," she complained, trying to get the skirt of her dress to cooperate as they walked up the steps to the Capitol.

"Ah, but you do look lovely," Moses swore under his breath as he almost stepped on her long skirt.

Quentin, who had been walking behind the couple, stepped forward to join them in their promenade. "She is the most beautiful bride I have ever seen," he said proudly. He patted his pocket to make sure he had the rings.

As he opened the door, Moses scanned the large group of people gathered inside. "Derek and Amelia are going to meet us here, but I don't see them yet."

They followed Quentin to the room where the ceremony was going to be held and were surprised to see that the room was packed with people--including a few newspaper reporters anxious for additional news about the candidate who was now a hero in their eyes because of the hotel ambush. Shoulder to shoulder and elbow to elbow they had come to assuage their curiosity.

"What do you think your chances are of beating your opponent?" one man asked. "Do you think not being white will be detrimental?"

"I would like to think that I will be measured by my character and what I can bring to Virginia, not by the color of my skin," Moses responded.

"What do you think should be done to curb the violence here in the city?" asked another newsman.

"I think we need to meet with those who are opposed to our ideas and discuss our differences in a rational manner," Moses answered, trying to push through the crowd.

"How can you bring people together?" This newsman was black like Moses.

"By setting a good example so that the populace can see that we are more alike than different. All people want the same things—food on the table for their children, a roof over their heads, respect and understanding. And most of all I think everyone wants peace and prosperity they just have different ways of obtaining those things."

Moses saw that Derek and Amelia were already inside the room. Politely excusing himself from more questions he took Forest by the hand and led her inside. Together they walked towards the Justice of the Peace, a man Forest recognized from the political meetings with Matthew Stewart, a man of mixed blood.

"We are come here today to witness and celebrate the union of Moses Abraham Douglass and Forest Faulkner in marriage," the Justice of the Peace began. "Marriage is more than simply joining two persons together through the bonds of matrimony it is also the union of two hearts and two families. It lives on the love you give each other and never grows old. It thrives on the joy of each new day. May you always be able to confide in each other, to laugh with each other, and enjoy life together. May you be blessed with a lifetime of happiness and a home of warmth and understanding. Today you declare your commitment to each other and your decision to share in a journey down the pathway of life."

Forest's cheeks glowed with happiness as she looked at Moses. Thinking about the first time they had met, she smiled. She had never envisioned that the frightened boy would one day become her husband. But she was so glad that he was going to be her mate in life.

"Do you, Forest Faulkner, take this man to be your lawful wedded husband?"

She didn't even have to think twice. She nodded. "I do."

Moses answered the same, reaching down to squeeze her hand.

"'For richer, for poorer, in sickness and in health, till death do you part."

Quentin handed Moses the plain gold band and he put it on Forest's finger, repeating after the Justice of the Peace, "with this ring, I thee wed. I will always love you, Jemma," he put his fingers to his lips then corrected himself. "*Forest*, my heart is yours."

She leaned toward him laughing softly. "I love you too."

The Justice of the Peace concluded by saying, "by the power vested in me by he State of Virginia, I hereby pronounce you husband and wife. You may kiss your bride."

For a timeless moment Moses looked at Forest, feeling as if he was the luckiest man alive. It was as if he were in a trance, but Derek's shout out of, "well, don't just stand there. Kiss her," broke the spell. Drawing Forest into his arms, he caressed her lips gently in a passionate kiss that took her breath away. It was a loving action that was captured for posterity by several of the photographers and newsmen in attendance.

"Just in case you win the election," he heard one

of them say.

Strange, Forest thought, how kissing Moses always made her heart flutter so. Now, as she stood beside her new husband, she knew that such dreams really could come true if you believed in yourself and in love.

\*   \*   \*   \*

All those people who insisted that the first month after marriage was the sweetest because there was nothing but tenderness and pleasure, had obviously not been involved in a campaign. Although Forest and Moses desired nothing more than being alone together, they were instead barraged with political rallies, parades, and events where both Quentin and Moses made so many speeches that they barely had any voice left.

Even though President Grant was not on the ballot, it was a time of excitement none-the-less. More people than Forest could count showed up, some even wearing colorful costumes, marching along with the bands and floats. Despite the fact that women could not vote that did not damper their enthusiasm, some sitting beside the men in their lives as they discussed the issues of the day. It appeared that these political gatherings were evolving into social events.

When Moses wasn't speaking before the crowds his views were being carried in the press. Newspapers where as plentiful as flies at a barbeque. Most of them favorable to Moses' and Quentin's ideas and ideals, but a few of them damning nearly every word Moses spoke.

"Unfortunately, there are still those who are angry that black men now have the vote and they will do everything they can to thwart you," Quentin told Moses after reading just such a bad review.

"I know what you say is true, but it is still tragic that there are men out there who will vote against their own best interests just because I am not exactly like them." Moses fought the emotions that facing such prejudice brought him. He wouldn't give up trying to sway their minds and prove to them that he was on their side.

Forest was there to cheer Moses on and to give him advice whenever she thought he needed to hear her perspective on matters. She had learned by listening to the talk in the crowd that some voters thought of political loyalty to a certain party as important as their religious affiliation. Others were determined to vote as their fathers and grandfathers had before them. Only a few had no party affiliation.

"I think it is going to be a close election," she heard more than one onlooker say.

Quentin's attitude was realistic. He knew that a small shift in votes, a drop in the turnout, or worse yet the fraudulent manipulation of returns could decide the winners. Not to mention the fact that the White League, Red Shirts, and other groups still hovered over the elections like vultures.

"It will be what it is going to be," Moses insisted, refusing to allow fear to rule the day. He had other issues on his mind as well—his farm. As the parades, speeches and events took up more and more of his time he was able to spend less and less time supervising the workers on his peanut farm. Then at last the election day was upon them and there was nothing more to do but wait.

Although Forest wanted to wait for the results at the cottage, Moses and Quentin preferred to wait it out in Richmond so that they would know the outcome as soon as possible. Seeking asylum at the Ridgewood Hotel they waited, and waited, and waited.

Sitting side by side, with Moses holding Forest's hand they tried to make light of the outcome. "Either you will be a congressman's wife or the consort of a peanut farmer," Moses joked, determined to lighten the mood.

"Either one is fine with me," she answered, wondering what a life as the wife of a politician entailed. "Just as long as we are together."

"If I win, we will need to find a place to live in Washington for several months of the year." Moses realized that winning meant uprooting their old way of life. Would it be worth it?

"And it will mean that I will have to wear a dress." Forest's expression of dismay caused both Moses and Quentin to laugh. The mood of merriment, however, evaporated as the hours dragged on.

"How long does it take to count little wisps of paper?" Moses asked Quentin as they waited and grew more impatient.

"I expect that they will not only be counting but recounting," he answered. "In the old days men were more vocal about how they voted but nowadays with politics so divisive and secrecy so damned important Men keep their ballots in their pockets until the last minute. Vest-pocket voting they call it. Tiresome is my name for it."

A knock at the door set all of their hearts racing. Bolting up from his chair, Moses answered the door, his hands trembling as he turned the knob. He was met by a small crowd of well wishers who gave him the news.

"Congratulations, Congressman Douglass." In a flurry of handshakes, back slaps, and words of praise, Moses was informed of his victory.

\*　　\*　　\*　　\*

Success can be bittersweet, as Forest and Moses were soon to understand. Although he had won a seat, the bad news was that in most of the other races those who were against the changes wrought by Reconstruction had won. For the first time since the start of the Civil War the southern Democrats were in control of Congress, although the Senate control was retained by Republicans. That meant it would be more difficult for Moses to have his ideas put forward.

Moses' election to congress meant a total change to their lives and the need to leave good friends behind, at least for part of the year. Moses planned to keep his farm and his house for those times when they were back from Washington D.C., however. He would keep the running of the peanut crop to one of the sharecroppers for a percentage of the profit.

"We will miss you." Derek didn't want to get too sentimental but the thought of not having his best friend close by was distressing. They had been through a lot together.

"Guess you are going to have to get into trouble

all by yourself," Moses quipped.

"Ah, but it won't be as much fun without you." Derek looked over at Amelia and Forest, chatting no doubt about the coming baby. "When are you goin' to start a family?"

Moses feigned surprise. "A family? Give me time. I just got married. Besides, I think I will be busy enough dealing with the squabbles between Republicans and Democrats."

It was a subject they brought up again at dinner. Honora had cooked a ham with all the trimmings to celebrate the victory of her favorite congressman, as she called Moses. "I always knew that you were special," she said, wiping an emotional tear from her eyes.

"I would say that he was ornery," Derek exclaimed. "You always thought he was a little angel, Mother, but I could tell you some stories......" He winked at Forest as he passed the sweet potatoes. "Remind me to tell you as well. It is best that you understand the wayward side of your new husband. That way you will have the upper hand."

Moses pretended to be angry. "Oh, is that so?" He looked across the table at Amelia. "If Derek is telling tales out of school, I have a few stories that I can tell as well."

"I am sure that you do," Amelia answered, "like the time you went in search of Blackbeard's treasure?"

"Ah, the treasure." Honora laughed. "That, I fear, ended up bein' a real goose chase for more than just one generation."

"And yet it is a subject that is mentioned in the

533

book on pirates that I found up in the attic," Amelia answered. "Stranger things have happened."

It was a topic that was overshadowed by other conversations—Honora, Amelia, and Forest were interested in talking about the latest fashions that were in *Godey's Lady's Book* as well as the coming baby. Moses told the story one more time about the Arcana Alliance and the plot to thwart the election. Derek kept Moses up to date on all that had happened on the plantation while he was campaigning.

"Before you head on up to Washington could you do me a favor?" It was Derek's intention to put all the ghosts of the past to rest. "Remember when we were diggin' the well and stumbled on that coffin?"

"I do." Strange, how it seemed such a long time ago.

"Would you help me dig up that old casket and move it to the family graveyard. Whoever the poor bastard is, I'd like to give him a proper burial now that I am the master here."

The word "master" caused Moses to stiffen. It was a grim reminder of the old days when he had been a slave. "Master? There are no more masters in this country."

Derek realized he had misspoken and hastened to make amends. "I didn't mean that the way it sounded and you know it. It was just a slip of the tongue. Perhaps my father's ghost is makin' his presence known."

"Ghost or what you really think deep down?" Moses was so annoyed that he had lost his appetite. The tension of the past few weeks had taken a toll on him.

Determined to calm the tension in the air Honora stood up. "Boys, boys, boys! Stop this bickerin' right this minute. You two have been friends through thick and through thin. You must not let foolishness upset the apple cart now."

Derek was contrite. "I shouldn't have used that word. I'm sorry. You are right—there are no masters now and there shouldn't have been masters in the past. I should have said that I am the head of the household."

Realizing that he had been too quick to find offense, Moses said, "and I should not have been so quick to take offense. It's just that dealing with so many haters during the campaign got to me more than I realized."

"Friends again?" Derek put out his hand.

Taking his friend's hand for a handshake Moses nodded. "Friends until the end."

\*    \*    \*    \*

The early morning sun was hiding behind a cloud as Derek and Moses met up at the spot where they had come across the wooden coffin. The air held the fresh, crisp scent of the earth that reminded Moses why he had always loved this area of Virginia so much.

"I am going to miss this land. I never realized it before, but I think that farming is in my blood," Moses said as he grabbed a shovel from Derek's wagon.

"You won't miss it once you are hobnobbin' with those highfalutin politicians in Washington. But just don't get your nose too out of joint and forget us down here," Derek exclaimed, picking up a pick and starting to dig.

"I couldn't forget even if I tried." Moses hadn't done any hard work in weeks and he was surprised by how quickly his body had gotten out of shape. After digging for awhile his muscles had started to hurt. He paused, watching as Derek continued to chip away at the ground.

Looking up Derek couldn't help getting in a little jibe. "What's the matter? Are you gettin' soft after just sittin' on your behind? I've heard that the only muscles those political types up in Washington exercise is their jaw muscles."

Moses laughed at the comment. "I'll have to be careful. If it looks like I'm in any danger of being like *them* I'll have to hurry back here for your comeuppance."

"That's what friends are for." Derek was quiet for a long time, just listening to the sound of their digging and thinking of the past. It just wasn't going to be the same without Moses close by.

Moses seemed to read his mind. "If I told you that I wasn't remembering all the memories we shared I would be lying. To tell the truth, I don't think I really thought I would win so I didn't contemplate what I would be leaving behind."

"Somehow I always thought you would get elected. Mother thought so too. But don't let that admission go to your head." Derek came across a few worms in his digging and that reminded him of all the times the two of them had gone fishing. "We never did get a chance to go to the lake. I found a new bait. Leeches."

"Leeches?"  Moses' expression was one of disgust. "I hate those bloodsucking creatures."

"They do remind a person of bankers and lawyers." They both laughed.

It took an hour to dig down to the casket but at last the task was accomplished. Jumping down into the hole Derek set aside his superstitions and brushed the dirt off the lid. The casket was so old that the wood was rotting. Whoever was inside deserved a better ending than this, he thought.

"Do you believe in ghosts?" Moses knew that he did. During the time he had been a soldier he had felt their presence on the battlefield. Even so, he jumped down in the hole with Derek.

"I'm not sure. But if there is a ghost near by, he will surely realize I am being very charitable in finding a new home for his bones." Taking the shovel, he scraped dirt off the end of the coffin while Moses scraped at the other end.

"Or her bones. It could be a female." Strange how that possibility was unnerving. "Do you think it could be a slave?"

"I don't think so. The slaves were buried in a special graveyard out by the edge of the fields. But anything is possible." It was just one more injustice, Derek thought. Slaves were buried in graves close together and often his father had not bothered with a headstone.

At last the entire casket was uncovered while Moses and Derek themselves were covered with dirt. They looked each other in the eye. Without saying a word, they knew what the other thought—did they really want to keep going or had they been crazy to start this project in the first place.

537

"Well, shall we open it and see if we can tell anything about who is buried here?" Moses asked at last. Sensing Derek's hesitation he said, "I don't think the skeleton is going to jump out at us."

"Do you think we should say somethin' over the casket first?" Derek felt a shiver flicker up his spine.

"Like a prayer or something?" Both of them said a silent prayer, then bent down but found that the casket was nailed shut.

"We could just lift the coffin up and put it in the wagon. I had a new casket built for the bones, but we could bury the coffin just as it is." That idea was agreeable to them both.

"On three we'll lift it up and out of here." Moses took a deep breath and flexed his fingers. "One. Two. Three!"

They tried to heft the coffin up, but it was much too heavy. "Try again!" This time Derek counted. "One, two, three….."

This time they were able to lift the coffin a foot or two off the ground, but it was obvious that lifting it out of the hole was out of the question. "Damn! All this work for nothing. Might as well set it back down." Moses tried to be careful but as he tried to steady his grip on the casket his foot slipped and he dropped his end. It came crashing down with a thud.

"The poor bastard!" With alarm Derek saw the casket split in two.

Moses couldn't believe what he was seeing. Instead of a skeleton or decomposing body there were gold coins spilling through the cracks in the casket.

"Do you see what I see?" Derek could hardly believe his eyes. Was someone playing a trick on

538

them? Picking up one of the coins he carefully examined it and was satisfied that it was made of gold, as were the other coins. "So, the rumors were true."

"Pirate treasure. You are now a rich man, my friend!" Moses couldn't control his laughter. Their childhood dream of finding Blackbeard's gold had materialized.

"You mean *we* are rich." Derek was determined to uphold the promise he had made when they were both boys, searching for the coins. "I told you that if we found it, I would share it with you. I mean to keep my word."

"No! This is your family's fortune. I won't hold you to that vow we made long ago. It wouldn't be right." He was tempted but his honor and loyalty won out.

Derek broke the casket open with the pick. Inside was a flag—the Jolly Roger—jewelry and coins of both silver and gold. "Nonsense. A promise is a promise. Besides, you can use some of this money to help those in need and to help push forward your ideas to help bring peace to Virginia."

Moses was stubborn in his resolve not to take any of the gold coins or jewels, but Derek kept after him. Winding Oaks Plantation had been built with the help of its slaves who had given their blood, sweat, and tears to help make it prosper.

"I'll give you half." Derek started the bargaining.

"That's too much." Moses was not a greedy man.

"A third." Derek stubbornly refused to take no for an answer.

# ASHES AND AWAKENINGS

After several minutes of haggling, they finally
decided that Moses would take a fourth which would
leave a fourth for Derek's sister, Allegra, a fourth for
Honora, and a fourth for Derek.

## Chapter Thirty-Nine

Money was said to be the root of all evil, but Moses and Derek were determined to prove that was not always the case. The treasure they found was going to be used for good. And perhaps others would learn from their example.

Derek intended to build houses for the workers on his farm and to pay them higher wages so that they could share in his good fortune. He also wanted to restore Winding Oaks to its former glory, a gesture he planned for his mother who had given up so much for others in the family.

Amelia's thoughts were on her students. She expressed her desire to have a real schoolhouse built on the property to replace the Avery house. In addition, she knew that the children would also need a chalkboard, books, pencils, paper, and desks. She also thought about the Negro children and asked Derek if they could also have a schoolhouse built near the church.

"They will also need a chalkboard, books, pencils, paper, and desks. And an organ for the church." Patting her stomach, she realized there would come a time when she would have to take a break from teaching so she asked if they could hire an additional teacher or two.

Derek finding the gold and silver coins still seemed like a dream to Amelia. For a week when she woke up in the morning, she expected to find it had all been a dream. But it was real. The coins were genuine. Never in all her fantasies had she thought when she was reading about pirates that one day she would hold some of their treasure in her hands.

"No more pinching pennies and going without," Derek had announced that day the treasure had been found. "We can pay all the money owed to the bank and never have another worry, at least for quite a long while."

The excitement Moses and Derek had brought into the drawing room that day had been contagious, their story of finding the treasure incredible. It was as if for just a moment in time they had become boys again, elated at having a secret to reveal. A secret that would change all their lives.

Amelia remembered Honora's frown as she had said to Derek and Moses, "If this is some kind of a joke it is not a humorous one you two."

"It's not a joke!" Derek could not hide his elation as he had handed his mother a handful of the coins, telling her all that had transpired.

"Your father told me that Avery Cameron is the one who was rumored to have hidden what was left from Jared's treasure. But Charles was not a believer in its existence, even if it was a mystery how Avery had the money to purchase the Avery Plantation House and the land for the original tobacco plants. And a wife."

"Well, now we know! And he was clever in his plan to keep others from finding it and taking it from him. He didn't think anyone would open up a coffin." Elbowing Moses in the ribs he laughed. "And we wouldn't have realized there was a treasure inside that casket if Moses hadn't dropped it."

Honora was not as elated as the others. "Wealth

can not buy happiness, love, respect, or common sense. But riches can bring heartache as well as joy," she exclaimed. "It appears that Avery was so obsessed with anyone else getting' their hands on his fondest possession that he forgot about the people in his life—his wife and sons. Accordin' to family history his last years were stalked by tragedy. I don't want this prosperous turn of events to harm either of you as well."

"It won't Mother. I promise. Moses and I have discussed it and we intend to use this money for good purposes only."

Amelia smiled as she thought how her husband and his friend had begun to make good on their promise. Already there were carpenters working on the Winding Oaks Mansion and building the two schools. She remembered that it was said that it was better to give than to receive and seeing the smile on her husband's face she knew that saying to be true.

*　　*　　*　　*

The train station was crowded with people, all carrying boxes and bags of various shapes and sizes. Pushing through the throng, suitcases in one hand, satchels in the other, Moses and Forest moved towards the platform as fast as they could. But it was no easy task to maneuver their way through the often immovable throng.

"I don't see Derek and Amelia," Forest lamented. "I was hoping to give them one last hug before we go off to Washington." It was an exciting adventure that awaited them, she thought, but there was also a sense of sadness to be leaving the

Camerons and Quentin behind.

It seemed that the past few weeks had moved like a whirlwind. There had been her astonishment when Moses had told her about the pirate treasure, then there had been planning to do. Moses had made plans to enlarge the size of their house near Richmond so that it would be ready when they were able to go back home. He had also wired money to a bank in Washington so that it would be at their disposal when they arrived. Like all of the other congressmen he had wanted to live near the United States Capitol building and so had rented apartments there. Although it would be a drastic change from living at the cottage in the woods, Forest knew that wherever she lived if it was with Moses, she would be content.

"There they are!" Derek proclaimed. Forest waved as she saw them but then the seemingly disappeared in the crowd.

The mixture of people waiting to board the train was a curious one—people of every color, but mostly the crowd was made up of men. A seemingly rowdy lot.

"Please let us through!" Derek's voice could be heard over the buzz of the crowd, but it was exasperating that they couldn't see over the hat tops. Forest's view was completely blocked by those who were much taller than she. All she could see was the dark grey smoke that belched from the incoming train's engine.

A whistle screamed. She heard the brakes screech as the train pulled into Richmond's Station. Her heart lurched as she realized that it must be the very train they were waiting to board.

"We don't want to miss it." The thought was

unsettling and caused Moses to be more aggressive in their quest to push through the crowd. His self-assertiveness paid off when he was at last afforded sight of the long, black train as it came to a full stop

Moses put his arm around Forest and they watched as a throng of passengers alighted from the flat-roofed cars that--resembled boxes on wheels--to be hugged and squeezed into the arms of those waiting on the platform.

"I remember another time aboard a train," he whispered in her ear. "That time when we first met so long ago. But I was just a frightened boy then. Who would ever have foreseen that I would meet and marry an angel?"

It took a long time to empty the train, a tranquil respite from the pushing and shoving, but as soon as the passengers had disembarked, the crowd began its impatient stampede again. The piercing whoosh of the steam engines blasted from full-bellied boilers continuing to send thick black smoke into the sky. The brakeman raised and lowered his kerosene lantern. The train was getting ready to begin its journey, to chug and puff down the maze of tracks that reminded Forest of a Chinese puzzle.

"Forest. Moses." Hearing Derek call out their names, they turned around and elbowed their way to where their friends were waiting. "Behave yourself in Washington now, you hear."

"And don't forget to write us and tell us all that is going on," Amelia added.

Moses did something he had never done before. He gave Derek a hug. "And don't you be strangers. There will be a bedroom waiting for you whenever you decide to come for a visit."

"We just might take you up on that," Derek said, patting Moses on the back then breaking away before he got too emotional.

They all heard the conductor call "All aboard!" and hurried to say a final farewell then waded through the stampede of people who at least were headed in the same direction now.

"Ouch!" Forest cried out as a misdirected elbow caught her in the ribs. The culprit didn't even say he was sorry. But she saw him eye Moses up and down and say the word "Nigrah" under his breath. She hoped that once they got to Washington DC that people would be more civilized.

"I will be glad when this is over," Moses whispered in her ear. But it was only the beginning. They were pinched and prodded, their toes stepped on several times along the way. It seemed to be every "man" for himself and Forest was certain that before this was over, she would be covered with bruises. And all the while her two pieces of luggage seemed to get heavier and heavier.

"Ah well, we'll have the rest of our lives to be together," she sighed, looking over at Moses and thinking that she could not help but love him.

"Tickets. Tickets....."

"It won't be long now, and we will be starting a whole new chapter in our lives," Moses said softly, handing over the tickets. He started to guide Forest to the area with comfortable seats but instead was told that he wasn't allowed to sit there.

"That is the area for your people," the conductor admonished, pointing to the back of the train car.

"I think I have a lot of work to do in Washington

to put an end to this kind of nonsense," Moses exclaimed, taking a deep breath to calm his irritation.

Most of the wooden benches aboard were filling up rapidly but Forest spotted two vacant seats at the farthest end of the passenger car. Moses insisted that she take the window seat, then secured his suitcases and both of hers underneath the bench just as the final whistle sounded. He took his place beside her just as the train pulled away from the platform.

Forest thought how the traveling cars reminded her of boxes on wheels. Certainly they were just about as comfortable. And crowded. Being cooped up with so many people made it so hot. Worse yet, it was up to the passengers to take care of their own needs.

It was noisy inside the train as bags clunked together and people chattered. Forest made use of the confusion to steal a long look at Moses. He looked handsome in a dark grey suit with matching vest, a white shirt, red tie and black leather boots. A gentleman to his core. It angered her that the conductor had been so disparaging. But she knew she would have to get used to that kind of treatment now that she was living in Moses' world.

Moses settled back in his seat. It was going to be a long journey, but with Forest beside him it would be more pleasant. "Any time you want, you can lean your head on my shoulder," he said softly.

The steady, pulsating rhythm of the train wheels was mesmerizing, and for a long time Forest contented herself in listening to the clatter, immersed in her own thoughts and memories. Was this all a dream? Would she wake up and find herself back in her bedroom at the cottage? No, this journey was real. And so was the promise of a happy life, a new beginning. She had to believe that people were really good at heart and that love was stronger than hate. It would take time but together she and Moses could change the world and make it a better place for everyone. It was a dream that gave her hope for the future as they left Richmond far behind them.

# KATHRYN KRAMER

**Author's Note:** Reconstruction was a success in that it returned the United States to a unified nation and added three Amendments – Thirteen, Fourteen, and Fifteen. But it ended in 1877 and marked the conclusion of the brief period of civil rights for black Americans in the South. Southern Democrats had promised to protect civil and political rights of former slaves, but the promise was not kept and there was widespread disenfranchisement of Black voters. When the last of the federal troops were pulled out of the South, formally ending the Reconstruction Era, black men and women were once again openly subject to unleashed discrimination and harassment. Black men were disenfranchised by state legislatures in every Southern state. The period of the "Jim Crow" laws came into effect and were enforced until 1965.

Jim Crow laws brought forth segregation and reinstated white supremacy. The law was named after "Jump Jim Crow" which was the name of a minstrel routine wherein the character was a dim-witted buffoon that made fun of Negroes. The word "colored" appeared and was used for signs that even instructed Black people to use separate drinking fountains. In addition, they were denied the right to vote, hold jobs, get an education, or expect equal justice. Those who even attempted to defy those laws faced arrest, fines, jail sentences, violence and even death. It marked a fierce return of the Ku Klux Klan. This led to Black populations moving to cities—north and west-- where unfortunately they became victims again as laws to limit their opportunities were installed. It was not uncommon to see signs posted at city limits warning that Blacks were not welcome there.

Not until the post-World War II era did civil rights activities gain traction under the leadership of Dr. Martin Luther King. Then in 1964 President Lyndon B. Jonson signed the Civil Rights Act which *legally* ended the segregation institutionalized by Jim Crow Laws. This was followed by the Voting Rights Act in 1965 and the Fair Housing Act of 1968.

I wish that I could write that the sixties saw the end of unfair laws and racism in the United States, but unfortunately it did not. Racism continued. Not even the election of the first black president was effective in ending discrimination. Following the election of Donald J. Trump blatant racism was exposed with the brutal deaths of several men and women at the hands of white police officers. Protests erupted mirroring those that were active during the 1960's and as of the completion of this book are still going on.

**Note from the author:**

I grew up in the "sixties" and remember hearing Dr. Martin Luther King speak many times. I was in awe of his intelligence, his courage, his grace, and his ability to give people hope. Hope is a sustaining human gift that was magnified by Dr. King's compassion and understanding of the human soul. I remember the total devastation I felt when he was shot and died because it was as if hope had also died with him. But hope was renewed when the Civil Rights Act was signed. Or at least I thought. As the years passed, I realized that I was wrong, and I mourned the continuation of the racism that was revealed.

Like many other citizens I was outraged by the death of George Floyd. But it was another death that prompted me to research the history of racism towards the Blacks in this country and to write this book. The death of Elijah McCain devastated me, tore at my soul, and urged me to add my voice to those crying out for justice.

Elijah Jovan McClain was a twenty-three-year-old massage therapist from Aurora, Colorado which was only a few miles from where I live. Elijah was black—a gentle human being who played his violin and guitar during lunch breaks for abandoned cats and dogs at animal shelters because he believed the music put them at ease. It was said by those who knew him that his gentleness with animals extended to humans also and that his spirit was a light in a world of darkness. He had never been arrested or charged with any crime and was a vegetarian, spiritual seeker, pacifist, and a peacemaker. His mother had moved her family to Aurora to avoid gang violence and so that Elijah could be home-schooled.

On August 24, 2019 as he was walking down the street from the grocery store (wearing a ski mask because he was anemic) -listening to music and swaying in time to the rhythm, he was confronted by police officers responding to a 9-1-1 call about a suspicious person. He was NOT armed. Even so, three police officers held him on the ground for fifteen minutes as he sobbed and kept repeating "I can't breathe". He vomited several times for which he apologized. He was handcuffed and a *carotid control hold* which intentionally cuts off blood flow to the brain was applied to him. One officer even threatened he would have his police dog bite the young McClain. Paramedics were called and injected him with a sedative for excited delirium and McClain suffered cardiac arrest while being taken to the hospital. He was pronounced brain dead on August 27th and died three days later. A police cover up ensued and the coroner could not determine the exact cause of his death. The event happened near his home.........

# KATHRYN KRAMER

## AUTHOR BIO

Kathryn Kramer is from Boulder, Colorado—home of the beautiful Flatirons Mountains, the inspiration for several of the stories. Kathy and her mother, Marcia Hockett also wrote under the pseudonym of Kathryn Hockett and Katherine Vickery. Together they have written a total of 43 historical romance novels which have been translated into German, Portuguese, Italian, Dutch, Japanese, Turkish, and Hebrew. They have won the Romantic Times Reviewer's Choice Award several years in a row. Marcia passed away in December of 2003 and Kathryn has continued writing alone.

A current project was formatting all 43 books into the ebook format. To date all novels are now available on Amazon. They include *Notorious, Destiny and Desire, Desire's Disguise, Lady Rogue, Midsummer Night's Desire, Desire's Masquerade, Notorious, Under Gypsy Skies and Flame From the Sea* (Kathryn Kramer); *Tame the Wild Wind, Desire of the Heart, Arrow to the Heart, Flame of Desire and Sea of Desire* (Katherine Vickery); *Gentle Warrior, Outcast, Conqueror, Explorer, Ragnar, Outrageous, Highland Destiny, Sweet Savage Surrender, River of Passion, Outlaw Seduction, Cherokee's Caress, Renegade lady* and *the Legend's Lady* (Hockett). *Ashes and Awakenings* is the sequel to *Destiny and Desire* and reveals more about the Cameron family. *Pirate Bride* tells the story of Jared Cameron and Blackbeard's daughter. *Highland Ghost* tells of the Cameron family in medieval Scotland.

Kathy's maternal great grandmother—Mary Margaret MacQuarrie--came to Colorado from

Kentucky after the Civil War. She had triplet uncles—two of whom fought on the side of the South and the other for the Union. Several accounts of battles were notated in the family bible, along with a mummified ear from one of the brothers that had been cut off during one of the battles. In addition, her grandfather's stories of the "old days" were extremely helpful in writing this book. Her paternal great grandfather was from Indiana and there was rich historical information in that family bible as well.

There are four websites: kathrynkramer.net and kathrynhockett.com as well as katherinevickery.com and kathrynhockett.com

Made in the USA
Coppell, TX
09 May 2021

55372300R00304